LOVE
LETTERS
on
Hazel Lane

ALSO BY JENNIFER PAGE

The Little Board Game Café

Jennifer Page

LOVE LETTERS on Hazel Lane

HEAD of ZEUS

An Aria Book

First published in the UK in 2024 by Head of Zeus,
part of Bloomsbury Publishing Plc

9 7 5 3 1 2 4 6 8

A catalogue record for this book is available from the British Library.

ISBN (PB): 9781804548332
ISBN (E): 9781804548318

Cover design: HoZ/Jessie Price

Typeset by Siliconchips Services Ltd UK

Printed and bound in Great Britain by
CPI Group (UK) Ltd, Croydon CRO 4YY

Head of Zeus Ltd
First Floor East
5–8 Hardwick Street
London ECIR 4RG

WWW.HEADOFZEUS.COM

To my wonderful husband,
Ryszard Andrzej Hermaszewski (77 points)

Prologue

'No-one will ever buy it,' said Mrs Thorp, wrestling the pinafore dress over the mannequin's bald head, 'but it'll look good in the window.'

'It was there for six weeks when it first came in,' the manager said. 'Nobody even tried it on.'

'We just need one customer who's going to a fancy-dress party.'

'Or someone who's crazy about Scrabble and happens to be a size 12.'

The pinafore was way too large for the ludicrously thin dummy – they ought to get some more realistically sized ones but new mannequins were a luxury the charity shop couldn't afford. Mrs Thorp pulled the waist in, securing it at the back with a pin, and fluffed out the skirt before going outside to see how it looked from the pavement.

It was certainly eye-catching, she thought. The dress was made out of fabric printed to look like a Scrabble board. It seemed fitting for the shop's board-game-themed window; the small Pennine town of Hebbleswick had gone board games crazy since that board game café had opened in neighbouring Essendale, yet she doubted that anyone would want that dress. Well, where *would* you wear it?

She'd barely been back inside the shop for ten minutes, when she noticed a red-haired young woman do a double take as she passed by. The woman stopped and gazed at the dress, taking a step closer so that her breath steamed up a small circle on the pane. She raised her hand, touching her fingertips against the glass. This small gesture reminded Mrs Thorp of a film she'd seen once; a woman had been visiting her wrongly incarcerated husband in an American gaol and they'd both put their hands against the reinforced window between them, desperate to touch. She knew then that the dress had found its new owner.

I

Friday evening. Everyone else had somewhere to go.

The younger members of the production team had spent half the afternoon in the ladies' toilets, changing their outfits and applying lip gloss, before disappearing at six on the dot for their night out. They'd stopped inviting her along since Leona joined the team.

David, executive producer of Pop! Productions, left at quarter past in a haze of overpowering aftershave.

'Hot date,' he said as he passed Jo's desk. 'You should give Tinder a try.'

Tinder! She had plucked up the courage to try one of the gentler dating apps, but she definitely wasn't ready for Tinder.

Caroline, the production manager, was the only other person left now in the open-plan office, eerily silent except for the occasional whirr of the printer.

Jo had completed all her work so reached for her phone and opened the WordPals app. She had loved Scrabble since she was a child and the app was almost identical. You could play against the app itself, against your Facebook friends – not that Jo had that many – or against random strangers. Few things in her life beat the thrill of playing on a triple word score. Particularly if the word contained a J, X, Z or Q, the highest scoring letters in the game. She began a game against someone in Tokyo.

Caroline was usually the last to leave, but even she was rushing away now as her husband was treating her to dinner in a new restaurant in Didsbury. A first wedding anniversary celebration.

'Paper,' she said, pausing by Jo's desk.

For a second, Jo thought she was referring to the state of her workspace. When she'd first arrived in this job several years ago, Caroline had wasted no time in telling her that her notebooks, printouts and Post-its would have to go. Jo saw them as essential to the way she worked, the way she kept everything organised. Caroline saw them as a fire hazard.

'Paper?'

'The anniversary. Like twenty-five years is silver and fifty is gold. The first is paper.'

Jo sighed. She should have known. She and her ex-husband had got as far as their third anniversary. She'd given him a pint glass, personalised with his name, but she'd never seen him use it. He'd given her a set of crystal wine glasses from John Lewis, which were too ostentatious for Jo's tastes. A few months later, she'd broken one of them washing up – they were too delicate for the dishwasher – and Si had berated her for days afterwards, accusing her of being clumsy. Jo had ordered a small apple tree for their fourth anniversary – fruit and flowers – but they'd divorced shortly before reaching it and she'd been single ever since.

Being single was fine, of course, if you wanted to be single. But now Jo had reached her mid-thirties, she longed to have

4

someone to share her life with. Or at least, her evenings and weekends.

Caroline reached into her bag and pulled out a newspaper. 'My anniversary gift for Paul. What do you think?'

'A copy of *The Times*?'

'From the day we met.'

'Romantic.'

If she was ever lucky enough to get to a first anniversary with someone again, Jo thought, she'd like to be given paper too. Preferably containing a hearty portion of fish and chips, purchased from a proper chippy at the seaside.

'Have a lovely time,' she called to Caroline's disappearing back. 'Can't wait to hear all about it on Monday.'

Jo was lying. She didn't want to hear about her colleague's romantic dinner – it would only remind her that she had no-one – but it was true that she couldn't wait till Monday. At least in the office there were people around.

She wouldn't feel so bad if: a) she still shared a flat with Gemma in the city centre, but Gemma had moved to Watford two months ago with her partner's job; and b) the man she'd recently started referring to as her boyfriend – albeit only in her head – hadn't texted, cancelling their date that evening with only a couple of hours' notice; and c) – yes there was a c) now she came to think of it – if she hadn't overheard Leona bitching about her earlier in the small office kitchen.

She picked up her phone and looked at Dan's message again.

Sorry. Can't make tonight after all.

It was over two weeks since she'd seen him.

He'd been perfect too. Attractive. Confident. (Jo felt she needed someone confident to make up for her own shortfall in that area.) Outgoing. (Ditto.) And quirky too with his spiky hair and flamboyant shirts.

Quirky. Now there was a good word – 22 points even before you counted any bonuses like triple letter or double word scores.

Meeting Dan had been a bit of a result. She'd been anxious about dating again, after all she'd been through – deep down, she didn't believe she was worthy of finding love – and even more anxious about joining a dating app. She found it so hard to trust anyone. No, more than that; she found it hard to trust her own judgement. But nor did she want to be alone for her entire life and how else were you meant to meet anyone these days? Especially if you weren't particularly extroverted. She wasn't the sort of woman who'd initiate a conversation with a man in the chiller aisle at Tesco, and as for chatting up someone in a bar... well, that was never going to happen.

So Jo had joined the dating app, and, anxious often to the point of nausea, had gone on a series of first dates, mostly terrible, wondering how on earth you were meant to be able to tell what someone was really like underneath the façade. She didn't want to end up with another Si.

But then she'd met Dan and he'd been confident and kind, and had quickly asked her for a second date and Jo had thought her luck was in.

She sighed.

Three dates and she'd started thinking of him as her boyfriend. Was she mad?

'Should I call him?' she said to Mona.

The *Mona Lisa* was one of three enormous canvases, grand masters butchered to reflect modern times, that dominated the office walls. Mona was depicted staring at an iPhone, whilst the figure from Munch's *The Scream* was watching a thriller on an enormous wide-screen TV and the hand of God from Michelangelo's *The Creation of Adam* stretched out to touch not Adam but an iPad. According to David, the paintings reflected the fact that Pop! Productions made content that could be watched anywhere at any time by anyone on any device. Not strictly true, Jo always thought. Their programmes were probably banned in North Korea and places like that, and her mum's old Nokia could only make phone calls and send texts. But she didn't point this out. Nobody liked a... what was the word? Pedant.

Pedant. A paltry 9 points.

'What do you reckon? Call him again? Or leave it?'

Mona stared at her phone.

'Okay, I'll take that as a no,' Jo said.

She'd already left one rambling monologue on Dan's answerphone asking when she could see him and yes, she knew she shouldn't have, and no, he hadn't rung back.

The thing was, Dan wasn't just the man she was dating; he was her entire social life. Now Gemma had moved away and her colleagues had stopped inviting her out – thanks to Leona, Jo suspected – her social calendar was decidedly empty. There was no-one she could call for a drink and she'd no plans for Saturday or Sunday either.

'You'll soon make new friends,' Gemma had said when she'd told Jo about her imminent move. 'You need to find your tribe.'

But making friends seemed to get harder the older Jo got, and let's face it, she'd never found it easy. At school, she'd been one of those children who preferred lessons to playtime. Socially awkward, one teacher had called it. Another had repeatedly asked her if she was being bullied.

Was it bullying? No-one was beating her up or stealing her lunch money. It was just a bit of name-calling. 'Sticks and stones,' her granny used to say. 'Sticks and stones.'

Words will never hurt me.

Although that just wasn't true. Not in Jo's experience. Words did hurt. Jo felt that hurt deep in every cell of her body, just as much, she thought, as if she *had* been beaten up. Wounds from a physical beating healed over time, but emotional scars didn't. They accumulated, one on top of another. The words her classmates had used echoed around her mind for years to come, taunting her throughout her teenage years, shaping her beliefs about herself, destroying what little self-confidence she had.

Ugly.

Fat.

Pathetic.

'You're such a swot,' said freckle-faced Sally Grainger at playtime one day after Jo had come top in the spelling test yet again.

'Your face is scabby,' said Stuart Bell, frowning at a nasty patch of childhood eczema on Jo's face.

'You're not invited,' said Melissa Dean, pointedly handing out birthday party invitations to every other girl in the class.

It was ironic really that words were the weapon the bullies used to make Jo's life a misery, yet at the same time, words were her consolation, her solace. As soon as she began to learn to read, Jo had been fascinated by how letters could be put together to form words, and how in turn, those words could be assembled into sentences, and those sentences into stories. Jo quickly learned she could escape from her misery into the pages of a book.

One Christmas, she'd ripped open shiny wrapping paper to reveal a Junior Scrabble set and her love of words for their own sake began. Jo loved Scrabble from the very first moment. Before long, her parents bought their serious little daughter the adult game too, and Jo began to collect words in her mind. Words that needed Qs and Zs and Xs and Js, so would gain her the most points. Those high-scoring words jostled for space in her brain alongside the negative ones: ugly, fat, pathetic, scabby, horrible.

Another good thing happened that same year; Gemma joined their class. It was midway through Year 3 and Jo finally had her first proper friend. Life became easier then. The taunts of 'Nobody likes you' subsided a little. The two girls were inseparable for the rest of their school days and into adulthood. Well, apart from when Jo was married; Si hadn't liked Gemma much. Jo never understood why. In fact, he had pretty much banned Jo from seeing her. After the divorce, the friendship had resumed – thankfully, Gemma had been understanding – and the two of them had shared a flat in Manchester. But then Gemma had left for Watford. Bloody miles away. Jo wondered if she'd ever stop missing her.

She tapped out a text to Gemma now.

He's cancelled on me.

The reply came back quickly.

Not again? What was his excuse this time?

No reason given. Vague as usual.

Think you should face it – he's not that interested. Get
back on the app. Find someone new! There are loads of
single men out there.

It was all very well for Gemma to say, 'Get back on the
app'. She'd never tried it. She'd met Jack in their first year
at secondary school and they'd been together since they'd
snogged at the school disco aged thirteen. Gemma had
never even been on a date, let alone a dating app.
She tapped out a reply.

Loads of single men but I always choose the wrong ones.

A minute later, her phone pinged again.

Saw an article online the other day that might help. I'll
send you the link.

Jo sighed. Not another article! She put her phone down
and opened the spreadsheet showing the programme budget
for Pop! Productions' latest offering to Channel Five: a show
that combined dating and cookery. She double-checked but
everything was accounted for, from the crews' overnights in
hotels near the location to the cost of the presenter's fake
eyelashes.

Her phone pinged again and she saved the spreadsheet and shut down her computer.

She clicked on the link that Gemma had sent:

Could Numerology Help You Find The One?

The article suggested applying the ancient art of numerology to the more modern world of internet dating, working out your compatibility with someone using numbers derived from the letters of both your names. It sounded like a load of hocus-pocus, but apparently Pythagoras himself had believed in this stuff. And if Pythagoras thought there was something in it, who was Jo to argue? After all, the man had a theorem and how many people could claim that?

You had to use the name you went by rather than your full name, and according to the chart, Jo's relationship number was seven. Lucky seven? Well, she hadn't been so far.

Jo scrolled down. Her ideal man would, she read, have a relationship number of three, five, seven or nine. She looked at the chart again and calculated that Dan's number was one. Maybe there was something in this.

She logged onto Buzzz, the dating app onto which she'd pinned her hopes. She'd left her profile up there, intending to remove it once Dan said the magic word: relationship. Or asked her to be exclusive. Only he was never going to say it, was he?

No new messages.

Still loath to make the forty-minute train ride back to her empty house, she decided to rearrange the contents of the stationery cupboard. What a lovely surprise that'd be for her colleagues on Monday morning; they'd actually be able to find an envelope, paper clip or drawing pin should they ever need one.

Monday morning: sixty-three hours and nine minutes to go.

The cleaner arrived.

'Hi, how are you?' Jo said, hopeful of a conversation, but he didn't hear her through his headphones. He hoovered under the desks, strutting to an inaudible beat.

Twenty-five to eight. She couldn't put it off any longer. Time to go home.

Her phone pinged as she pulled on her coat. Gemma again probably, thought Jo pulling it from her bag. But it wasn't Gemma; it was a new message on Buzzz.

You look lovely. Fancy meeting for a drink tonight?

The sender's main photo showed a dark-haired man. Serious-looking but attractive nonetheless. Jo skimmed his profile: six-foot, graduate, wants children. And based here in Manchester.

She hesitated. What about Dan?

She clicked on Dan's photo. Stared into his brown eyes. Then she noticed the little green dot in the corner. He was online.

Too busy to meet her tonight, yet here he was. Online. Right now. Using the app.

We aren't exclusive yet, she reminded herself. But perhaps Gemma was right. Perhaps it was time to face the fact that Dan wasn't that interested and date someone new.

She could get the train home and curl up with a favourite

episode of *ER* – she was particularly partial to season five of the popular medical drama when George Clooney aka Dr Ross was starting to get a little hint of silver in his beautiful dark hair – or she could join the ranks of People Who Had Somewhere To Go and meet an actual human being for a face-to-face conversation.

She would go on the date, she decided.

2

Jo looked at herself in the mirror of the ladies' toilets where, a couple of hours earlier, her colleagues had got ready for their Friday night out. Without her. It would be nice to get ready *with* someone. To say, 'Can I borrow your lippy?' or 'How does this look?'

Passable, she decided. She looked passable.

Looks wise, Jo had always considered herself average. Si had said she was gorgeous, when they'd first met, but over the years they were together, his constant criticism of her weight and her clothes and her hairstyle had made her feel anything but. Gemma, loyal as always, was always telling her she was beautiful. 'You've a lovely open face and curves in all the right places.'

Jo had remembered this when she'd written her dating profile, describing herself as 'curvy'. Pleasingly curvy, she tried to tell herself, though officially she nudged into the overweight category on that BMI chart at the doctor's.

Her eyes weren't bad, she thought now, looking in the mirror. A striking shade of green: the colour of peridot. She always attributed them to her Irish granny, along with her pale skin. And her hair was okay. Long and thick and a gorgeous shade of red. Not naturally red – thanks, Nice 'n'

Easy – but still lovely, according to Gemma. And maybe it was better that she hadn't been born with red hair; she'd come in for enough teasing at school as it was.

She lived too far away to go home and change so would have to go on the date in the clothes she'd been wearing all day: M&S jeans with added stretch, a plain T-shirt and her favourite (only) cashmere cardigan. Was a cardigan too frumpy for a Friday night out in Manchester? Probably. But it would have to do.

In any case, she had no aptitude for choosing clothes – as Si often used to remind her – and always stuck to jeans. They suited all but the most formal of events. Until recently, she hadn't possessed a single dress.

She applied a hint of mascara, praying that this new man would be so wonderful that he'd make her forget all about Dan cancelling on her. Or at the very least, that this would be a good date, i.e. one where he at least vaguely resembled his photo, was easy to talk to and didn't have half of his dinner down his shirt, in his beard or stuck between his teeth.

The bar was easy to find, with its migraine-inducing lights illuminating the whole street. Jo crossed over, pulling her earbuds out; she'd been listening to Etta James's 'At Last' as she always did on the way to dates to put herself in the right mood. Flirting didn't come naturally to Jo – she couldn't pull off coquettish looks or witty remarks – but Etta helped her feel she could bat her lashes or make eye contact for longer than one second, or whatever it was you were supposed to do to capture his heart. Or at least cause a little stirring in his groin area. She always dreamed that if she ever did manage to meet the right man, they'd choose 'At Last' for the first dance at their wedding. Though knowing her luck, he'd be more into Black Sabbath or the Grateful Dead.

She peered through the window, hoping to spot him. There was nothing worse than arriving in a crowded venue, not being able to spot your date and standing there on your own looking conspicuous. It took her right back to those early school playground days, hanging around with no-one to play with. It made her vulnerable somehow, as if she half-expected the other people in the bar to pick on her the way the kids at school had, to torment her for being alone. She couldn't see him, but took a deep breath and opened the door anyway, before pushing her way through city types in tailored suits and blond people in designer jeans.

To her relief, she spotted him quickly. He was sitting at a table, watching the door. He looked not unlike his profile picture; that was one good thing at least. He'd taken off his jacket and was wearing a loose-fitting, striped shirt. He stood up when he saw Jo, but didn't smile. Perhaps she didn't meet his expectations. Must be the cardigan.

'Hi, I'm Neil,' he said, offering his hand.

'Jo. Nice to meet you.' She shook his hand, his skin dry and cold against hers. Dan's hands were always warm.

'What would you like? A cocktail? Wine?'

'Pinot grigio, please.'

He went up to the bar to order and Jo sat down on an ultra-modern Perspex chair. Perspex. Now there was a good word – 18 points without bonuses but you'd be lucky to pick up two Ps at once. Anyway, she thought, it was a proper noun so wouldn't be allowed in Scrabble.

She glanced around the bar. Generally speaking, she preferred bars with softer seats, softer lighting and softer music so you could actually hear the conversation. Bars where you could buy a round without taking out a mortgage.

Neil returned, placing a glass of wine in front of her. He had some kind of beer in a fancy bottle. That shirt really was loose. Untucked too, so it hung over the top of his jeans. He smiled – finally – revealing white, straight teeth, and Jo suddenly realised how much she wanted him to like her. Then she saw him cast a glance at one of the blondes at a neighbouring table.

'I love that we're meeting on the spur of the moment,' she said, trying to regain his attention and hoping this showed she was spontaneous rather than someone who didn't have enough friends and therefore had nothing planned on a Friday night.

'Glad you were free.' He was peering at the blonde woman's impossibly high shoes.

Jo took a large gulp of wine. 'Have you been on Buzzz long?'

'Two weeks. Bit of a laugh, isn't it?'

That wasn't how she saw it, but she nodded.

'What was it that you liked about my profile?' he said.

She racked her brains. 'Profile? Puh-lease. I didn't get beyond those gorgeous photos.'

She cringed as the words came out of her mouth. She wasn't the sort of person who said puh-lease. Or told a man that his photos were gorgeous. Not even Dan, and his photos actually were.

But Neil seemed to lap up her flattery. 'Have you eaten?'

She'd been intending to pick up a ready meal on the way home. 'No.'

'Bit busy to eat here, but I know just the place.'

They drained their glasses. Jo followed him out into the fresh, spring air, imagining a bijou restaurant in a hidden alleyway. The sort of place Dan might choose.

But rather than a secret alley, Neil led the way into a pedestrianised shopping area, with a selection of chain restaurants.

'¡Tapas! ¡Tapas! okay?' he said, indicating a branch of the popular Spanish chain.

When it came to food, Jo didn't like to share so tapas wouldn't have been her first choice, but he was already halfway through the door.

A waiter led them to a table and Neil ordered a bottle of Rioja.

He could have at least asked she fancied red, Jo thought, as she started to study the menu. Alongside the tapas, there was a small selection of main courses. She decided on a slow-roasted Iberian pork with garlic potatoes and green beans.

'I'd prefer just a main course if that's all right?'

He nodded but reeled off a long list of tapas when the waiter arrived. Undeterred, she ordered her pork and a small orange juice.

A series of plates began to arrive. As she sipped her juice and waited for her one dish, he began to munch his way through pimientos, gambas and patatas bravas, washing them all down with red wine and gesturing to the waiter to bring a second bottle. The loose shirt made sense now.

The more he drank, the more he talked about his ex.

'...sleeping with my best friend...'

Jo bit into a piece of pork. Surprisingly tasty for a chain restaurant.

'...then expects to keep the apartment...'

And the garlic potatoes – mmm.

'Mother always said I could have done better...'

Soggy beans. Bit of a shame.

'So...?'

He was waiting for her to answer.

'Delicious, thank you.'

'I asked what your ex-husband was like,' he said.

An image of Si's anger at the broken wine glass flashed through her mind. 'We er... wanted different things.'

Fearing he might ask more about her marriage, she excused herself and slipped to the ladies', leaving him chewing on the last meatball.

Neil. What was *his* relationship number? she wondered as she sat on the toilet, remembering Gemma's numerology dating article. She recalled the chart showing the value of each letter and did a quick mental calculation.

4. His number was 4.

Incompatible.

Funny, she thought as she walked back to their table, his relationship number was the same as the number of points his name would score in Scrabble.

She sat down. Neil was polishing off churros con chocolate. An idea occurred to Jo as she watched him wiping chocolate and sugar from around his mouth with a napkin before gesturing to the waiter.

A crazy idea.

She almost dismissed it.

But then… well, it might be fun.

What if she only dated men whose names would score highly in Scrabble?

Of course, this new approach had no scientific basis whatsoever. Names weren't even allowed in Scrabble. It was a completely random algorithm. She'd effectively be leaving it up to fate, but maybe that wasn't such a bad idea given that selecting men on the basis of a combination of their looks, profile and messages hadn't proved successful so far. Quite the opposite in fact.

Take Dan. She liked him – a lot – but she had to face it sooner or later; he wasn't that into her. In fact, she'd probably never hear from him again. And what would his name score in Scrabble? Just 4 points. Pathetic.

Or Neil, her date tonight. Again, 4 points.

And as for her ex-husband?

Si – 2 points.

Only 2!

You couldn't get a lower-scoring name.

The lowest score and the worst man she'd ever had the misfortune to be involved with.

Perhaps there was something in this Scrabble dating idea.

The waiter placed the bill on their table. Over ninety quid! Her pork and orange juice were less than twenty.

'Fifty each should cover it,' Neil said, 'including a tip.'

Fifty quid? She didn't mind paying her fair share – this was the twenty-first century, after all – but fifty quid?

'I only had…' she began, but the waiter arrived back at the table and thrust the card machine under their noses.

Neil entered his PIN and said, 'She'll pay the other half.'

As soon as the waiter had torn off her receipt, Neil announced that he didn't want to see her again.

'No chemistry,' he said, rubbing his belly with both hands.

Dating someone with such a large appetite would bankrupt me anyway, Jo thought, as they left the restaurant.

They stood on the pavement for a moment before he said, 'I guess this is it.'

'Okay, goodnight,' Jo said.

She turned to walk away but felt his hand on her arm. He pulled her back towards him and pressed his wet lips onto hers.

3

It was a while since a man had seen her in this state of undress.

'What time is it?' Jo mumbled, rubbing her eyes.

'Quarter past ten,' he said.

'Already? I don't normally sleep this late.'

'Could you sign here please?'

As she tried to write her name on the postman's little electronic pad with her fingertip, she wondered who the strange-shaped parcel could be from. She hadn't ordered anything online. Her birthday wasn't coming up. But there was nothing like an unexpected delivery to liven up an otherwise dull Saturday morning.

'Oh,' she said as he handed her the package. 'It's not for me.'

'It's for three doors down, but everyone else is out.'

She had crawled out of bed and was standing on the doorstep in her one and only dressing gown that was, quite frankly, too short and skimpy for anyone but a lover to see her wearing. And the parcel wasn't even for her.

She left it on the floor in the lounge, made a cup of instant coffee and flicked on the radio. A chat show. Perfect. The illusion of company on this weekend morning. Some expert was talking about loneliness. Being lonely was, apparently, worse for your health than smoking. It raised your levels of cortisol – good Scrabble word, 10 points – and too much cortisol wasn't good.

Great. Her single status was not only making her downright miserable; it was also causing her more harm than a packet of Marlboros. She flicked the radio back off; she didn't need to know this.

She logged into WordPals, played – and lost – a game against a woman in Ontario and then opened Buzzz. No new messages.

She finished her coffee. It was almost eleven o'clock on a Saturday morning. She was in a new town in a lovely area that she'd barely explored yet, but here she was, still sitting in her PJs, staring at a screen, playing word games.

Joining Hebbleswick Library had been practically the first thing Jo had done when she'd moved here. She'd loved libraries since she was a child. Libraries didn't require you to 'join in'; well, obviously you had to join if you wanted to borrow books, but you didn't have to participate in anything. You could tuck yourself away in a corner, lose yourself amongst the shelves and disappear into other worlds of mysterious kingdoms hidden inside wardrobes.

She decided she would visit the library now and while away an hour or two. She dressed quickly, and – armed with her card, two romance novels that she'd recently finished and an old crust for the ducks on the canal – set off down the hill towards the town centre.

The small town of Hebbleswick appeared to have tucked itself into a narrow valley where there wasn't room for a town at all. Three, sometimes four storeys of terraced houses, built of Yorkshire stone, zigzagged their way up the hillside, giving rise to a peculiar West Yorkshire phenomenon known as underdwellings and overdwellings: the houses on one street were built on top of those on the street below.

Jo's house was an underdwelling – with a lounge and tiny kitchen on its ground floor, its bathroom and one bedroom on the floor above. And above that was an entire other house. She never saw her upstairs neighbour; the entrance to their house was on the street above hers, on the opposite side of the building. Her house was a little dark and poky, but it did have a magnificent view over the valley. There hadn't been many rental properties available. Jo had been torn between this one, and a more modern flat, but the flat had little character, no view and it wasn't on Hazel Lane.

Hazel Lane.

Jo liked the word 'hazel'. It had a certain ring to it and would score a whopping 17 points in Scrabble.

Hebbleswick had a town hall, three pubs and a parish church called St Cuthbert's. It was popular with commuters thanks to its good rail links – well, rail links anyway – to both Leeds and Manchester, and with tourists thanks to its quirkiness, country walks on the doorstep and locally brewed real ale.

Almost every other shop was an art studio. You could buy several types of lentil – all organic, of course – and herbal remedies that could cure everything from indigestion to impotence. Also on offer were hand-made soaps, hand-crafted chocolates and hand-knitted sweaters made from the finest alpaca wool, but you'd be hard-pushed to find a can of Heinz baked beans should you want one.

Jo had wondered at first if she was a bit too – well, ordinary – to live in a place like Hebbleswick. When Gemma had announced that she was leaving Manchester, Jo had realised she'd have to move herself; she couldn't afford to rent their two-bedroom flat on her own and didn't fancy sharing with a stranger. She needed a change, a fresh start. Initially she'd intended to move to Essendale, attracted by the fact it had a board game café; she'd be sure to find like-minded souls there who'd be up for a game of Scrabble. But when she'd visited the café, there wasn't a Scrabble board in sight; the only letter tiles had been iced gingerbread biscuits. Jo had eaten a Q and decided that maybe Essendale wasn't the place for her after all.

Feeling more than a little despondent, she had wandered along the canal and soon found herself in the neighbouring town of Hebbleswick. She'd looked round a few shops, marvelling at how anyone could spend a fiver on a single bar of soap, and trying on a funky – 15 points – beanie made out of recycled plastic bottles. She'd been on her way to the station when something had caught her eye in the window of the hospice shop: a rather unusual dress. She'd peered through the window; the fabric had been printed to look like a Scrabble board.

The dress was too small, way too small – Jo could see that. But she'd wanted a closer look, so had ventured into the shop.

To her surprise and delight, the dress had been pinned to fit the mannequin and was a bigger size than it had first appeared. So of course, she'd tried it on and discovered that it was a near-perfect fit. It was a sign surely, Jo had thought, staring at herself in the changing room mirror. A sign that this was the town where she should settle, where she'd 'find her tribe' as Gemma always said.

(So far, she hadn't found anyone. Not a single friend. But still. Early days and all that.)

She had taken the dress up to the till to pay for it, relishing the fact that these days she could spend her money how she wanted. If she chose to buy a dress that she'd probably never wear, there was no-one to stop her. She'd been almost gleeful as she handed over a twenty-pound note, waving away the change that the shop assistant offered. Well, it was for a good cause.

Jo smiled to herself now as she walked along the canal, remembering how fate, the Universe or whatever you wanted to call it, had led her to live in Hebbleswick. She knew that many people might think it was silly superstition to decide to move somewhere because of a dress. And maybe it was. Maybe the perfect dress for her being in the shop window on the very day she happened to walk by *had* just been a coincidence, but Jo wasn't ready to give up on her signs just yet. She needed them. She needed them because she didn't trust herself to make decisions without them.

She'd made bad decisions in the past – well, one spectacularly bad decision. She'd married Si.

After that, she hadn't needed to make many decisions at all, because Si had made them all for her. And so Jo's confidence in her own ability to make choices for herself had slowly but surely been eroded, and now she liked her signs. They were like a comfort blanket somehow, a reassurance that she was doing the right thing.

She threw the last of the bread to a hungry-looking

mallard but a Canada goose got there first. Jo sighed and sauntered on towards the library.

The library was situated in an old stone building that had been given a bit of a facelift with modern glass doors and a little courtyard area with a bench. She checked her phone one last time – still no messages on Buzzz – then put it on silent. Loads of people didn't bother putting their phones on silent in libraries these days, but Jo had always been a bit old-fashioned like that.

She returned her old books, perused the shelves for a while, then checked out three new ones – two romances and a thriller. She was about to leave when she spotted a flyer on the community noticeboard.

Are you living Your Best Life? it asked.

Well, no. Obviously not.

Do you want to know the secret to getting everything you want?

A boyfriend would do.

And perhaps a job where she felt valued.

And some friends.

The 'Your Best Life' talk was today, she realised. It started at midday and it was already ten to. She punched the address into Google Maps. Eight minutes' walk. She could make it.

The church hall was almost full when she arrived. She paid the entrance fee and slipped into one of the few remaining seats. She didn't realise it then, but she'd walked straight past a poster on the church noticeboard advertising Hebbleswick's Scrabble group.

4

An American woman in flouncy dress and four-inch heels was strutting across the small stage, explaining how everyone could lead their Best Life. Her hair was piled up in an enormous, blonde bouffant, which wobbled as she moved.

Bouffant, thought Jo – 16 points.

'Visualise what you want from your life. Set your intentions, trust the Law of Attraction and the Universe will deliver,' the Bouffant said.

Jo was a firm believer in the Universe giving her signs, but less confident about its ability to deliver whatever she wanted on demand. Was she the only one feeling sceptical? She glanced around. Most people seemed to be hanging on the speaker's every word. Two rows in front, a man was filming the talk on his phone and the woman beside Jo was making notes in an expensive-looking notebook – the kind that used to cost over a tenner in Paperchase – her long, dark hair falling in a sleek, shiny curtain as she leaned forwards to write. And not just notes but *copious* notes, Jo thought – 11 points.

Was no-one else thinking, but what about paying the gas bill? She doubted that simply visualising it being paid was going to work.

She got out her trusty polka dot Filofax – true, it was old-fashioned but she loved all its little sections: so organised – and contemplated making a few notes herself, but this wasn't worth the paper.

'The Law of Attraction will not work if you do not value yourself,' the Bouffant was saying now. 'If you have a low sense of self-worth, this will affect the way you communicate with the Universe. By not believing that you are good enough, you are telling the Universe that you don't deserve anything. And if you tell the Universe that you don't deserve anything, nothing will come. Nada. Niente. Zilch.'

This was waffle. There was nothing about what to do if your best friend was now living two hundred miles away, if you were being ostracised at work and made to look silly in front of your colleagues, and if every man you went on a date with turned out to be a complete toerag.

'You cannot rely on other people to bolster your sense of self-worth – it has to come from within. From your heart,' the Bouffant said, clasping her hand to her chest in a dramatic fashion in case anyone wasn't sure where their heart was.

Jo found her mind drifting. How had the speaker got her hair to stand up like that? Not a look she wanted to emulate – a bit too Marge Simpson for her – but impressive nonetheless.

Was it blow-drying? Or backcombing? Or hairspray? Must take hours.

'When you have self-worth, you are ready to ask the Universe for what you want. Imagine achieving your goals. Make a vision board of your ideal home. Picture yourself nailing that job interview or clinching that business deal.'

Or using all seven tiles on a triple word score, Jo thought.

'Or finding the right man,' she murmured to herself.

Whoops. She hadn't meant to say that out loud. The woman next to her shot her a look.

'But my most important piece of advice...' Marge scanned the audience like a teacher making sure the entire class was listening '...is to live each day as if it were your last. Thank you for listening.'

Applause erupted from the audience.

'If this was her last day,' Jo mumbled, 'bet she wouldn't spend so long on her hairdo.'

She didn't intend anyone to hear, but her shiny-haired neighbour whispered, 'Too right.'

This seemed strange coming from someone who had clearly spent quite some time on her own coiffure. You didn't get it that shiny without a conditioner or that straight without straighteners.

Now the talk was over, a massive queue began to form along one side of the hall. Marge was signing books.

The shiny-haired woman turned to Jo and said, 'Are they mad? She didn't say anything I hadn't read before.'

'Honestly? But you were making notes.'

'No, I was updating my journal. I keep a review of each date I've been on.'

She was single too? Rather surprising. Not only did she have the kind of sleek, shiny hair that Jo could only dream of, she also had high cheekbones, large, blue eyes and a delicate nose. She was elegant too, in a green dress in soft jersey fabric with brown, knee-length boots.

'You must get a lot of dates,' said Jo.

Her neighbour flicked through the notebook.

'I write one page for each date. It's kind of a research project.'

'And is it working? Have you met anyone nice?' Jo asked.

'Not so far.'

'Me neither. Demoralising, isn't it? Each new message gets your hopes up and then you go on the date and he says, "There's no chemistry".' She made inverted commas with her fingers.

The woman laughed, snapping her notebook shut. 'Perhaps it's lucky we met. I'm Kate.' She held out a manicured hand.

'Jo.' She stretched out her own hand with its stubby, unpolished fingernails.

'Don't suppose you fancy grabbing lunch somewhere?'

They left the church hall. Jo was so busy talking to her new acquaintance that once again, she walked straight past the poster for the Scrabble club without noticing it.

Over a lunch of a huge green salad with no dressing (Kate) and burger and fries (Jo) in one of Hebbleswick's trendier cafés, the two women compared dating experiences.

'I hope you let him pay,' said Kate after Jo had regaled her with the saga of dinner with Neil at ¡Tapas! ¡Tapas!

'Well, no…'

'Oh, Jo, honestly.' She put her head in her hands for a few seconds then looked up again. 'Paying your own way would be one thing, but paying *more* than your fair share? Why on earth didn't you object?'

'He didn't give me chance. He told the waiter to take half from his card and half from mine.'

'Why didn't you stand up for yourself?'

Jo shrugged. 'I dunno. I never do.'

'Hmm, well, you need to start. All the books advise letting the man pay on a first date,' continued Kate. 'And also, you should keep first dates short. Only stay long enough to pique their interest.'

Perhaps she should be writing this down. *Let them pay on the first date. Pique their interest. Stand up for yourself.* She'd never manage that last one; she never had.

'And let them do the chasing, at least initially. Don't message them after a date,' Kate said. 'Wait for them to contact you.'

'My friend Gemma would say this is the twenty-first century…'

'And is she still single by any chance?'

'No, she's not, but she hasn't done much dating.'

'Well, then. Oh yes, and don't appear too keen.'

'Perhaps that's where I went wrong with the last guy, Dan. I really liked him, but he cancelled our last two dates. I haven't seen him in over a fortnight. And he's stopped returning my texts.'

'Forget him then,' said Kate. 'Move on.'

'How about you? Met anyone interesting recently?'

Kate sighed. 'There was this one guy – Rob. We dated for a while and I was so into him, but he was obsessed with fitness. I mean, I like to keep in shape, but he was out running or in the gym every single night. I barely saw him. Since we split, I've had loads of dates, but nothing serious. When were you last in a serious relationship? Ever been married?'

Jo took a sip of her Coke. This was something she

preferred not to talk about. 'I was married but it didn't work out.'

'How come?'

'He was...'

Did she reveal the truth? Or the version that she usually told people?

The usual version, she decided. She'd only just met Kate; it was too early to divulge the full horror of those years with Si. And in any case, well, it never sounded as bad as it actually was. Si had never hit her. He raised his voice sometimes, but only if she'd been very annoying. He was sometimes a little too insistent when it came to sex, claiming that Jo was frigid if she wasn't in the mood. He criticised her, but said it was for her own good. It had been such a confusing time; he was so convincing. Even now, Jo still wondered if he had been trying to help her, as he always used to claim.

'We just wanted different things,' Jo said. Yes, it was best to stick to the usual version.

Kate nodded. 'Who left who?'

'I left him.'

It sounded so easy; it had been anything but. It had taken her months to pluck up courage. There'd been the practicalities to sort – she'd opened a separate bank account, squirreling away as much as she dared, hoping he wouldn't notice the extra cash withdrawals, and she'd arranged to stay at Gemma's – but the emotional side of leaving her marriage had been by far the most difficult. He'd told her so many times that she was nothing without him that Jo believed it. She spent many a sleepless night wondering how she'd cope without him. She couldn't have managed without Gemma's support.

Suddenly, Jo realised that Kate had asked her something and was waiting for an answer. 'Sorry, I didn't catch that,' she said.

'I said, what was he like?'

'He was...'

How to describe him? He was gorgeous. Out of her league, she'd thought when they'd first met. He oozed charisma. Everyone liked him. When they met anyone new, Jo always clocked their surprise that this attractive, popular man had such an ordinary woman on his arm. Afterwards, when it was over, she'd realised that was probably why he'd chosen her. He wanted someone who wouldn't draw any attention away from him; he liked having the spotlight on himself.

She'd been easy to manipulate too. Her parents had by then taken early retirement, pursuing their dream of moving to a Scottish island, and Jo only saw them once a year at Christmas. There wasn't a rift; there'd been no big argument. It was just that Angus and Susannah had never really understood their bookish daughter. Jo often wondered if things might have been different had she had a closer relationship with her parents or a wider circle of friends, but as it was, there was only Gemma sounding the alarm about Si, and Jo had ignored her.

'He was...?' Kate prompted.

'Gorgeous-looking. He made me feel special. At least at first. But... it doesn't matter. Let's talk about something else. The future, not the past. I want to meet someone new. Someone who's kind to me. But I always seem to choose wrong 'uns. Not that I get loads of choice. I mean, there are a lot of men on Buzzz, but most of them aren't interested in me.'

Kate frowned. 'I don't see why not. Show me your profile.'

Jo took out her phone, opened the app and clicked onto her profile, before handing it over. Kate shook her head as she started to read and the furrows on her forehead deepened. '*I like watching box sets – especially* ER *– and reading romance books. ER?*'

Jo glanced around the café, hoping no-one was listening in. 'It's an American medical drama. With George Clooney.'

'I know what it is.' Kate continued, '*I enjoy eating out and especially love cakes*. Honestly, Jo. And your photos...'

'What's wrong with them?'

'They don't do you justice. You have to sell yourself. Overhaul your profile. Include some interesting hobbies, and better photos. Have you been anywhere exotic? Machu Picchu? The Great Wall of China? Uluru?'

Jo shook her head. Llandudno probably wouldn't cut it.

'How about putting that you're interested in art?' Kate said. 'I mean, who doesn't love looking at a few waterlilies or a vase full of sunflowers?'

''Spose. We have spoof copies of *The Hand of God, The Scream* and the *Mona Lisa* hanging in our office. I often talk to Mona.'

Kate looked puzzled for a second, before continuing. 'And you could put "adventurous activities." It's so vague it could mean anything.'

Jo wasn't so sure; she couldn't be less adventurous if she tried.

'Good thing you've met me, Jo,' Kate said. 'And perfect

timing. My best friend Emily recently met the love of her life.'

'Mine has too. Well, she's known him ages, but she's moved in with him now. In Watford. Crap, isn't it?'

'Yeah, well, of course, I'm pleased she and Ludek have found each other...'

Ludek, thought Jo. Lucky Emily – 10 points.

'...but I need a new wingman. You up for that?'

Jo wasn't exactly sure what being Kate's wingman would entail, but she nodded enthusiastically. At least – at *last* – she'd found her first friend in Hebbleswick.

'I'll have them queuing up to date you,' Kate continued.

Men queuing up? Jo wasn't sure about that. She just wanted one man. One man who'd appreciate her, who'd love her for who she was.

In those early days with Si, he had done that. He had made her feel that she was a person worth talking to, worth listening to, worth making love to, and more than anything, Jo wanted that feeling again. She wanted it so badly.

'Yep, count me in,' she said.

5

Monday afternoon. Not a single one of Jo's colleagues had noticed how tidy the stationery cupboard was.

And not a single new man had noticed her newly improved profile on Buzzz; she'd lost the references to boxsets and romance books, kept the cakes and added an interest in art and 'adventurous activities.' But to no avail. There were no messages and she hadn't had so much as an online wink. It was ten to three and her phone had been silent all day. Jo checked for the fourth time that it wasn't because it was *on* silent.

Waiting.

Waiting.

Waiting.

Ping.

She pounced on her phone. It was Gemma.

Love your Scrabble score dating idea! Any new messages on Buzzz?

Jo was tapping out a reply to say that no, there'd been no new messages, when David bellowed from his office, 'Jo!'

He sounded angry, she thought, dropping her phone

and scrambling to her feet. He did have a bit of a temper, but it had never been directed at her. There was no time to stop and wonder what she'd done wrong; she grabbed her Filofax and scuttled into his office, leaving the door open behind her.

'Where the hell is the budget for the Channel Five dating show?'

Oh, was that all he wanted? He never had got to grips with Caroline's obscure filing system on the shared drive.

'If you look on the shared drive, it's in the Channel Five folder, and then you need to go to another folder – Caroline called it...'

'I've looked through *all* the folders and it isn't there. Are you sure you saved it?'

'Definitely,' said Jo, moving round to his side of the desk to look at his screen. 'It was the last thing I did on Friday night...'

'Well, it isn't there.'

Jo clicked frantically, staring at the monitor. He was right; it wasn't there.

'Did you save in the wrong place?' said David.

She shook her head. She *never* saved things in the wrong place. Organised was her middle name. Although she had been distracted. That message from Neil had arrived on Buzzz... was that before or after she closed the spreadsheet?

Odd though, because whenever you closed a document in Microsoft Office, it prompted you to save your work if you hadn't already.

'I definitely saved it, David,' she said again.

She couldn't understand it. She didn't make silly mistakes like this. She just didn't.

'Well, bloody find it,' he said, slamming his fist down on the desk and making Jo jump back. 'I have a Zoom meeting with the channel tomorrow, Jo. I need to check through those figures. Like now.'

She stared down at the screen, blinking back the tears. She hated it when someone raised their voice at her; hated the memories it brought back.

'Don't just stand there,' he said. 'Find. It. Now.'

As she rushed out of his office, everyone busied themselves, trying to act as if they hadn't been listening to David's every word. Everyone, that was, except Leona, who stared at Jo, a tiny smile beginning to form on her lips.

Sitting down at her desk, Jo checked the shared drive again, but the missing document wasn't there. It wasn't in her personal drive either. And yet she was sure – well, 99 per cent sure – that she *had* saved it. She looked up at Mona hopefully. 'You saw me,' she mouthed. 'You know I saved it. How could it disappear?'

She'd have to redo it, but first, she needed coffee.

She could have gone to Costa – the fresh air would probably have done her good – but to save time, she filled the kettle in the office's tiny kitchen. A cup of instant would do. Anything with caffeine.

She waited for the water to boil, deep in thought. How could it vanish? And then she had that strange feeling that you get when you know someone is watching you. She turned to see Leona standing in the doorway, a barely concealed smirk across her face.

'Ah, great, you've put the kettle on already,' said Leona, brandishing an empty mug.

Jo had only put enough water in for one cup of coffee.

With a sigh, she picked the kettle up and filled it some more, although she knew full well what Leona wanted and it wasn't caffeine. She wanted: a) to find out more about why David had been angry, b) to gloat or c) both. It was probably c) both.

Anyone else would have asked their colleague if they were okay, but not Leona. She cut straight to the chase with, 'David sounded mad at you. What d'you do?'

'I… he…' Jo bit her lip. 'He couldn't find a file, that was all. Saved in the wrong place.'

Leona nodded. 'And you found it?'

'Well, not exactly.'

'How odd,' said Leona. 'Perhaps Little Miss Organised isn't so organised after all.'

The kettle began to boil. She would normally make Leona's coffee for her, but sod it. Her colleague was clearly revelling in the fact that Jo was in trouble. She spooned Nescafé into her own mug, poured in the hot water and left the kitchen. She preferred coffee with milk, but just this once, she'd drink it black. She wouldn't spend a second longer than necessary in such close proximity to Leona.

Had Leona deleted that spreadsheet deliberately? Jo wondered as she sat back down at her desk. Would she stoop that low? From the moment they'd met, Jo had sensed that the woman didn't like her, but had no idea why; she'd tried so hard to help Leona when she first joined Pop! Productions, but since then, they'd barely spoken. Leona had quickly appointed herself the social secretary of the little office, ensuring that Jo was no longer included on girls' nights out. That wouldn't have bothered Jo too much in the days when she'd shared a flat with Gemma, but since her best friend had moved so far away, it *did* bother her. It bothered her very much.

But it was one thing to omit to invite a colleague out for Friday night drinks, quite another to deliberately sabotage their work. Whatever grudge Leona held against Jo, she wouldn't go that far. Would she?

It was twenty to eight that evening by the time Jo finally boarded the train back to Hebbleswick. Caroline had kindly stayed late and the pair of them had managed to recreate the missing spreadsheet. Jo had checked and double-checked that it was saved this time, had emailed it to David and blind-copied herself in, to be on the safe side.

It had been a terrible day. As well as losing the spreadsheet and David getting cross, Jo had overheard Leona telling the whole team about it. 'Can you believe it?' her nemesis had said. 'The Queen of Spreadsheets has *lost* a spreadsheet!'

They'd all laughed.

Or rather, cackled – 16 points.

As the train left Manchester Victoria Station, Jo's phone pinged. A new message on Buzzz. It was from someone who, according to the app, lived within two miles of her. Strange. He'd never come up in any of her searches.

She realised why when she clicked on his profile: he was five foot eight, the same height as her, so below her minimum height specification. She preferred men who were taller than her. Who made her feel safe and protected. Ironic, she thought. Si had been six foot two and she'd felt anything but safe with him. She'd spent every minute walking on eggshells.

Forget Si, she told herself. She was making a fresh start. She was going to meet someone new.

It had taken her years to pluck up courage to even contemplate another relationship, and she couldn't face dating after what Si had put her through. For one thing, she didn't think anyone would want her anyway; years of first the other kids at school and then her husband telling her she was ugly and unlikeable had made her believe that. For another, Jo wasn't sure she'd ever be able to trust another man; what if she met another Si? How could you tell? He had been charming at first – she'd been so smitten; couldn't believe her luck – but then he'd changed, and she'd always blamed herself that she hadn't realised sooner what he was really like. There must have been warning signs.

She'd been too fearful to start dating again, but when Gemma left, Jo had been overcome with loneliness, so had taken the plunge and signed up for a dating app. She trusted words more than pictures, so wanted an app where the emphasis was more on the words you wrote about yourself, rather than your appearance, and having read all the reviews, she'd decided that Buzzz was the app for her.

'Take things slowly,' Gemma had advised. 'Don't get attached to anyone too soon. Keep your eyes peeled for red flags. Always meet them somewhere public and don't, whatever you do, go back to their place or get in a car with them until you really know them. Watch out for players. And control freaks. You do not want another Si.'

She certainly didn't, Jo thought, remembering her friend's words as the train trundled on. She turned her attention back to her phone and the profile of her new admirer. He hadn't written much; it was – like her new profile – rather vague. Kate would have approved, Jo thought. She couldn't glean much from his photo either; it had been taken in a mirror and the flash obscured half his face. From what she could make out, he had the messiest hair, a large nose and geeky glasses like the awful free ones they used to give schoolchildren on the NHS. Not exactly a heart-throb, but then she had wanted a dating app where you didn't judge on appearances. She skimmed through his profile then reread his message.

He hadn't sent the usual *Hi, how are you?* or *You look nice* or *Can we shag?* He'd come up with a decent question that showed he'd read what she'd written:

If you had to eat one type of cake for the rest of your life, what would it be?

She mentally gave him an A* for effort – it was original at least – and decided that, even though she didn't fancy him, he at least deserved a reply.

Can I choose afternoon tea? That way I'd get a variety.

Variety – 13 points.
His reply came quickly.

No, that's cheating!!!

Okay then. I'll go for scones. Fruit ones one day, plain the next. With different jam.

Their online chat – still all about food – continued as the train dawdled through the outer suburbs of Manchester.

Favourite breakfast?

Croissants. No, pain au chocolat. Yours?

As the terraced houses and blocks of flats gave way to the dark hills of the Pennines, Jo's phone pinged again.

Cold, leftover pizza.

Urgh

she texted back. She smiled to herself, her woes at the office almost forgotten.

The best meal I've ever eaten was a simple spaghetti bolognaise in a simple back-street café in Florence

he wrote as her train finally neared Hebbleswick station. It sounded heaven and Jo suddenly wanted spag bol for dinner, even though it was already late. She dropped by the corner shop, picking up soya mince (they didn't sell animal products), an onion, a tin of tomatoes (organic as it was all they had) and dried spelt spaghetti. Why couldn't you buy a packet of *normal* spaghetti around here? Was everyone on a vegan, organic, whole-grain diet?

Jo finally reached Hazel Lane. Her key sounded hollow as it turned in the lock. The front door wouldn't open; it had been sticking for weeks but DIY wasn't her thing and the landlord was yet another man who didn't return her calls. She managed to shove it open as her phone pinged again.

She threw her coat onto the threadbare sofa. Despite the fact that her belongings were everywhere, this place still didn't feel like home. She kept intending to put pictures up and buy a throw for the sofa to cover up the coffee stain – at least she hoped that's what it was – that the previous tenant had left.

She plonked herself down on the sofa and pulled out her phone to read his latest text.

Perhaps we'll go there together one day.

Together? To Florence?

She went into the tiny kitchen to begin cooking. That latest message had surprised her. She hadn't contemplated meeting him in real life; as far as she was concerned, they were only passing the time with a bit of online chat.

She was browning the soya mince – were you meant to brown soya mince? – when there was another ping. She turned the gas down and went to retrieve her phone.

Fancy meeting on Saturday afternoon? I know the perfect place for our first date.

Their first date?

Did she want to go on a date with him?

She'd enjoyed his messages; they'd been chatty – like the sort of messages you'd send to a friend, rather than a stranger from a dating app – and a welcome distraction on the train home. Without them, she'd have spent the journey dwelling on the shenanigans – 15 points – in the office.

And she was curious about this 'perfect place' he'd mentioned. It had to be food-related since that was all they'd talked about. Probably some fabulous café that served afternoon tea on a three-tiered cake stand: neat little sandwiches, chocolate eclairs, tiny sherry trifles.

It was tempting; he seemed like a lovely guy but he wasn't her type and she didn't want to lead him on.

She didn't know what he was called, she realised suddenly, remembering her Scrabble dating idea. If his name would score double figures, she decided, she'd go on the date. If it wouldn't, she'd let him down gently.

You haven't told me your name

she messaged and waited for his reply.
Nothing.
She put her phone down and began chopping an onion.
She picked up her phone a minute later and checked his profile again. The little green dot on his profile had disappeared. He was offline.
She was adding the tin of tomatoes to her culinary masterpiece when there was a ping.

My name is Rasmus. My grandad was Danish.

Rasmus – 8 points. So not double figures.
But only 2 points off.

6

Saturday. For once, Jo was relieved it was the weekend after the trauma of the missing document on Monday, although the rest of the week had been non-eventful: nothing else disappeared, David seemed to have forgiven her, and Leona hadn't made any snide comments. Plus, she was looking forward to her date with Rasmus. Especially the afternoon tea element.

Jo made an effort for this date, hoping he'd be taking her to one of Hebbleswick's smarter cafés. She donned her favourite jeans – deep indigo with lighter patches down the thighs that the woman in the shop had assured her would have a slimming effect – and a crisp white T-shirt under a tailored green jacket. She even ditched her usual trainers in favour of navy flats.

After a brief tussle with the front door, which did not want to close, Jo set off towards the centre of the little town. A long, stone staircase led down from her street, alongside the allotments with their neat rows of carrots and lettuces. Jo shoved her earbuds in and cranked up the volume on Etta James. She was pretty sure that today *wouldn't* be the day her love came along, but it wouldn't hurt to get herself in the right mood.

But she almost turned straight around when she spotted Rasmus waiting on the town hall steps, glancing around nervously in the way that men on first dates often did. She knew she shouldn't judge on appearances, but no way was he five foot eight. Five foot seven, maybe. At a push. Definitely shorter than her. The NHS glasses had gone – contacts perhaps? But his orange anorak had seen better days – an anorak? Really? On a date? – and was about three sizes too big for his slim frame. His baggy jeans weren't much better. His hair was a nondescript shade of brown – admittedly the same colour hers would be if she didn't use Nice 'n' Easy – and hadn't seen a comb recently. And his eyebrows could have done with a trim. Or a pair of garden shears.

If she had to describe him in one word, that word would be 'awkward' – 18 points.

He took first-date awkwardness to a whole new level.

He was awkwardness personified.

He shuffled towards her, fiddling with the zip on his jacket. Here was a man who worked in IT if ever there was one. No kiss on both cheeks. No handshake. Just a mumbled 'hi' as he looked at his feet.

'Hi, Rasmus,' she said, trying to sound cheerful. 'Lovely to meet you.'

'Call me Ras. Everyone does.'

Ras? He went by the name of Ras.

The letters R, A and S each scored only 1 point in Scrabble so that made a pathetic total of 3 points.

If only he'd said that to start with... well, she wouldn't be here.

'We'd best get a move on,' he said, still making no eye contact. 'Don't want to miss our slot.'

Slot? He meant table surely?

He was still looking down but at *her* feet rather than his own. 'Er... I think you might need different shoes.'

'Different shoes?'

'Yeah, when we get there, it's a bit of a walk. And those shoes... well, they aren't suitable for where we're going.'

'Where *are* we going?' Jo's hopes of fluffy scones and clotted cream and sandwiches with the crusts cut off were fading fast.

'It's a surprise,' he said. 'I'm hoping you haven't done it already. I'm so excited about this – you're going to love it.'

'You sound very sure,' she said, 'considering you've never met me before.'

'You said in your profile that you liked adventures. And this... well, it's definitely an adventure. A world-famous, record-breaking local attraction.' He paused and looked at her. 'Well, perhaps not world-famous. Or record-breaking. But people come from miles around to see it. So are you up for a mystery tour?'

'A mystery tour?'

'Yes, the car's over there.' He gestured towards the car park.

Jo frowned. No way was she climbing into a car with a man she didn't know. He could be anyone.

He sensed her hesitation. 'Sorry, sorry, I should have thought. Obviously, you don't want to get into a car with a stranger. And quite right. Stupid of me.'

'It's just... well, you could be anyone. An axe murderer.'

He laughed. 'Do I look like an axe murderer?'

She looked at the orange anorak. 'You don't. But axe murderers don't look like axe murderers. If they did, they wouldn't get away with the murdering.' She was rambling now. Why was she rambling? Not nerves, surely. She didn't even fancy him.

'Listen. Google the health centre – Hebbleswick and Essendale Group Practice – and click on the link to "medical staff".'

She looked at him for a moment, puzzled, but then did as he suggested. The first picture that came up was Dr Ludek Ulanicki. Ludek? Kate had mentioned the name Ludek. Her friend's husband, wasn't he? Must be the same guy. And underneath, there was a picture of the man standing in front of her. Dr Rasmus Rasmusson. So he was one of the local GPs. Astonishing. He looked even less like a GP than he did an axe murderer.

'You're a doctor?' She tried to keep the surprise from her voice.

He nodded. 'Yep. Look, if you still don't feel safe, we can leave it. Go and get a coffee or something instead.'

A coffee would be nice, thought Jo. And perhaps there'd be cake. But it would also be like every other internet date she'd ever been on, sitting in a café or a pub, with a latte or a Pinot Grigio, making inane small talk. No man had ever offered to take her on a mystery tour before. And surely if he was a doctor, it would be perfectly safe. They did background checks, didn't they, before they employed someone in a role like that?

'I'd like the mystery tour please,' she said.

'You sure?'

He looked up and his eyes met hers for the first time. And they *were* kind eyes. And he looked so hopeful, like a Labrador pleading for a morsel of food. Excited even. Sure, he wasn't her type, but he'd taken the trouble to arrange something that he thought she'd enjoy. And he mightn't be boyfriend material, but perhaps he'd turn out to be friend material. And she didn't know anyone in the area yet, except for Kate. And Jo had texted her three times now, suggesting a drink, but got the same reply each time:

Sorry, off on another date.

Kate seemed to go on a date every night of the week.

'I feel perfectly safe,' Jo said. 'Come on, let's go.'

'Great.' He seemed relieved. 'Let's pop by your place so you can change your shoes.'

Another no-no with a man she'd only just met; he'd know where she lived. But still, he was a doctor. Although she'd best not mention any of this to Gemma; she had promised not to take any risks. 'Yeah, that'd be great, thanks. It isn't far.'

'Have you got hiking boots?'

'Hiking boots? No.'

'Trainers?'

'Sure,' she said. 'I've got trainers.'

Ras drove Jo to Hazel Lane where she changed her shoes and, on his suggestion, swapped her smart jacket for a warmer coat. They set off up a steep road out of Hebbleswick, zigzagging between rows of terraced houses. Ras negotiated several hairpins with great skill until they emerged onto open moorland, covered with heather.

'What do you do for a living?' said Ras.

'I work in TV.'

'That's exciting. You must be very creative.'

'Not especially,' Jo said. 'I book taxis, write schedules and keep the budgets up to date. I'm not at all creative.' She paused for a moment. Perhaps she was selling herself a bit short. 'But I am good at organising,' she added. 'In fact, I *love* organising.'

'Good to know. Can I call on you if I ever need anything organising?'

She laughed. 'Of course.'

'And how was your week? Did you organise an awful lot of things?'

'I've had a terrible week,' began Jo, then stopped herself. Why hadn't she said her usual, 'Fine, thanks. Yours?'? She couldn't tell him about the lost spreadsheet, David slamming his hand on the desk and Leona smirking about him. She didn't need to consult Kate to know that telling your date about your problems, moaning, complaining, whatever you wanted to call it, wasn't a good tactic.

'How come?' he said.

'Oh, it's nothing. A colleague I don't get on with. Your messages on Monday evening cheered me up.'

'Did they? I'm glad.'

The stark beauty of the moorland gave way to gently undulating hills, their green slopes dotted with trees.

'Almost there,' he said. 'See the old-fashioned signal box? That's the Settle–Carlisle railway.'

She might have known he'd be into trains. With that anorak, he'd fit right in with the little crowd of middle-aged men she sometimes saw on the end of the station platform in Manchester, jotting down numbers in their little books.

But so what if he seemed a bit geeky? There was something she rather liked about Ras.

7

A car park.
They were in a car park. Granted it was in a pretty village. Popular too, judging by how difficult it was to find a space and the number of people brandishing walking poles and studying ordnance survey maps.

A hill, she decided. This famous, local attraction he'd mentioned must be a hill.

Well, that wouldn't be too bad. Given that she'd put that she liked doing 'adventurous things' on her profile, he could have chosen anything. Skydiving. Bungee jumping. Waterskiing. At least her arms weren't going to get wrenched out of their sockets. And hopefully, it wouldn't be too steep a hill.

Besides, the exercise would do her good. She loved her curves – they were the only thing she liked about her body – but for health reasons, she could do with being a little fitter.

'Ready?' said Ras, and he managed to make eye contact.

Jo nodded. Okay, so he was too short for her, but those eyes were sparkling with excitement and they were a rather lovely shade of blue. The same shade, in fact, as a double letter score square on a Scrabble board. And although he was scruffy, there was something rather cute about him, rather endearing, like a hairy puppy in the dogs' home that jumped up and down with excitement every time a potential new owner went past.

Definitely not axe murderer material, which was lucky since she was about to head up into the hills with him and he was giving her a lift home later.

They set off along the road, in the same direction as all the other walkers, and took a path into a woodland. A sign ahead said: 'Waterfalls'.

Aha, thought Jo, so that's what he's brought me to see. Kind of romantic. Well, it would be *if* she fancied him.

She couldn't remember the last time she'd been for a walk. A proper walk, rather than a short stroll along the canal to feed the ducks. It was such a simple pleasure: breathing fresh air; counting the different shades of green on the trees, hearing the ground scrunching underneath your feet, the birds singing. She ought to do this more often. It was a bit silly, living somewhere like Hebbleswick, surrounded by beautiful countryside yet only ever seeing it from the train window on her daily commute to and from Manchester.

And it was a lovely thing to do on a first date. Far better than sitting opposite someone in a pub or a restaurant. How many times had she done that?

Suddenly, an unwelcome image popped into her head.

Her first date with Si.

Her ex-husband.

He'd taken her to the poshest of restaurants. She'd been half-impressed, half-intimidated, certain that the waiting staff were all looking down on her. It must have been obvious from her clothes that this wasn't the kind of place she usually frequented.

But Si had strode in as if he came here every day. She'd almost expected the wine waiter – or what was it Si had called him? The sommelier (13 points) – to say, 'The usual, sir?'

'What would you like, Joanne?' he had asked, when he'd seen her frowning at the complicated menu.

She'd hesitated, wondering whether to remind him that she preferred being called Jo. She'd mentioned it once already.

'Shall I order for you?' he'd said.

It had seemed kind of gallant at the time, and she'd nodded gratefully. Only later did she realise it was the first of many choices that he'd made on her behalf. At least on their first date, he had asked.

'Wow, look at that,' said Ras.

Jo jolted back to the present with a huge sense of relief. They were standing by a waterfall, white froth deluging over steely grey rocks.

'It's lovely,' she said, raising her voice to be heard over the noise of the water. 'Thank you for bringing me here.'

'You're welcome. Although this isn't what I've brought you to see. We've still got a couple of miles to go.'

'Let me guess. We're climbing a hill?'

'Nope. We can do that afterwards if you like. Although I rather thought we might go for tea and cakes.'

Tea and cakes. Now he was talking her language.

'Afterwards... after what?'

'Wait and see. You'll love it.' He held up crossed fingers.

They yomped on. A wide pathway led upwards, along the path of the river, with fields of sheep on either side, and drystone walls criss-crossing the hillsides. The path grew narrower, winding steadily upwards into a gorge with limestone rocks towering on either side of them.

After scrambling up some loose rocks, they found themselves on open moorland, the slopes of Ingleborough now visible in the distance, and beneath it, a large, white tent, not unlike the kind you saw on TV detective shows.

'Is that where we're heading?' she said. 'Or have they found a body?'

'A body?'

'They look like those tents you see on crime dramas on the telly. You know, that they put over the murder victim whilst they do their forensic tests or whatever.'

He laughed. 'I see what you mean, but no-one's been murdered. Hope not anyway, as that's where we're going.'

As they drew closer, Jo could see it was more like a marquee – 18 points – than a forensics tent. For a second, she imagined it was some kind of village fete, up here on the hillside, and that a committee of women from the local WI were at this very moment judging the Victoria sponge competition. Ridiculous idea. But it was baffling. Why would someone go to the trouble of lugging a big tent all the way up here?

'What is it?'

Ras tapped the side of his nose. A large nose but it suited his face. Quite Roman. He wasn't conventionally good-looking but he was rather striking.

'You'll see.' He was clearly intent on maintaining the 'mystery' element of this mystery tour for as long as possible.

They'd reached a small wooden fence now, with some steps leading down. Down to what exactly?

There were people milling about. Quite a lot of people.

And an air of excitement. Some kind of structure built of scaffolding had been erected near the tent and beneath it was an enormous hole in the ground. She looked at Ras, puzzled.

'Gaping Gill,' he said.

'Gaping Gill?'

'One of the largest underground chambers in Britain. You'll see when we get down there.'

Jo's jaw dropped. 'We're going down there?'

'I hope this is adventurous enough for you.'

Kate! Jo thought. Why on earth had she listened to Kate? It was one thing writing 'art' as an interest – she wouldn't have minded traipsing round the odd art gallery – but 'adventurous activities'? Being winched into a hole in the ground? No thanks.

'There's only two weeks a year when the public can go down it and this happens to be one of them,' said Ras. 'Look, someone's going down now.'

Jo watched with horror as a man of about twenty fastened his hard hat, walked down the steps, across the scaffolding and sat himself down in a yellow, metal chair.

Scaffolding, she thought. Appropriate. She felt like she was going to her execution. Was it safe? What if the rope broke?

'They don't weigh you first, do they? To check you're not too heavy?'

'I don't think so,' said Ras. His eyes flicked down her body. 'Anyway, I'm sure you're not too heavy.'

She blushed, and turned away so he wouldn't notice, watching as the young man was harnessed into the chair. He gave a thumbs up to his watching friends, one of whom was filming the whole ordeal on a mobile, and began his descent into the hole, soon disappearing out of sight.

'How far down is it?' said Jo. Perhaps it was only a few feet. She could manage that.

'About a hundred metres, I think.'

A hundred metres!

Why? she thought again. Why had she listened to Kate?

Then she remembered something else that Kate had said: that she should stand up for herself. She could start now; could say, 'That's not my idea of fun. I'm sorry but no.' He could go down, but she wasn't going to put on a hard hat that would make her hair look even flatter and more lifeless than it usually did, or be strapped into a tiny chair and lowered a hundred metres on a chain that might snap.

Although…

Well, perhaps she could do it.

Because a) she didn't mind heights.

And b) a woman of around her size was now being winched up out of the enormous hole; she had the biggest beam on her face that Jo had ever seen and the chain seemed to be holding up okay.

And c) this would make a great anecdote. When she went into the office on Monday morning, if anyone bothered to say, 'How was your weekend, Jo?' she'd have something interesting to tell them. For once.

'You don't have to do it,' said Ras. 'It does look a bit more… well, it looks scarier than I thought it would.'

'Of course I'll do it,' Jo heard herself saying. 'It'll be great.'

8

'Ladies first,' said Rasmus when their turn came.

Jo pulled the hard hat down onto her head, checked the strap three times to be sure, and walked down the steel steps and across the scaffolding to the waiting yellow chair. The seat of doom, she thought, wriggling into it. It was barely big enough for her arse.

One of the cavers helped her fasten herself in and checked the straps were secure. She glanced across at Ras, who was waiting at the top of the steps, and gestured to him to take a photo of her. He rummaged in his pocket and pulled out his phone.

'Have fun, Jo,' he called, as he took a snap.

She took a deep breath and gripped the chair as she began her descent. Looking up through the grey limestone rocks that formed the mouth of the hole, she could see blue sky and the face of one of the cavers receding into the distance. Below her was black. Endless black.

At times, the shaft was so narrow that Jo thought she might graze her elbows, but after a surprisingly short amount of time, it widened out and she reached the bottom. One of the caving team unhooked her and she climbed out of the chair, tottering a little on trembling legs. She blinked, her eyes not yet accustomed to the darkness, but slowly began to get a sense of her surroundings.

'Amazing, isn't it?' said the caver. 'You can fit the whole of York Minster in here.'

Jo had never been to York Minster but imagined it was pretty big.

The air inside the cavern was cool and fresh. A shaft of light streamed down from the hole a hundred metres above. There were a few electric lamps around, and other visitors were using the torches on their mobile phones, but even so, it was dark; Jo felt like she'd entered another world.

Another adventurer was strapped into the chair now, and it made its way back above ground to where Ras was waiting. Jo felt a surge of gratitude towards him. He was a quiet man, not her usual type at all, but bringing her here, planning this activity, because he thought she loved adventure was a thoughtful thing to have done. He wanted to please her, not merely sit across a table from her in some anonymous pub, boasting of his achievements like so many of her previous dates had. She couldn't wait for him to get down here so she could tell him what an amazing time she was having.

She didn't have to wait long. The chair was soon on its way back and Jo watched as the figure of Ras descended towards her. Looking at him from this angle, he seemed taller.

There was a reason for that, she realised as he got closer. He wasn't Ras.

Another man, an older man, climbed out of the chair and seemed surprised to find Jo waiting for him.

Where was Ras?

'I was expecting my… friend,' she said to the new arrival. 'I thought he'd be down next.'

'Short bloke?' said the man. 'Scruffy?'

'Yeah, that's him.'

'Lost his bottle. They strapped him in, but he changed his mind. He went a funny colour. Thought he was going to be sick.'

Poor Ras. Was he scared of heights? Odd that he chose this for their date if he was. Or perhaps he'd been taken ill? Something he'd eaten? She'd take a quick look round, then go back to him and tell him all about it.

She felt a pang of disappointment, wishing she was sharing this experience with him. It *was* like being in a cathedral, she thought, remembering what the caver had said about York Minster. She wished Ras could see this; much as she loved words, Jo knew that when she tried to describe this magical place to him later, words wouldn't do it justice. She could never capture the mystery of it, how it felt to stand here, in this echoey, cavernous space, hidden away underground.

When she reached ground level, Ras was sitting on a rock, head in his hands. She put her hand on his shoulder, making him jump.

He looked up at her, pale-faced. 'I'm sorry, Jo. I've let you down. I've always been afraid of heights.'

'Then what made you bring me here?'

'Two reasons. I've been having hypnotherapy and thought it would be a kind of test for me, to see if the hypnosis had worked. I was sure I'd manage it.'

'And the other?'

'I knew you'd like it.'

Her heart went out to him. He'd been willing to put himself through this ordeal for her? Well, willing to try, at any rate.

'I did like it – I loved it, in fact. So thank you. This definitely ranks as my most unusual first date ever. Although…'

'Although?'

'I'd have enjoyed it more if we'd done it together.'

She didn't say that to make him feel bad – the opposite, in fact. She wanted him to know that he'd been missed.

'Sorry,' he mumbled. 'What was it like?'

She paused for a moment. There was only one word. 'Breathtaking,' she said.

She almost added, '22 points,' but she didn't want Ras to think her boring; he was bound to think that, if she admitted she loved Scrabble. She'd never met a man yet who'd understood her obsession with word games. She couldn't admit that she sat around most evenings playing on the WordPals app; well, it hardly made her sound like scintillating company, did it?

It was, Jo decided as they sped along the windy lanes back towards Hebbleswick, not only her most unusual first date ever, but her most enjoyable. After an unpromising start – well, he was a bit on the quiet side – she'd found she could relax with him and she hadn't felt nervous, except when she'd first seen that bloody great hole. She hadn't felt the need to impress him or to be anyone other than who she was. Apart from not mentioning the Scrabble obsession and she probably *could* have told him about that; he didn't seem judgy.

She glanced at her watch. Over six hours. Her longest first date too. And there'd been no awkward silences – at least, not if you didn't count the first couple of minutes.

Come to think of it, he wasn't saying much now, but this didn't feel like an awkward silence. She glanced at him. He was focused on the road, lost in his own thoughts, as she was lost in hers. He was frowning slightly, probably because they were stuck behind a caravan and the road was too bendy to overtake.

When he asked for a second date, would she say yes?

She was sure he'd ask her out again; after all, he must have liked her profile to have arranged this trip to Gaping Gill, and they'd definitely got on well.

She weighed up the pros and cons. He was a) shorter than she was; b) not conventionally good-looking; and c) the scruffiest man she'd ever been on a date with.

But on the other hand, a) she'd felt safe with him; b) attraction could grow, couldn't it? He was definitely more attractive than she'd initially thought; and c) who cared about clothes? She wasn't exactly stylish herself. In fact, it would be a refreshing change to be with a man who wasn't so hung up on appearances; with Si, *everything* had been about appearance and his need to show the rest of the world that he had made it, with his flash car and designer suits.

So yes, she would definitely say yes to that second date.

Only he didn't ask. He pulled up outside her house and said, 'Thanks for a lovely day, Jo. It was fun meeting you.'

That sounded a bit... final. Not like a man who wanted to see her again.

Should she ask him in for coffee? Or was that a bit silly if he'd expressed no interest in seeing her again? What would Kate do?

She unfastened her seatbelt and it pinged back into place. Kate wouldn't ask him in. She'd remain a bit aloof. Keep her dignity.

'Thank you again,' she said, climbing out of the car and closing the door behind her.

9

Jo thought about Ras as she waited at Hebbleswick Station on Monday morning. And as she boarded the train when it finally arrived. And as she grabbed a seat next to a man eating a rather pungent sausage sandwich and wearing cheap earbuds, which afforded the entire carriage the dubious pleasure of hearing the tinny backing track of whatever song he was listening to.

When she stood up to let sausage man past – he was getting off at Essendale – she wondered if it mattered that he wasn't her usual type. Ras, that is. Not sausage man.

Move on, she told herself. *You didn't like him* that *much anyway.*

You like men who are taller.

More confident.

But he'd been so thoughtful. Such a good listener. And had encouraged her to step out of her comfort zone. On reflection, she'd had the best time.

On Sunday, she'd still been clinging to the hope he might contact her and had been disappointed when her phone didn't ping. She'd picked it up seventeen times (at least), tapped out a short message thanking him for a wonderful date, then put it down again without sending. What was the point? He hadn't messaged her. She wasn't sure what had gone wrong, but something had, judging by his demeanour as he'd driven her home. The promised tea and cakes had never materialised. Something seemed to have changed between them on the walk back to the car. Had she said something that offended him? She couldn't for the life of her think what.

She managed to put him out of her mind as the train trundled towards Manchester. She avoided looking out of the window at the Pennines; they'd only remind her of him. Instead, she focused on her phone, playing game after game on WordPals, and wondering if she'd have the guts to pitch her programme idea this morning in the team meeting.

They began every working week with a full-team planning meeting at eleven o'clock. One of Pop! Productions' programmes was a weekly magazine show, which needed constant feeding with ideas, and those Monday morning meetings were pitching time. The researchers would have scoured the morning papers in search of inspiration, unusual stories that might make a good short film or celebrities who had a book out and were doing the interview rounds, but everyone – not only the 'creatives' like the researchers and producers but the admin staff like her – was encouraged to put their ideas forward. Since Leona had arrived, Jo had been reluctant to speak up in meetings, but she was determined to find the courage to do it today. If she could allow herself to be lowered one hundred metres into the ground on a little chair, she could speak in a meeting. Of course she could.

There was a bit of a scramble for chairs as the team piled into the meeting room – it was far too small for the growing company – and a few people ended up standing around the sides. Jo managed to get a seat next to Caroline. Opposite Leona, but you couldn't have everything.

She listened as David ran through the agenda – last week's viewing figures, audience feedback, which programmes were being filmed this week – and then seized her opportunity as soon as he said, 'Anyone got any new programme ideas?'

'I have,' she said quickly before she could change her mind. She felt her cheeks reddening as all eyes in the room focused on her.

'Let's hear it then,' said David, giving her an encouraging smile.

'I wondered about a series of programmes where people face their fears. For example, someone who's scared of heights could do what I did this weekend; I went down Gaping Gill. It's a huge hole in the ground in North Yorkshire – a hundred metres deep.'

She hesitated, unsure if she should give them another example and decided that she would. 'Maybe someone with arachnophobia could spend a day at the zoo working with the tarantulas. Or…'

'Oh, puh-lease,' said Leona. 'Same old, same old.'

'All ideas are welcome,' said David firmly. 'It's a good one, Jo, though there might have been something similar on TV already. Anyone else? Come on, people. We need more ideas.'

'I could organise a brainstorm?' said Leona.

'Thought shower,' said Caroline. 'We don't say brainstorm at Pop! Productions. But an ideas meeting is a fantastic idea. Thanks, Leona. Can you sort that?'

Jo dropped her eyes to her Filofax and kept them there for the remainder of the meeting. She hadn't expected her boss to immediately start pitching her idea to the channels; she wasn't that naïve. But she had thought there might at least be some discussion about it.

'She said what?' said Kate.

'"Same old, same old". David – he's my boss – reminded her that all ideas are welcome, but he always says that and I still feel like an idiot if I pitch something they don't like.'

They were in the George, Hebbleswick's most traditional pub. Jo needed cheering up and had been relieved when Kate had said she could meet that evening; it was the first time that she'd seen her new friend since the day they'd met as Kate was always busy. Always dating. Evening after evening. Jo wasn't sure how she managed it. Still, they were here now, and Jo was tucking into her favourite dinner, steak pie and mash with a generous helping of gravy – best comfort food ever – whilst Kate had another green salad. Was that all she ever ate?

'It hasn't been the same since she joined the team,' Jo said. 'She talks about me behind my back. I never get invited any more for a drink after work.'

'She sounds awful.' Kate sliced an already tiny tomato into quarters. 'Just ignore her.'

'That's easier said than done. Perhaps I've never fitted in at Pop! – I'm not really cut out to work in the media. I'm not trendy enough.'

'Nonsense. You're fine, Jo. Don't do yourself down.'

Jo nodded but she didn't believe that for a second. She thought of her colleagues – of how they hurried around talking loudly on their mobiles, giving off an air of self-importance, an assurance, a confidence that Jo had never had – and she wondered, not for the first time, how on earth she'd she ended up working in television. It wasn't the place for a mouse like her.

It was Si who'd encouraged her to apply for that first position in a small TV company on the outskirts of Manchester. Jo had been quite happy doing her old job, working for a small firm of solicitors, but he'd wanted his new fiancée to have a more impressive-sounding job than that.

'They want someone "highly organised",' he'd said. 'That's you, Joanne. No previous media experience necessary. It's ideal.'

'But I'm happy at Smythes,' she'd told him.

'You can stay *there* forever.' He'd grimaced, as if he'd stepped in something nasty. It had been clear that he'd looked down on her current workplace, but she couldn't for the life of her think why. 'It'd be a step up from what you're doing now. They don't value you, Jo. They don't see your potential. You're just a typist to them.'

Just a typist? She shouldn't have let him get away with that. Should have pointed out that she did so much more than typing letters. She practically ran that company. Mr Smythe had had tears in his eyes when she'd handed in her notice. *Reluctantly* handed in her notice. Si had harangued her for days about the telly job until she'd applied to keep him quiet. She'd never expected to actually get it.

And then, still not satisfied, a year or two later, he'd 'encouraged' her to apply for the post at Pop! Productions. 'Production co-ordinator', he'd said. 'Surely that's better than what you're doing now? And it's a bigger company too. Much more prestigious. Not quite the BBC, but still… you'll get there eventually.'

Jo had never had any intention of applying to work at the BBC. It was far too big. Far too intimidating.

'How's your steak pie?' said Kate.

'Delicious. How's your salad? Is that all you ever eat?'

Kate stuck her fork into an olive. 'I'm trying ayurveda. Have you heard of it? You eat different things according to what type you are. I'm kapha. D'you know your type?'

'Probably heifer,' said Jo, tipping the last drops of gravy from the jug onto her mash.

'I don't think that's one of them.' Kate looked baffled; Jo hoped she hadn't written GSOH on her dating profile. 'Seriously, it's very healthy. You should try it.'

Jo shook her head and cut herself a generous chunk of pie. She'd always promised herself she'd never go on another diet as long as she lived. Not after the final two years of her marriage when Si had watched every calorie she ate, monitoring each morsel that she put in her mouth. 'It's for your health,' he'd said. 'And you want to make the best of yourself, don't you?'

How often had he said those words?

The best of yourself.

Why wasn't she good enough as she was?

The pounds had come off, but when Jo looked in the mirror, she'd liked herself less and less with each passing day. Her chin was too large. Her shoulders too broad. Her hands not feminine enough. Her stomach was flatter, but her hips and thighs had remained resolutely chunky.

'I'm only thinking of you, Joanne,' he'd said, after he'd chosen a salad for her in their favourite restaurant, whilst opting for rump steak and chips for himself.

And that was another thing: she had hated the way he

insisted on calling her 'Joanne' yet was happy to shorten his own name.

'Joanne sounds much more feminine,' he'd always said when she protested. 'Jo sounds like a man's name.'

'Been on any dates recently?' Kate said.

Jo snapped herself back to the present moment and regaled her with the story of her trip down Gaping Gill.

Kate snorted with laughter. 'Sounds awful. Was he good-looking?'

'Not especially.'

Although he had grown on her over the course of the day.

'So why did you agree to the date? You're not that desperate, surely?'

'He sounded nice in his messages and...' Jo paused. No, perhaps not. She wouldn't mention her Scrabble dating plan; Kate would think it was daft.

And probably best not to reveal Gaping Gill man's true identity; Kate might know him since he worked at the health centre with Ludek, who was, Jo felt sure, her friend Emily's partner. There couldn't be two Ludeks – not in their little valley.

'How have your dates been?' Jo said. 'You're out every evening.'

'Terrible. But I have hope. Do you fancy going to a pub quiz?'

'A pub quiz?'

'Well, a pub quiz with a twist. You did say you'd be my wingman?'

Jo wasn't sure why Kate would need a wingman for a pub quiz, but it might make a pleasant change. 'Sure,' she said. 'Why not?'

IO

'Speed-dating?' said Jo when she saw the sign on the door of the pub. 'You said it was a pub quiz.'

Kate laughed. 'I said a pub quiz with a twist. The speed-dating is the twist. Come on.'

She opened the door, and Jo followed her inside, wondering what she'd let herself in for. Another sign directed them towards the room upstairs.

She'd been a bit suspicious when Kate said they were going to Huddersfield, rather than the weekly quiz at the Red Lion in Essendale. But speed-dating? She'd never have agreed to that. Twelve first dates – and potentially twelve rejections – in one evening? It was her worst nightmare.

Still, she liked a good pub quiz; maybe she could concentrate on the questions. Judging by the number of cocktails being knocked back by their fellow competitors, the height of their heels and the cleavage on display, everyone else would be focusing on the dating element of the evening and she'd be in with a good chance of winning.

'I'll buy the first round,' said Kate. 'Margarita? Sex on the beach?'

'Shouldn't we keep a clear head for the quiz?'

'Don't be daft. Who cares about the quiz? I've heard the mojitos here are amazing.'

'Go on, then. I'll have a mojito.'

Jo sat in a corner and played on the WordPals app whilst Kate fought her way through to the bar. She returned a few minutes later with four mojitos.

'Saves queuing later,' she said, placing them down on the table.

Jo had intended to have only one drink but had to admit that Kate was right about how good the mojitos were. They were also strong and her head was already spinning a little by the time the host for the evening tapped the mic with his finger, and then began to speak.

'Good evening,' he said. 'Can everyone hear me all right?'

A few people shouted, 'Yeah,' and he continued. 'Are we all excited for the speed-dating?'

This time no-one replied, but he carried on regardless. 'There are sixteen women and sixteen men.'

Sixteen first dates, Jo thought. Great.

'Now, I've forgotten the name badges this evening, so you'll have to do that old-fashioned thing of introducing yourselves. There'll be eight rounds of quiz questions: two general knowledge, a current affairs round, music, history, sports, food, and arts and culture.'

He explained how the evening would work: one pair of men would join Jo and Kate's team for the first round, and then they'd move on to the next table for the second round, and two more men would join them. And so on.

'It's a bit of a lottery,' Jo said to Kate, surveying the blank answer sheet. 'If we happen to get men who have Sky Sports for the sports round and men who listen to the *Today* programme for current affairs, we've got a good chance. But knowing our luck, we'll get the *Today* programme listeners for the sports round and the Sky Sports guys for the current affairs.'

'And that matters because…?'

'We won't win the quiz.'

Kate gave Jo a withering look. 'It's about the men, not the quiz. The quiz is an ice breaker. Whilst we're discussing what the answers might be, we suss the guys out and decide if we like them.' She waved a piece of paper. 'This is the important thing that we're filling in tonight.'

Alongside the blank sheet for their quiz answers, they each had a second sheet numbered one to sixteen with a tick box alongside each number. If Jo ticked 'yes' to a man, and he ticked 'yes' to her, the speed-dating company would email them each other's contact details, so they could arrange to meet up again. If either – or both – of them didn't tick the vital box: no exchange of details.

Jo and Kate had been among the first to arrive so were numbers three and four. Men numbers three and four would join them for the first general knowledge round; they wouldn't meet numbers one and two until the end of the evening.

A bell sounded and the men began to head for their first tables.

Two tall guys, both balding, both wearing jeans and rugby shirts, sat down opposite them. Kate smiled coyly. Jo was about to ask their names but the quiz began.

'Zn is the symbol of which chemical element?'

Jo had the pen and the answer sheet, but as soon as the question had ended, Number Three grabbed them from her and scribbled down the answer. Neither Jo nor Kate got the chance to say who'd co-written *Gavin and Stacey* with Ruth Jones, what a Geiger counter measured or which type of wood a cricket bat was made from. Not that Jo knew that last one anyway, and she felt pretty certain that Kate wouldn't either.

'So much for the questions being an ice breaker,' she whispered to Kate, looking over at Number Three, who was zealously guarding the answer sheet.

'What is a zax?' said the host.

Jo leaned over and peered at the answer sheet. Number Three had written 'musical instrument'.

'He said *zax* not *sax*,' she said, pulling the answer sheet back across the table. She held her hand out for the pen. For a second, it looked as though he wasn't going to relinquish it, but then the bell rang and he couldn't get to the next table fast enough.

They each put two crosses on their 'men' sheets, next to Numbers Three and Four. Number Four might have been a lovely guy but they hadn't had the chance to find out.

Jo crossed out *musical instrument* and wrote *tool for cutting slate tiles*. She'd looked it up once; it was a useful little word in Scrabble if you happened to have both the Z and the X, and would score a respectable 19 points, though she'd never actually played it. Or seen anyone else play it, come to that.

It was sport next – Jo's weakest subject by far.

As Kate and Number Five answered questions about who'd won which medal in the last Olympics, Jo made polite small talk with Number Six about what they thought of the evening so far. They quickly reached a consensus: not much.

As the host read out the last question of the round, Jo wondered whether she should tick his box. He was a little pasty-looking, but perhaps he'd look better in daylight, and he seemed like a pleasant enough guy.

'What's your name?' she said to him.

'Sam.'

Only 5 points. That'd be a no then. She resolved to ask the men at the start of each round what their names were, but the next two guys seemed intent on using their numbers.

'Double-O-Seven at your service, ma'am,' said the shorter of them. He couldn't have looked less like James Bond if he'd tried.

Jo fared no better in the music round than she had in the sports. Number Eight was unimpressed with her complete inability to recognise songs by Rihanna, Arctic Monkeys and Busted, to name the movie that had featured Taylor Swift singing 'Eyes Open' or to state which British girl group had done a cover version of 'The Tide is High' which had stayed at number one for several weeks.

'Was it Blondie?' she suggested.

'They were American,' said Kate.

'And they weren't a girl group,' added Number Eight.

As the round ended, he stood up, looked at Jo and said, 'Seriously, what *do* you listen to?'

Number Seven shrugged his shoulders and followed him to the next table.

'Hello, ladies,' Jo heard him say as the two men sat down. 'I'm Double-O-Seven, at your service.'

'I think we can safely say we're not ticking either of those two,' said Kate as Numbers Nine and Ten slipped into their seats opposite Kate and Jo.

Between them, Noel (4 points) and Ian (3 points) managed to name the energy secretary and the celebrity who'd died the previous month aged ninety-three, which film had won the most Oscars this year, and which country the Pope hailed from, but there was a bit of debate about which city was currently the UK's city of culture.

By the time the next round began, Jo was feeling a little worse for wear, having almost finished the second mojito, so forgot to ask the names of Numbers Eleven and Twelve.

Numbers Thirteen and Fourteen looked far younger than the thirty to forty age group stipulated on the entry tickets so she didn't ask them either. It was the food round. She let Kate make conversation with the guys and busied herself with the questions, writing that burrata was a type of mozzarella and the Isle of Wight held an annual garlic festival.

'They were a bit lairy,' said Kate, as Numbers Thirteen and Fourteen stumbled towards the next table. 'Did you know all the answers?'

'Some,' Jo said, looking down at the sheet and checking her answers. Out of the corner of her eye, she saw a tweed jacket being slipped over the back of the chair opposite her.

She looked up. Perhaps it was her mojito goggles, but this man was perfect. Short, dark hair. Lightly tanned skin. The brownest eyes. A strong jawline and dazzlingly white smile. She'd only ever seen teeth that white in magazines and had always assumed they were Photoshopped. And his ears. Such neat ears. Ears weren't something she generally noticed. But this man's ears... she wanted to nibble them. Now. Right now.

And if that wasn't enough, he was definitely quirky. His

look was kind of country squire: a herringbone waistcoat – who wore waistcoats these days? – with a bow tie. And was that a pocket watch? It was. This man had come to a speed-dating event in a back-street pub in Huddersfield wearing a pocket watch. As someone who always dressed to blend into the background, Jo was full of admiration for this man who was clearly intent on standing out.

If she were to spend time with someone like him, maybe his confidence would rub off on her.

'Hi, I'm Kate.'

Kate held out her hand to the squire's friend, a blond guy wearing a business suit. He shook it a bit too vigorously.

'George,' he said.

'I'm Jo,' she said, holding out her own hand to the man in the herringbone waistcoat.

He took her hand and kissed it. Actually kissed it.

'Lovely to meet you, Jo,' he said. 'I'm Tarquin.'

11

'Tarquin?' said Jo. 'With a Q?'

A Q. One of the two highest scoring letters in Scrabble. Making his name worth a massive 16 points.

'Yes, Tarquin,' he said. His voice would have given Hugh Grant a run for his money in the poshness stakes. Rich. Velvety. The kind of voice that melted her insides.

Jo barely heard the first question of the round; she was concentrating on trying not to gawp at Tarquin. It was silly getting all worked up like this when he was clearly out of her league. If he ticked either of their boxes this evening, it would be Kate's.

'Have you given up on the questions?' said Kate, taking the pen off Jo. She began to write.

'Do you like art?' Tarquin said, looking directly at Jo.

Was this the art round?

'Of course. Who doesn't love sunflowers and waterlilies?'

He laughed. 'I know *nothing* about art.'

'Nah, me neither.'

He twinkled at her. 'Good to know we've got something in common.'

They watched as Kate and George established between them that Frida Kahlo was born in Mexico and that *My*

Bed was by Tracey Emin. Tarquin sipped his wine. Jo noisily sucked up the last dregs of her mojito from the bottom of her glass, like a child trying to get the last drops of a McDonald's milkshake. From time to time, she could feel his eyes upon her and felt her cheeks reddening, but kept her gaze firmly fixed on Kate and George, who were arguing about who had won the previous year's Turner prize.

They settled on Grayson Perry.

'Who painted *The Scream*?' said the host.

'Edvard Munch,' Jo said.

Tarquin raised his eyebrows at her. 'So you do know about art?'

'Only cos that one hangs in our office,' she said.

The question master's voice boomed through the speakers again: 'Who first developed the pottery known as Jasperware?'

'Was it Jasper?' Jo said.

Tarquin laughed. Initially, she was pleased that she'd amused him – a GSOH was a highly sought-after commodity in the dating world – but he laughed a little too loudly for a little too long, and Jo realised he was faking it. Her quip hadn't been *that* funny. Still, he probably wanted to be nice.

Kate frowned and said, 'No, too obvious.'

George said, 'Wasn't it Wedgwood?'

'Oh yes, my gran had some Wedgwood,' said Kate. 'Joseph Wedgwood?'

'Josiah,' said George. 'We're a great team, aren't we?'

Kate and George exchanged smiles as the bell rang, signalling for the men to move on.

'See you later, Jo,' said Tarquin as he left for the next table.

With Tarquin sitting only metres away, Jo wouldn't have noticed if either of their final dates of the evening had been George Clooney himself, and she certainly couldn't concentrate on the final round of questions: more general knowledge.

Numbers One and Two knew that the first successful vaccine was used to prevent smallpox, that Julia Gillard was the first female Prime Minister of Australia and that 'E' was the only vowel not used as the first letter in a US State. None of them had a clue which English city used to be called Duroliponte or how many states there were in India.

But Jo didn't care about the quiz anymore. She had only one thing on her mind. Tarquin – 16 points.

12

Friday lunchtime. Caroline had dashed off to do some shopping. David was probably eating a sandwich at his desk; his office door was closed, a sure sign that he was busy working on something important and couldn't be disturbed. And the rest of the office had disappeared off to lunch somewhere without inviting Jo. Leona's doing, of course.

Jo refreshed her emails for the dozenth time that day. There was still nothing from the speed-dating company to tell her if she'd had any matches. Or one match. There could only be one match, because she had only ticked one box.

And that box belonged to Tarquin.

Every other woman in the room probably ticked his box too, she thought. Well, every woman except Kate. Jo still wasn't sure if her friend simply hadn't fancied Tarquin (honestly, did the woman not have eyes?) or if she'd spotted how much Jo liked him so had done the decent thing.

Jo finished off her lunch – a jacket potato heated up in the office microwave with generous dollops of butter and cheese – and picked up her phone and opened Buzzz. Would Tarquin be on there? she wondered. She entered Huddersfield, chose 'within a five-mile radius' and clicked Search. And there he was, the first face on the page; the app's algorithm put the most popular profiles at the top.

God, he was gorgeous; he looked too good to be true. If she hadn't already seen him with her own eyes, she wouldn't have believed he was real. Gemma had sent her at least three articles about dating scams: fake profiles and men who pretended to be someone else then conned you out of your life savings. But Jo didn't have any life savings to be scammed out of and besides, she already knew that Tarquin existed.

Her phone pinged.

Are you checking me out?

It was the man himself. The app must have alerted him to the fact that Jo was looking at his profile. She felt as if she'd been caught out, doing something she shouldn't have been doing.

Another ping.

Hey, didn't we meet last night? At the pub quiz?

He remembered her then. Well, that was something at least.

Heart pounding, she tapped back,

Yeah, I think we did.

She added a smiley, pressed send and waited.
His reply came back swiftly.

Fancy a drink? Monday evening?

She could hear voices now and turned round to see a gang of her colleagues returning. For once, she was glad that she hadn't been invited along. If she'd gone out for lunch, she might never have looked at Tarquin's online profile and he might never have asked her out.

There was no sign of Tarquin outside Halifax station, but then she was five minutes early. She hopped from foot to foot as she listened to Etta James, not with cold but with nerves.

At dead on seven, a flashy black sportscar stopped in front of her. The window opened and a familiar posh voice called out, 'Come on, get in.'

Jo hesitated. She barely knew him. Getting in a car on a first date was ill-advised. Of course, she'd got in Ras's car, but that was different. She'd checked him out, verified that he was who he said he was: the local GP. Okay, so she'd met Tarquin once before but even so, he could be anyone.

A small silver hatchback pulled up behind him and tooted its horn.

'Get in! What are you waiting for?' His voice sounded impatient now.

Jo put her fears to one side and opened the door, slipping into the passenger seat beside him. Well, not slipping exactly. More falling into. This car was quite low; it wasn't going to be easy getting out again. Not elegantly anyway. Not in these tight jeans. Thank God she wasn't wearing a skirt.

'Hi, Tarquin,' she said, savouring the sound of his lovely, high-scoring name as it left her lips.

'Lovely to see you, darling.'

He kissed her on both cheeks.

The car behind gave another toot, then pulled past them.

'Arsehole,' said Tarquin. 'So where to?'

Jo racked her brains. There was a small pub on the main road going towards Hebbleswick. It was a couple of miles away, but probably more intimate than a town centre bar. And she wanted their first date to be somewhere special; if things worked out, this might be an evening they'd look back on with fondness for many years to come. They hardly wanted to be saying, 'Remember our first date in that Wetherspoons in Halifax? When those two lads had a fight and a bar stool got broken?'

Tarquin seemed pleased with her suggestion.

'So what do you do, Jo?' he said as they drove along.

'I work in television. In Manchester.'

'Must be exciting. All that filming.'

Jo bit her lip. She'd hardly ever been filming, but it sounded dull to admit she was always stuck in the office. 'How about you?' she said. 'What do you do?'

'I'm in property.'

A developer probably, she thought. That would explain the fancy clothes and the fancy car. He was obviously doing well for himself.

He turned into the pub car park and swung into the only available space. It was reserved for disabled badge holders, but he didn't seem to notice and was out of the car before Jo could point it out. She followed him into the pub.

She found a table whilst Tarquin went up to the bar to

order. He was wearing a brown jacket this time, with pink trousers. Pink! Not bright pink, more of a salmon colour, but even so, it was a bold statement. He was obviously aiming for the country squire look again and Jo decided that she rather liked it.

'Here you go,' he said. 'One Pinot Noir.' He placed a glass in front of her. She'd asked for Pinot Grigio but not to worry. He sat down opposite her and raised his half pint. 'Cheers.'

'Cheers. Thank you.'

'You're welcome. You look beautiful this evening.'

Jo fought the urge to turn round to see who he was talking to. She wasn't used to receiving compliments.

'You look great yourself. The clothes... well, I love your style.'

'Thanks,' he said. 'Everyone dresses like everyone else these days. Like bloody clones.' He laughed and Jo found herself glancing down at her completely unoriginal outfit of jeans and T-shirt and wondering if he thought *she* looked like a clone.

'So what kinds of things are you into...' he began, then paused.

She realised he'd forgotten her name. 'Jo,' she prompted.

'I knew that.'

'I couldn't forget your name. Tarquin. So unusual.'

And so high-scoring.

'Latin, apparently.' Tarquin took a sip of his low-alcohol beer. 'It means ruler.'

'Are you good at measuring?'

'Ha-ha. Very good.' He rolled his eyes. 'Believe it or not,

there were *two* Tarquins in my year at boarding school. The other one was an absolute hoot.'

Jo hoped he wasn't about to ask about her school experiences – the less said about those, the better – but he launched into a long-winded story of some prank he and the other Tarquin had once pulled.

As he spoke, she studied his face. Those eyes. And his cheekbones – she hadn't noticed those at the pub quiz. A hint of stubble. And soft, full lips. Well, they looked soft anyway. It was hard to tell without touching them. What would it be like to kiss him?

She realised suddenly that he'd reached the end of his story and was waiting for an answer. 'Hilarious,' she said, hoping it was the right response.

It clearly was as Tarquin nodded, happy.

'Where do you live, Jo?' he said.

'Hebbleswick.'

'Nice little place. Lived there long, have you?'

'No, I moved quite recently. It was hard to find somewhere – every other house is an Airbnb.'

Tarquin looked thoughtful. 'So there's a shortage of housing there, is there? Interesting. Might have to go and have a look round sometime. See if there's any opportunities.' He paused and had a sip of his beer, still looking deep in thought. 'And what do you like getting up to?'

There was something about the phrase 'getting up to' that sounded a little bit suggestive. Jo's stomach turned to butterflies and she pushed thoughts of what she'd like to get up to with Tarquin to the back of her mind.

She wondered how to answer his question. They'd

established at the pub quiz that neither of them were into art. Should she say adventurous activities? Or opt for the truth?

She settled on the truth. Gaping Gill had been fun, but in the unlikely event of a second date with Tarquin – though she doubted she'd be *that* lucky – she didn't want him organising abseiling or skydiving.

'This probably sounds horribly boring,' she said, 'but I love Scrabble. In fact, I'm a bit of a fanatic.'

'Scrabble? As in the board game? How quaint!' He smiled. 'Jo, you're adorable, d'you know that?'

She shook her head. Adorable? Was he being serious?

'We'll have to have a game sometime,' he said. 'Another drink?'

'Thanks, yeah. I'll get them.'

'No, allow me. Same again?'

And with that, he stood up and returned to the bar, leaving their empty glasses on the table to be collected by the bar staff later.

Kate would approve; she'd said to let the man pay on the first date. Although Jo would have preferred to at least buy a round.

A couple of minutes later, Tarquin returned, placing the drinks on the table. He sat down opposite her, and took her hand. It was a little clammy, she thought, but you couldn't judge someone for that. Perhaps he had a medical condition.

'What are you looking for, Jo?' he said.

'I er…'

She wasn't sure how to answer that question. Saying she was looking for love sounded a bit too full on.

'Because I'm looking for a serious relationship,' Tarquin

said. 'I like to establish that from the word go, so we aren't wasting each other's time.'

Was he for real?

She gazed into his eyes, hoping to discern whether or not he was genuine, but he was focused on something beyond her, over her shoulder. She turned around to see what he was looking at. There was a mirror behind her that she hadn't noticed before, and Tarquin was staring at his own reflection. He licked his fingertip and smoothed one of his eyebrows then ran his fingers through his hair, angling his head as he checked himself out. He caught her watching him and turned back to her, a mischievous smile on his lips.

'Vanity.' He laughed. 'One of my many sins. Though not the one I enjoy the most.'

Jo felt her cheeks reddening. She took a hasty swig of wine and tried to push the thought of what it might be like to 'sin' with Tarquin to the back of her mind. She couldn't remember fancying a man quite this much.

She hadn't quite finished her Pinot Noir when he said, 'Listen, I have to call it a night – early start tomorrow – but I'd love to see you again.'

'Sure,' she said, trying to keep the excitement out of her voice. Kate had said. *Don't be too keen. Men like the chase.* 'Although I'm pretty busy.'

'How about Friday?'

Jo knew full well she was free but decided to check her diary to keep up the illusion of not being too available. She reached into her bag and pulled out her trusty Filofax, opening it to the calendar section.

'A Filofax,' said Tarquin. 'Cute. Haven't seen one of those in years.'

Jo couldn't tell from his tone if he was admiring her old-fashioned organiser, or mocking her for having one, so she simply said, 'Yes, I could make Friday.'

'Perfect.'

They stood up and he put a proprietorial hand in the small of her back – she shivered at his touch – and he guided her out of the pub, pressing his key fob to open the car.

Jo glanced at the road. It was about three miles back to Halifax, but Hebbleswick lay in the opposite direction. It didn't make sense to let him drive her to Halifax, only to catch the train back again. Perhaps if she pointed this out, he'd offer her a lift; it would take him no time at all to run her back to Hazel Lane. Not in that car. And then perhaps he'd kiss her goodnight on the doorstep and…

'Aren't you getting in?' he said. 'I'll run you back to Halifax.'

'I'm in that direction,' she said, pointing towards Hebbleswick. 'Only five minutes away.'

'Sure, fine. Darling, it's been wonderful. I can't wait for Friday.'

He kissed her on both cheeks then got into the car. Jo watched, dumbfounded, as he started up the engine. Loud music began to blare from the car's stereo as he reversed out of the disabled space. He gave her a cheery wave then drove away, swinging left out of the car park. She watched his red rear-view lights disappearing.

How was she supposed to get home? She'd have to walk, a thought she didn't relish at this time of night. She knew exactly what Gemma would have to say about this. If she told her. 'Well, you shouldn't see *him* again.'

Although… well, it was her own fault. Perhaps when

she'd said she lived five minutes away, he'd thought she meant five minutes' walk. Yes, that would make sense.

And he *had* offered her a lift to Halifax; she should have accepted, then caught a train home. Or been more explicit. She could have asked him to run her home.

But she hadn't. It was her own fault.

Now was there a bus stop somewhere round here?

13

The bus stop was, it turned out, a hundred metres away from the pub, but there was no timetable and no-one else was waiting, so Jo had no idea if a bus would actually arrive. Still, she didn't relish the thought of a three-mile walk back to Hebbleswick, so she'd give it ten minutes. Or maybe quarter of an hour.

She had just balanced herself on the thin bit of plastic that purported to be a seat – clearly not meant for anyone with a normal-sized arse – when a poster caught her eye. The lettering was small and she couldn't read it from where she was, but it appeared to be written in Scrabble tiles. She stood up to get a closer look.

The tiles spelled out SCRABBLE CLUB, with the word SCRABBLE written horizontally, and the word CLUB written vertically, the two words intersecting and sharing the letter C. Underneath, written in normal typeface, were the words:

ST CUTHBERT'S CHURCH HALL, HEBBLESWICK.
EVERY FRIDAY. 7.30 P.M.

Scrabble club? There was a Scrabble club in Hebbleswick?

And she'd lived there – how many weeks was it now? – and not discovered this?

She had to go. This week.

Although damn. Friday was her date with Tarquin, and much as she loved Scrabble, she couldn't cancel that. The week after then.

She was still gazing at the poster when the bus arrived and its doors opened, taking her by surprise.

'Hebbleswick, please,' she said, stepping on board. She swiped her card on the reader, and practically skipped to down the aisle to a seat.

A date with a gorgeous man *and* the discovery that the little town she'd decided to call home had its very own Scrabble club. Things were definitely looking up.

'Sounds promising,' said Kate on Tuesday evening.

'It's early days,' said Jo. 'I'm amazed he wanted a first date, let alone a second. I'd have thought every woman in that room would have ticked his box.'

'I didn't.'

'Oh no?' Jo decided she wouldn't let on that she'd stolen a glance at Kate's paper.

'I'm sure he's lovely but those clothes... bit flash.'

'I like the clothes. They're quirky.'

Kate harrumphed. 'That's one word for them. He's a good-looking guy and he sounds charming. Well, I suggest that if you really like him, you pull out all the stops. Be flirty in your text messages. And ask him to pick you up from yours and make sure the place smells of cinnamon when he arrives. I'm sure I read that somewhere.'

'Cinnamon?'

'Men associate the scent of cinnamon with love.'

'How do I do that? One of those plug-in things?'

'No, it has to be real cinnamon. You sprinkle it on some bread soaked in milk and put it in the oven on a low heat. It'll slowly infuse through the house.'

This had to be the most ridiculous piece of dating advice that Jo had ever heard.

'Can you eat the bread afterwards?'

'No idea,' said Kate. 'Anyway, you'll be far too busy gazing into Tarquin's deep brown eyes to want to eat the bread.'

It was Thursday before Jo heard from Tarquin; she was starting to wonder if he'd forgotten her.

What shall we do tomorrow? Fancy getting together for some Scrabble?

Scrabble? He wanted to play Scrabble?

He *must* like her.

As she walked back to Hazel Lane from the station, up the hill and past the allotments, Jo decided that she wouldn't just send him a boring, old text message. When she reached home, she laid her Scrabble board on the little dining table and spelled out YOUR PLACE OR MINE with the letter tiles. Then she took a C, turned it back to front and added a dot underneath with a black marker pen to make a question mark.

YOUR PLACE OR MINE?

It wasn't exactly flirty, but it was original. Cute, even. He had said she was 'adorable' when she'd first admitted to liking Scrabble. Hopefully, he'd think this was adorable too.

She got out her phone, took a photo and WhatsApped it to Tarquin before she could change her mind.

She didn't have to wait long for his reply.

Your place. Friday evening. I'll be in Hebbleswick on Friday afternoon anyway to check out some potential development opportunities.

Jo sprinkled a liberal amount of cinnamon on a hunk of old bread that she'd been saving for the ducks and then poured over the last of the milk from the fridge. She popped it into the oven at one hundred sixty degrees – Kate had said a low temperature and that was low, wasn't it? – and went upstairs to get changed.

She hurried to the door as soon as she heard his knock, but then, as per usual, it took her several seconds to open it. It really did need fixing. She made a mental note to hassle the landlord again.

'You ought to get that sorted,' said Tarquin when she finally managed to open it.

Presumably, since he worked in property, he could have fixed it easily enough, but he didn't offer.

He stepped across the threshold, kissing her on both cheeks.

Not only late, she thought, but also empty-handed.

She felt a pang of disappointment. Surely you didn't tip up at someone's house without bringing a bottle of wine or a bunch of flowers.

Although... well, maybe that was a good thing.

Si had showered her with gifts. Small things at first: a box of chocolate or a bouquet. Then bigger things. A charm bracelet. An enormous bottle of perfume, something by Yves Saint Laurent, wasn't it? And a Space NK advent calendar. Jo wasn't into cosmetics and had been a little surprised that he hadn't known that. But it was kind of him, she'd thought at the time. He was trying to please her. To spoil her.

Love-bombing, Gemma had called it and, with hindsight, she'd been right. Jo wished she'd heeded her friend's warning.

So yes, it was definitely a good thing that Tarquin was empty-handed. A sign that he was a normal, decent man.

And an attractive man at that, she thought, looking at him standing there in her scruffy little lounge, in his mustard-coloured trousers.

'Wine?' she said.

She watched him clock the stain on the sofa and perch himself awkwardly as far from it as possible, a look of distaste on his face. Then she went into the kitchen, poured the drinks and sat down beside him. He immediately reached across to her and took her hand.

'I loved your message,' he said. 'Very clever. You're witty as well as beautiful.'

He stopped stroking her hand, took his jacket off and laid it across the sofa next to him. No cufflinks, she noticed. Ordinary buttons. And that shirt was a little creased too.

But then, he had been working all day. And working hard, by the look of it; were they patches of sweat underneath each armpit?

Tarquin had a look on his face. Hunger. And not for food, she realised. For her. He was about to kiss her.

She had always liked those moments in romantic films, where the hero was about to kiss the heroine and they both knew it was about to happen. There would be a bit of gazing, perhaps his hand would brush her cheek, stroking a hair away from her face. Their mouths would nearly meet, but not quite. They'd linger, savouring the moment. The anticipation... well, it was almost as good as the kiss itself, she always thought. Not that anyone had ever kissed her like that. But she longed for the day when someone would.

This was not that day. Tarquin plunged straight in, clamping his mouth onto hers. He was barely an improvement on Neil, the tapas guy. After less than a minute of soggy smooching, Tarquin's hand was on her thigh and she could feel it edging higher. It was all too much, too soon, and Jo thanked heaven that she always wore jeans and not a skirt. She pulled back, taking his hand firmly in hers and placing it on his own thigh.

'Slow down,' she said.

He blinked at her. 'Sorry, Jo. Got a little carried away there. You can't blame a man for trying. I find you so attractive. Irresistible. I want you, Jo.'

'I thought we were going to play Scrabble?'

He laughed. With a snort. 'Scrabble? God, no. That was a euphemism.'

A euphemism?

(18 points.)

So he hadn't meant it?

'You knew that, right?' he was saying now.

Suddenly he launched himself at her, his mouth covering hers, and his hand fondling her breast.

She turned her head so his mouth was no longer on hers, and said, 'No, Tarquin. Stop.'

But like Si, all those years earlier, Tarquin didn't seem to understand the word no. He tried to kiss her again, his hand now squeezing her breast.

'I'll scream,' she said. 'The woman in the house upstairs...'

'*House* upstairs?'

'This is an underdwelling. There's a house upstairs.'

'How quaint,' he said, his lip curled in a sneer. 'I thought you owned the whole place.'

'No, the bottom two floors. And I rent it. I don't own it.'

Tarquin shrugged. 'Now where were we?'

'I think you were going,' she said, wriggling away from him and struggling to her feet. She picked up his jacket – it was rather garish, she noticed – and handed it to him. 'This isn't what I want. I like to take things slowly in a new relationship.'

'Who mentioned a relationship?'

Jo stared at him. He had seemed so attractive, so gorgeous, that first evening at the speed-dating pub quiz. But now, for all the fancy clothes, the chiselled cheekbones, the deep brown eyes, he seemed sleazy somehow. Like a second-hand car dealer trying to palm you off with a dilapidated old banger. Or an estate agent extolling the spaciousness of a studio flat you couldn't swing a cat in.

'What do you mean who mentioned relationship? That was you. Was it a ploy to get me into bed?'

With as much dignity as she could muster given that her bra had somehow ridden – or rather been pushed – above her right boob, Jo walked to the door. In her mind's eye, she would open it and make a gesture indicating for Tarquin to leave, and he'd disappear out of her life. In reality, she tussled with the handle for what felt like ages – but was probably only a few seconds – and when she finally wrenched it open, she fell back against the wall. And she didn't need to gesture. Tarquin stepped out.

'You're frigid,' he said.

The word stung. It had been one of Si's favourite words. For a second, Jo wondered if the two men were right. Perhaps she had a low sex drive. Had she led Tarquin on?

No, she decided. She'd agreed to a date, not a shag. 'You could have been honest,' she said. 'If casual sex was what you wanted, you could have said that.'

He turned to look at her. 'Jo.'

'Yes?' she said, wondering if he was about to do the decent thing and apologise.

'I can smell burning.' he said. He clicked his key fob and his car chirruped back from further down Hazel Lane.

Jo watched him walk away, then channelled all her anger, all her frustration into one almighty shove against the front door, closing it with a bang that seemed to shake the entire row of terraces. She put the chain across. He was right; there was a burning smell. She went back into the kitchen, opened the oven door and removed the blackened remains of the cinnamon bread.

She opened the window to let the smoke out of the tiny kitchen and scraped the charred mess into the bin. The ducks could have had that bread. They'd missed out for what? Because she'd been stupid enough to believe that the scent of cinnamon might make a guy like Tarquin fall in love with her. He had only ever been after one thing: to get her into bed.

All that spiel about wanting a serious relationship – that had just been a line. No, make that a lie.

Gemma had warned her about men like him; at least two articles on the subject had pinged into Jo's inbox when she'd first announced she was signing up to Buzzz. She should have paid more attention.

At least he had stopped. She shuddered; it could so easily have turned out differently. But it had taken the threat of screaming; he hadn't taken 'no' for an answer. Still, she was used to that; Si had never taken 'no' for an answer either.

She sat down on the stained sofa. Her legs were still shaking but her heart rate was beginning to return to normal. Perhaps she wasn't ready. Yes, it had been years since she'd split up from Si, but one incident like this brought it all back to her, as if it had happened yesterday.

How could you know? How could you know when you met someone on a dating app or at speed-dating whether they were a decent guy or whether they'd turn out to be a Si or a Tarquin? That was the trouble; she just couldn't tell.

She wiped her damp cheeks on her sleeve. Tarquin hadn't wanted a relationship with her; he had wanted her for sex. Ras hadn't wanted her at all. Nor ¡Tapas! ¡Tapas! man nor Dan before him, come to think of it.

Men made her feel bad about herself.

No, make that people. Other people made her feel bad about herself, she thought, and the unwelcome image of Leona came into her mind.

(Okay, not everyone. Gemma didn't. Nor Kate. Although she did sometimes feel a little inferior looking at how immaculately groomed her new friend was.)

She couldn't avoid people altogether, appealing though that thought was at this moment in time, but she could give up dating.

Yes, that was what she'd do. She'd give up dating. She'd give up men.

Unless the Universe gave her a sign – and it had to be a big one and not something that could be explained away as a mere coincidence – that a man was right for her, then Jo Knox was going to stay single.

14

The first person to learn of Jo's decision was Mona.
'I've given up dating.'

Mona looked decidedly unimpressed.

'Well, I was never going to find anyone, was I? You know that. I know that. I was kidding myself. Signing up to Buzzz. Agreeing to be Kate's wingman. It was never going to work.'

For all she yearned for company, Jo relished the mornings when she was first to arrive at work. When she could make a mug of coffee before anyone else arrived, check her emails and chat to Mona, before the open-plan office filled with the chatter of Leona regaling the others with the fantastic night out she'd had the previous evening and David marching down the corridor talking loudly on his mobile, as he invariably did.

'So yeah, I've given up dating.'

Mona stared at her phone.

'Rude,' said Jo. 'Plain rude. Looking at a mobile when someone is talking to you. I might start talking to them instead.'

She gestured at the other two canvases. Maybe the anguished figure in *The Scream* would be a better listener than Mona. Jo could identify with him. Perhaps he was screaming with frustration after another bad date from Tinder or being ghosted by someone on Buzzz.

The second person to learn of Jo's decision was Gemma.

'You're giving up dating?' she said when Jo phoned her later that morning. 'Why?'

As Jo related the story of Tarquin and his clumsy pass at her the previous evening, the tears began to roll. She hastily moved a stack of A4 paper out of the way before it got soggy.

'That's terrible, Jo,' said Gemma. 'But at least you got rid of him. You stood up to him, made him leave. Good for you.'

'Yeah, I did, didn't I?'

'But not all guys are like that.'

'The trouble is, I don't know how to recognise the good ones. Hang on.' She put her hand over the phone as footsteps approached. The sound of David's voice, getting closer. He seemed to pause by the door, but then continued on his way, his voice growing fainter. 'It's okay now. The coast is clear. My boss was going past but he's gone now.'

'Where are you?'

'Stationery cupboard. Oh, hang on...'

Leona's voice now. 'It would be good for my career development...' Jo could hear her saying.

'Of course.' That was Caroline.

Jo didn't catch any more. 'Okay, they've gone now,' she said to Gemma as the voices receded.

'Giving up completely seems a bit drastic. Just because of a few bad dates.'

'But it hasn't been a few bad dates, has it? It's been a lifetime of choosing the wrong men. I'm like a magnet for them, for some reason. Dan. Tarquin.' Jo hesitated before adding, 'Si.'

'Well, perhaps that's your answer. Fathom out *why* you choose those men rather than giving up completely. Then choose someone different. Someone who isn't your usual type. Someone you feel comfortable with, can strike up a friendship with. Even if there isn't immediate physical attraction – cos that can grow.'

'I tried that,' said Jo, thinking of Ras. She had never mentioned him to Gemma. Hadn't wanted to let slip that she'd done exactly what she'd promised she wouldn't do and got into a stranger's car. Besides, there'd been no point; it had only been one date. One insignificant date.

'Look, I've got to go, Gem. There's a big shoot happening next week and I've tons to do – got to make sure everything is organised down to the tiniest detail. The director's a stickler.'

'And will you be going on the shoot? That could be fun. You might meet someone there. Some hunky actor.'

'It's documentary, not drama.'

'Hunky cameraman then.'

'No, you know I hardly ever get to go filming,' said Jo. 'Bye, Gem. I'll text you later.'

Friday evening. Everyone else had somewhere to go. Leona had gone out for a pizza with the researchers. Sam, the producer, had gone last-minute shopping for a birthday present for his wife and David had practically skipped down the corridor, off on another Tinder date no doubt. Only Caroline and Jo were left, frantically tapping away on their keyboards, under the watchful eye of Mona.

'Jo, have you got a minute?' Caroline called over.

'Sure.'

Jo went over to her manager's desk. 'How can I help?'

'All organised for next week?'

'Yeah, double-checking the schedule now and then I'll email it out to the crew.'

'Great, I can always count on you,' Caroline smiled. 'Can you book another hotel room? For the entire shoot – Wednesday through till Sunday. Leona's going to go along to help.'

'Leona?'

Jo frowned. If anyone should be going, it should be her. She'd organised everything for next week, knew all the arrangements off by heart. Leona hadn't even been working on this particular programme.

Caroline's eyes were fixed firmly on her screen. 'Yes, Leona. David and I thought it would be good for her career development. She's never been filming.'

In all her years at Pop! Productions, Jo's career development had barely been discussed. There was always an annual appraisal meeting, which mainly consisted of filling in a form with Caroline. *What I could do more of. What I could do less of.* Caroline always said the same thing: 'David and I have no complaints, Jo. None whatsoever. You're doing brilliantly.'

Brilliantly, but there was never any mention of career development, promotions, courses or pay rises.

'I could have gone,' Jo said. 'If Sam needed an extra pair of hands.'

'You could,' said Caroline. 'But as I said, David and I felt this would be good for Leona. An opportunity for her.'

What about an opportunity for me? thought Jo.

'Anyway,' Caroline continued, 'I'm not sure I could manage without you in the office for a whole three days.'

Three days, thought Jo. Well, that was one good thing. Three days without Leona being here. It'd be like it used to be.

But it was nevertheless galling. The documentary was a behind-the-scenes peek at a festival. They'd already shot a few scenes: planning meetings and the like. On Wednesday and Thursday, they'd film the last-minute preparations – the marquees going up, Jo presumed, and the Portaloos arriving – then over the weekend, they'd focus on the festival itself. Jo wasn't into festivals – big crowds and loud music weren't her thing – but it would have been interesting. A change. A break from her usual routine. And a welcome distraction from the loneliness that was her life. Even more lonely now that she'd resolved not to go on any more dates.

Jo went back to her desk and phoned the hotel where the crew would be staying the following week and requested an extra room.'

'We've only a suite left,' said the receptionist. 'But I can do it for the same rate as an executive double.'

Typical. Leona was one of those people who had all the luck. If Jo *had* been going on the shoot, the only room left would have been a small single.

Jo made the booking, added Leona's name to the schedule and saved it twice, once to her personal drive and then to the shared drive. She always did that these days, determined that no more vital documents would go missing.

When Caroline had left, Jo phoned Gemma again.

'Twice in one day?' Gemma said when she answered. 'To what do I owe the honour? You normally text.'

'Leona's going on the shoot,' she said. 'The shoot that I organised. They didn't even *consider* sending me. Honestly, since she joined Pop! things haven't been the same. She talks about me behind my back and I never get invited for after-work drinks. Never. And then when I suggested a programme idea at the team meeting, she said, "Same old, same old".'

'She said what?' said Gemma.

There was a pause.

Jo knew that pause. It meant Gemma had something to say but wasn't sure if she should say it.

'Jo, I think you're being bullied.'

'Bullied? No-one's beating me up, calling me names or nicking my sweets.'

'Bullying isn't just a playground thing, Jo.'

Another silence. Jo knew what Gemma was thinking. She was thinking it herself. They were both remembering what Jo's schooldays had been like before Gemma had befriended her.

'I can't help wondering if...'

Another pause.

'Go on, Gem.'

'I wonder if perhaps it's all linked. Being bullied at work. Attracting the wrong men.'

'You mean, it's my fault somehow?'

'Of course not. Get that out of your head right now. It's definitely *not* your fault. Look, I'm going to send you...'

'Let me guess. Another article?'

Gemma laughed. 'You know me too well. Look, why don't

you get the train home and do something to cheer yourself up? Make a nice dinner? Or how about that woman you met? Could you meet her for a drink rather than being on your own? You've had a rough twenty-four hours.'

'Kate'll be busy. Friday night. Peak date night.' Jo thought for a second. 'There's the Scrabble club.'

'Scrabble club?'

'Yeah, I saw a poster. Hebbleswick has a Scrabble club.'

'Perfect, get yourself down there. And in the meantime, I'll ping you over that article.'

The eighteen thirty-seven was leaving the suburbs of Manchester behind when Jo's phone pinged. She glanced at the screen: the promised article from Gemma.

Jo had lost count of the number of self-help links that Gemma had sent her over the years. She'd sent the first one, Jo recalled, soon after her marriage to Si; it was something about coercive control. This wasn't a term Jo had heard before and she'd found it rather puzzling. And then he had stumbled across it one day when he'd been looking for an email in her inbox. He hadn't been too pleased, said Gemma had always had a downer on him and that she wanted their marriage to fail. At the time, Jo could understand why he hadn't wanted her to see much of Gemma after that.

Those articles! Perhaps it would be better if Gemma had never started sending them. Although now... well, looking back, she'd been right to be concerned, hadn't she? Si had been rather controlling.

She put the novel she'd been reading back in her bag and opened this latest article:

How to Handle Adult Bullying

Bullying. Was it bullying? Or simply a personality clash? She scanned down the list of suggestions.

Avoid places and situations where the bullying might happen.

Great, so what was she supposed to do? Not go to work?

Surround yourself with cheerleaders – people who encourage you and love you for who you are.

Cheerleaders? Where the hell was she supposed to find cheerleaders? People didn't cheer when you won a game of Scrabble. They cheered for marathon runners crossing the line, footballers scoring a penalty in a cup final and pilots landing planes in high winds.

Practise self-love. Self-love? Really? What was that meant to achieve?

Another ping. Gemma again.

Don't forget to go to the Scrabble club. Don't sit at home being miserable on your own this evening. It's Friday!

The club met in the hall at the back of St Cuthbert's Church. She stopped halfway up the driveway, steeling herself. It was never easy meeting new people. But if they all liked Scrabble, they were bound to be nice.

Jo was early. The second to arrive in fact; there was a man there already, unstacking the chairs. Even though he had his back to her, she recognised him immediately. The orange anorak. The scruffy hair.

Ras.

Ras. At the Scrabble club?

Ras. Lovely Ras. Whom she had a wonderful first date with. And he shared her favourite hobby all along and she'd never known?

Ras. The man who didn't like her; at least not enough to request a second date.

It would be wonderful to meet people here in Hebbleswick who liked playing Scrabble – what a world of difference that would make to her life – but Jo couldn't face seeing him. So humiliating, to come face to face with a man who had rejected her.

Especially after the earlier debacle of her date with Tarquin.

She would leave, she decided. And she was about to when he must have sensed her watching him and turned around.

Bugger. Too late now. He had seen her.

15

'What are you doing here?' he said.

His awkwardness was back, she noticed. And she felt just as awkward. 'I er… came to play Scrabble.'

'You like Scrabble?'

'Yes. Do you?'

'Well, obviously. This is my Scrabble club. I mean, I'm the organiser.'

They stood gawping at each other. Jo couldn't quite believe it. She'd never written Scrabble on her dating profile; it had seemed too geeky. And it had never even occurred to her to actively look for a man who loved the game as much as she did; it was hard enough finding a man she fancied who fancied her back, without hoping he'd share her hobby. And yet here he was. Ras. A man she fancied who liked Scrabble so much that he ran his own group.

Usually, Jo would have seen this as a sign from the Universe, only Ras, she knew, didn't fancy her back.

It's just a coincidence, she reminded herself. *He didn't want a second date, remember? Wouldn't even come in for coffee.*

'I'm sorry about…' Ras began, but then the door opened and voices echoed round the hall.

'Doctor Ras,' someone called.

Jo turned to see two older ladies making a beeline for him. They were both wearing the kind of clothes her paternal grandmother would have called their 'Sunday best'. Skirts, scarves and sparkly brooches that twinkled in the harsh strip lights of the hall.

Ras seemed to change gear, from awkward mode to convivial – if a little on the quiet side – host. He shook their hands and then gestured to her and said, 'This is Jo. Jo, meet Florence and Sylvia.'

He began unstacking more chairs. One of the women eyed Jo up and down. She was slim – the type who'd go to Zumba for the over-sixties and do Pilates every morning in her living room – with blonde highlights in her short, greying hair. She shook Jo's hand, murmuring, 'Nice to meet you, Jo,' before disappearing off towards the kitchen.

'I'm Florence,' the other one said. 'Are you the doc's girlfriend?'

She was a jolly-looking woman, with dark, curly hair, probably dyed, and one continuous bosom. Jo looked at her pale-pink, silk shirt and patent black court shoes and felt somewhat underdressed in her jeans and trainers.

'Er, no. We're friends,' she said.

The door opened again, and they both turned to see another woman tottering into the room on stilettos. She must have been in her fifties, but was dressed in a clingy, purple catsuit, with a low neckline revealing an admirable cleavage.

Florence raised her eyebrows at Jo and whispered, 'That's Linda. She fancies Ras.'

And then she added, 'And so does Sylvia.'

She nodded in the direction of the kitchen. Through the open hatch, Jo could see Sylvia filling a large urn. Who'd have thought? Two women clamouring for Ras's attention. Although they were both at least two decades older than him. Probably more.

An elderly man arrived. He was suited and booted, not unlike Tarquin, and he was wearing a purple bow tie.

'Florence.' He nodded as he walked past.

'That's Stan,' she nodded back, 'also known as Mr B.' She glanced round the room then whispered to Jo, 'I hope you've brought a dictionary. That man tries to cheat, every single week.'

Jo hadn't thought to bring a dictionary. Was it really that competitive?

A stream of people began to trickle through the door. A blonde-haired woman, perhaps a little older than her, bearing a stack of cake tins. A spiky-haired lad of about sixteen who hopped from foot to foot, twitching with nervous energy. An older man in a stained, green jumper who looked round the room anxiously and appeared relieved when he spotted Ras. She was going to fit in here, Jo decided.

'That's Malcolm,' said Florence, pointing at the man in green. 'He's lovely but don't ask him about insurance. You'll be here all night if you do. And don't ask Sylvia about her grandchildren or her ailments, and if she asks, say you don't like poetry or she'll start giving you a recital.'

So much to remember.

Ras clapped his hands and said, 'I think we're nearly all here.'

'Doctor Ras, before we start, I've been having some trouble with my ankle this week,' Sylvia piped up.

A collective groan ran round the room.

'You know what I'm going to say, don't you, Sylvia?'

'Yes, yes, I'll make an appointment,' she trilled. Jo heard her mumble to Mr B, 'Always worth a try.'

'Everyone, grab yourselves a cup of tea and then we'll make a start,' Ras said.

Florence left Jo's side, seemingly determined to reach the urn first. A queue began to form behind her.

'Only nine tonight,' said Ras, sidling over to Jo. 'Sometimes we get a couple more.'

'Is there an entry fee?'

'No, no charge.'

'Who pays for the hall?'

'I do. It isn't much. I've done a deal with the vicar.'

'You must love Scrabble,' Jo said.

'I do. But it's not only about the Scrabble.'

'Isn't it?'

'No, it's about community. I want to help people who are lonely. A little social contact is surprisingly effective in helping maintain someone's mental health, and it can even have a positive effect on physical health too. It's important for people to feel socially embedded.'

Jo followed his gaze as he looked round the hall, at the people greeting each other, chatting and laughing.

'So, it's kind of a work thing for you?'

'Kind of.' He hesitated for a moment. 'I don't know about you, Jo, but we all get lonely sometimes, don't we?'

Jo was about to admit that she certainly did, when the man in the green jumper thrust a cup of tea into her hand – and one into Ras's – and said, 'Who's this, Ras?'

'I'm Jo.' She shook his hand with her empty one. 'Nice to meet you, Malcolm. It is Malcolm, isn't it?'

He nodded. 'Joanna,' he said. 'Or Josephine?'

'Just Jo.'

'Well, if you ever need to know anything about insurance, I'm your man.'

'Thanks, Malcolm. I'll bear that in mind.'

Ras put down his tea and clapped again, and the room fell silent.

'How shall we do this tonight?' he said. 'Three tables of three?'

'Or you and I could play together,' said Linda to him, somehow managing to make the words 'play together' sound suggestive, 'and the others could make a four and a three.'

There was a general murmuring of dissent about this idea. Most people, it seemed, wanted to play on Ras's table.

'I'll challenge Sylvia to a two-player game,' said Malcolm.

'You're on,' said Sylvia.

'In that case,' said Ras, 'I'm going to play with Jo, since she doesn't know anyone here. Florence, will you join us? And Mr B perhaps? And Linda, Annie and Ray can form a three.'

Everyone found their tables and sat down. The hall fell silent as every player in the room began to contemplate their letters.

'We're missing one thing,' said Florence, 'as usual.'

Ras began to root through his pockets. 'I've forgotten again,' he said.

'He never remembers to bring pens or paper to keep score,' Florence whispered to Jo.

Jo reached down for her handbag and pulled out her trusty Filofax. She never took pages out but decided to make an exception on this occasion. She handed blank sheets to the neighbouring tables and, using the pen she kept clipped in the Filofax's handy penholder, drew four columns on a blank page in the 'Notes' section, heading them Ras, Florence, Mr B and Jo.

'Very organised,' said Florence.

'Organised is my middle name,' said Jo, then a second later, hoped that hadn't sounded like she was bragging. 'It's just… well, I have to be organised with my job.'

'What do you do?' Mr B asked.

'I work in television. Nothing exciting – I'm not a producer or anything. I do all the behind-the-scenes stuff, organising everything like hotels and taxis and every last detail so that the shoots run smoothly.'

'Think you might have found the perfect person for…' began Florence, but Ras put a finger to his lips as if he were an infant teacher and she mimed zipping her lips.

What had she been about to say? The perfect person for *you*?

They began to play. Ras took an early lead playing JOURNEY in his first turn and using up all his letters, thereby achieving a massive bonus of 50 points. They'd have their work cut out to catch him after that.

At the adjacent table, Jo could hear Sylvia saying, 'And then, last week, I had these palpitations. Several times, in fact.'

'Have you thought about critical illness cover?' Malcolm said to her.

As Jo turned her attention to her letters, her embarrassment at seeing Ras again began to ease. So what if he didn't fancy her? She still felt a little stung at his rejection, but he seemed happy enough that she'd come along this evening. And she hadn't been 100 per cent sure she fancied him anyway; yes, over the course of their date, her attraction towards him had grown, but he definitely wasn't her usual type. So what if she wasn't his? That was okay, wasn't it?

Perhaps they could be friends – they shared a hobby, after all, she thought as she used the J on the board to make JOKER on a double word score. Heaven knows, she needed friends. Maybe here at Hebbleswick Scrabble Club, she might finally 'find her tribe'.

Florence used the K to make SPIKE. Unfortunately, this gave Mr B access to the triple word bonus space.

He ummed and ahhed for a bit before spelling out PAXOS.

'You can't have that,' Florence objected immediately. 'It's the name of a Greek island. Proper nouns aren't allowed.'

'It means several packets of sage and onion stuffing,' he said.

Jo caught Ras's eye and bit her lip, to stop herself from laughing.

'Paxo is a brand name,' hissed Florence, 'and therefore also a proper noun.'

Mr B reluctantly took his letters back.

'Your go, Ras,' Florence said firmly.

'What about me?' said Mr B.

'You forgo your turn if you play a word that isn't allowed,' Florence said to him. 'Stick to the rules, please, Stan.'

Ras looked like he was about to intervene, but she silenced him with a glare and he turned his attention to the letter tiles on his rack.

They were partway through the game – Ras still in the lead – when there was the sound of a chair scraping on the floor and Jo looked round to see Linda standing up.

'Got to go,' Linda said. 'My salsa class starts at nine.'

'But we're mid-game,' said the spiky-haired lad.

'Sorry, Cosmic,' she said and tottered out on her heels.

'Cosmic?' said Jo.

'Nickname,' said Ras. 'His name's Ray.'

He turned to the group. 'Is this a good time for a tea break, perhaps? And some of Annie's cakes?'

Annie's cakes were like something you'd get at a fancy French patisserie: huge mille-feuilles oozing vanilla custard and tiny tarts filled with shining, glazed fruits.

'These cakes are amazing,' Jo said to Ras, as she tucked into her second tart.

'Annie's a pro,' said Ras. 'She works at the (Not So) Little Board Game Café in Essendale, but says Scrabble's the only game she likes.'

Teacups drained and cake tin emptied, they resumed their games. In the end, the scores on Jo's table were pretty close. Ras narrowly beat her with Florence coming in third place, and Mr B a few points behind her.

'Would either of you like the score sheet?' Jo said. 'I can rip it out. Or I can leave it in there and we can write next week's scores on the back.'

'Save it for next week,' said Florence. She stood up and went over to Sylvia, who was waiting near the door.

'See you on Monday with my ankle, Doctor Ras,' called Sylvia as they left. 'Mind you've got that prescription pad ready.'

Cosmic appeared at their table.

'Did you say you're coming next week?' he said to Jo.

'Yeah, hopefully,' she said.

'Great. I was getting fed up of being called the *new* member. I've been coming for five months now.'

He headed towards the door, whistling atonally to himself.

When everyone had gone, Ras looked at Jo and said, 'So you're coming next week?'

'I think so.'

He had a look on his face now that Gemma would have described as 'pretty chuffed with himself'.

As they stacked the chairs and folded up the trestle tables, Jo couldn't help wondering about what Florence had said. *Think you might have found the perfect person for...*

For what exactly? Jo had to know.

'What was it Florence meant earlier?' she said.

Ras looked blank.

'When she said, "Think you might have found the perfect person." The perfect person for what?'

'Oh, that,' he said. 'Tell you what. I'll explain over a drink.'

16

As Rasmus stacked the chairs away, as he did at the end of every Scrabble evening, he pondered on the strange coincidence that Jo of all people had turned up here.

Hebbleswick wasn't a large town. It was the sort of town where everyone knew everyone else. Furthermore, Rasmus was the local GP so he, more than anyone, tended to meet most of the local residents. He'd always known that sooner or later, their paths were bound to cross. That was fine. He was hoping that it would be later.

It wasn't that he didn't like her. The opposite, in fact. He liked her a lot. There was something about her dating profile that had resonated with him, even though on the face of it, they had nothing at all in common. He normally didn't go for adventurous women, not because he didn't think he'd like them but because he was pretty sure they wouldn't like him. If someone had written that their ambition was to climb Everest or they enjoyed skydiving, he scrolled on by. What was the point in doing otherwise? Rasmus wasn't tall, dark or conventionally handsome. He didn't have a particularly outgoing personality either; on a date, he couldn't dazzle a woman with his charm and charisma. He couldn't do comedy either. He enjoyed a laugh as much as the next person but telling jokes wasn't his forte.

He wasn't down on himself; he was realistic. He had his good points; he knew that. He was a great listener – his patients were always telling him that – and was easy to talk to. He liked helping people and making others feel good about themselves. But those weren't the kinds of things you generally wrote on your internet dating profile. They were underrated qualities, he thought. The women he'd encountered in life so far seemed to be looking for more alpha male traits and Rasmus knew he was probably a beta. If not a gamma or a delta.

Could you buy Scrabble with Greek letter tiles? he wondered as he folded up the legs of the last of the trestle tables. Presumably you could. Was the scoring different?

Scrabble. Jo liked Scrabble.

And Rasmus liked Jo.

He still couldn't quite get his head around the fact that she liked Scrabble too. And not only liked it in the sense that she enjoyed the occasional game, but really liked it. He'd noticed how focused she'd been as they played, how she'd watched everyone's moves, studied her letter tiles intently, never once distracted by her mobile phone or what else was happening in the hall. Rasmus rather suspected that Scrabble was as much of a passion for her as it was for him.

He'd been obsessed with Scrabble since he was seven, when one of his aunts had gifted it to him for Christmas. He'd loved it from the minute he opened the box and saw all the little letter tiles; in fact, it had been his favourite present that year, much to his parents' consternation as they'd bought him a rather fancy bicycle. He'd felt bad for disappointing them, but he couldn't hide his fascination with his new game.

'What was it Florence meant earlier?' Jo said, as she put the last chair on top of a stack.

Rasmus cast his mind back to what Florence had said.

Think you might have found the perfect person.

Honestly. He loved Florence, he really did. The constant arguments between her and Mr B over illegal words and proper nouns were hilarious, but why had she had to say that?

Jo was bound to have assumed that Florence meant 'the perfect person' in a romantic sense.

And now he knew she loved Scrabble, well, he had to admit he thought that too.

But their first date had gone so badly, he couldn't allow himself to think like that. He'd better explain to Jo what Florence had meant, though it seemed a little forward to ask for her help when this was the first time she'd come along to the group. He didn't want to appear pushy.

'Oh that,' he said, trying to sound casual. 'Tell you what. I'll explain over a drink.'

To his surprise, she agreed immediately. In fact, she'd sounded keen, but as they walked to the pub together, he told himself not to read anything into that. Jo was out of his league; why had he ever thought otherwise? He'd never stood a chance. He'd been silly to ask her out in the first place. She was gorgeous, with that red hair and those green eyes. A little curvy. As a doctor, he should probably have advised her that her BMI might be slightly on the high side, but as a man, he thought her figure was just perfect.

Yes, he'd been silly to ask her out. And even sillier to take her on a date that involved heights. What the hell had he been thinking?

He'd had hypnotherapy to overcome his fear and he'd thought it had worked, but it clearly hadn't. Or not enough anyway for him to go plunging down an enormous hole in the ground. He'd chosen to take Jo to Gaping Gill because he thought she'd really love it. And okay, he had to admit, he'd also thought it would impress her. Then he'd ended up doing the complete opposite, showing her what a complete wuss he was. God, that had been embarrassing. Mortifying, even.

He'd tried to put her out of his mind, but he had thought about her a lot since that date. He'd often looked at the photo he'd taken, of Jo sitting strapped into that chair with the helmet on her head, about to descend into that enormous hole in the ground. During the car journey to North Yorkshire, and the walk up to Gaping Gill, he'd really enjoyed her company. They'd clicked, hadn't they? After an awkward start, the conversation had begun to flow and he'd felt so relaxed with her. Things had been going well. But then afterwards? Well, he could barely bring himself to speak to her as he was so embarrassed about his phobia.

But they were here now, he thought, pushing open the door of the George.

He was sure he had blown any chance he had with her romantically – if he'd ever had a chance at all – but since they shared a hobby and since she was by her own admission someone who loved organising, well, it wouldn't do any harm to run his idea past her and perhaps enlist her help. She could say no if she didn't want to get involved.

And they could be friends, couldn't they? Rasmus

needed to make more friends in the area; he hadn't lived in Hebbleswick long. He'd come to work at the Essendale and Hebbleswick Group Practice as a locum initially, when one of the other GPs, Ludek, had been in an accident. When Ludek came back to work, he'd decided to go part-time so he could help his partner Emily with her new business, the (Not So) Little Board Game Café in Essendale. (Rasmus had been there a few times and it was a wonderful place, but he had never seen the point of playing games other than Scrabble.) So with Ludek working part-time, Rasmus had stayed on, doing three days a week initially, which had now been increased to four.

'Do you fancy grabbing a table and I'll get you a drink?' he said to Jo, gesturing towards the bar. 'What would you like?'

'Just a white wine, please,' she said.

'Any particular type?'

'Sauvignon Blanc or Pinot Grigio. I'm not fussy.'

He nodded. 'There's a table over there.'

Jo headed over to the last unoccupied table in the place, which was tucked into a corner. He watched as she sat down on one of the stools. She looked uncomfortable, he thought, and hoped that was the stool rather than the fact she was with him. She'd seemed happy during the Scrabble evening, though. Very happy.

He went over to the bar and waited to be served.

'Doctor,' said the landlord as soon as he saw him. 'The very man! I have this rash and was wondering if you could take a look. Save me a trip to the surgery.'

Before Rasmus could stop him, the man had rolled up his sleeve and was holding out his forearm. The skin looked red and angry, but it was hard to see properly, given that the lighting in the pub was designed for cosiness rather than medical examinations. Rasmus leaned over, standing on his tiptoes, trying to get a better look.

'It could be eczema, but it's hard to tell,' he said. 'Have you changed your washing powder or anything?'

The landlord shook his head and Rasmus continued. 'Perhaps it might be best to make that appointment and let me take a proper look. Could I have a glass of Sauvignon Blanc and half a shandy please?'

'Coming right up.'

Rasmus waited whilst the drinks were poured, fighting the urge to look round at Jo. He didn't want to give away how he felt about her. If she knew he was attracted to her, that might put her off helping him. He didn't want her thinking that he was only seeking her involvement in the hope of getting into her knickers. That really wasn't his style at all. He would keep his feelings to himself and focus on his project. If the two of them became friends, that would be wonderful. He knew anything more was out of the question and resolved that he wouldn't allow himself to think otherwise.

17

Less than twenty-four hours after she'd resolved to give up dating, Jo was sitting on a tiny – and somewhat uncomfortable – stool, waiting for a man she rather liked – Ras, in other words – who was getting the drinks in.

This wasn't a date, she reminded herself. Just a drink.

What was taking him so long?

She looked across at him. He was standing on tiptoes, leaning over the bar and peering at a nasty rash on the landlord's arm.

Jo wished he'd hurry up. She was on tenterhooks. What had Florence meant?

Consultation finally over, she watched as the landlord refused Ras's ten-pound note. A brief argument ensued whilst Ras tried to press it into his hand and the landlord shook his head. Then Ras shoved the note into his back pocket, picked up his half of shandy and her Sauvignon Blanc and began making his way back to their table. Jo looked down at her phone, trying to pretend that she hadn't been watching all along.

'Sorry that took so long,' said Ras. 'It happens sometimes. People seize the chance for a quick consultation. He had a bit of a rash.'

'Should you be telling me that? Or does doctor-patient confidentiality not apply when you're in the pub?'

Ras laughed. 'Everyone waiting to be served saw that rash.'

'And what was your diagnosis?'

'Could be eczema,' he said.

Jo took a sip of her wine. 'You were going to tell me what Florence meant.'

'Oh yes.'

Was it her imagination or did he look a little nervous?

'I want to promote the Scrabble club, get more people along,' said Ras.

'You want me to put up a few flyers?'

'No, much more than that. I thought we might hold some kind of Scrabble-themed event. Perhaps on a Saturday afternoon? Attract some families? Only I don't have much time – it's horrendous being a GP these days, even working part-time – and none of the others want to take it on. They'd all help, of course, but we need someone to organise us. To galvanise us into action.'

'You want me to organise a Scrabble event?' She took another sip of wine, unsure whether to be flattered or disappointed. At the back of her mind, she had thought – hoped? – that Florence had meant she'd be the perfect person for him *romantically*.

A crazy idea.

She reminded herself once again that she hadn't heard a peep from him after that first date.

Although once he'd got over his initial shock at her appearance at the Scrabble club, he'd seemed pleased to see her. And he had suggested this drink and was now asking her to organise an event for him. She'd never understand men.

'You're obviously organised,' he said, 'and I'm not.'

Getting a big event off the ground, Jo thought, would need more than just good organisational skills.

'You need someone more creative to pull off something like that,' she said, 'and I'm not an ideas person.' Her recent experiences at Pop! Productions had taught her that much. Nothing she'd suggested had ever made it to the screen.

'Everyone would pitch in,' he said.

'Or a people person.'

'I'm sure you…'

'Or a natural born leader. Besides, I wouldn't know where to start.'

'I have every confidence in you. I'm sure you could do it.'

I have every confidence in you.

David had said that once. Back before she'd lost that spreadsheet.

It was a good feeling, having someone believe in you.

And organising an event for the Scrabble club would ensure she felt like a real part of the group, rather than being the 'new member'. She didn't fancy bearing that title for the next five months like Cosmic Ray had.

Not to mention the fact that it would give her something to do with her time now she'd given up dating.

And would distract her from thinking about what a complete mess her life was.

'Okay, I'll do it,' she said.

Ras's face lit up with a huge smile. 'Honestly?'

'Yeah, it might be fun.' She took out her Filofax and turned to a blank page. 'First things first. What's going to happen at this event?'

He took a sip of his drink. 'We play Scrabble.'

'You already do that,' she said, 'on Friday nights. How will this be any different?'

'I thought if we did something on a Saturday afternoon, families might come along. We could put up some flyers.'

'But you said you wanted to do *more* than put up a few flyers?'

'We could offer Junior Scrabble perhaps, as well as the adult game.'

This was disappointing. If it was going to distract her from her failed love life and all the nonsense going on at work, the Scrabble event needed to be big, not a pimped-up version of what he was already doing. It needed to be something that would give her something to sink her teeth into. Something that would need so much organising that it'd fill all the hours she used to spend scrutinising men's profiles on Buzzz. Something that would occupy her mind and stop her dwelling on the fact that she was a complete failure when it came to relationships and was doomed to be single forever.

Putting up a few flyers to attract more people wasn't going to do that.

Jo fiddled with her Filofax, absentmindedly clicking the metal rings open, then clicking them shut again. 'If all you want to do is hold an afternoon of Scrabble in the church hall on a Saturday, I'm not sure why you need me. I thought you wanted to do something a bit more ambitious.'

'I definitely need you,' he said, and his eyes met hers. 'Let's think big. Think outside the box.'

'I know. We'll have a brainstorm.'

'You can't say brainstorm. It's not PC. It's offensive to people with epilepsy. We say "thought shower" at work.'

Ras harrumphed. 'An epileptic fit is nothing like a storm.

It's the opposite of a storm. In a storm, everything happens chaotically, whereas it's the synchronous firing of neurons that causes an epileptic episode.'

'Okay, Doctor, enough science. Let's jot down our ideas.'

She wrote *Scrabble Event* at the top of a blank page, and looked at him expectantly, her pen poised.

'We… play Scrabble,' he said.

Was it her imagination or were his eyes twinkling at her? The last thing she needed when she had resolved to give up dating was twinkling eyes.

She looked down at her Filofax and wrote, *We play Scrabble*. 'And then?'

'We… play some more Scrabble?'

'Oh, come on, Ras. And then…?'

'We… go to the pub?'

'Do we play Scrabble in the pub? Or have a drink?'

Ras laughed. 'Or both?'

'I think we need to come up with something that'll put Hebbleswick on the map,' said Jo.

'Let's think it over. Talk about it next week at Scrabble club.'

That was one advantage to David having chosen Leona instead of her to go on that shoot; if Jo had gone, she'd have been away next Friday at that festival…

'I've got it,' she said suddenly. 'A Scrabble festival.'

Ras had his glass to his lips as she said this. He took such a large gulp of shandy that Jo could have sworn she could almost see it descending down his throat like a cartoon cat swallowing a mouse. She decided not to mention this in case he pointed out that it was medically inaccurate.

'A festival?' he said, with a bit of a splutter. 'That sounds rather... large-scale. Could we manage that?'

Could they? Or was she being ridiculous?

But then a television programme was a bit like an event. She mightn't be the creative brains behind anything they did at Pop! Productions but now she was the organisational power behind most of it. The person who booked everything from taxis to camera crews. The person who ensured that every piece of music that a director chose to use was cleared for copyright. That the celebrities they interviewed had every single item they wanted in their dressing room, whether that was waffles, whisky or Werther's Originals.

'I'm not thinking Glastonbury,' she said.

'What no bands? No mud? No stinky toilets?'

'Not sure about bands but I can probably sort out mud and stinky toilets if you want them.'

Ras laughed. 'So, what are you thinking, Jo? What's your vision?'

'Something like a church fete or a village show. Only over an entire weekend and with letters rather than lettuce.'

'Lettuce?'

'Don't they have vegetable growing competitions at those events? Biggest marrow? Most knobbly carrot? We'll need some kind of competition too to inject a bit of drama to the proceedings. A tournament perhaps.'

Ras frowned, his lips pursed as if he couldn't quite work out what to say. 'It's... a little bit... competitive. That's not the ethos of the club. It's not about who wins. It's about bringing people together and enjoying the game.'

'The tournament could be one element. There'd be all sorts of other things going on at the same time. We can have one room devoted to more casual games. With several tables so people can wander in and play. In another room, we could have Scrabble-themed crafts and in...'

'Sorry to stop you, Jo, but where are all these rooms?'

'In our venue.'

'Sounds expensive. I'm not sure, Jo.'

Jo lifted her wine glass to her lips and took a mouthful. And swallowed. Her Sauvignon Blanc. And her disappointment.

'Okay,' she said, standing up. 'We'll do it your way. Saturday afternoon Scrabble club meeting. Shall we have another drink?'

The landlord didn't engage Jo in any conversation, let alone show her his rash. When she returned to the table, Ras looked deep in thought.

'Crafts,' he said. 'You mentioned crafts.'

Jo took out her phone, opened Instagram and typed #*Scrabble* into the search bar. She clicked on a photo and held her phone out to show him. It was a framed picture with hearts and flowers and the words LOVE and YOU spelled out in letter tiles, intersecting as they would on a Scrabble board.

'Love. You,' Ras read out loud and then cleared his throat. 'It's pretty.'

'They're popular,' she said. 'They sell for quite a bit on Etsy but they'd be easy enough to make. You can buy bulk bags of letter tiles on eBay and people could create their own versions. Pictures, greeting cards and so on. Personalise them with names. Make them as gifts. And before you say that we don't have the budget, we'd charge them something. Not much but enough to cover our costs. We'd have to shell out a little at the beginning, but we'd make the money back.'

'If enough people come.'

He sighed. He wasn't interested. He wanted his small event. Jo wasn't sure why he'd tried to rope her in in the first place if all he wanted to do was hold Scrabble club on a Saturday afternoon.

She swigged the wine. Might as well call it a night and go home. She'd be far happier back on the sofa, playing a few games of WordPals, than trying to persuade someone who clearly wasn't up for being persuaded.

'If you build it, they will come,' he said.

'What?'

'It's from *Field of Dreams*.'

She must have looked blank.

'The 1989 film with Kevin Costner. It's a classic.'

'Hmm… 1989,' she said. 'Well, these days, if you build it, then promote it like crazy on Twitter, Instagram and Facebook, then yes, they might come.'

'Are you any good with social media?' he said.

'Not especially.'

'The guy I work with, Ludek, his other half's best friend, Kate, works in marketing. She might lend a hand.'

'I know Kate.'

'Small world. Do you think she'll agree?'

'I'm sure she will,' said Jo, crossing her fingers under the table. She didn't know Kate well enough yet to be sure. 'So is that a yes? A yes to the festival?'

'It's a yes.'

She wanted to lean over and hug him, but since she was perched on a tiny stool that was a bit too small for her arse, it would have been risky. Instead, she said, 'Hebbleswick Scrabble Festival. It has a bit of a ring to it, doesn't it?'

18

'You sound more cheerful than yesterday, said Gemma. 'Was the Scrabble club good?'

'I'm organising a festival.'

'A festival? I didn't think festivals were your kind of thing.'

It was Saturday morning and Jo was sprawled on the sofa. She wanted to tell Gemma her big news before taking a wander down to Hebbleswick to scan the shelves of the library on the off chance that they had *A Dummy's Guide to Organising a Festival* or *Festival Organisation Made Simple*.

'It's a Scrabble festival,' Jo said, as if Scrabble festivals were a completely normal thing.

'Wow. And how did this come about?'

'Well, the guy who organises the Scrabble club turned out to be Ras.'

'Ras?'

'Gaping Gill man.'

'Who?'

Damn. She'd forgotten that she hadn't told Gem about Ras.

'A man I had a date with. Um... a week or two back.

Only the one date. I didn't hear from him again so it wasn't worth mentioning him.'

'Why's he called Gaping Gill man?'

'He drove me up to North Yorkshire...'

'You got in his car? On a first date?' Gemma sounded panicked. 'Honestly, Jo. You've always promised you'd be careful.'

'He's the local GP. I saw his picture on the health centre's website so it wasn't much of a risk. Anyway, he took me up to North Yorkshire and we walked up to this enormous hole in the ground called Gaping Gill. It's a hundred metres deep and I went down it.'

'Like abseiling? On a rope?'

'Not exactly. I was strapped into a chair and winched down. I was terrified, but it was brilliant.'

'And the guy? What was he like?'

'Lovely. At first, I thought he wasn't my type but he was so easy to talk to and he'd made a massive effort to choose an activity he thought I'd like...'

Gemma laughed. 'He thought you'd like going down a hole? What on earth made him think that?'

'I wrote on my profile that I like adventurous activities.'

'Oh, I see. That makes sense. Sort of. Except... why would you write that? You don't like adventurous activities. You like Scrabble.'

'Kate – you know that woman I met at the Your Best Life talk – she suggested that I made my profile a bit more interesting. To attract new men.'

'You've got to be honest though. What if you attract someone who likes ski jumping or skydiving and he expects you to share his enthusiasm?'

'Yeah, I suppose. But I did enjoy Gaping Gill. I enjoyed the whole date. He was lovely company.'

'But you didn't go on a second date?'

'Well, no. He never asked.'

'You could have asked him.'

'Kate said it was better to let the guy make all the first moves. Initially at least.'

'This is the twenty-first century, not the nineteenth!'

'I knew you'd say that.'

'And why are you listening to all her advice when you hardly know her?'

'She's kind of a dating expert.'

Gemma harrumphed. 'Anyway, tell me more about Gaping Gill man. What was his actual name again?'

'Ras. Only 3 points. So he didn't fit with my Scrabble dating rule.'

'Pah,' said Gemma. 'That was just a bit of fun, surely? I mean, I know I sent you that numerology article, but you can't seriously rule out a decent guy whose company you enjoyed on the basis of how many points his name would score. What was he like? Besides being easy to talk to, lovely company and good at coming up with unusual activities for first dates. Was he attractive?'

'Not especially. Although... he kind of grew on me. The longer I spent with him, the more I thought... Well, it doesn't matter.'

'Personality?'

'Quiet. Kind. I felt... I dunno... comfortable with him.'

'And he likes Scrabble. You said he was at the club?'

'He's the *organiser* of the club.'

'He sounds like he's exactly what you need.'

'How d'you make that out?'

'Because he likes Scrabble and – now I know you won't like me bringing him up – but Gaping Gill man sounds like the complete opposite of Si.'

Jo paused. 'I've got to go.'

'Don't hang up,' said Gemma. 'I'm sorry. I shouldn't have mentioned him. Tell me about the festival.'

'Later. Tomorrow. The library's only open till two on a Saturday.'

Gemma was right, Jo thought after she'd hung up.

That date with Ras… it was as if she'd asked the Universe to bring her a man who was the complete opposite of her ex-husband and the Universe had listened, just as Marge Simpson aka the Bouffant had promised it would.

And it had delivered Ras.

The two men couldn't have been more different.

For one thing, with Si, there'd been instant attraction.

Jo was bowled over when she first met Si. He'd come into the solicitor's offices where she worked, looking for legal advice: some boundary issue with a neighbour, she seemed to remember. She wouldn't have thought that a man like him would look twice at a woman like her. Or even once.

And he didn't just fancy her; he fell in love with her. It seemed too good to be true. (And in hindsight, it was.)

He flattered her, telling her within three weeks of meeting her that he thought he'd met The One.

'Do you feel that too?' he asked. 'Please, Jo. Put me out of my misery. Tell me it's mutual.'

If truth be told, Jo would have felt more comfortable if they'd taken things a wee bit slower. But she hadn't liked to put the brakes on; he might have thought she wasn't interested. She didn't dare risk losing the best thing that had ever happened to her. So she'd smiled and said that yes, she felt the same and mumbled, 'But let's take things slowly. I want to savour every moment.'

He'd ignored her and proposed a few weeks later. A flash restaurant, an ostentatious solitaire. Jo had put her doubts aside, intoxicated by the feeling that someone wanted her this much. And not just any old someone but someone like Si: attractive, successful, confident.

For a while at least, all the gifts, the engagement ring on her finger and, a few months later, the lavish wedding had made her feel – for the first time in her life – that she was, to quote that shampoo advert, 'worth it'.

But once they were married, it hadn't taken long for things to change. Pretty soon, Si began to make Jo feel worthless.

19

Sunday morning. Jo's phone pinged. Gemma.

Sorry if I upset you yesterday.

Don't worry. I'm fine.

Tell me more about this festival you're organising. Sounds like a mammoth task. But if anyone can do it, you can.

Jo smiled. Hebbleswick Library hadn't had a single book about organising festivals, but it didn't matter. She knew exactly what her first task should be: finding a venue. There were several conference-type hotels nearby that would be ideal – a large room for the Scrabble tournament and smaller rooms for casual games and the craft activity – but they were too expensive. And out of town. She knew Ras wanted the event to happen in Hebbleswick itself. That was the whole point: it was for the community.

I need to find a venue. And it needs one large space where the main tournament will happen and smaller rooms for other things. And preferably facilities for catering – we'll have to serve tea and coffee at least.

Church hall?

Not big enough. No side rooms either.

I have one suggestion. But I don't want to upset you again.

Tell me?

Local primary school?

Jo gulped. She hadn't been inside a school since the day she'd left the comp and had vowed never to set foot in one again. (She hadn't yet figured how she'd manage if she ever had children of her own. Dropping them off at the school gates in a morning and picking them up of an afternoon would be one thing, but venturing inside for parents' evening or a nativity play? She'd need therapy to do that.)

She tapped out a reply to Gemma.

There must be somewhere else.

Yeah, there's sure to be. Put your thinking cap on.

Jo spent the whole day wandering around Hebbleswick. She browsed the bookshelves in the hospice shop. She peered through the windows of the art gallery, with its landscapes of the local countryside, patchwork scenes of sheep fields and drystone walls. She marvelled at the many different types of lentils in the wholefood shop and wondered if anyone actually ate quinoa, but she couldn't think of anywhere other than the school.

She had to put all her bad memories aside – the interminably long, lonely playtimes and the relentless teasing. She had to push the humiliation of being kicked out of the school choir for singing out of tune and always being the last to be chosen for the netball teams to the back of her mind. If she couldn't do that, then Hebbleswick Scrabble Festival wouldn't happen.

Jo's old primary school was over forty miles away from Hebbleswick but the two buildings were strikingly similar. Dark-grey stone. Victorian architecture. High windows. A main entrance and two side entrances, one marked 'boys' and one marked 'girls'.

Of course, much had changed since she was a child. Playgrounds that once were squares of tarmac surrounded by stone walls now accommodated football nets, basketball hoops, a climbing frame and benches.

Hebbleswick Primary even had a nature zone complete with pond, and vegetables were being cultivated in a small allotment area. Jo stood outside the gates, trying to pluck up courage to go in.

Schools might have changed, but she suspected that children could be as cruel now as they were back then. If your face didn't fit, if you didn't know quite what to say or how to join in a game...

Her legs felt weak, almost as if they might give way from under her. She hated the smell of schools: the lingering aroma of school dinner cabbage with overtones of unwashed children, sweaty socks and cleaning fluid.

And the sounds too: voices echoing down corridors, the sound of others enjoying themselves at playtimes whilst she cowered behind a tree, the taunts.

She wondered – not for the first time – if her life might have been different if she'd had a more positive experience at school. If she'd grown up with a little more confidence, maybe she wouldn't have leapt at the first chance of love; maybe she wouldn't have ended up with a man like Si.

She shuddered. Was she really going to do this, to step inside? It was tempting to walk away, but she wanted the festival to happen perhaps even more than Ras did. From the second she'd come up with the idea, it had brought such a strong sense of purpose to her life, something she hadn't even realised had been missing. Besides which, she didn't want to waste her free afternoon. David had been most surprised when she'd asked him; it was the first time in the many years Jo had worked at Pop! Productions that she'd asked for some time off without at least two months' notice.

She pressed the shiny chrome button.

'Jo Knox to see the head teacher,' she said in her most confident voice.

If the head teacher agreed to her request, she'd be going inside this building rather a lot over the next few weeks. Did she really want to do this?

There was a buzzing noise for a few seconds. Jo pushed the black metal gates open and stepped inside. Taking a deep breath, she strode purposely up the path towards the sign saying *Main Reception*.

'Good afternoon, Miss Knox,' said a voice as she walked in. 'Or is it Mrs?'

The reception area was bright and cheerful, a far cry from the austere hallway of her old school. But that didn't stop the memories from flooding back.

Her surname had always been the butt of jokes. At first, it hadn't been too bad: variations on knock knock jokes that simply weren't funny. But later... she shuddered remembering how the teasing had started in earnest when she was the first in her year to need a bra. A vile bit of graffiti on the cloakroom wall. *Seen the size of Knoxs knockers?* it had read.

Jo had been upset not only by the personal remark about *her* body, but also by the missing apostrophe.

'Are you all right, Miss Knox?'

She snapped back to reality. The receptionist, seated behind a curved modern desk, was staring at her. 'Do you need a glass of water?'

'No, thank you,' Jo said. 'Sorry. I'm fine.'

'Well, if you're sure... Would you mind signing in please?'

She gestured at a large open book on the top of the desk, and Jo wrote her name and noted down the time.

'The head's seeing someone at the moment,' said the receptionist. 'But take a seat and he'll be with you shortly.'

One of the bright-blue, upholstered chairs was already occupied by a ginger-haired, bespectacled child who was swinging his legs at a frenzied pace. Jo sat down a few seats away and wondered if it looked bad to get her phone out.

This wasn't the first time she had sat outside a head teacher's office, waiting. Not by a long shot. She was regularly summoned to see the head teacher for retaliating when someone had teased her so much that she couldn't contain her temper any longer.

Jo glanced over at the boy. There was something in his expression that she recognised; here was a child who did not fit in. Most likely a victim of bullying too. She wanted him to look up, to meet her gaze, so she could smile at him. Communicate some sympathy, perhaps. Show that she understood. But he remained resolutely staring at his feet.

Five minutes passed. And then ten.

The receptionist said, 'Sorry about this. He won't be long.'

At that moment, a door opened behind her and woman in a garish, floral dress came out, followed by a flustered man in a grey suit, who, Jo assumed, was the head teacher.

'Thank you so much for coming in to see me, Mrs Hamilton-Jones,' he said, 'and for raising your concerns.'

'I do hope you can sort something out this time,' said Mrs Hamilton-Jones. 'A boy of Alfred's ability needs to be stretched.'

'As you've said,' said the head teacher.

'We don't want to have to move him to another school,' she said.

'Quite.'

'I don't want to go to another school, Mother,' said Alfred.

'It needn't be a big thing,' she continued as if her son hadn't spoken. 'He could join Year 6 for mathematics. Or you could run a chess club at lunchtimes. He needs more stimulation, Mr Morgan.'

'Yes, I'll certainly consider your suggestions. Now I'm sorry to rush you but my four thirty appointment is here.

And Alfred has been patiently waiting for you. After-school club finished nearly fifteen minutes ago.'

Mrs Hamilton-Jones looked at Jo resentfully, gave a sigh of resignation and left, the boy following behind her, his eyes fixed on the ground.

The head teacher glanced at Jo and said, 'I'm so sorry to have kept you waiting, Miss...'

'Jo,' she said.

'Jo, good to meet you. Come in.'

He shepherded her into his office and gestured at a chair in front of his desk. Jo perched on the edge of it, crossing then uncrossing her legs.

He slumped in the chair opposite her, loosened his tie, then had second thoughts and removed it completely.

'I have no idea what this is about,' he said. 'Clare said you had a proposal that I might find interesting.'

Well, that was a good start at least. His receptionist thought he might be disposed to the idea.

She had rehearsed this in her head, but now she was actually sitting in front of him, she wasn't sure where to start. 'Do you know Doctor Rasmusson?' she said. 'From the health centre.'

'Yes, vaguely. The mums all rave about him. Say he's a good listener.'

That was a good start, Jo thought. 'Well, Ras and I would like to... are hoping to organise an event to bring everyone together. To raise community spirit.'

'And what sort of event did you have in mind?'

Jo took a deep breath. 'A Scrabble festival.'

'A Scrabble festival?'

'Yes, a big Scrabble-themed gathering over an entire

weekend. A tournament would be the main event, but there'd be informal games for less serious players too. Refreshments, of course. A craft room too.'

'A craft room? What's that got to do with Scrabble?'

Jo unbuttoned her jacket and revealed a necklace she'd purchased from Etsy, which spelled out her full name, Joanne, in letter tiles. She hadn't wanted to choose Joanne – she never used her full name – but having only two letters had looked a bit silly.

'People make bracelets too and sometimes pictures for the wall.'

'I see. Great idea. So where do we come in? Do you want us to tell the children about it? Try and get some families involved?'

'I was rather hoping you'd let us use the school.'

'The school?'

Jo tried to read his expression. It wasn't a definite no, but he wasn't blown away by the idea either.

'Let me get this straight,' he said, sitting up in his chair and picking up his pen. 'You'd like to hire the school for an entire weekend.'

'Well, I was hoping... that it might be...'

'Here's our pricing.' He rummaged in a desk drawer and pulled out a laminated piece of card. He pushed it across the desk towards her, and Jo saw it was printed with hourly rates.

'That's way more than we could afford.'

'How much could you afford?'

'We haven't got much of a budget.' She paused. 'Well, to be honest, we haven't got a budget at all. I was hoping that we could do this... as some kind of... joint venture?'

'A joint venture. What's in it for us?'

He tapped his fingers on the desk. Jo took this as a sign he wanted to get rid of her and began to speak faster now, trying to get as many words out as possible in the hope of persuading him. Mentally, she ran down the list of points she'd made: reasons why the school should agree to this.

'Well, as I said, it'd be great for the community. And for your reputation. Other schools would think how innovative it was.'

She glanced at him. He wasn't buying it.

'And money,' she continued. 'We'd need to recoup our costs, but any profit we make, the school can keep.'

She should have checked this first with Ras.

'The PTA already have an active programme of fundraising events,' said Mr Morgan.

She had one last card to play. If this didn't persuade him, nothing would.

'Scrabble is very educational. There could be all sorts of word-based activities. We'd have a children's zone with Junior Scrabble games for younger participants. Could be the perfect thing for kids like Alfred.'

20

Tuesday morning. As the train left the Pennines behind and sped – well, bit of an exaggeration – towards Manchester, Jo got her Filofax out. For once, she'd been lucky enough to bag herself a table seat so she could go through all the plans for the festival.

She had a long to do list with only the first item – venue – crossed off.

Second item – although not actually on the list: tell Ras the good news. They had a venue for the festival.

Next, she needed to look into how to go about running a tournament. There were, she'd discovered after some googling, regular Scrabble tournaments across the whole country – how had she never found this out before? – and some hardcore players who spent their weekends travelling to each and every one. Perhaps she'd join their ranks after the festival.

The list went on. To anyone else, it might have been daunting, having so much to do on top of their day job, but Jo felt confident that she could manage it. Not only confident, but excited.

In the office, she went through the rigmarole of booking taxis and hotels and typing up a schedule for a forthcoming shoot, but all the while, her mind was running through the plans for the festival. How many helpers would they need? Who could print the tickets? Design the posters?

At five to eleven, she stretched and decided it was time for a coffee. She could hear voices as she approached the kitchen: Leona was holding court again, telling the others about the filming trip she'd been on. Jo paused by the door to listen.

'...it was so muddy,' she was saying. 'My favourite shoes were ruined.'

'I usually wear trainers on a shoot.' That was Hannah's voice. 'You're on your feet so much.'

'And the cameraman was so grouchy. Treated me like I was his slave. Fetch this, fetch that.'

'Well, you were there to help.' Hannah again.

Jo coughed and walked into the room.

Leona's cheeks reddened slightly. 'Yeah, I had the best time. You should have seen the size of my hotel room – it was more of a suite. And Hannah, you won't believe this, but Adam asked me out. You know, the presenter. I'll be in *OK!* magazine before long.'

A hotel suite? Yes, but only because that was the last available room. And as for *OK!* magazine...

Jo felt the irritation – anger, even – bubbling up inside her, and before she could stop herself, she blurted out, 'Adam the presenter is gay, Leona.'

Leona shook her head and left the room, leaving Hannah and Jo staring after her.

'Perhaps I shouldn't have said that,' Jo said.

'I thought everyone knew,' said Hannah. 'He has pictures of his partner all over Instagram.'

'His rather gorgeous partner.' Jo nodded, filling the kettle. 'Coffee?'

'Yeah, please. How are you, Jo? We never get chance to speak these days.'

'I'm good, thanks. Mad busy as usual.'

'At work? You always seem on top of things.'

'No, not at work. At home. So much going on. But it's great,' she added. 'I love being busy.'

She left the office that evening the second it turned six o'clock – something she hadn't done since she'd shared a flat with Gemma – and ran for the train. It was a bit of a struggle to make the train at twelve minutes past, but she made it with seconds to spare.

By five past seven, she was sitting in the waiting room of the health centre. Surgery had finished over an hour ago, but Ras had said he'd still be there, finishing off his paperwork.

He finally emerged from the corridor leading to the consulting rooms. 'Sorry to keep you waiting, Jo. Now, what's this good news you mentioned?'

'I went to the school and we have a venue.' She couldn't keep the excitement from her voice, and it echoed around the empty waiting room.

'The head teacher agreed?'

'He took quite a lot of persuading. But I pointed out it would be good for the children. And...'

He looked at her quizzically.

'I'm not sure you're going to like this,' Jo said.

'Tell me.'

She took a deep breath. 'I agreed the school could keep all the profits.'

Ras breathed a sigh of relief. 'That's okay. It was never about making money.'

'No, I know, but it *has* to make some money now. The festival is going to be combined with the school summer fayre. Turns out they hadn't yet come up with a theme for this year. It's good because it means the PTA will help, but it also puts the pressure on because we'll need to make at least as much money as the fayre would have done. We can charge people a fiver to enter the tournament, but I think we need something big for the Saturday evening. Something a bit different. Something that'll entice people to part with their cash.'

'I know,' said Ras. 'We could play Scrabble.'

'Ha ha. Obviously, it has to involve Scrabble, but it needs something more. Something that'll generate interest. Create a bit of a splash.'

'Hmm. Tell you what... let's think about it over some dinner. I didn't have time for lunch today and I can't think on an empty stomach. My place?'

Ras's place turned out to be the top floor of a mill, now converted into apartments. Its huge windows overlooked the canal, the old mill chimney and the cobbled streets of Hebbleswick, all set against the spectacular backdrop of the Pennines. It was sparsely furnished – 'I've not been here long,' he said apologetically – but had all the essentials: a comfy (unstained) sofa in a vibrant shade of teal, a huge, copper-coloured floor lamp for reading and a table big enough for a Scrabble board.

Ras rustled up tortellini and a side salad, poured them

each a glass of chilled white wine, and they ate in the kitchen, sitting on bar stools.

'This is delicious,' said Jo. 'Thank you.'

'Well, it's not quite that little trattoria in Florence that I mentioned in our first texts,' he said, 'but I do make a decent bowl of pasta, if I say so myself.'

Jo smiled at the mention of their early messages. *Perhaps we'll go there together one day*, he had said. That seemed vanishingly unlikely, given that he hadn't asked her for a second date.

As he cleared the plates away, Jo got out her Filofax.

'We've tons to do, Ras,' she said. 'I thought first…'

'I think first, we should have a game of Scrabble,' he said. 'Relax. We've plenty of time.'

'We only have a few months.'

'That's plenty of time,' he repeated. He leaned over and took her Filofax from her, smiling as he glanced down at the long to-do list on the open page before closing it gently. 'Let's go and sit on the sofa and I'll set up the board on the coffee table.'

Jo and Ras played Scrabble all evening – they each won one game – and didn't do a great deal of festival planning, so they agreed to meet again the following evening. This time, Ras cooked them a simple supper of pan-fried salmon, but again, as soon as dinner was over and he'd put their plates in the dishwasher, he got out the Scrabble box again.

'What about the festival?' Jo had said, opening her Filofax.

'Just one game. It's like mindfulness meditation,' he said,

handing her the bag so she could draw her letter tiles. 'Helps me let go of the stresses and strains of the day and clears my mind, ready for whatever festival questions you're going to throw at me.'

Of course, once again, one game led to another and they managed very little festival planning, so Ras invited Jo over the following evening. Once again, he prepared dinner for her – quesadillas – but Jo insisted that the Scrabble box remained on the shelf. Instead, she took out her Filofax and ran through her very long festival to-do list with him.

'I'm having coffee with Kate in Essendale on Saturday morning and I'll ask her if she'll help with the marketing,' said Jo, 'and I've a meeting with the chair of the PTA tomorrow before Scrabble club to go through everything and work out who's doing what.'

'That all sounds fantastic. What can I do?' Ras's eyes twinkled at her across the table. The awkwardness of first-date Ras had disappeared now. The last three evenings had felt easy. As easy as evenings with Gemma when Jo had shared that flat with her in Castlefield; they'd cook together most nights, chat about their day and watch box sets on TV.

'If we could come up with a poster design this evening,' said Jo, 'then perhaps you could print some out and we could ask the Scrabble club members to start putting them up.'

'Sure.' He opened up his laptop. 'Now what do we want? Hebbleswick Scrabble Festival spelled out in Scrabble tiles?'

'Perfect. And a picture of the town. The dates. My email address so people can message for further information. I could put my mobile number…'

'Best not. You might be inundated with calls.'

Jo sighed. 'Or not. Maybe no-one will be interested.'

'I have a good feeling about this,' said Ras. 'Now how about this photo?'

He'd opened a shot of the town that must have been taken from high up – possibly from Hazel Lane, in fact – with the rows of stone terraces zigzagging up the hillsides, and the little town nestling below. You could see the canal with its brightly coloured narrowboats, the church spire and the mill chimney too.

'That's perfect,' she said. 'Add that on. And the times as well as the dates.'

He tapped away at the keyboard, moving the image around till it was positioned in the perfect place, deftly adding the dates and times, and experimenting with different fonts to see which made the most impact. He knew his way around a computer, Jo thought, remembering how her first impression of him had been that he looked like he worked in IT. Unkind of her, she thought. True, he was a little geeky, but he was also kind and warm and...

Ras stifled a yawn.

'I should go,' she said, scrambling to her feet.

'No, sorry, that was rude of me. It's just... well, work. You know. I'm shattered.'

Despite his obvious exhaustion, Ras walked with her up the hill to her little underdwelling overlooking the allotments. He had insisted on doing this every evening, even though she always protested, saying she felt perfectly safe walking back on her own.

Jo unlocked her front door, then tried to wrestle it open. It seemed to get worse each day. She'd sent two texts to the landlord and rung the letting agency but had heard nothing.

'I'll see you at Scrabble club tomorrow,' she said as the door finally swung open.

'Sure,' he said. 'And then, I was wondering if we shouldn't get together on Saturday afternoon. You can update me on what Kate said and how it went with the PTA. I'll come here, if you like.'

Jo hesitated. Her place was so scruffy compared with his, but to refuse him would seem inhospitable. 'That'd be nice.'

'Jo, I'm very grateful for all the time you're putting into this.'

Their eyes met. Jo thought for a second that he was about to kiss her, but then he pulled her into a hug. She nestled into him, relishing the sensation of another human's body warmth. She hadn't had a hug since Gemma had moved down south. In fact, as a single adult, she didn't get much physical contact with other human beings at all: an air-kiss on both cheeks or a handshake when she went on a date; unwelcome fumblings from the likes of Tarquin; a pat on the back from Caroline at work when Jo had finished a particularly tiresome spreadsheet; and an awkward hug from her parents on her annual trip up to the Isle of Arran for the festive season.

And now here she was, standing outside her little house on Hazel Lane, with the lights of Hebbleswick twinkling below and Ras's arms around her. Surprisingly strong arms for a man of his stature. She didn't want this moment to end.

21

This time, Jo wasn't nervous as she pressed the shiny chrome button outside the school gates and heard the buzz of the catch opening; she was excited.

Focus, she reminded herself, *focus*. But her mind kept wandering back to Ras, and how it had felt to be held in his arms. Her feelings for him now went beyond attraction; there was attraction, of course, but there was connection too. A deeper connection than she'd expected to have with anyone after such a short time of knowing them. But she had no idea how he felt about her. No, that wasn't true; she did know. He didn't fancy her; there hadn't been a second date.

'Anyway, you've given up dating,' she mumbled to herself as she walked up the path. 'Concentrate on the festival.'

She was bursting with ideas to share with the chair of the PTA. Her favourite was the tombola. Instead of tickets, they'd buy a load of blank letter tiles and put in twenty-six actual letters. If you drew a tile with a letter on, you would win the corresponding prize. A high-scoring letter like a Q or a Z would win you a better prize than a low-scoring one like a T.

The chair of the PTA turned out to be a woman a little older than Jo: slim, with a mop of loose, blonde curls – a few dark roots showing, Jo noticed with relief; she always felt more relaxed with women whose hair wasn't perfect – and a creased T-shirt.

'I'm Sal,' she said as she greeted Jo in reception.

Sal – 3 points, Jo thought.

'Ignore the state of me,' Sal continued. 'Four kids, all under ten, and the PTA to run. I don't have time to iron.'

Sal was as excited about Hebbleswick Scrabble Festival as Jo was. She raved about the tombola idea and cooed over the greeting cards and pictures created using Scrabble tiles and said she'd persuade the Year 4 teacher to be in charge of the craft room. 'You're so creative, Jo. Exactly the sort of person Hebbleswick Primary needs.'

You're so creative.

Jo automatically opened her mouth to object, to say that no, she wasn't creative, she was more of an admin kind of person, but then she closed it again. What would it be like just to accept a compliment for once?

'Thanks, Sal,' she said.

They agreed that the PTA would provide coffee and cakes, and that Sal would persuade the school dinner ladies to provide light meals.

'Could we serve alcohol on the Saturday evening?' said Jo.

'We've no licence, but we can get round that. We could buy in beer, wine, perhaps make a few cocktails and then ask for donations. What are you planning that evening?'

Jo paused. She still hadn't come up with a killer idea, despite thinking of nothing else – well, practically nothing else; Ras kept creeping into her thoughts – all day. 'You'll have to wait and see,' she said. 'Might the PTA run a bookstall? Books are full of words, so it sort of fits with the theme.'

'Fab idea,' Sal said. 'And a Scrabble-themed fancy dress competition?'

'Yeah, sure,' Jo said, though she wasn't quite sure how that would work. What would people come as? A board, a letter or a tile rack? Of course, she had that Scrabble-themed pinafore dress at home, but she couldn't ever imagine having the courage to wear it.

'Scrabble-themed fancy dress?' said Florence later. 'I've not got a clue what I could go as.'

'I think it's more for the children,' Jo said.

Her meeting with Sal had overrun and Jo had dashed back to Hazel Lane, grabbed a piece of cheese on toast and hurried back down the hill twenty minutes late for Scrabble club to find that a) Ras had had to leave – he was on out-of-hours duty, apparently, and there'd been an emergency – and b) word had already got round about the festival and everyone was far more interested in hearing about her plans for that than they were in playing an actual game.

'Our Robert's kids go to that school,' said Sylvia. 'Suppose I'll end up sewing their costumes. I always have to for World Book Day – their mother claims she's too busy. Trouble is, these days I can't see to thread the needle. I'll have to see Doctor Ras about my eyes.'

'Our Knit 'n' Chat group could make scarves featuring letter tiles,' said Florence.

'Great idea,' said Jo, somewhat absently. She was really disappointed that Ras wasn't here – after she'd been thinking about him all day – but at least she'd see him tomorrow.

'You'd be surprised how much knitwear twenty-eight

retired women can generate,' said Sylvia. 'Although knitting does play havoc with my joints.'

'Letter tile scarves,' said Jo, finally managing to push Ras from her mind. 'I like that idea. We need to make as much money as possible for the school.'

'I could make biscuits,' said Annie. 'With iced letters on. To look like Scrabble tiles. Like the ones we sell in the (Not So) Little Board Game Café.'

'Thanks, Annie.' Jo made a note in her Filofax to check this with Sal; she didn't want Annie stepping on the toes of whoever was running the PTA refreshment stall.

'And there'll be a tournament?' Mr B said.

'There will.' Jo nodded.

'Can anyone enter?' said Cosmic.

'Yes, but there'll be a small entry fee,' Jo said.

'I hope you'll be bringing plenty of dictionaries,' said Florence, glowering at Mr B.

Jo knew that Florence and Mr B argued every time they played together, Mr B trying it on with proper nouns, words of his own invention and, on one occasion, a Polish word – it was his mother tongue – and Florence spending entire games with her nose buried in the *Oxford English Dictionary*.

'I will.' Jo added 'dictionaries' to her list. How many would they need? And where could she get them from? The school, perhaps? Or perhaps they could use an online dictionary?

'Have you thought about insurance for this festival?' said Malcolm.

Everyone groaned.

'No, hear me out,' he said. 'What if there's a major

incident? An earthquake? Or a terrorist attack? What if the school burns down the day before the festival?'

'In the unlikely event of an earthquake, we'll cancel,' said Jo, but made a mental note to check with the school in case they did need insurance.

Saturday morning. Jo hadn't ventured into the (Not So) Little Board Game Café in Essendale since she'd first decided to move out of Manchester and had been hunting for somewhere to live. She'd been preoccupied then – with Gemma moving so far away, with the search for a new place, with Leona's recent arrival at Pop! Productions – and hadn't noticed what a lovely place it was. The walls were painted in a delicate shade of grey and hung with enormous photo canvases showing close-ups of board games pieces. Red and white bunting hung from the ceiling and a long shelving unit stacked full of games ran along the entirety of one wall.

Kate was sitting at one of the brightly painted tables, talking to the waitress that Jo vaguely remembered from her first visit. She was pretty, with a long, wispy fringe, pale-blue eyes and an elfin face, and she was wearing an olive-green dungaree pinafore.

'Jo, this is Em,' Kate said. 'Em, meet Jo.'

'Pleased to meet you,' said Em.

'Great place you've got here,' Jo said.

'Yeah, it took a lot of hard work to get it like this, but it's paid off in the end. And I'm opening a second one in Hebbleswick. You'll have to come along.'

'Yeah, that'd be good,' said Jo. 'Providing you've got a few Scrabble boards.'

'Don't talk to me about Scrabble,' Em said. 'I've lost all my best customers on Friday evenings since Ras started that club of his. Florence and Mr B used to meet to play here. Are they still arguing over every word?'

Jo nodded.

'Well, I don't miss that,' Em said. 'Now what can I get you?'

When they'd placed their orders – latte and a muffin for Jo, green tea for Kate – and Em had disappeared off into the kitchen, Kate and Jo turned their attention to the festival.

'If you give me all the details,' said Kate, 'date, time, venue, bullet points detailing the main attractions, I can write a press release for the local newspaper and the local radio station. Might be able to get an interview slot too.'

'That'd be good,' said Jo, wondering who would be brave enough to go live on air. They could cross that bridge when they came to it.

'And I'll do some social media stuff too. Have you put posters up everywhere?'

'Not yet, but we're planning to.' Jo reached into her bag and pulled out a rolled-up printout of the poster she and Ras had designed.

'Looks good,' said Kate.

'Ras and I did it.'

'Been seeing much of him?'

'Yeah, well, you know. With all the planning.'

Kate raised her eyebrows. 'Come up and see my plans for a Scrabble festival,' she said in an exaggerated, seductive tone.

'It's not like that,' said Jo. 'We're friends. I've given up dating.'

'Since when?'

'Since I realised that Tarquin was just trying to get me into bed. Since Ras didn't ask for a second date even though our first one was lovely. Since every man I date turns out to be a bad choice. Perhaps I'm not ready, Kate. Not after the disaster that was my first marriage. Perhaps I'll never be ready.'

Jo walked along the canal back to Hebbleswick and up the hill to her little house. Although she'd resolved to give up dating, told Kate she wasn't ready, she went straight upstairs to the bathroom and checked out her appearance. Ras would be here soon and there was no harm in looking her best.

That hug on Thursday evening – that had felt special. It had awakened something in her: a longing to be held. It had somehow made her feel both calm and excited, if that was possible. She couldn't quite explain it, not even to herself. Excited by his physical presence. Those strong arms around her, the sense that he would protect her, should he need to. The scent of him; that messy hair mightn't look great, but it smelled wonderful, citrussy fresh. If she had turned her head a little, she could have kissed him. It would have been so easy to slip her fingers under his T-shirt and touch his bare skin.

She'd felt aroused, yet at the same time, safe and comforted.

Hormones, Jo decided. Both the calmness and the sexual excitement had simply been hormones. Oxytocin (20 points) and... well, something else. Ras would know. Not that she intended to ask him.

*

Jo tugged the door open to find Ras standing outside wearing…

What *was* he wearing?

Overalls. Scruffy, paint-spattered, blue overalls.

The colour did nothing for him.

Well, this was disappointing. Okay, so this wasn't a date – just another festival planning meeting – but she had spent the best part of an hour trying to curl her hair, before deciding it looked better straight, and applying make-up before deciding she'd put on a bit too much and scrubbing it off,before opting for a more natural look. Whereas he had clearly made no effort whatsoever.

He was never a smart dresser. She knew that. And that was fine.

But overalls?

Although he was carrying a plastic bag. Had he bought her a gift?

Beware of men bearing gifts, she thought, remembering Si. But this was Ras. Different kettle of fish. A gift from Ras would be rather lovely.

'Hi,' she said, stepping aside for him to come in.

'Look what I've brought.' He reached into one of the bags and pulled out some kind of electrical power tool. 'I thought I might fix your door. If you'd like me to?'

So that explained the outfit.

He rummaged in the bag again and pulled out a screwdriver. 'I'll take it off and plane it. It won't take long and then you can update me about the festival over a game. How does that sound?'

'Sounds amazing,' she said. 'Thank you.'

She watched him take the door off its hinges, then she held it steady whilst he shaved off slivers of wood from the bottom. She watched him work, hoping the landlord wouldn't mind, and fighting the urge to make some kind of double entendre about liking a man with a big tool.

'That should do it,' he said, screwing the door back into position. 'I was worried about you. I mean, what if there was a fire and you couldn't get out?'

'I'd escape through a window.'

Even with this arse, she added mentally, before saying out loud, 'But Ras. I am grateful. It's so kind of you.'

'Well, I'd hate anything to happen to you, Jo.'

He'd been worrying about her? And would hate anything to happen to her?

Was he...?

Did he...?

'And I'm so grateful for all the effort you've put into organising the festival.'

No, this was one favour in return for another.

'I'm enjoying it,' she said.

'You are?'

'Yeah. And I like spending time with you.'

Love spending time with you.

'In fact,' she added, 'I haven't had this much fun in ages.'

Make that ever.

'Me neither,' he said.

There was a pause. For a second, Jo thought again that he was going to kiss her, right there and then, in his overalls. But then he said, 'I'll put my tools away. Is there somewhere I can change?'

'Bathroom's upstairs. Shall I get the kettle on?'

I'd hate anything to happen to you.

What did that mean exactly? she wondered as she put the kettle on. She opened the kitchen cupboard, pulled out two Mr Men mugs – Mr Tickle and Mr Perfect – and made two mugs of strong tea. So strong, it might have been described as builder's tea. Rather apt after he'd fixed her door.

Did he care about her?

Or were they simply the words of a friend? A good friend?

She was going round and round in circles thinking about it. She took the mugs through to see Ras coming downstairs in chinos and a white T-shirt, looking decidedly smarter than he usually did. He sat down on the sofa, right on top of the stain, and Jo handed him the steaming Mr Perfect mug.

They played a game of Scrabble and Jo updated him on her meetings with Sal and Kate.

'It feels like everything's sorted,' he said. 'Nothing left to do.'

Jo snorted. 'There'll be something we've forgotten.'

'What, with all your lists? I doubt it.'

His eyes met her across the board.

'I still need to come up with something for the Saturday evening,' she said. 'It has to be something different. Something with a wow factor. Something a bit more unusual that we can charge a bit more for and that will rope in people who wouldn't normally be interested in Scrabble. But it still has to be Scrabble-themed.'

'So you want to get people who don't like Scrabble to part with a wodge of cash to play Scrabble?'

Jo laughed. 'Basically yes. Any ideas?'

'Rude Scrabble,' said Ras. 'Bonus points for naughty words?'

'Hmm. Could be fun, but I can't see it going down too well with the head. It's a church school after all. What else?'

'My mind's a blank,' he said. 'No Scrabble pun intended.'

'I'll think of something,' she said, laying down all seven of her tiles to form the word LOVEFEST. 'A 50-point bonus. I used all my tiles.'

'Lovefest?' said Ras. 'You sure that's a word?'

'Check it if you like.'

Jo raised her eyebrows at him, challenging him to get out the dictionary. She was certain the word would be in there.

'No, I'll believe you. So who did you used to play against?' Ras said. 'Before you met me and joined the Scrabble club.'

'Sometimes Gemma, before she moved away. If I could persuade her. But usually the WordPals app. Are you on that?'

'I am, but I hardly use it. I prefer playing face to face. Although occasionally, if I've a free minute at work – if a patient doesn't show up – I'll have a quick game. I mean, there's always tons of paperwork to catch up on, but sometimes I need a breather. A few minutes to myself.'

Perhaps they had played each other, Jo thought, and never realised. But there wasn't time to dwell on that now. They had to come up with something – and something good – for the Saturday evening of the festival, and it would need to generate a bit of publicity, create a splash. But Jo didn't have a single idea what that something might be.

22

Over the next few weeks, the stuff in the office mattered less and less to Jo as the festival mattered more and more. She didn't mind when Leona went off on another filming trip, proclaiming loudly that Adam the presenter had requested her presence. Jo doubted that somehow, but Leona could tell herself that if she wanted. Hannah suggested that Jo came along for Friday night drinks one week, but she declined, saying she already had plans. Well, she did. Friday night was Scrabble club.

With the exception of the Saturday night – Jo still hadn't come up with anything special to offer and it looked like they'd have to go with a simple social evening – the plans for the festival were going swimmingly. Kate had the marketing 'all in hand' and had somehow persuaded Emily to loan them some alternative word games like Codenames, Bananagrams and Upwords. The pile of Scrabble-themed knitwear was reaching mammoth proportions, though Jo hadn't seen it yet. She was now a frequent visitor to Hebbleswick Primary School. There were regular meetings to update Mr Morgan, the head, on her progress, plus planning sessions with Sal that were more social than planning these days. The PTA were taking care of all the refreshments with the exception of Annie's biscuit stall. Sal had organised tombola prizes, the year 4 teacher had agreed to run the craft room and had loved Jo's pictures of cards and necklaces made with letter tiles, and some of the other teachers had worked out a rota for running a Junior Scrabble room.

'You wouldn't believe it if you saw me,' she said to Gemma on the phone. 'Walking in and out of that school like it's nothing.'

'You're putting your past behind you and that's great,' said Gemma. 'And if you can do that with the school stuff, you can do it with your marriage too. You can move on from the trauma you suffered with Si, find someone new and be happy again.'

But Jo wasn't so sure. Putting the bullying she'd suffered at school behind her was one thing; recovering from an emotionally abusive marriage was quite another. There were times when she looked at Ras and wanted him so badly. She thought she could trust him – they knew each other pretty well by now – but she'd thought that about Si once, hadn't she? He too had been lovely at first.

Anyway, she still didn't know how he felt about her. Sometimes, when he looked into her eyes over the Scrabble board, it was easy to believe that he did want something beyond friendship with her. Wishful thinking probably, and she reminded herself – again – that she had given up dating. Unless the Universe gave her a sign, an unmistakable sign.

Nevertheless, she couldn't help wondering one morning, as she walked to the station, if things might have been different had she and Ras 'met' on WordPals rather than on Buzzz. What might that first date have been like if they'd known they shared a hobby? Might he have asked her out a second time? Would they be together now, well on their way to being a proper couple, instead of just two good friends organising a festival together?

Scrabble brought us together, she imagined herself saying to Caroline. *We've been inseparable ever since.*

And then an idea popped into her head.

Scrabble speed-dating.

It could be the perfect event for the Saturday evening of the festival.

If you could have a pub quiz crossed with a speed-dating event, why not Scrabble?

Obviously Scrabble and speed weren't two words you'd normally associate with each other – at least not in Hebbleswick where certain members of the club seemed to take an age over each and every turn. They'd be there for a week if each man played a whole game with each woman, but if each couple only made five words each, it might work. When the bell sounded, the woman would reset the board and the next man would arrive at the table to play. How long would each couple need to play their five words and have enough of a chat to know whether they wanted to see each other again?

She needed to test it out, and to do that, she needed someone to play with. She texted Ras.

Fancy a game of Scrabble tonight?

Jo decided she wouldn't reveal her idea until she was sure that it would work. She set the Scrabble board up on her tiny, fold-out dining table before he arrived. Her plan was to time how long it took to play the first ten words. She was hoping ten minutes would be long enough. If they had twelve pairs of daters that would mean two hours of playing Scrabble, with a half hour break for drinks in the middle. They could open at half seven to register everyone, start playing at eight, and be finished by half past ten.

With her phone secreted on her lap and the stopwatch app activated, they began to play. Ras chose difficult letters at the start of the game. Ten minutes went by and he hadn't played his first word. Or uttered a word, come to that. If this were a date, she wouldn't be ticking his box. This idea was a non-starter.

The first four words took seventeen minutes.

As Ras laid his fifth word – COBBLER on a double word score – he said, 'Why do you keep looking at your phone? And pretending that you're not?'

'No reason.'

'Are you waiting for a text from someone? Have you met someone new on Buzzz?'

'No,' said Jo. 'I'm through with dating. I'm crap at it.'

Ras hesitated, as if he was about to say something but thought better of it. She couldn't quite read his expression.

'So why do you keep looking at your phone?' he said eventually. 'Are you timing my moves? Am I being too slow or something?'

'Yes and yes.'

'I didn't know this was speed Scrabble all of a sudden.'

She couldn't keep the idea to herself any longer.

'Not speed Scrabble,' she said. 'Speed-*dating* Scrabble. For Saturday evening at the festival.'

'Speed-dating? In a primary school? Are you sure the head'll be up for that?'

'He isn't expected to join in.'

'I didn't mean...'

'He'll be fine, Ras. Don't worry.' She explained how she thought it might work. 'I was timing how long it takes to play ten words, to check it would work.'

'Then we need to do it properly,' said Ras. 'Timing the moves on a normal game doesn't tell us anything. If people know they've only got ten minutes, they'll play quicker, especially if it doesn't matter who wins the game. Each round will take less time, but you've got to factor in some small talk. They've got to chat to work out if they like the other person.'

'I suppose.'

'Let's play again and this time, we'll pretend we've just met. Ask the sort of questions you ask on a date and try and make a few words at the same time.'

'I feel silly,' Jo said.

He was putting all the letter tiles back in the bag again, ready to start a new game.

'Come on, set the timer.'

She set a timer for ten minutes and pressed 'start'.

'Hi, I'm Ras,' he said.

'Hi, I'm Jo.'

'We should choose our letters. Seven each, isn't it?'

'Yes, seven.'

He was far better at this than she was, Jo thought. Why hadn't he been this confident at the start of their real date?

'Would you like to go first?' he said.

'Shouldn't we take a letter from the bag and the one nearest the start of the alphabet goes first?'

'You'd come across a bit nerdy if you said that on an actual Scrabble speed-date.'

She glanced at the timer. A minute had already passed and they hadn't laid a single word down yet. Her letters weren't all that easy either. 'Q' with no 'U'. Only one vowel, in fact.

She played FELT in the end and added up her points, jotting them down on a fresh sheet in her Filofax, with the time '1 min 32 secs' next to it.

'Great word,' said Ras.

'It isn't. You're being weird.'

'I'm being a nice date. Hoping you'll put a little tick in my box and agree to go out with me.'

He was play-acting, she reminded herself. And she had given up on men.

She drew four new letter tiles.

In a mere thirty-two seconds, Ras spelled out FANCY on a double word score for 26 points.

She could now spell out YES using the Y of FANCY. *Yes, I would tick your box. Yes, I would agree to go out with you.*

As she placed the 'S' on the board, Ras stretched his hand out and placed it over hers, displacing several of the tiles on the board and pretty much ruining the game. His skin felt soft and warm. But not clammy. Definitely not clammy. She looked up into his eyes.

He coughed. 'I'm testing what would happen, if someone got a little amorous and decided to hold hands with their date across the board.'

Jo's heart sank. He moved his hand away from hers and gestured at the jumble of letters.

'And there you have it. The game is spoiled. We'll have to make a rule: no hand-holding till the boards have been packed away. I mean, it could be disastrous. A tile could get knocked on the floor and never be seen again. Would you like to play another round?'

They tested the Scrabble speed-dating idea several times that evening. And the evening after that. And the one after that too.

Jo was pleased that she won the majority of their ten-word matches, but disappointed that he didn't take her hand again. Not once.

23

As Ras had predicted, Mr Morgan was less than enamoured with the speed-dating idea.

'I'm not sure that's appropriate,' he said. 'This is a primary school.'

'It's a bit of fun, Nick,' said Sal. 'Not an orgy.'

'Keep your voice down. There might be children about.' He stood up and closed his office door.

Jo had taken two hours off that morning so she could pop into the school and outline her latest plan to Sal and the head teacher. But so far, he didn't seem too keen.

'It'll be very respectable,' said Jo.

'I thought the festival would be more family orientated,' he said.

'And during the day, it *will* be family orientated,' said Jo. If he said no to this, she was going to be stuck. Neither she nor Ras had any other ideas for something a little different – and lucrative – for the Saturday evening; it had taken her weeks to come up with this one.

'Look at it this way, Nick,' said Sal. 'If people don't meet and fall in love, there'd be no families. Any matches from Jo's speed-dating night might result in a few more pupils on the roll in the next few years.'

He harrumphed. 'But our reputation…'

'Oh, for heaven's sake,' said Sal. 'The after-school football coach you took on last term is bonking the lollipop lady. One of your infant teachers is dating the mum of a child in her own class. And at the last parents' evening, a father of a boy in 3C got chatting to a mother of a boy in 4A and they are now having a torrid affair that will probably break up both their marriages before too long. And you're worried about a bit of speed-dating? I know this is a primary school but you are a bit of a prude sometimes. You'll be banning the Year 6 end-of-term disco next.'

'But I…'

'Jo promised us all the ticket money and all the donations from the drinks. You want to buy new iPads? And revamp the library? Scrabble speed-dating is a brilliant idea.'

'I suppose…' he began.

'Great,' said Sal. 'I'm glad we're all agreed. Jo, you can count on me to spread the word amongst the single parents.'

'Scrabble speed-dating?' said Sylvia at Scrabble club the following Friday. 'Can I have you as my date, Doctor Ras?'

Ras laughed. Linda shot Sylvia a ferocious look, and tugged the hem of her top so that even more cleavage was on display.

Jo took a bite of her chocolate éclair. Annie had surpassed herself with the cake offering this evening. These were superb.

'You have cream on your lip,' said Ras. He leaned over and wiped above her mouth with his forefinger, then looked away awkwardly. She found herself blushing and looked away too, to see Linda scowling at her.

'How will people know about the speed-dating?' said Florence.

'Kate's told the local paper,' said Jo. 'And I think she's organising an interview on local radio about the festival so it can be included in that.'

'I'll give the interview,' said Linda.

'It's got to be Jo,' said Ras. 'Jo, you're the one who knows everything that's happening, it was your idea and you've done most of the work.'

Her? On local radio?

'I don't think…' she began.

'It should definitely be you,' Florence beamed and patted Jo's arm. 'You've worked so hard. And we're all excited about the festival, aren't we? Now, Annie, are there any more of those salted caramel cupcakes?'

Later, when everyone had gone and Jo and Ras were stacking the chairs, he said, 'You are happy to go on the radio, aren't you?'

'I dunno. I've never done anything like that. And I'm not exactly outgoing.'

'You could write down the main points in case you go blank. And I could practise with you.'

He grabbed a letter rack from one of the tables that someone had failed to put away in its box and held it up to his mouth like a microphone.

'So, I'm here with Jo Knox who's going to tell us all about Hebbleswick Scrabble Festival. Welcome, Jo.'

She cringed. This was worse than role-playing Scrabble

speed-dating. Drama had been one of her least favourite classes at school.

He was holding his pretend microphone out to her now.

'Thanks, Ras.' She could feel her cheeks reddening. 'Yes, we've got a lot going on at Hebbleswick Scrabble Festival. Something for everyone. You'd be crazy not to come along.'

'You certainly would,' he said.

Then he held her gaze for a little too long until she said, 'I wonder which box is missing a letter rack?'

Monday lunchtime. With most of her colleagues out of the office and only five days to go until the festival, Jo sat at her desk, eating her sandwiches and double-checking the plans in her Filofax for the umpteenth time. She ran her finger down the to-do list. Refreshments? Tick. Rota for who was monitoring the door? Tick. Posters? Tick. Programmes? Being printed this week. Tickets for speed-dating? Only two more to sell. Blank Scrabble tiles for the craft workshop? Arriving tomorrow courtesy of eBay.

'Jo,' said David, emerging from his office.

She looked up, exchanged glances with Mona and swivelled her chair to face him.

'How can I help?'

'The Plymouth shoot...'

'Yes, everything's ready for that. Scripts and schedules all printed.' She tapped the coloured cardboard folders beside her on the desk. 'All the transport arrangements checked and double-checked. All sorted.'

'Thorough as usual, Jo,' he said. 'I can always rely on

you. I need you to book another hotel room. You're going with them.'

'But I never go filming.'

'I know. And that seems so unfair. I thought this time you would like to.'

'I would like to. Only not this time.'

'I need you to go.'

Jo sighed. She didn't want to be difficult but she couldn't possibly go. 'I've booked a day off on Friday and I have plans over the weekend.'

'You have plans?'

'Yes, I have plans.'

Was that so inconceivable?

'You knew when you accepted this job that there might be some weekend working.'

'I did, but so far there hasn't been. And you can't expect me to cancel my plans at the last minute like this. I won't do it, David.'

Was this really her voice? Standing up to her boss? Saying no?

'I see,' he said. 'So that's how it is.'

She glanced at Mona again; she could almost feel the mysterious, Italian noblewoman egging her on. 'That's how it is.'

He turned away from her and barked across the office. 'Caroline, she won't do it. You'll have to go.'

A little later, she was making a coffee in the kitchen when Caroline came in.

'Jo,' she said in the tone of voice you'd use to soothe

a crying child. 'This shoot over the weekend... you don't really have plans, do you?'

'Yes, I do. Is that so hard to believe?'

'Well, I have noticed that you often hang around in the evenings, as if you don't want to go home.'

Jo was a bit stung. Caroline had noticed? Yet never once asked her to go for a coffee or a drink? Never once asked if she was okay?

'When my best friend moved away,' she said, 'I may have hung around a little. I was a bit, you know, lonely. But I've made new friends now. And I have plans.'

'Couldn't you postpone whatever it is you're doing?'

Jo paused. The festival *could* run without her; she had planned it to the nth degree and didn't actually need to be there. Sal, Mr Morgan – she still couldn't get used to calling a head teacher by his first name – and Ras were more than capable of managing everything. And she'd be on the other end of a phone, in case of emergencies.

But she'd worked so hard for this. It was the biggest thing she'd ever done in her entire life. There'd be other jobs, if she lost this one, but Hebbleswick wouldn't have another Scrabble festival.

'Sorry, Caroline,' she said. 'I'm giving an interview on local radio tomorrow and...'

'You're giving an interview?'

'Yes, and after that I'm running a festival. Over the whole weekend. I can't possibly go to Devon.'

That Friday, she wished she *had* gone filming in Plymouth. Anything would be better than this torture.

She was sitting in the 'reception area' at Hebbleswick Radio – an ordinary kitchen in an ordinary stone terraced house in a typical Hebbleswick cobbled side street – her palms sweating, her mouth dry. This was madness. She was the person who found speaking up in meetings difficult. How had she ever imagined she could give an interview on live radio?

'Jo, would you like to come through?'

She looked up to see a spotty youth staring down at her.

'Sure,' she said standing up.

Feeling distinctly wobbly, she followed him outside and into what was basically a garden shed kitted out with techy equipment, where a balding, middle-aged man wearing huge, black headphones was leaning back in his chair as a song began. A song she recognised. Soaring violins playing the familiar opening of 'At Last'.

In an instant, Jo was transported back to all those evenings when, dressed in her best jeans with her heart full of hope and her stomach full of butterflies, she'd ventured into various bars and pubs to meet yet another stranger off the internet. Etta had given her hope back then – the belief that one day her love really would come along – and confidence too: the confidence to overcome her nerves and her fears and her shyness and to approach her date and say 'hi'. As Etta's voice rang through the air now, Jo decided she could do this. Enthuse about her beloved festival for five minutes? Of course she could. Or at least, she could give it her very best shot.

24

'So how long have you been having the headaches?' he asked, fighting the urge to look at the clock on the wall.

'A month maybe,' said Mrs Green. 'Or it might be more like two months? Or even three? Do you think they might be serious, Doctor Rasmusson? I'm worried it might be a brain tumour.'

She'd been googling, he thought. The internet seemed to bring up every worst-case scenario possible. The rarest of diseases. The most unlikely of cancers. Any innocuous little symptom *could* in theory be a sign of something dreadful, but it usually wasn't.

'There are many things that it's *much* more likely to be. Let's see if we can figure out what's causing it and make sure you're all right.' He tried put on his most reassuring tone, which normally he knew was a very reassuring tone indeed, but today there was a note of impatience in there. He hoped Mrs Green didn't notice.

He couldn't resist it any longer; he glanced at the clock. He reckoned the interview would be starting in about three minutes.

Jo's interview.

He couldn't quite believe that she'd agreed to it. She'd been so nervous, so shy, when he'd first met her, but he'd watched her confidence grow recently; this Scrabble festival seemed to have ignited a passion in her. It made her even more alluring. He wished *he* could ignite a similar passion. He'd liked shy, introverted Jo, but he liked this new Jo too. He'd often wondered what had happened in her past to make her such a nervous person; if practising medicine over the years had taught him anything, it was that people who lacked self-belief usually lacked it for a reason. There'd been a bullying parent in their past, perhaps, or a former partner who took pleasure in belittling them. Something like that had happened to Jo, he felt sure of it. But she was slowly becoming more self-assured, and Rasmus liked to think that he'd perhaps played a part in that in his own small way by enlisting her help in organising a Scrabble event. He'd never for one moment imagined that she'd organise something this big.

He was suddenly aware that Mrs Green was looking at him, waiting for him to say something.

'Do you have any other symptoms when you have the headache?' he said.

'No, just the headache.'

'Flashing lights? Nausea? Vomiting?'

'No, none of those. But it's really painful. What do you think is causing it?'

Rasmus sighed. Headaches were such difficult beasts. What he wouldn't give right now for a child with chicken pox or even a boil that needed lancing!

They'd said they'd give the two o'clock news bulletin, it would be followed by a song and then it would be Jo. It was three minutes past two and he reckoned an average track was about three minutes long so that meant...

'My husband thinks it could be cheese,' said Mrs Green. 'Do you think it could be cheese, Doctor Rasmusson?'

'Do you keep a record of when these headaches occur, Mrs Green? Do they happen at a particular time of day?'

Four minutes later, he dispatched Mrs Green with an assurance that there was no need to give up Cheddar just yet and instructions to take the occasional paracetamol if the pain was really bad, keep a headache diary and make a follow-up appointment if things didn't improve in a fortnight. He then phoned through to reception and requested a three-minute break between patients, saying he had to write up some notes. Then he flicked screens to the online local radio station and raised the volume on his computer.

'...and that was, of course, the wonderful Etta James singing "At Last",' intoned the DJ, 'and our lovely guest this afternoon, Jo Knox, was just telling me that that song was very special to her. Jo, would you like to tell the listeners why?'

'Er, no, not really,' said Jo. 'It's a bit personal.'

Rasmus couldn't help smiling to himself. He could imagine Jo's face as she said that. He could feel the awkwardness in the radio studio as acutely as if he were there.

There was silence for a moment before the presenter said, 'So you're here to tell us about a very unusual event that's happening this weekend in Hebbleswick.'

'Er, yeah.'

Rasmus realised that he was holding his breath. He was as nervous as if he were giving this interview himself. 'Come on, Jo, you can do this,' he said out loud. 'Tell them it's a Scrabble festival.'

'And what's the event?' said the presenter.

'A Scrabble festival.'

'Tell them about the tournament.' Rasmus was practically shouting at the screen now. 'The speed-dating. The craft room.'

'There'll be a Scrabble tournament,' said Jo.

There was a moment's silence. Rasmus could picture her in the studio. She'd be fiddling with her hair or her hands. She always did that when she was feeling anxious. His heart went out to her. Jo. Lovely Jo. She might have grown in confidence recently, but this was quite clearly out of her comfort zone.

He was very much a man of science and didn't believe in telepathy, but he willed her to continue now. *Go on, Jo. Go on. You've got this.*

Through his speakers, he heard her clear her throat. Then suddenly her voice came again, hesitant but clear. 'Though not everyone is competitive so if you just want to come along…'

She cleared her throat again. '…and play a game of Scrabble for fun, there'll be plenty of opportunities to do that. There's also a craft room…'

'A craft room?' said the presenter.

'Yes. You'll be able to make necklaces and pictures and greeting cards using letter tiles.'

She sounded more confident now.

'Well done, Jo. Keep going,' urged Rasmus. His fists were clenched and he was shaking his hands, as if he were cheering on an athlete in a race.

'That's an interesting idea,' said the presenter.

'And then tomorrow evening, we'll be running Scrabble speed-dating.'

She was really getting into her stride now, thought Rasmus. He felt a surge of pride; he knew she could do this.

'Scrabble speed-dating?' said the presenter. 'How does that work?'

'In normal speed-dating, you basically get three minutes to talk to each of the men in the room – or each of the women, if you're a man obviously – and then the organiser rings a bell and you move on to the next person...'

Rasmus had rehearsed with her several times, but she was managing somehow to say all this as if she were saying it for the first time. It not only sounded natural but he could hear the excitement in her voice and hoped that other people would pick up on that too.

'During those three minutes,' she continued, 'you can talk about whatever you like, only not everyone is good at small talk and it's sometimes a bit awkward. So we're doing Scrabble speed-dating. You have ten minutes with each person instead of three so you have a little longer to get to know them and see if you like them, but you also have to play Scrabble at the same time. The Scrabble is a kind of ice-breaker.'

Rasmus punched the air. She was nailing it.

'That's a genius idea. Did you come up with it?'

'I did actually. I'm glad you like it. If you're single, you could come along yourself.'

The presenter gave a nervous laugh. 'So where is the festival taking place?'

'It's in the primary school, and if any families want to

come along during the day, there'll be junior Scrabble games too, and other word games. There really is something for everyone. And the school canteen will be serving lunch and light refreshments so if people want to join us for the whole weekend, they can and we really hope they will.'

She sounded so warm and engaging. He pictured her again in the studio, her eyes bright with enthusiasm, and he wished he were there, could hug her afterwards, could tell her how brilliantly she'd done.

He remembered how it had felt to hold her in his arms, how good she'd smelled, how she'd nestled into him. He was falling for her; he knew that. Had fallen already, perhaps. He wasn't quite sure when that had happened. It had sneaked up on him. Initial attraction on their first date and, he liked to think, a spark between them. At least there had been till he'd wimped out of going down that hole.

Gaping Gill! If only, he thought for the umpteenth time, he hadn't chosen Gaping Gill for their first date. Would they be together now if he hadn't?

Perhaps. But at least he'd made a friend. And a good one at that. He really cared about Jo. This festival had to go well, for her sake, not his own. She'd put her heart and soul into organising this, and he couldn't bear to think of how dejected she'd feel if the whole thing was a flop. Personally, he'd have been happy with a small, Saturday afternoon event to attract the children and parents crowd who wouldn't normally come on a Friday evening. Then Jo had suggested the festival and it was such a good idea that he hadn't had the heart to say no. They had both worked so hard to bring everything together – Jo especially – and it would be a crying shame if no-one turned up.

'And is there a charge for admission?' the presenter said, just as Rasmus's phone began to ring.

He hastily muted the volume on his computer and picked up the phone.

'Are you ready for your next patient, doctor?' Jackie the receptionist said. 'Only we don't want you to be running late when you've got your Scrabble festival starting this evening, do we? You said you wanted to be away by five at the latest.'

'Sure,' he said. The interview would probably be over soon anyway. 'Send them in.'

25

'You were brilliant, Jo,' said Ras. 'I didn't hear all of it, but I managed to catch some between patients.'

They were sitting in the staffroom of Hebbleswick Primary. In a little over an hour, the doors would open and the festival would begin.

It was a cosy staffroom: a couple of large, comfy sofas and a long dining table so the teachers could eat lunch together. Cheerful, motivational pictures hung round the walls with slogans – admittedly cheesy slogans like *Failure is success in progress* and *Stay positive and good things will happen*. Gemma would approve, Jo thought.

'Was it really okay?' Jo said. 'I was so nervous. I know it's only a small local station, but I was so worried I'd say the wrong thing. Or dry up completely.'

'You were fabulous. Far better than I would have been.'

He patted her arm in a reassuring way. Not flirty. More the way he'd reassure an anxious patient. But nonetheless, she felt a frisson of excitement at his touch.

No, she reminded herself for the umpteenth time. There'd been no big sign. She mustn't let herself think of him like that.

'Let's hope loads of people heard your interview and decide to come along.'

Jo held up crossed fingers. Ras's eyes were bright with excitement; she knew how much he wanted this festival to be successful, to draw in people from all over Hebbleswick and beyond, and foster that sense of community that he believed was so important to health and well-being. And, of course, they needed to make money for the school. Jo knew from things Sal had told her that educational budgets were tight these days and the fundraising efforts of the PTA made a real difference to lives of the children.

'Now, where's this final checklist you said we had to run through?' said Ras.

Jo took out her Filofax and turned to the festival section. In forty-eight hours, she'd be removing this section completely and putting it in the recycling bin. What on earth would she do when the festival was over? There'd be nothing to plan and no excuse for seeing Ras several times a week.

She ran down the list, ticking everything off, as he peered over her shoulder.

'You have such neat handwriting,' he said as she crossed off the final item. 'I've always had a bit of thing about women with neat handwriting.'

A thing about women with neat handwriting?

Was he flirting? Or making a joke?

She turned to look at him. Their eyes met, then the staffroom door opened suddenly and Mr Morgan appeared. They jumped apart guiltily; Jo felt as if she was seven years old again and had been caught doing something naughty at school.

'Visitor for you, Jo,' said Mr Morgan, and a familiar face poked out from behind him.

'Gem,' Jo said, standing up and rushing to hug her friend. 'I didn't know you were coming.'

'No way was I going to miss this.' Gemma beamed. 'And you must be Ras. Aka Gaping Gill man.'

Ras frowned slightly – Jo could have kicked Gemma – but then he smiled and said, 'Nice to meet you,' and Jo watched as her oldest friend shook the hand of her newest.

'I'm sure that knowing you, Jo,' said Gemma, 'everything will already be organised, but is there anything I can do? When does it all start?'

'Less than an hour to go,' said Ras. 'And my car boot's full of Scrabble boxes.'

'Then what are we waiting for?' said Gem.

Somehow the sight of all the Scrabble boxes in Ras's boot made the whole thing real. They were doing this. Actually doing this. All those plans that she'd spent weeks making in her Filofax were about to become reality. Ras must have been thinking along similar lines because he put an arm round her and gave her a squeeze. 'I can't believe it, Jo. It's actually going to happen.'

'Aye, aye,' said Gemma, when Ras had disappeared into the school hall with an armful of boxes. 'He seems touchy-feely.'

'We're just friends, Gem.'

'And the rest.'

Jo shook her head. 'I said I'd stay single, unless the Universe gave me a sign...'

'Do you need a sign to know that he's right for you? There's chemistry, Jo. And you share a hobby. You could try trusting your instincts.'

'My instincts? I don't have good instincts when it comes

to men. You know that, Gem. Anyway, let's forget about romance. I've a festival to run.'

The next hour was frantic. The school hall – the main venue for the festival – was used by the after-school club until five o'clock so could only be set up then. Jo, Ras and Gemma began putting up tables. The spring mechanisms on the legs of the school's large fold-up tables were so vicious that Jo came close to losing a finger on one or two occasions. Mr Morgan, nobly assisted by one of the PTA mums – who, judging by the way she laughed at everything he said, seemed to have a bit of a crush on him – put up the letter tile bunting all around the walls. Jo had been worried about the bunting: the cheap cream curtain lining fabric cut into rectangles, with the letters drawn on with black marker pen, had seemed rather crude. But now it was hanging up, each rectangle *did* look like a Scrabble tile; she had to admit the whole thing was rather effective.

Sal was busy filling helium balloons in loads of bright colours with Mrs Woods, the Year 4 teacher who happened to love anything arty-crafty, standing beside her drawing letter tiles on each one with another black marker. There were already two bouquets of them in the far corners of the hall. The splash of colour gave the place a touch of festivity.

'The whole place looks amazing,' said Gem. 'Jo, you're so clever.'

'She certainly is,' said Ras.

'I can't claim credit for the balloons or the letter tile bunting,' Jo said. 'Mrs Woods thought of those.'

'Well, it looks beautiful whoever thought of it,' said Gem. 'Everyone's going to love it, Jo. You'll see.'

*

Mr Morgan tapped the microphone and began to speak. It squeaked, causing piercing feedback to reverberate round the hall and two children to clamp their hands over their ears.

He looked into the wings of the small stage.

After a brief pause whilst Mr Timms, the caretaker, adjusted the PA levels, he began again. 'Welcome, everyone.'

By everyone, he meant Gemma and four mums with seven children between them who were hovering at the back of the hall.

'Please, do take a seat,' he said.

There was some discussion and the families sat down, squashing onto the two tables at the back of the hall. A bit of shuffling ensued as children changed their minds about who they wanted to sit next to. Eventually they were all settled and Mr Morgan began his speech.

'Thank you so much for coming. We have so much on offer this weekend.' He looked down at the programme Jo had given him and began to outline everything that was happening.

She glanced around the huge, almost empty hall, then over at Ras. He looked deflated, like a broken man. Her heart ached for him. She wanted to wrap her arms around him, to stroke his hair, to console him.

'Ras, did you want to say a few words?' said Mr Morgan from the stages.

Ras shook his head. 'Let's get on with the Scrabble,' he called back.

They set up four boards between the eleven attendees.

'Fancy a game?' Jo said to Gemma.

Gemma hesitated. 'We could, I suppose. Although I fancy a chat more. I haven't seen you in ages.'

'Why don't you two go and have a cup of tea?' said Ras. 'It's going to be full on all weekend, so you might as well grab your chance to have a break.'

Full on? She doubted that – and judging from his flat tone of voice, he did too – but it was kind of him to suggest they had a break, so they left him to it and wandered over to the staffroom.

As they neared the door, she could hear Mr Morgan inside, talking with Sal.

'Disappointing,' he said. 'Our events are always so well supported. I don't understand why no-one's here. I shouldn't have said yes. It was silly of me, in hindsight, to entrust this to someone we don't even know.'

'She's done everything she could possibly do to make this a success,' said Sal. 'I mean, we work hard in the PTA, but I've never seen anyone put in so much effort. She's incredible.'

Jo looked at Gem.

'Yes, that's *you* she's talking about,' whispered Gem.

'Didn't you hear what he said? That he should never have trusted me,' hissed Jo.

'And she said you're incredible.'

'She's an organising wizard, I'll grant you that.' Mr Morgan's voice now.

'See?' whispered Gem. 'You're an organising wizard. When are you going to realise how fantastic you are? Come on, let's go in and get that cuppa.'

Before Jo could stop her, Gemma walked into the

staffroom. Sal looked up as they went in and put her hand on the head teacher's arm, as if trying to silence him, but to no avail. 'We were saying,' he said, 'how disappointing the turnout is.'

'We were also saying,' said Sal, giving him a stern look, 'how hard you've worked and how much we appreciate it.'

'Don't worry about the turnout,' said Gem. 'We'll put Jo's plan B into action.'

'There's a plan B?' he said.

'Of course. And knowing Jo, a plan C and D and...'

'Yes, okay. I get the picture. So what's your plan B, Jo?'

Thanks for landing me in it, Gem, Jo thought. She hadn't got a plan B at all. Although...

'Well, I'll get Kate to do a final push on social media,' she said.

Mr Morgan looked doubtful.

'I can do a phone chain,' said Sal. 'I ring or text six mums, they text six more who text six more and so on. In case anyone's forgotten.'

Jo doubted that Sal's phone chain or a final push on social media was going to work; perhaps the good folk of Hebbleswick had better things to do with their weekend than play Scrabble. How could she have ever thought otherwise? But she had to try. As Gemma made two mugs of tea, she texted Kate and explained that things had got off to a bad start, and asked if she could post something in the local Facebook group that might encourage a few more people to come along.

When Jo and Gemma went back in the hall, a couple more

families had arrived. Ras was surrounded by children. Three were playing a game and the others were all spectating. Jo had never seen him with children before; he almost seemed to be one of them. She watched as he laid down two letter tiles and all of the children erupted into giggles.

'Good with kids,' said Gem, raising an eyebrow at Jo. 'Make a good...'

'Yeah, I know. He'll make a good dad one day.' She shook her head. She couldn't imagine ever getting beyond a couple of dates with someone again, let alone one day settling down and having a family.

They walked over to see what had made the children laugh so much; Ras had played the letters B and M on either side of a U that was already on the board.

'And don't forget,' he was saying, 'you've got to tell all your friends how great Scrabble is, so they come along tomorrow.'

A few adults were arriving now, Jo noticed, but it was only the usual members of the Scrabble club, and not even all of them. No Sylvia. No Cosmic.

'This is useless, Gem,' she said. 'We get more than this on a normal Friday evening in the church hall.'

'You know what we need?'

'Tell me.'

'Rain,' said Gemma. 'If it pours down tomorrow, people will be looking for indoor activities. Fancy doing a rain dance in the playground?'

26

On Saturday, Jo woke to the sound of rain – heavy rain – beating down on her lounge window; she had slept on the stained sofa and let Gemma have her bed.

They hadn't exactly done a rain dance in the playground on the way home – neither of them knew what a rain dance actually looked like – but Gemma had made up some silly song praying for rain, and they had bopped about a bit to it, after making sure no-one was looking.

It couldn't have worked, could it? Jo wondered, drawing back the curtains and looking at the angry grey clouds in the sky.

Nah, of course not. It was daft enough believing in signs, but rain dances?

In fact, it was pouring so hard that despite raincoats and umbrellas, Jo and Gemma both had wet jeans by the time they'd walked down the hill past the allotments and along to the school.

'The rain dance worked,' said Gemma, as a car drove past them and they dodged to avoid being splashed.

'Yeah, right. But will people come just to get out of the

rain? They could stay in and watch NetFlix.' Jo shivered as
a raindrop found its way under her coat and slid down her
neck.

Gemma held up crossed fingers. 'Or they might decide to
check out the festival.'

Even if the inclement (13 points) weather didn't bring
more people to their door, Jo thought, they were guaranteed
a few more attendees today. There were thirty-two places
in the tournament and all but one was filled. If everyone
showed up, that would be a big improvement on the
previous evening, although nothing like the number they'd
been hoping for. At this rate, the event was going to cost the
PTA money, rather than making it. She knew for a fact that
they'd shelled out a considerable amount for refreshments.
Refreshments that they weren't going to be able to sell.

The doors of the school weren't open to the public yet. Jo
spent an anxious fifty-five minutes patrolling the hall and the
classrooms, checking that everything was in place. Gemma
traipsed after her, making optimistic comments about how
more people were sure to come and admiring everything.
Jo had to admit it all looked great. The bookstall was well
stocked, with a mixture of adult and children's titles. The
tombola was ready with the prizes on display, each labelled
with a letter; if you were lucky enough to draw the one letter
Q from the barrel, you'd win a huge bottle of Pol Roger
champagne; draw an A or a T, and you'd get a small box of
chocolates or a potted cactus. Annie was arranging her neat
Scrabble tile biscuits on her stall in one corner. In the art
room, Mrs Woods had made a small selection of necklaces,
greetings cards and framed pictures using letter tiles to
illustrate what could be created, and two teachers had set

up one of the classrooms with a variety of alternative word games kindly loaned by the (Not So) Little Board Game Café in Essendale: Bananagrams, Upwords and Just One. Another room was set aside for Junior Scrabble and a third for ordinary Scrabble, for those who wanted to play but didn't feel up to entering the tournament.

Yes, it looked fantastic. But if no-one was going to see it, what was the point?

'Look over there.' Gemma gestured to the double doors of the hall, where, through the glass panes, Jo could see a few people gathering in reception.

Mr Morgan strode over to them. 'I know it's only twenty past,' he said, 'but can we open the doors? They're queuing all the way out of reception and down the path and everyone's getting soaked. It's very strange – the forecast didn't give rain.'

Jo could barely believe it. Queuing all the way down the path?

'How odd,' said Gemma. 'You can't trust the Met Office these days.' She glanced at Jo, who was too stunned to say anything.

Mr Morgan scratched his chin. 'Think we'll have to abandon the fancy dress competition – they've all come as letter tiles, made from cardboard boxes – and they're all soggy.'

'Okay, let's open up,' said Jo. Her disappointment about the fancy dress was far outweighed by her excitement that so many people had come.

Mr Morgan opened the doors and the room was soon swarming with people.

'Can you believe this?' said Ras, emerging from the

kitchen. He had a cake crumb in the corner of his mouth. 'It's incredible.'

'I was wondering where you were,' said Jo.

'Quality control,' he said. 'Checking the refreshments were up to standard. It's going to be a success, Jo. It is, isn't it?'

She nodded as several children made a beeline for Ras.

'Will you play a game with us, Doctor Ras?' said one girl, grabbing his hand.

'Someone's popular,' said Gemma to Jo as they watched him disappearing off towards the classrooms, with a small band of kids traipsing behind him like rats following the Pied Piper.

The hall was buzzing. The queue for the tombola snaked halfway down the hall, several people were already tucking into Annie's biscuits and the bookstall was doing a roaring trade. Soggy children sporting cardboard letter tile tabards were chasing each other around the hall. The helpers from the PTA were already serving up teas and coffees from the hatch. People were grabbing Scrabble boxes and setting up games. Jo hastily placed her 'RESERVED, 11 – 5.30' signs on the sixteen tables she'd earmarked for the tournament.

'You've done a wonderful job, Jo,' came Florence's voice from behind her.

Jo turned round to see her and Sylvia.

'Amazing,' said Sylvia. 'You should be proud of yourself. Sorry I didn't make it last night. I was helping Annie with her lettered biscuits. She's so talented. I wish my Robert had married someone like that.' She looked towards the back of the hall, where Annie was already doing a brisk trade in biscuits. 'He dated a lovely woman when he was at university, but she left him. And then he ended up with Jilly. She's not much of a homemaker. Never has been. Now where's that Doctor Ras? All that baking has exacerbated my arthritis.'

'In the children's room,' Jo said, mentally working out that 'exacerbated' would score 23 points. 'He's found some new fans.'

Cosmic appeared, hovering anxiously around Jo and Gemma.

'Sorry I wasn't here yesterday,' he said. 'I needed an early night. Before the competition.'

An early night? He was taking it *that* seriously? Jo hoped he'd at least get through to the second round.

There was only one fly in the ointment now: they were one player short for the tournament. Thirty-two was the ideal number: it meant there'd be three initial rounds before the semis and the grand final. The Scrabble club had all signed up, of course, except for her. She had to be on hand to adjudicate, should that be necessary – and it probably would be with Mr B and Florence involved – so she couldn't play as well.

She'd arranged to print the list of first round matches in Mr Morgan's office before the tournament started.

At ten to eleven, she knocked on his door.

'Am I still okay to use your printer?' she said poking her head round.

'Oh, yeah, sure,' he said.

'Trouble is, I'm still one player short,' she said. 'I don't suppose...'

'No.'

'Go on, it'll be fun. Half the school is here. The kids would love seeing their head teacher in a competition.'

'No.'

'You're not scared of losing, are you?'

'Of course not.'

'Only I thought you'd be one of those heads who told the children it was all about taking part and not about winning.'

He looked up from his computer. 'I really don't think...'

'Please,' said Jo.

He sighed. 'Go on then.'

'Great, thanks.' She pulled her USB stick from her pocket. 'Can I jump on your computer to print the list of players for the first round please?'

'Sure.'

He stood up and she slipped into his seat. An Excel spreadsheet was open on his screen, the school budget she guessed. Most of the figures had question marks after them. There were boxes highlighted in red, and others in green and yellow. It looked like a complete jumble.

'Have you saved this already?' she said. 'Or shall I save it in case?'

'It's a mess anyway. I'm hopeless with spreadsheets. It keeps telling me I've put a circular reference in and I've no idea what that means. The school manager normally deals with all this but she's off sick.'

'I could have a look later,' Jo said. 'If you want me to. Unless it's confidential or something. Not that I'd divulge anything to anyone, obviously.'

She clicked save, plugged her USB stick into his machine and opened the document showing who was playing who in the first round. She typed Mr Morgan into the final box – he'd be playing an outside entrant in the first round – and clicked print. The A3 printer beside his desk whirred into action.

'Fabulous,' she said. 'I'll go and pin this up. We start in five minutes, by the way.'

She stuck the list of first-round matches on the display board in the hall, which one of the teachers had kindly cleared of its original display of children's Van Gogh style sunflower paintings. A rush of people gathered round, several of whom were clutching their own dictionaries.

'They're the professionals,' whispered Ras in her ear as she moved to one side.

She turned to face him. 'Professionals?'

'Well, not professionals exactly, but they go round all the tournaments in the north. They take it ever so seriously. You won't catch any of them in your craft room making gifts for Mother's Day.'

'How do you know?'

'Because I used to go round all the tournaments too, when I wasn't on call over the weekend. I recognise some of them.'

It crossed Jo's mind that this was something they could do together when the festival was over. Would he want to?

'I've drawn the head teacher,' a tall man in jeans was saying to the woman next to him. 'Bet he'll be miffed to go out in the first round, in front of all his pupils.'

'I seem to be playing someone called Cosmic Ray,' she said.

The members of the Scrabble club and the handful of parents who had plucked up courage to enter were all holding back, she noticed. With the exception of Florence, who'd pushed herself to the front and was jotting down the matches. She recognised Alfred too, the boy she'd seen waiting in reception on her first visit to the school; he was the only child to have entered the tournament and was now standing nervously near the display board, with his mother giving him some kind of pep talk.

'It's time, Jo,' said Ras, tapping his watch.

Jo checked that the 'Quiet Please. Tournament in Progress' signs were on the doors leading into the hall then went up to the stage. She tapped the mic and cleared her throat. This wasn't something she'd have envisaged herself doing three months ago. It was every bit as daunting as being winched one hundred metres down into Gaping Gill or speaking live on local radio, yet she'd managed those things so she could manage this.

She took a deep breath. 'Er... could everyone please... er...'

No, that sounded wimpy. *Be confident, Jo*, she willed herself, and began again. 'Good morning, everyone. Thank you for...'

A chorus of children's voices chimed back at her, 'Good morning, Mr Morgan. Good morning, everyone.'

Jo hadn't expected that. She cleared her throat and began again. 'Welcome to Hebbleswick Scrabble festival and thank you for coming. Due to the terrible weather, we've decided to cancel the fancy dress competition as so many of the lovely costumes are just too soggy. But there's lots of other things for you to do, children. There's some craft activities and junior Scrabble games in one of the classrooms so please do visit those. And in the hall this morning, we have the tournament about to start. So, competitors, please can you take your seats at your numbered table, so we can begin?'

As the tournament got underway, Gemma went off in search of coffee, whilst Jo, feeling like an exam invigilator, perched herself on the edge of the stage and watched. Halfway through, she decided to have a look to see how the games were going. It was neck and neck on Mr Morgan's table. He was giving the professional a bit of a run for his money. Alfred was winning his game hands down against one of the parents. Ras had taken the lead on his table by playing ZAX on a double word space – Jo knew the word but had never seen anyone play it before – and even Cosmic Ray was winning his game so far. That early night had clearly been worth it.

When the first round came to an end, Jo and Gemma raced around the hall, jotting down the name of the winner at each table. Jo was delighted that both Ras and Cosmic were through to the next round, as were almost all of the professionals: the one who'd been bragging about beating Mr Morgan had lost. Florence, Sylvia and Mr B were still in, too.

During the lunch break, Gemma and Jo sat on the edge of the stage, eating ham and tomato sandwiches and surveying the scene. The dinner ladies – or 'lunchtime supervisors' as Mr Morgan had always referred to them – were doing a roaring trade in beefburgers, cheese pies and jacket potatoes. The PTA's cake stall seemed to be doing well too, and there was quite a crowd gathered around Annie's biscuits.

'It's a roaring success, Jo,' said Gem. 'I knew you could do it. Oh, look. There's Gaping Gill man again.'

They'd just finished eating, when Jo noticed Ras walking over to them, carrying something in his hands. He looked rather pleased with himself.

'I made these in the craft room.' He held out his hands, revealing three necklaces made of letter tiles.

'I didn't have you down as an arty, crafty kind of person,' said Jo.

'The kids dragged me in there, so I thought I'd make us each a souvenir of this weekend.'

'Wow, thanks,' said Gemma. She and Jo each took their necklaces, fastening them on.

'Can you do mine, please, Jo?' Ras said. 'I don't normally wear necklaces – I don't seem to be able to do it myself.'

He turned his back to her and offered up each end of the necklace. Jo tied it for him, her fingers brushing his warm, smooth neck as she did. She wanted so much to touch more of that soft skin but pushed the thought away.

Ras turned to face the two women. 'Ta-dah,' he said. 'What do you think?'

Jo stared at the necklace. It didn't say RAS. It said RAZZ.

'Weren't there any letter S's left?' she said. 'I bought plenty.'

He looked baffled for a moment. 'Oh, my name? I've always spelled it like this – since primary school. I even have a sign on my door at the surgery that says, *Doctor Razz*.'

So Ras wasn't Ras at all?

He was Razz – 22 glorious points.

How had she not known this? If only she'd walked down the corridor to his consulting room at the health centre, rather than sitting in the waiting room.

'Time for round two of the tournament, Jo.' Ras – or rather, Razz – tapped on his watch. 'I'd better go and find my table.'

'Sure, I'll... er... go up and make an announcement.'

But Jo didn't move. She watched him walk away then looked at Gemma. 'R-A-double Z.'

'Now I'm not as into Scrabble as you,' said Gemma, 'but even I know that Z scores 10 points. On your Scrabble dating chart, he scores a massive 22 points. That's not just a sign from the Universe. That's a Bloody Big Sign.'

27

A Bloody Big Sign.

In a daze, Jo announced the beginning of the second round of the tournament and sat back down on the edge of the stage with Gemma, surveying proceedings.

'R-A-double Z,' said Gemma. 'The Universe has given you your sign. Not that you needed a sign in my book, but well, you've got it now. You'll have to tell him.'

'Tell him?'

'How you feel about him. You clearly have feelings for him, Jo. I don't know him, obviously, but I reckon he has feelings for you too.'

Jo wasn't so sure. 'We do get on, Gem, but as friends. I did think he was about to kiss me in the staffroom yesterday, seconds before you arrived, but that was probably wishful thinking on my part. I mean, after that first date, I didn't hear from him. If I hadn't gone along to the Scrabble club, I'd never have seen him again. If he liked me in that way, surely he'd have got in touch.'

'There could be all sorts of reasons why he didn't,' Gemma said. 'Maybe he was waiting for you to get in touch with him. I think you should tell him how you feel.'

'But we're friends now. If I tell him and he *doesn't* feel

the same way, then it could be tricky. It might ruin our friendship. I'd feel really awkward at Scrabble club – it was bad enough realising that first time that he was the organiser. I nearly left. But if I tell him now and he doesn't feel the same way, well, I'd feel even more embarrassed. I'm not sure I'd dare go back, to be honest. And that Scrabble club's become a big part of my life.'

'I know you love Scrabble, Jo, but if he *does* feel the same way, this could be life-changing. What if he's The One? And both of you are too reticent to declare your feelings. Isn't it worth risking potential embarrassment at Scrabble club to find out what he thinks about you? Oh, hang on. Someone's got their hand up.'

Jo settled an argument about whether the word YOWZA was allowed – it was, according to the most up-to-date copy of Collins' Scrabble dictionary, which one of the professionals had brought along – and returned to her seat beside Gemma.

'You should tell him,' said Gemma.

'Kate says that it's better to let men make the first move.'

'Maybe with some men, but Razz seems kind of shy. And as I've said before, this is the twenty-first century. Why shouldn't a woman tell a man if she likes him?'

The discussion continued for the entire second round. Jo was so lost in her thoughts about Razz and her dilemma about what she should do that she didn't notice at first that every table had finished. She and Gemma sprinted around the hall, jotting down the results. Razz, Florence and Mr Morgan were all through to the last round of the day, along with one of the parents, two of the professionals, and little Alfred, who had beaten his opponent easily, using up all his letters not once but three times, and racking up masses of bonus points.

Mrs Hamilton-Jones was beside herself with excitement. 'My Alfred could win the whole thing,' she said to Jo.

'He could. Definitely.'

Personally, she thought it was unlikely. The professional Alfred would be up against next had quite a ruthless look in his eyes.

After a short break, the third round kicked off. The hall was even busier now, with hordes of people milling about, many of whom were standing around the tables, avidly watching the games. Razz took an early lead in his match against Mr Morgan but was beaten with only three points in it. Florence went out, despite arguing over at least four words and being proved right on two occasions. Miraculously, Mr B was still in the running, but he had got lucky in the draw and hadn't been up against any of the pros yet. And little Alfred saw off the ruthless professional; someone had to fetch his mother a glass of water as she looked a little faint.

And then it was time to say goodbye to Gemma; it was Jack's parents' wedding anniversary lunch the following day and she'd been unable to wriggle out of it.

'I wish I could stay for the whole thing, but you know what his mother's like – she'd never forgive me if I missed it. Besides, you've got this, Jo. It's all going brilliantly. Everyone's enjoying themselves and you've had your big sign from the Universe that Razz is the one for you. Promise me you'll tell him.'

Jo looked at her. 'I dunno...'

'You don't have to declare undying love. Drop him a hint

or something. Or ask him if he'd like to go on that second date with you, once the festival is over.'

'Okay, I can do that. Perhaps tonight, whilst we're running the speed-dating.'

'Promise?'

'I promise.'

Three hours later, the crowd of parents and children had gone home, many promising to return the following day, and the doors opened for the Scrabble speed-dating event. Sal was the one-woman welcoming committee, ticking off each person on her list with brisk efficiency and handing out name labels, whilst Jo and Razz put the game boards on each table.

'All set?' said Razz.

'I think so.'

He looked lovely this evening. He'd slipped home and changed into an open-neck shirt and chinos but was still wearing his Scrabble necklace proudly around his neck.

He took her hand and gave it a squeeze. 'Today's been brilliant, hasn't it? I can't believe how many people came, can you?'

Jo squeezed his hand back. 'I can't.'

And she couldn't. Couldn't believe how many people had come. Couldn't believe how much money they'd already raised for the school. Couldn't believe that Razz had spelled his name Razz all along and she hadn't even known. Couldn't believe that she was going to tell him how she felt.

But she was. She was going to dig deep, find the courage from somewhere to risk rejection and admit her feelings to the man she was beginning to fall in love with. She'd let the dating event get underway, then, as they both stood and watched from the sidelines, she would tell him.

Or at least drop a heavy hint.

Jo didn't recognise any of the speed-dating participants. The Scrabble club – thankfully – had all decided to give it a miss, even Linda acknowledging that she wasn't in the age range. Mr Morgan was keeping his beady eye on proceedings, greeting one or two people by name. Single parents, Jo guessed.

Kate arrived with a young, blonde woman. She'd mentioned that she might bring someone; a colleague, Jo vaguely recalled her saying. Or had she said cousin? Whoever she was, she was even more petite than Kate, with a tiny waist, enviably pert breasts and straight, shiny hair down to her waist. Impeccably dressed too, Jo noticed, in a short, black dress with lots of gold jewellery. A little much for an evening in a school hall in Hebbleswick, but she somehow managed to pull it off. Jo reluctantly let go of Razz's hand and went over to them to say hello.

'Jo, this is Zoey,' said Kate.

'Zoey with a y,' said Zoey.

'Thanks for coming,' Jo said. 'How do you two know each other?'

'Work. Zoey's recently started in the accounts department.'

Colleague then.

Over Kate's shoulder, Jo noticed Razz talking to a small group of women. Kate and Zoey with a y turned to see who she was looking at.

Razz was a far cry now from the scruffy-looking man in the orange anorak that she'd met on that first date. How had she ever thought that he wasn't attractive? Okay, so he didn't have the easy charm of someone like Tarquin who knew how to put a woman at ease on a first date, but – unlike Tarquin – Razz meant every word that he said.

'That's Doctor Razz,' Kate was saying to Zoey. 'He works with Ludek, Emily's boyfriend. I've told you about Emily, haven't I?'

'Your friend with the café?' said Zoey, nodding. She looked at Razz again. 'So he's a doctor? Wow.' She raised her eyebrows.

Jo felt a sudden sense of unease at the way that Kate's new friend was checking Razz out. So openly, as if he were a commodity. More prized because of his profession. And there was another feeling bubbling up inside Jo that she couldn't quite put her finger on.

'We organised this festival together,' she said, but the blonde woman's attention had been diverted by a new man entering the hall.

'Ooh, look at him,' said Zoey. She nudged Kate and they both looked towards the door.

The man was tall and lean, with sun-kissed, blond hair, a golden tan and several leather bracelets on one wrist. He was wearing just-above-the-knee shorts in faded denim and a tight-fitting, pink T-shirt. He looked like he'd be more at home on the beach in Cornwall with a surfboard in his hands than playing Scrabble in the hall of a little Yorkshire primary school.

'Mm, your type,' said Zoey, nudging Kate again, and Jo felt a stab of irritation that Zoey knew what Kate's type was. Kate had played her cards close to her chest when it came to her own love life and Jo hadn't got a clue what kind of man she liked.

'I'd better go and... er, organise things,' Jo said.

'Introduce us to your friend Razz,' she heard Zoey call after her but she ignored her.

Protective, Jo realised. That was how she'd felt watching Zoey checking out Razz. She didn't want Razz – lovely, kind Razz – to get hit on by this woman who was only interested in him because of his job.

And, if she was honest with herself, she had felt possessive too. She'd never considered how she'd feel with Razz here in a hall full of single women. Single women all looking for a man. Single women who might spot what she hadn't seen when she'd first met him: that he mightn't be conventionally good-looking or a smooth talker, but he was cute, kind and genuine.

She began to walk towards him, hoping to... hoping to what, exactly? Warn him off Zoey with a y? Ask him not to talk to any of the women? Announce that she wanted to be more than friends?

A tall man stopped her, wanting to know where he could put his jacket.

'On the back of your chair,' she said.

She escaped and edged closer to Razz, still unsure of what she was going to say, when another man put his hand on her arm, wanting to know if he should have brought his own dictionary.

'No,' she said, 'the Scrabble part is secondary to the evening.' He looked disappointed.

She had nearly reached Razz when she bumped into

Mr Morgan, hopping nervously from foot to foot. Jo couldn't ignore the head teacher, not when he was hosting their event.

'All okay so far?' he said.

'So far.'

'There's rather a long queue for drinks.' He gestured at the line of people snaking their way to the serving hatch.

'I'll go and help out.' She sighed and headed over to the kitchen.

As she poured drinks, she glanced across the hall. Kate and Zoey were looking around, assessing all the men. Razz was scrutinising the list of daters over Sal's shoulder. When she'd served this last customer, she would take mojitos over to them, then draw him aside and tell him how she felt about him before she lost her nerve.

But then two women approached the counter and started dithering about what to order. By the time she'd served them, Razz was talking to Zoey with a y and Kate was standing right in front of her.

'There's a real buzz about the place, Jo,' Kate said. 'Congratulations. You're a whizz at organising. Could I get three mojitos, please?'

Jo poured the drinks and looked over at Razz and Zoey again. They looked good together too, she thought grudgingly. Zoey was the perfect height for him; Jo felt large and gawky in comparison.

Zoey laughed at something he said and pushed him playfully in the chest. Jo placed Kate's cocktails on the counter a little too forcefully, sloshing some onto the counter.

'Sorry,' she said. 'Donations in the tin. In aid of the PTA, so please give generously.'

And please stop your glamorous friend from chatting up Razz, she wanted to add, but she didn't.

Kate shoved a twenty-pound note into the pot and turned away. Jo felt a hand on her arm and heard Sal say, 'Could I have a word, Jo? I've registered everyone, but one man and two women haven't shown up. My niece is coming over to take one of their places, but you'll have to take the other one.'

'Can't we run it with eleven tables?'

'We could, but I've been telling everyone they'll have twelve dates. Besides, I've already asked Razz to take the missing man's place and he seemed rather pleased.'

Jo's heart sank into her trainers.

She'd never considered the possibility that she might take part in the Scrabble speed-dating, and she definitely hadn't considered that Razz might too, let alone that he'd be pleased to do so. Did this mean he was still actively looking to meet someone? And therefore that he wasn't interested in her?

28

'I̶s that okay, Jo?' said Sal.

'Sorry, is what okay?'

'I said, since you're now a participant, I'll do the timing and ring the bell at the end of each round. Ten minutes, wasn't it?'

'Yes, that's fine,' said Jo. 'Thanks.'

'Of course, the power might go to my head. If I see a couple are getting on, I might give them an extra five minutes.'

'No, don't do that,' Jo said quickly. 'Please.' The last thing she needed was Sal giving Razz and Zoey more time. 'I've worked it all out so it ends at half ten exactly. Then you've half an hour to sell – I mean, serve – a few more drinks and get a bit more cash before we close at eleven like we agreed with Mr Morgan. He doesn't want complaints from the neighbours...'

'Relax, it'll all be fine. This is the most exciting event the school hall has seen since Year 6 put on *Chitty Chitty Bang Bang* and persuaded Mr Morgan to play the Child Catcher. The reception class was terrified.'

Jo managed a smile. 'I bet they were.'

Jo and Sal climbed the steps onto the stage. By now, Jo

wasn't in the slightest bit nervous about standing in front of a crowd. She was getting used to it, and besides, she had more things to worry about. On the same day that she'd discovered that Ras was Razz and decided that this was the sign she'd been waiting for and it was time to confess her feelings, she'd also realised she had competition in the desirable form of Zoey. From her high vantage point, Jo could see Zoey standing beside Razz, unable to take her eyes off him. She was fiddling with her long hair in a coquettish kind of way. Definitely flirting, Jo decided. What she couldn't quite ascertain – 11 points – was whether Razz was flirting back.

Jo rang the little bell that she'd bought from the hospice shop especially for this evening. The room fell silent.

'Welcome to Scrabble speed-dating,' she said. 'When we start, please take a seat at the table with your number on it and start playing Scrabble and chatting to your date. Sal is doing the timings tonight. She'll give you ten minutes with each person – that should be enough time to play five words each. When she rings the bell, ladies, stay at your table and reset the board. Men, move to the next table. So, if you're man number one, go to table number two next. If you're man number twelve, go to number one.'

She looked round at the audience, trying to make sure everyone understood.

'Please remember it's not about the Scrabble,' she continued, looking pointedly at Dictionary Man. 'The idea is that whilst you're playing, you suss each other out like you would at conventional speed-dating. The Scrabble is an ice-breaker, so you're not stuck making small talk and wondering what on earth to say next. We've all been there on dates. I know I have, anyway.' She tried to catch Razz's eye at this point but Zoey was whispering something to him. Razz and Zoey. Zoey and Razz. She had to admit that their names went well together.

'I'm not running things tonight as I'm taking part to even up the numbers.' She hesitated. Perhaps she shouldn't have said that. The men might feel they were being cheated, not getting a proper date. But she wanted Razz to know that she wasn't looking for anyone. At least, not looking for anyone else.

'I'll hand my little bell over to Sal,' she continued. 'Don't forget to tick the box if you'd like to see someone again.'

Sal rang the bell and Jo made her way down the steps and over to table eleven. She opened her Scrabble box.

Razz was Number Twelve, so he'd be her last date of the evening. She glanced over at him; he was shaking hands now with a young woman whom Jo presumed was Sal's niece.

He caught Jo's eye and held up crossed fingers for luck.

What did that mean? Fingers crossed that she'd meet someone? Or that he did? Or fingers crossed that the event would be a success?

Man Number Eleven slid into the seat opposite her.

'I'm Zach,' he said.

'Jo.'

'This is a brilliant idea,' he said.

'Actually, it was my idea.'

'Seriously? Well, that's a tick in your box already.'

A few weeks ago, she'd have been thrilled by this. Zach's name scored an impressive 18 points. He wasn't bad-looking: dark hair, albeit receding a little, a kind face and chocolate-brown eyes. But he wasn't Razz. She was only interested in Razz.

'Come on, let's play,' she said. 'Can I start? GAMES on a double word score. I make that 16 points.'

They'd only played seven words between them when the bell rang and it was time for him to move on. Dictionary Man sat down opposite her next. He was tall and dark-haired, with round glasses. Good-looking in a grown-up, Harry Potter kind of way.

'This is great. I won the last game.'

Jo refrained from reminding him that it wasn't about the game and concentrated on making sure that he didn't win this one.

Numbers Nine and Eight were both pleasant, but Jo couldn't help glancing over between turns to see how Razz was doing. She was relieved to see that he was engrossed in the game every time, rather than in the woman opposite him.

Number Seven was the surfer dude whom Zoey had said was Kate's type.

'Lovely to meet you,' he said as he sat down opposite her. 'I'm Matthew.'

'Jo.'

'I've heard a lot about you, Jo.'

'Oh? Who from?'

'Sal and Mr Morgan,' he said. 'They're always singing your praises. I'm a teacher here.'

'Let me guess. PE?'

'Why does everyone assume that? Don't judge by appearances.' He smiled. 'I'm the technology co-ordinator. Sal promised me that if I came along this evening, there might be a couple of extra iPads in it for Year 6. I'm counting on you and your festival to raise loads of dosh this weekend. Gotta have those iPads.'

'Technology co-ordinator? So, you know about IT?'

An idea was beginning to form in her mind. There'd been so many people here today and it had been difficult for people to watch the games in the tournament. But with an IT whizz on board…

'I do,' he said. 'I mightn't look it, but I'm a real computer nerd.'

'Are you busy tomorrow?'

'Teachers are always busy. Marking. Planning. Everyone thinks we finish by half past three and enjoy ridiculously long holidays, but that couldn't be further from the truth. I could be free tomorrow, though. What did you have in mind?'

'Could you rig some kind of camera over the Scrabble boards in the semi-finals and the final? And connect it to a screen so more people can watch it?'

'Easy. What time do you start?'

'We open at half past nine.'

'There goes my Sunday lie-in. Sure, I'll do it.'

The bell rang then before they'd even had chance to begin the game.

As Number Six sat down at her table, she noticed Razz taking his seat opposite Zoey. Jo introduced herself to her new opponent but kept glancing over at Razz. She was too far away to see their Scrabble board. They were leaning towards each other across the table, laughing. He looked confident and completely at ease. What had happened to him? What had happened to the nervous man who'd been so awkward, so reticent, so shy, when Jo had first met him? What had Zoey done to him?

'Jo, it's your go,' said Number Six.

They'd managed to make nine words between them when the bell went again. It was half-time. Number Six said, 'Thanks for the game' and Jo realised – too late – that she hadn't paid him much attention. She chastised herself; she could have at least tried to be pleasant.

The queue for drinks was growing longer and longer. She wanted to go over to Razz, to interrupt his conversation with Zoey, to drag him away on some pretext or other, but she couldn't leave the mums from the PTA struggling to serve everyone. She slipped into the kitchen area and turned to the first customer. It was Kate.

'Four mojitos, Jo, please,' she said. 'This is a great event. Far better than that pub quiz.'

Jo poured her drinks from the enormous jug and Kate popped another twenty into the tin. When everyone had been served, Jo handed Sal a ginger beer and grabbed one for herself, as the bell rang to signal the start of part two.

Razz was still talking to Zoey. Man Number Eleven, who'd been Jo's first date of the evening, was standing behind him, but Razz seemed reluctant to relinquish his seat. Eventually, he stood up and joined Kate at her table. Jo hadn't realised she'd been holding her breath, but it came out suddenly, leaving her light-headed. She took a sip of her ginger beer and turned her attention to her letters and to Man Number Five.

After this round, she only had Numbers Four to One to

get through and finally Razz, Number Twelve, would be across the table from her. What on earth was she going to say?

She'd tell him straight, she decided. Be honest and say that she wanted to be more than friends. If she could pluck up courage, she might even tell him that she was falling in love. Because she was, wasn't she? She hadn't acknowledged it before, but that was what had been happening these last few weeks as they'd organised the festival together. She'd grown closer and closer to him, and she'd started to fall in love. She hadn't dared admit it, not even to herself, because she was so sick of failed relationships, so sick of embarking on something with someone, of falling for someone, only to realise that she'd chosen the wrong guy to fall for – yet again. Only now, the Universe had given her a sign and anyway, she *knew* Razz; knew that he was a kind, gentle bloke who'd never treat her the way Si had. She knew she could trust him so yes, she would tell him. Now. Before it was too late. Before Zoey got her claws into him.

The next three games dragged. Really dragged. Jo did her best to be good company, to chat between placing tiles on the board. This was her event, after all, and she wanted these men to enjoy themselves even if she wasn't interested in them romantically.

As Number One took his seat at her table, she couldn't help but be aware of Razz sitting down opposite Woman Number Ten, only a couple of feet away from her.

She placed her fifth word down on the board, her hands shaking as she did. I.

'What's that?' said Number One.

'Again,' Jo said.

'Incorrect spelling! No points for you for that one.'

She was going to argue, to tell him she'd placed the letters the wrong way round by accident, but then the bell rang and the next minute, Razz was sitting in front of her, smiling.

'It's going brilliantly, isn't it?' he said. 'Such a fantastic idea of yours. I'm having the best time.'

Jo smiled and started to clear the letters from the board, left over from the previous game, and as she did, she glanced at Razz's tick sheet. He had only ticked one box. Number Five. Zoey.

He had ticked her. That meant he wanted to exchange contact details with her. He wanted to see her again. Jo's heart plummeted; she could hardly declare her feelings now.

'Do you want to go first?' She tried to sound upbeat but her voice sounded alien. False.

'Let's do it properly,' said Razz. 'Draw from the bag.'

'You said I'd come across as nerdy if I insisted on doing that,' she said, thinking back to the evening when they'd rehearsed the speed-dating. If only she'd told him then. If only she'd responded when he'd taken her hand. What a missed opportunity.

'I *am* nerdy,' he said. 'And you already know that.'

They each drew a letter. She drew R. He drew J. She would have taken this as a sign – them drawing each other's initials like that – if she hadn't already seen him with Zoey.

'You make the first move,' she said, wishing he would make a move on her.

She couldn't focus on the game. She scored a miserable forty-seven points – less than ten points per word – whilst he more than doubled her score.

'You're never normally this easy to beat.' Razz smiled and she tried to smile back.

'I'm tired,' she said and suddenly she realised that she was. Exhausted. And defeated.

The final bell went, signalling the end of the evening. Jo stood up. 'I've got to collect all the forms,' she said, holding her hand out for his. Perhaps he hesitated before he gave it to her. Or perhaps he didn't. She didn't know anymore.

She went round the room in a daze, asking people if they'd enjoyed the event and gathering forms, but she was only interested in one form: Zoey's. Had she ticked him too? Would Jo have to email her details to him tomorrow evening? To let them both know that they were a match?

Like Razz, Zoey had ticked only one box. It was easy to see whose it was: the last box on the page. She'd written 'Razz' alongside it too. Jo was surprised she hadn't gone the whole hog and drawn a little heart next to it.

Zoey.

Zoey with a y would score 16 points.

Jo's own name would only get 9. She knew when she was beaten.

29

S unday morning.
 Jo opened her eyes and was happy for a few seconds.
Her phone pinged: a text from Gemma.

How did it go with Razz?

He met someone else before I had a chance to speak
to him.

WHAT?!!!

At Scrabble speed-dating. He ticked her box. She ticked
his. He didn't tick mine.

Oh God, Jo. I don't know what to say.

Gemma didn't know what to say and Jo didn't know what
to think. It had all felt so right yesterday, like everything was
about to slot into place. To have that Bloody Big Sign, as
Gemma had called it, pointing right at Razz, the man she'd
grown so fond of as they'd planned the festival together,
only to have Zoey swoop in on him, right in front of her.

Anyway, there wasn't time to lie in bed dwelling on it; she had to be at the school by nine at the latest.

She'd been intending to wear her Scrabble pinafore dress, the one she'd bought in the hospice shop, for the final day of the festival, but she felt too deflated and pulled on her usual jeans and T-shirt instead. Then she made an instant coffee in the Mr Perfect mug, the one that Razz had drunk out of, and picked up the speed-dating forms that she'd left there the previous night. Yes, Razz had definitely ticked Zoey. And she had definitely ticked him.

Kate had only ticked one man: Matthew the technology co-ordinator. And he had ticked her box – and only her box – too.

Jo glanced through the forms, looking to see if anyone had ticked her. A grand total of three. Three out of twelve: 25 per cent. Not bad. She'd have been pleased with that a few weeks ago. But Razz wasn't one of them. Her admirers were Dictionary Man, Zach – he'd been quite good-looking, hadn't he? – and Number Six. Jo couldn't even remember Number Six.

She ought to be happy. Three matches from speed-dating; not that she wanted anyone other than Razz, but it was still flattering. Far more attendees at the festival than she'd ever imagined. As far as she knew, Malcolm hadn't bored too many people about insurance and there'd been no fist fight between Florence and Mr B over proper nouns in the tournament. Admittedly, Jo had fixed the draw so that there was little chance they'd play each other. And the PTA were delighted with the amount of money that was coming in. Sal couldn't quite believe her eyes as she'd counted up the money last night from the alcohol 'sales'.

'Those mojitos were well worth the effort,' she'd said. 'Even though there's no mint left in my herb garden.'

She, Jo Knox, introvert and Scrabble fan, had managed to organise an entire festival. She had stood on a stage and addressed a crowd. She'd given an interview on live radio and had found her tribe in the Scrabble club.

But Razz liked Zoey.

Jo checked his form again to be certain, but he had ticked Zoey. Of course he had. Later, when she sent everyone their matches, she could miss them out, 'forget' to let them know that they were a match. But if Razz liked Zoey and she liked him, who was she to stand in their way?

The cooks were already working in the kitchen when Jo arrived. Matthew had rigged up an enormous screen on the stage and was fiddling with cables, and Annie was laying out a fresh batch of letter biscuits on her stall.

Alfred was sitting on a chair in the corner, his mother leaning over him. She looked like a boxing coach, stoking a fighter up before a big match. It was still only quarter to nine and they didn't officially open till half past so Jo wasn't sure who'd even let them in.

In the opposite corner, Malcolm was talking to – or rather at – Mr Morgan.

'Do you know what sort of policy you've got?' he was saying. 'I'd be happy to have a look at it if you like.'

'I see Malcolm has collared Mr Morgan.'

Jo hesitated for a moment before turning to see Razz standing behind her.

'Yes, desperate to sell insurance as usual,' Jo said.

'He's not selling it.'

'He's not?'

'He used to but he's retired now. He just likes talking about it.'

Razz looked tired. Had he gone out with Zoey last night after speed-dating? To a late-night pub in Halifax, perhaps? Or a club? She didn't think clubs were his thing, but how well did she really know him?

'We need to clear all the tables but one and put the chairs out,' she said. 'In a kind of U shape around the table for the tournament matches, but not too close. We want to give the players some space. Matthew's rigging cameras up so everyone will be able to see the board on the screen.'

'Hi-tech,' said Razz. 'I didn't know that was happening.'

'Last-minute idea,' she said. 'I couldn't believe Matthew was kind enough to give up his Sunday lie-in. Such a nice bloke and a techie whizz too.'

She nearly added, *Did you enjoy the speed-dating?* but she was scared she'd hear a bit too much enthusiasm in his voice, so said instead, 'Come on, let's sort those chairs.'

When all the chairs were in place, when she'd checked that the crafts room was ready, that the children's room was all set up with Junior Scrabble boards on each table and one of the teachers supervising, she grabbed herself a cup of coffee and went outside for a few minutes of fresh air. The rain clouds of the previous day had vanished and the skies were clear and blue.

Jo sat down on the friendship bench, wondering about the children who usually sat here during playtimes and lunchtimes. Remembering how it felt to not fit in, to find making friends difficult. She thought she'd turned a corner, thought she'd found a real friend – and maybe something more – in Razz. Would things change between them now he'd met Zoey? Why had she ever dreamt up the idea of Scrabble speed-dating? Why had she suggested a festival in the first place? If they'd gone with a simple Scrabble afternoon one Saturday in the church hall, he would never have met Kate's glamorous colleague.

'May I join you?' said a voice.

As she looked up to see Matthew, the IT teacher, towering over her, she realised that a tear was rolling down her cheek and wiped it away hastily. She hoped he hadn't seen.

'Yeah, sure.'

He sat down beside her and took out an e-cigarette.

'Are you okay, Jo?'

He had seen the tear then.

'I'm fine. Thanks.'

He glanced around him then waved the e-cigarette at her. 'You don't mind, do you? I'm trying to give up. Probably shouldn't do this on school premises but no-one's looking, are they?'

'No, no-one. Go ahead.'

Jo wiped another tear away with her sleeve and Matthew rummaged in his pocket and pulled out a crumpled tissue.

'It doesn't look it, but it's clean,' he said offering it to her.

'Best offer I've had all morning.'

'A problem shared, Jo. What's up?'

She took a deep breath. It might help to tell someone.

'There's a man I like – I mean, *really* like. He was at speed-dating last night. He only ticked one woman's box, and it wasn't mine.'

'Ah,' he said. 'Look Jo, you're lovely, but you're not my type.'

Jo suddenly remembered that Matthew, like Razz, had only ticked one box. Oh God, he thought she fancied *him*. This was even more embarrassing than him catching her crying.

'It's not you, Matthew,' she said.

He laughed. 'I know. I was winding you up.'

She gave him a faint smile.

'I've cheered you up at least,' he said. 'Jo, I'm sorry the guy you like likes somebody else, but you'll meet someone. Honestly. You will.' He glanced at his watch. 'Twenty-five past nine. We should head back inside.'

The seats they'd laid out around the tournament table filled up quickly. Alfred was playing Mr B. Jo had had the feeling that Alfred wasn't exactly a popular child, yet half the school seemed to have turned up to cheer him on. She felt sorry for Mr B with his small band of supporters consisting only of the ladies from the Scrabble club and Cosmic Ray.

Alfred took an early lead. Mrs Hamilton-Jones was sitting with a stocky, bespectacled man who looked, Jo imagined, exactly how Alfred himself would look in thirty years' time. She was gripping his hand so hard that her knuckles were white.

Early in the game, Mr B managed to play the word QUICK with the Q on a triple letter score and he began to edge ahead of Alfred.

'I can't bear to watch,' she heard Florence whisper to Sylvia. Jo wasn't quite sure whose side Florence was on.

Was she now supporting her arch rival? Had she put their past quarrels behind her?

At one point, Alfred had all consonants and no vowels and had to forfeit a turn to change his letters. Mr B drew the J, worth a massive eight points, and managed to make JUGGLING using a blank title and an N that was already on the board. This netted him a fifty-point bonus for using all his letters.

There was no way for Alfred to catch him after that, and Mr B was declared the victor.

'How could you, Stan?' Jo heard Sylvia scolding him afterwards. 'You should have let the child win. He'll be gutted.'

Jo looked over at the Hamilton-Joneses. Mrs H-J was in tears on her husband's shoulder but she couldn't see Alfred. Eventually, she spotted him, surrounded by a crowd of schoolchildren. He appeared to be signing autographs.

She pushed her way through them.

'Are you okay, Alfred?' She put a hand on his shoulder.

'I reached the semi-finals of my first Scrabble tournament,' he said. 'Mother's disappointed, but I think I did pretty well. I'm only nine.'

'Where did you get such a grown-up attitude?' she said.

A small girl standing beside him said, 'Mr Morgan always says it's the taking part that counts. Not the winning.'

'Well, Mr Morgan is up next in the second semi-final,' Jo said, 'if you want to cheer him on?'

'Nah,' said Alfred. 'We're all going to play Junior Scrabble in one of the classrooms. I'm offering coaching sessions. Oh, and by the way, it's Alfie now. Not Alfred.'

Jo left them to it, and went to warn Mr Morgan and

Harry, the only 'professional' left in the tournament, that their match would be starting in five minutes.

It's probably fair to say that Harry wiped the floor with Mr Morgan. As soon as the game finished, Mr Morgan headed out of the hall and disappeared in the direction of his office.

Jo went up to the stage and picked up the microphone. 'Thank you all for watching. The final starts at half past two. In the meantime, grab yourself some lunch, see what's on offer in the craft room or play a game of Scrabble yourself in one of the classrooms.'

Then she went after Mr Morgan and tentatively knocked on his door.

'Humiliated,' he said. 'That's what I am. Humiliated. In front of my entire school. The chair of the governors was watching. Not to mention the parents. And all the children.'

He was sitting at his desk, his head in his hands.

'The children weren't watching. Alfie's giving coaching sessions. They're crammed into one of the classrooms.'

'Even so...'

'You reached the semi-finals,' Jo said. 'That's pretty good going.'

'But I lost,' he mumbled through his fingers.

'Isn't it the taking part that counts? Not the winning? Isn't that what you tell the children?'

He looked up at her. 'I suppose so.'

'Come on,' she said. 'Fancy getting some lunch? I hear there's cheese pie and beans today.'

An expectant hush fell through the hall as the final began.

Latecomers tiptoed to their seats – not that there were many seats left – and customers at the PTA refreshment stall whispered their orders.

The two opponents stared at each other, weighing up the competition, last-minute game plans and strategies no doubt running through their minds, and the audience waited in silence. It was like the Snooker World Championships at the Crucible, thought Jo. Only without any cues. Or any green baize. Or coloured balls. So not like the snooker at all, in actual fact.

During this final game of the tournament, Jo stood at the top left-hand corner of the table in her role as adjudicator. For most of the match, her eyes were fixed on the board and the players so she didn't notice Zoey and Kate arrive. But she looked up when Mr B was taking a particularly long time to figure out his next move and spotted them: Zoey was sitting in the back row, between Kate and Razz. Jo bit her lip hard, praying that her eyes wouldn't fill with tears again, and forced herself to focus on the tiles that Mr B was now placing on the board. He moved his hand with a flourish and stopped his clock. He'd used all his letters, scoring the fifty-point bonus. A collective gasp ran round the audience.

Jo didn't look back at Zoey or Kate for the rest of the game, nor as she declared Mr Stanisław Baranski the winner.

Florence rushed straight over to Mr B. 'I'm so proud of you, Stan,' she said, dabbing at her eyes with a hanky.

Then Harry, the losing player, shook hands with Mr B and said, 'It's great that someone from the local club has won the whole thing. I'm already looking forward to the rematch at next year's festival.'

Next year's festival?

This was a one-off as far as Jo was concerned, but she didn't like to say.

She looked at Mr B. He'd been a different player in the tournament compared with the one she knew at the club. As well as using up all his letters and scoring that bonus, he'd managed to play three, four and even five scoring words in one turn. He didn't make a single proper noun or word of his own invention, a fact that didn't go unnoticed by Florence.

Later, as Jo tidied some of the tables, she overheard Florence saying to Sylvia, 'I don't understand it. Stan never plays that well on a Friday evening yet he beat that pro hands down. He didn't try any of his usual nonsense.'

'Bit of a dark horse,' said Sylvia. 'I reckon he's been fooling us all this time.'

The two older women moved away and Jo couldn't catch the rest of their conversation.

'He has, you know,' said a voice from behind her.

She turned round. Razz.

Why did he keep sneaking up on her like that?

'He has…?'

'Been fooling us,' said Razz. 'Stan – Mr B – is one of the pros. I met him in the (Not So) Little Board Game Café when I first moved to the area, but I'd already seen him at one or two tournaments. In fact, he gave me the idea for the Scrabble club in the first place.'

'So why does he play all those silly words?'

'Can't you figure it out?'

'No.'

'I suspect he rather enjoys the banter with Florence.'

'Banter? More like arguments. And I'm not sure she enjoys them.'

'Oh, she does. She loves it. Anyway, is there some kind of announcement? Are you doing that?'

'I could,' Jo said, 'but it might be nice to ask Mr Morgan. It is his school.'

She was rather wishing she'd thought to get a prize, or, at the very least, a certificate.

Mr Morgan had recovered from his defeat in the semis and was happy to announce the winner. 'It'll show the children that I've no hard feelings, because as I always say, it's the taking part that counts, not the winning.'

He gave a speech to that effect as he stood on the stage, before finally declaring what they all already knew: that Stanisław Baranski was the winner of this year's festival tournament.

This year's festival tournament, thought Jo. As if there'd be another. It had been fun, but it had also been a lot of hard work.

'And the prize,' said Mr Morgan, 'generously donated by one of our sponsors, the Brookfield Hotel in North Yorkshire, is a spa weekend for two.'

Sponsors? They had sponsors?

Florence shouted, 'Well done, Stan! Jolly well done!' as Mr B climbed the steps.

Razz was directly in front of stage, cheering and clapping. Zoey was nowhere to be seen, but Kate was standing next to Matthew. Rather close to Matthew. And as Mr B took the microphone, Jo saw Matthew lean over and whisper something in her ear.

'I'd like to thank everyone who took part in the

tournament,' Mr B said, 'and the PTA and Brookfield Hotel for this generous prize. I didn't even know there was a prize.'

There was a smattering of laughter round the hall.

'And I'd like to thank Mr Morgan for allowing us to use his school for this festival. But most of all, I'd like to thank the two people who have worked so hard to create such a wonderful festival. It wouldn't have happened without them. Jo and Razz, everyone.'

He raised an imaginary glass as if toasting a couple at a wedding.

Jo looked over at Razz. He turned, as if sensing her, and their eyes met across the crowded school hall. And then Zoey suddenly appeared by his side and patted his back. His eyes moved to Zoey, at the same moment that everyone raised an imaginary glass as Mr B had done, and said, 'Jo and Razz.'

But there was no Jo and Razz, was there? And perhaps now there never would be.

30

Once the tournament was over, Hebbleswick Scrabble Festival ended quickly. The spectators and participants drifted away. An army of PTA volunteers packed away chairs and tables, took down the bunting, and replaced the festival notices with the children's paintings that had been there originally. Mr Timms began sweeping the floor, tutting over imaginary dints in the wood from the previous evening's stilettos.

Razz was packing away his games, carrying piles of boxes out to his Ford Focus in the school car park. Matthew was on the stage, taking down the screen. There was no sign of Kate and Zoey; they must have left. Jo wondered if she should go over and help Razz. She could casually ask if he'd enjoyed the speed-dating. Maybe even enquire if he'd met someone. Yes, that's what she'd do. She'd find out if he was intending to date Zoey. It'd be better to know.

Or was it better *not* to know?

'Jo.' She turned around; it was Mr Morgan. 'It's gone so well. You must be pleased. It's been great for the school.'

'I'm glad,' she said.

She glanced over at the exit where Razz, his arms full of boxes, was nudging the double doors open with his foot.

'I don't suppose you could look at that spreadsheet for me, could you? I mean, if you're too tired, that's fine, but I'd appreciate it.'

Mr Morgan was looking at her expectantly. After he'd been kind enough to let them use the school all weekend, well, she could hardly refuse, could she? And it wouldn't take long. She could talk to Razz once she'd finished.

But by the time she had finished untangling Mr Morgan' circular references, Razz was nowhere to be seen.

Monday morning.

Jo had once spent her weekends looking forward to getting back to the office; she liked having people to talk to. Even when Leona joined the company, Jo had still preferred the working week to the long, lonely Sundays.

But something had changed. Since she'd met Razz, got involved with the Scrabble club and taken on the mammoth task of organising the festival, she'd begun to enjoy her weekends. And the more she'd enjoyed her weekends, the more she'd realised that she didn't enjoy her job. At Pop! Productions, her organisational skills were mocked, not appreciated. No-one ever listened to her ideas. And when her colleagues went off for an after-work drink, they never thought to invite her along.

All things considered, her workplace had become toxic. Yes, that was definitely the right word. Toxic – 14 points. No, place that on a double word score and make it 28 points. Because the environment at Pop! Productions was, as far as Jo was concerned, doubly toxic.

And now something had changed again. Hebbleswick

Scrabble Festival had come to an end. Razz was with Zoey. Probably, anyway. She still didn't know for sure.

She picked up her phone and looked at the time: 5.57 a.m. The alarm would go off in one hour and three minutes. She rolled over, pulled the duvet over her head and wondered what Razz was doing now. He couldn't be in bed with Zoey already, could he?

Probably not. Not yet. He wasn't the sort of man who leapt into bed with a woman the minute he met her. He'd be wooing her, taking her out to dinner, getting to know her.

She really must stop torturing herself with these thoughts.

She felt deflated. And it wasn't only the thought that Razz and Zoey were now dating each other, or the fact that she'd soon be walking into her toxic workplace. She had the same flat feeling that she'd had the day after her Grade 2 violin exam and the day after her GCSEs. All that build-up to the festival. The excitement. The energy. The adrenaline surging through her veins. Or was it arteries? (Razz would know but he wasn't there to ask.) And now, suddenly, wham. It was all over.

It had been odd yesterday that he'd left without saying goodbye to her. Disappeared without a word. They'd never arranged anything, but she'd always envisaged that once everything was tidied up after the festival, they'd go for a drink – or a cup of tea at least – and discuss how it had gone. Celebrate their achievement, no matter how tired they both were. Had he rushed off to be with Zoey?

What the hell was she going to do with herself? she wondered as she walked to the station. Every spare minute had been devoted to organising the festival. How would she pass the evenings and weekends now?

She'd assumed that once it was over, she and Ras – Razz, now – would continue spending time together. Even if he didn't want her in a romantic way, she'd imagined that they'd still meet as friends. That he might invite her over to play Scrabble at his place. That she might give her tatty house a bit of a makeover and invite him over to hers. That they'd hang out.

That was what she wanted more than anything. Even more than she wanted a boyfriend, she wanted a friend to hang out with.

But she couldn't imagine Zoey being the type who'd be happy with her new boyfriend – assuming Razz was now her boyfriend – spending time with another woman. Even if they were only playing Scrabble.

Later, as her packed train trundled towards Manchester, Jo realised she was going back to her old life. A life of lonely evenings playing word games on her phone and watching box sets of nineties medical dramas. Maybe she'd try *Grey's Anatomy* instead of *ER*; she wasn't sure Dr Ross did it for her anymore. You could keep your Dr Ross; it was Dr Razz who occupied her daydreams these days.

She pulled out her phone and clicked on WordPals. As the train left the hills behind, Jo spelled out SAD and scored a miserable 4 points. As it crawled towards the high-rise buildings of Manchester, she scored another 9 points with HOPE, and as it pulled into Victoria Station, she used a blank tile and added LESS to HOPE and scored another 13 By the time she reached the ticket barriers, she had lost the game.

The office was buzzing with the usual Monday morning hum about who'd done what over the weekend. For once, she wanted someone to say, *How was your weekend, Jo? What did you get up to?* so she could say, *I organised a Scrabble Festival and hundreds of people came and it raised loads of money and was a great success and everyone had a fantastic time.*

Well, everyone apart from her when she saw the man she was in love with tick someone else's box at the speed-dating event. But they didn't need to know about that bit.

No-one asked her anyway.

'Morning,' she called, trying to sound cheerful as she sat down at her desk.

Only Caroline replied, 'Morning, Jo,' back to her. That was something at least. There'd been some mornings when no-one had replied at all.

At eleven o'clock, they all filed into the meeting room as usual, notebooks in hand. Well, Jo had her Filofax and the others all had notebooks. David closed the door behind them and took his place as he always did at the head of the table.

'Fabulous show last week,' he said. 'Good viewing figures too.'

He said this every week, regardless of the actual viewing figures. Probably thought it was good for team morale.

'What have we got for this week?' he said. 'There's a pre-recorded interview with the director of that new film... what's it called again?'

Hannah was the first to jump in with the name.

'What else is on the table? What's topical at the moment?'

The ideas began to fly around, David nodding enthusiastically. Jo jotted everything down on the back of one of her festival ideas sheets – she couldn't find a blank page in the work section of her Filofax, or any other section come to that – to email round the team later. The merits of every idea were debated.

'Anything else?' said David. 'Before I make a rather important announcement.'

On the spur of the moment, Jo decided to pitch a half-baked idea that had occurred to her during the preparations for the festival; she hadn't had time to think it out properly. 'I was wondering about a mini-series. A strand, running across several programmes, each episode featuring something people do to overcome loneliness. Like board games groups. Or Knit 'n' Chat mornings.'

She glanced round everyone's faces to see how the idea had landed. Both researchers looked bored. She caught Leona rolling her eyes at Hannah. Sam stared impassively ahead as if he was in a different world entirely.

'That's not a bad idea,' said David, 'but I'm not sure it's right for us. Loneliness isn't sexy.'

'It's topical,' Jo said. 'The newspapers often have articles about it.'

'That's true,' said Caroline. Jo smiled at her across the room, but she was looking at David.

'It wouldn't appeal to our demographic,' he said.

'But we know that 63 per cent of our audience are female and more than half of them are over fifty-five,' said Jo. 'It's exactly the kind of thing that would appeal to them. Most are probably retired and have time on their hands.'

'We're trying to appeal to a *younger* audience,' said David.

'Okay, but it's a common misconception that loneliness only affects the elderly. In surveys, more than a quarter of people in the UK aged eighteen to twenty-four report that they often feel lonely.' Jo wasn't quite sure where she'd got those stats: probably one of Gemma's articles.

David laughed. 'We can always count on you, Jo, to come up with the numbers. Anyway, moving on.' He closed his notebook and Jo felt her entire body deflate as she realised he was indicating that that was the end of the matter. 'Caroline, would you like to make the announcement?'

'Yes, okay,' said Caroline beaming round the table. 'I wanted to let you all know that Paul and I are expecting our first baby.'

A couple of people clapped.

'Woo-hoo,' said Leona.

'Congratulations,' said Sam.

'When are you due?' said Hannah.

'Who'll do your maternity cover?' said Jo.

Caroline took Jo to one side after the meeting and explained that David had decided that Leona would cover her maternity leave.

'She's competent,' she said, 'and enthusiastic.'

'But she hasn't been here long,' Jo said, 'and she hadn't even worked in TV before that.'

'David feels that you haven't had your eye on the ball recently. I mean, there was the programme budget that you forgot to save...'

'But I didn't forget. I'm certain that I saved it.'

'It wasn't there though, was it? And then when we needed you to go filming, you had another commitment.'

'It was short notice.'

'Yes, but Leona cancelled *her* plans for the weekend so that she could go in your place.'

Jo sighed. It was pointless arguing. All those years of devoted service to Pop! Productions, all that time hoping that one day she'd get the chance of a promotion, and Leona had waltzed in and snatched it from under her nose.

And what was worse, far, far worse, was that this would make Leona her line manager.

'Look, I know you must be disappointed...'

'Yes, I *am* disappointed,' Jo said. 'For years, I've done everything perfectly. Everything you've asked me to do. Made sure that every shoot runs like clockwork. Every t crossed, every i dotted. I think of the tiniest details to ensure everything goes smoothly. I'm the obvious person to step up and do your job, but I make one little error and am unavailable for one shoot, and I get passed over like this.'

She felt out of breath when she'd finished and could feel her heart pounding, but it felt good. A few weeks ago, she'd have meekly accepted that she hadn't got the job. At least now she was standing up for herself, even if it wouldn't change anything.

'David's decided, Jo,' said Caroline. 'I'm sorry but there it is. Already organised.'

Jo returned to her desk. It was a cliché but the past seventy-two hours had been a roller coaster. There'd been the highs – summoning up the courage to do the local radio interview, the excitement and triumph of the festival, the discovery that Ras was actually Razz, and the decision to tell him how she felt about him – and then the lows – seeing Razz with Zoey and now Leona's promotion. Her life had taken a sudden and unexpected downturn.

The festival had finished. It seemed pretty certain that she'd lost Razz; since the festival, she hadn't had so much as a text from him And now the woman who spent most Friday afternoons giggling in the ladies' loos, trying on different outfits and reapplying her mascara, was going to be her line manager. For a whole year.

31

Razz sighed, pulling the pile of papers from his desk towards him. This was going to take forever. It was the last thing he needed after seeing a steady stream of patients all day, but he'd neglected the admin part of his job – and admin was an increasingly large part of his job these days; far more than when he'd first qualified – during the run-up to the festival.

His phone beeped and Razz pounced on it, hoping it would be Jo. He opened WhatsApp and saw there was a message not from Jo, but from that friend of Kate's from the speed-dating event. Zoey. With a y. So funny how she'd introduced herself that way.

He glanced at the message; it seemed she wanted to meet. He'd reply later when he'd finished this mountain of work. He'd never expected her to tick his box and for them to end up being a match.

In the meantime, he tried to focus on what he had to do. There were several letters from hospital consultants. He ran his eye over them quickly, trying to ascertain if there was any follow-up required on his part, but he couldn't concentrate. He kept thinking of Jo, wondering what was going through her mind. Wondering why she'd left so abruptly after the festival had finished without so much as a goodbye. Had it been anything to do with that teacher, Matthew?

He'd happened to glance over during the speed-dating and had noticed that Jo and Matthew were so wrapped up in their conversation that they weren't playing Scrabble at all. And then yesterday morning, he'd seen her heading outside – for a breather presumably – and he'd followed her out, wanting to get things off his chest, to tell her how he felt about her. He'd been intending to wait until *after* the festival – if she didn't feel the same, it could make things awkward – but he couldn't bottle his feelings up any longer. But then Matthew had got there first, and once again, Razz noticed, the pair of them were engrossed in their conversation. So much so that he hadn't liked to intrude.

He should have intruded.

He'd told himself that there mightn't have been anything between them at all, that perhaps they were only talking, but then Jo had raved on about Matthew, full of admiration and enthusiasm, saying wasn't it wonderful how he'd stepped in and rigged up those cameras for the semis and the final at such short notice. 'Isn't he clever?' she'd said.

Razz had looked over at the tall, blond man who looked like he'd stepped out of an episode of *Love Island* rather than being an IT co-ordinator in a small primary school in the Pennines, and decided that he had no chance. Matthew definitely looked like the outdoorsy type. He could picture them together, surfing in Cornwall, whizzing down parallel zipwires, camping in the middle of nowhere in the Scottish Highlands. Now that the festival was over, Jo was presumably longing to get back to her adventurous activities – not that she'd ever mentioned it.

There was no doubt in Razz's mind; he had lost her.

Why on earth hadn't he told her how he felt sooner?

He'd been intrigued by her from the start. And attracted to her. And confused by her. (Although he was, to be fair, someone who was often confused by the opposite sex.) On the one hand, judging by the way she dressed, she was someone who liked to blend into the background, but then she dyed her hair bright red. Judging from her dating profile, he'd expected someone more outdoorsy, more outgoing, but she'd seemed shy and anxious. At first, she hadn't seemed that keen on descending into Gaping Gill, but she'd done it, which was more than he'd managed.

For the umpteenth time, he thought back to that day, to the drive home afterwards, when he'd been feeling embarrassed – no, more like mortified – about losing his bottle the way he had. He'd convinced himself that she'd never want him now; someone who said they liked adventurous activities wouldn't have time for a man who was scared of heights. Nevertheless, when he'd dropped her off on Hazel Lane that day, he should have asked her if she'd like to meet up again. There'd been nothing to lose back then. No friendship at risk. If she'd said no, he'd have got over it, but she might have said yes. He'd thought for a moment that she was going to ask him in for coffee, and his heart had leapt, but then she hadn't. That had decided him; he wouldn't contact her again. If she got in touch, he'd ask for a second date. If she didn't – well, he'd know she wasn't interested.

He'd clung onto a small grain of hope for a day or two that she might text and thank him for the date. But she hadn't.

And then she'd turned up at the club. He'd been so excited to see her again, and to discover that she loved Scrabble too, but he tried not to let it show too much. Women didn't like men who were too keen, did they? Kate had told him that once, when he'd been having a coffee with Ludek in the (Not So) Little Board Game Café, so Razz had played it cool.

Instead of asking her out as he was itching to do, he'd asked her to help him organise a Scrabble event. It had been the perfect excuse to spend some time with her, to get to know her better, but now it was over.

Razz put aside the consultant letters. This was hopeless; he couldn't keep his mind on the job. There was a stack of blood test results and repeat prescription requests to go through, but maybe he should go home, get an early night and tackle it all tomorrow.

He switched off his computer and turned off the lights in his consulting room.

On his way home, Razz's thoughts turned to Jo once again. They'd grown so close during all those weeks of planning the festival together. They'd become friends, good friends, but he'd thought there was something more. There'd been so much eye contact. He could have sworn that on at least a couple of occasions, he'd seen her pupils dilate, a sure sign of sexual attraction.

Kate had told him once to make subtle moves on a woman: a hand on an arm, perhaps, or brushing away a loose strand of hair. That way, he could gauge her response, rather than ploughing straight on in there with some clumsy, cack-handed attempt at seduction. So he'd taken Jo's hand over the Scrabble board that evening when she'd first suggested speed-dating; she hadn't taken it away. He'd brushed cream from the side of her mouth when she'd been eating one of Annie's eclairs. She'd looked away but hadn't seemed too uncomfortable. But not looking uncomfortable wasn't exactly a green light, was it? He had never been sure how she felt about him.

Jo had changed during the past few weeks, which had been lovely to witness but made working her out even more problematic. The rather nervous young woman he'd first met outside the town hall had become confident; she'd sailed through that live radio interview and stood on the stage at the festival as if it were nothing. And with every ounce of confidence that Jo seemed to gain, Razz became even more attracted to her. It was like watching a flower blossom, he thought. A cliché but perfectly true.

And then the festival had happened and it had all been a roaring success, and he'd wondered if they might go out after it ended to celebrate how well it had gone. Maybe he could order champagne – a little Dutch courage wouldn't go amiss. But then he'd seen her with Matthew.

In any case, she had vanished afterwards without a word. He'd been loading his car with all the Scrabble boxes and she'd definitely been there, but then when he'd returned to the hall, there was no sign of her. He'd gone round all the classrooms searching, but she was nowhere to be seen. Mrs Wood had been packing up the art room; she'd said that no, Jo hadn't been in. She wasn't in the staffroom either, nor the kitchen nor any of the classrooms.

How could she leave without saying goodbye after everything they'd achieved together?

Matthew wasn't there either and Razz couldn't help wondering if Jo had left with him.

Maybe there was some other explanation. A sick relative perhaps, or some other emergency. Or maybe she'd just been tired. Had a headache. It had been an exhausting couple of days.

He contemplated texting her to check she was okay but decided to wait until Friday when he'd see her at Scrabble club. She probably needed a few days to recover from the weekend.

Yes, he would talk to her on Friday, and in the meantime, he'd think of some subtle way to find out if she was seeing Matthew.

Perhaps he'd ask Annie to bake a special cake in Jo's honour, to thank her for everything; she had, after all, undertaken the lion's share of the work for the festival. She could have easily done it without him, but Razz knew, without a shadow of a doubt, that he couldn't have done it without her.

32

Right when I thought things couldn't get any worse, they did.

Jo tapped out a WhatsApp to Gemma later on the train home.

David promoted Leona instead of me. What am I meant to do, Gem?

Her phone pinged a few minutes later. Gemma had written,

Impress him. Make him regret his decision.

And inevitably, as she always did, Gemma attached an online article:

Six Ways to Make Your Boss Love You.

Great. Just what she needed.
And the first way? Enthusiasm apparently.
So, when Leona took over from Caroline, she was supposed be enthusiastic?

No chance.

She scanned down the article. *Go above and beyond what your role requires and your boss expects.*

And how was she meant to do that, exactly?

Jo placed the drinks on the table and slipped onto the banquette seat beside Kate.

It was Tuesday evening. After another tricky day in the office and feeling frustrated at Leona's imminent promotion, Jo had needed a shoulder to cry on and a listening ear. She wanted to text Razz, but something had stopped her. She hadn't heard from him at all since the festival and was beginning to feel rather hurt about that; even if he was with Zoey, well, they were friends, weren't they? And yet he'd left without so much as a goodbye after the festival. She felt rejected by him. Again. So rather than texting him and risking further rejection, she had messaged Kate instead, who, surprisingly, had turned out to be free that night.

'Have you met up with Matthew yet?' Jo asked.

There was hardly anyone in the George that evening: a group of older women in the corner who shrieked with laughter every few minutes and some lads knocking back pints of dark, locally brewed ale.

'Yeah, last night as it happens.'

'And how did it go?'

'Well, he's lovely but he's a bit of a nerd. Always banging on about techie things. But we'll see. How about you? Any matches from the speed-dating?'

'Three ticks in my box.'

'And did you tick any of them?'

'I didn't tick anyone.'

'Oh? How come?'

Jo wondered if she should mention Razz. Admit how much she liked him. After all, she didn't know for sure how he felt about Zoey. It was jumping to conclusions to assume that a tick in a box meant they'd start a relationship. They might have had a first date and decided they weren't each other's type after all. But the fact remained that Razz had ticked Zoey's box whilst he hadn't ticked hers. What was the point in telling Kate about her feelings for him now? She needed to put him to the back of her mind and focus on her work situation. That was why she'd asked Kate to meet her for a drink this evening. Not to talk about men.

'I want to focus on work,' she said, 'rather than men. It's all gone a bit… well, tits up.'

'My work's crap at the moment too.'

'Seriously? I thought you liked your job.'

'I used to, but it feels pretty pointless. I spend all day dreaming up ways to market products that no-one needs. It's not what I want to do with my life.'

'What *do* you want to do?'

'Well,' said Kate. 'What I want to do – and I've never told anyone this before, not even Emily – is become a life coach. I love giving advice. As you may have noticed.'

'Yeah, a bit,' said Jo, thinking back to how Kate had started giving her dating advice, practically from the minute they'd first met. None of it had helped – not so far anyway – but she didn't like to say. Maybe Kate's work advice would be better than her dating tips.

'Anyway, we're here to talk about you. Tell me about your job.'

'The production manager's going off on maternity leave and they've asked Leona, not me, to cover for her. I've been there longer and have way more experience so it's a bit of a blow. It's too late to change their minds about the maternity cover, but I want to make sure I'm not overlooked in future.'

Kate looked thoughtful. 'Put your resentment aside about not getting the maternity cover and think of a way to impress your boss. What's his name again? David?'

Jo nodded.

'You've got to make David kick himself that he didn't give *you* that promotion.'

'Yeah, but how? I've always done a good job. Well, I slipped up once and lost a document – still can't see how that happened – and then I said I wasn't available for a shoot. But it was short notice and it was the weekend of the Scrabble festival. Other than that, I haven't put a foot wrong. Everything organised. Double-checked. Triple, even. I don't see what more I can do.'

'You need to go the extra mile.'

Had Kate read the same article that Gemma had sent? Jo wondered.

'The extra mile?'

'Yep! Do something to make yourself stand out. What could you do that you haven't done yet?'

'I've never come up with a killer programme idea,' said Jo. 'I've suggested a few but they're never good enough. If I suggested a fascinating documentary or devised a brilliant format for a new game show, he'd be impressed. Although… well, I'm not a particularly creative person. My strength lies in organising things.'

'Rubbish,' said Kate. 'Look at the festival. Yes, you did a brilliant job of the organising, but it was much more than that. You came up with the idea of Scrabble speed-dating. And the tombola with letter tiles. The craft room activities...'

'That was copied from Instagram.'

'You thought of the whole idea in the first place. You're very creative.'

'Yeah, but that was about Scrabble. I love Scrabble so much – I felt inspired.'

'Then think of a programme idea about Scrabble.'

'Like a Scrabble game show?'

'Why not? *I* think Scrabble's a bit geeky but there are millions of people around the world who disagree with me.'

Even before Leona joined Pop! Productions and started scoffing at every syllable she uttered, Jo had never had much luck pitching her ideas at the team meeting. But this idea... surely this was a good one?

A TV show based on Scrabble.

Scrabble had been around now since the 1930s, Jo knew. Almost a hundred years old, although it wasn't called Scrabble back then.

And WordPals was a popular app. There was no doubt about it. People loved the game, so why wouldn't they love a TV version?

For the past few weeks, Jo had thought about nothing but Hebbleswick Scrabble Festival. Well, nothing but Razz and the festival. Now the Scrabble game show idea filled her head on the train every day as she journeyed to and from Manchester. She thought about it in the bath, as she heated up each evening's ready meal, and at work, as she ploughed through her usual tasks of booking hotels and taxis and typing up schedules. Those tasks seemed so mundane now; she was far more excited about the idea of coming up with a concept that might one day become a programme.

At least seven times a day, she almost texted Razz. Almost.

I'm trying to come up with a programme idea to impress my boss. Wondering about a Scrabble game show.

Would you watch a Scrabble game show on TV? I want to pitch it at our next team meeting at work.

Trying to devise a new TV game show based on Scrabble. Would you have time to play-test a few ideas with me please?

But she never pressed send on any of these messages. She imagined – assumed – he'd be too busy with his new romance. He wouldn't want to be bothered with her. If she sent it and then he didn't reply, or said it sounded great, but he hadn't time to play-test it with her, well, she'd feel rejected all over again.

Perhaps she would ask him on Friday at Scrabble club. She could rope in the other members then and run her ideas past them too.

Even though she didn't work on the creative side of TV production, she'd worked in the industry for long enough to know that simply televising a game of Scrabble wouldn't work. Everyone had been enthralled watching the final of the festival tournament on the big screen in the school hall, but this wasn't a sustainable format on television. Game shows had rounds, with different activities in each round. She needed to think of different letter- or word-based activities.

Viewers liked elimination rounds. There might be four or six players in the first round, but at least one of those would be knocked out so only some went through to the second round. By the final round, there should only be two people left. Facing each other one-on-one, going head-to-head over the Scrabble board, to see who would emerge victorious.

Jo could picture the set: predominantly grey – the same shade as the Scrabble board itself – with accents of red, pink and blue to reflect the coloured squares on the board. The contestants would stand behind lecterns and an illuminated display board would spell out each of their names in letter tiles.

And what would the rounds consist of? Playing against the clock was always popular. It added drama.

The first round could be an anagram round. Each player could be given a set of seven letters and they'd have to find the anagram of those letters. Or was that too similar to *Countdown*?

How about giving each player the same set of letters and their own board? They'd have a minute to make each word. And, she thought triumphantly, it could link with an app – a bit like the WordPals app – so people could play along at home. David was always banging on about engaging the audience. Viewers could even tweet their answers during the show using a hashtag. David would love that; 'interactivity' was one of his buzzwords. That was sure to win her brownie points.

Since Scrabble was a word game, there could be a round where the players had to guess the correct meaning of some unusual words. Perhaps unusual words that would score highly in Scrabble. Like zax, she thought, smiling as she remembered Razz playing that in the tournament.

The ideas were flowing thick and fast now, jostling for space in her brain. She couldn't write them down quickly enough.

A true or false round; is this word allowed in Scrabble or not? They could present the players with a mixture of foreign words, now assimilated into English, and proper nouns. Was 'google' allowed in Scrabble these days? It had made it into the dictionary.

Perhaps a round where the aim was to make the most words in one go. Points would be awarded for both the number of words and the length of each one.

By Friday afternoon, Jo had several scribbled pages of ideas in her Filofax. When all her colleagues had left – David was meeting a woman off Tinder, it was date night for Caroline and her husband, and Leona and the others were going out on the town – she read them through, chose the best ones and typed them up into a Word document.

She yawned. If she didn't leave soon, she wouldn't make the Scrabble club on time.

She saved the document and was about to turn off her computer when it occurred to her that Razz might bring Zoey along to the club that evening.

Damn. If he was with Zoey, well, she'd have to get used to that, but she wasn't quite ready to see the two of them together just yet. Perhaps she'd give it a miss tonight. She should probably keep working on her pitch anyway, make sure it was word perfect.

It was five past eight when she finally decided to call it a night. She made sure to save her document – she wasn't going to make that mistake again – and clicked print to create a hard copy to take home. She planned to memorise it and rehearse it over the weekend, so as to present it in the best possible way at the team meeting on Monday morning.

The door to the office opened, and the cleaner arrived. He never usually acknowledged her as he strutted round the office in his headphones, vacuuming under the desks. But this evening, he wasn't wearing the headphones.

'Evening,' she said.

To her surprise, he actually replied. 'What an evening! Last job – well, the place was such a mess. Then two buses didn't show up…'

He glanced up at the enormous canvas of Mona above Jo's desk. 'Don't you find her creepy? It's like she's watching your every move.'

Jo shook her head. 'Nah, she's too busy looking at her phone. I talk to her sometimes.'

'Get away, you don't.'

'I do, it's true. Anyway, it's been nice talking to you, but I need to get home.'

She picked up her bag, gave him a quick goodbye wave and headed out of the office. She didn't notice her pitch document still sitting on the tray of the printer.

Jo's phone was silent all weekend. She'd been hoping Razz would text her, might ask why she hadn't been at Scrabble club or check she was okay, but he didn't.

She tried to put him to the back of her mind and spent the time rehearsing her pitch in front of the bathroom mirror. It was tricky without the printout – she'd been halfway to

Hebbleswick before she'd realised she'd forgotten it – but she managed nonetheless. She worked out how to explain each round in a succinct way and practised smiling as she spoke. She tried to second-guess what questions David might have and pondered how best to answer them. She was ready for this. Thoroughly prepared and utterly convinced that he would say yes.

Monday morning.

Jo could barely sit still in the team meeting as they ran through the usual agenda: this week's viewing figures, audience feedback, what filming was happening during the week and who was involved. This was her big chance; her Scrabble game show was her best idea yet. She had to keep calm and present it in a clear, concise manner, like she'd practised at home. Her mouth was dry, her heart thudding; she wasn't sure if this was nerves or excitement or a mixture of both.

'And now we move on to ideas,' said David.

Finally. The moment Jo had been waiting for. She took a deep breath, visualised the Word document in her mind, the bullet points, the details of each round, and said, 'We could...'

'I've been working on an idea,' said Leona. 'I thought we could do a game show based on the board game, Scrabble. It's an extremely popular game; 150 million sets have been sold and it's been around since the 1930s.'

'Fantastic,' said David. 'Tell me more...'

33

Jo couldn't believe her ears.

'There might be four or six players in the first round,' Leona was saying, 'but at least one of those would be knocked out so only some would go through to the second round. Viewers like eliminating players like that, don't they?'

She looked round the room, smiling at everyone, but avoided making eye contact with Jo.

'By the final round,' she continued, 'there would only be two people left. Facing each other one-on-one, going head-to-head over the Scrabble board, to see who would emerge victorious.'

'And these rounds?' David said. 'What would they consist of? Because watching people playing a game of Scrabble wouldn't be that exciting. Rather slow, I'd have thought.'

'I'm coming to that.' Leona smiled again. 'For the first round, each player would have their own board and the same set of letters. They'd have one minute to make each word. And now here's the good bit...'

She paused.

Jo glanced at her colleagues; they were all hanging on Leona's every word. She wanted to say, *Hang on a minute, that's my idea*, but her mouth was dry and Leona was presenting the whole thing so well, so confidently. Better than she would have done, for all her rehearsals.

No-one would believe you, she thought. Leona's really nailing this pitch. She's owning it. No-one would believe it wasn't her own idea.

'We'd devise an app to link with the show,' Leona was saying now. 'A bit like the WordPals app. Have you all heard of that? Jo's always on it, aren't you, Jo?'

'Yes, but not when I'm meant to be working,' Jo mumbled through gritted teeth.

'Of course not, Jo.' Leona smiled sweetly. 'I wasn't implying that. So this app that I've thought of – it would allow viewers to play along at home. Our audience wouldn't be passively watching from their sofas; they'd be actively taking part. You're always saying how it's good to engage our viewers more, David. And – you'll love this bit – it would be interactive. We'd encourage the audience to use social media to tell us their highest scoring words.'

Jo looked down at the table. As Leona continued, Jo mouthed the words. She knew exactly – *exactly* – what was coming next. She must have found the document that Jo had left on the printer on Friday and managed to memorise the entire thing before the team meeting.

'I thought we could call it *Love Letters*,' Leona was saying now, 'because it's for people who love letters!'

'Brilliant,' said David. 'Absolutely brilliant. Genius idea.'

Jo sighed. She'd known David would love the audience participation stuff. Trouble was, this was winning Leona brownie points, not Jo.

'I have more details,' said Leona. 'If you'd like to hear

them. I've worked out what the other rounds might consist of.'

Jo listened, barely able to supress her fury as Leona outlined every single one of her ideas, brazenly presenting them as if they were her own. She wanted to speak up there and then, to confront Leona, to point out what she'd done in front of the whole team, to reveal her for the ideas thief that she was, but somehow, she couldn't find the words. She would talk to David later. When she had calmed down.

'Zeitgeist,' said David.

Zeitgeist, thought Jo. Good word: 19 points. Although was it German? Or had it been assimilated into English? She would have to check later.

'Zeitgeist?' she said.

'Yes, it literally means "time mind" or "time spirit".'

'I know what it means.' Jo had stayed silent in the meeting, but afterwards, when her heart had stopped racing, she knew she had to stand up for herself, had to tell her boss what had happened.

'It explains why more than one person often comes up with the same idea at the same time,' said David. 'There are several famous cases in history. I made a documentary about it once. Isaac Newton and Gottfried... I forget his name. Anyway, they both discovered calculus. Newton was first, but he hadn't spoken about or published his ideas so Gottfried thingy couldn't have copied him.'

'But Leona *did* copy mine.'

'And on the exact same day that Alexander Graham Bell arrived at the patent office having invented the telephone, someone else came in with the same invention. It took lawyers to sort it all out. So you see, Jo, you might have come up with the idea of a Scrabble game show, but Leona did too. Hardly surprising given that you've been banging on about your Scrabble festival in the office for the last few weeks. I bet it was that which gave her the idea.'

Jo frowned. She'd barely mentioned the festival in the office.

'But David,' she said, 'this isn't simply a question of two people coming up with the same basic idea. All those details that Leona came up with in the meeting, the different rounds, they were *all* my ideas. We might both have thought of a Scrabble game show, but the details wouldn't be identical. I printed my pitch out on Friday evening. I must have left it on the printer and she must have found it.'

'Jo, Jo, Jo,' said David. 'Why on earth would Leona steal your idea? This is most unlike you. You've had a problem with Leona, from the moment she first joined Pop! Productions...'

'No, it's the other way round. She's never liked me.'

'...And I can see that it probably rankles that I chose her, rather than you, to fill Caroline's shoes when you've been here the longest. But accusing her of stealing your ideas? That's going a bit far.'

Stony-faced, David sat at his desk, swinging his chair a little from side to side.

Whatever she said, he wouldn't believe her. She couldn't prove that Leona had found the print-out that morning. Time to admit defeat.

'You're right,' she said. 'Probably zeitgeist.'

And with that, she stood up and headed back into the

open-plan office, fighting back the tears because the last thing she wanted was to give Leona the satisfaction of seeing her cry. Because that was what they always wanted, didn't they? Bullies. They always wanted to make you cry.

Jo sat on the toilet, mulling over her options. She could confront Leona, but what was the point? Cunning would triumph over honesty, any day of the week. And her colleague was definitely cunning.

No, she'd say nothing. She'd get her work done as quickly as possible and leave the office on time. She'd ring Gemma or maybe Kate. One of them might know what to do, and, at the very least, they would offer some consoling words.

She'd barely sat back down at her desk when her phone pinged.

It was Razz. Finally.

We missed you at Scrabble club. Are you okay?

She hesitated before texting back. She wanted to tell him how much she was missing the festival, missing him, about the programme idea and how it felt like everything had been going right in her life, but now everything was going wrong. But he was probably in a new relationship now; he wouldn't want to be bothered with her problems.

Fine thanks. I was working late.

I've a letter for you.

A letter? Who from?

A woman who came to Scrabble club looking for you.

That was strange. Jo couldn't think who it might be.

Did she say who she was?

Jo was puzzled. She waited for him to text her back but her phone went silent. Perhaps a patient had arrived at Razz's door.

Still baffled over who the mystery woman was and what the letter could be about, Jo opened her Filofax to the work section and ran her finger down her to-do list. She needed to double-check next week's filming arrangements, book hotel rooms in Winchester for a big shoot happening next month and figure out travel arrangements for the presenter too, but that wouldn't take too long.

She was looking at Booking.com and working out which was the nearest hotel to the location when her phone pinged again. Razz's patient must have left, prescription in hand, on route to the pharmacy.

No idea.

She was curious. Who could it be from? It was about time she saw Razz again. Even if he did have a girlfriend – well, they could still be friends, couldn't they? She started to tap out a reply.

Wondering when you might be free…

'You're not busy then?'

She looked up to see Leona standing behind her.

Jo quickly put her phone back on the desk.

'No, I'm on top of everything,' she said and then added, 'As usual.'

'Great,' said Leona. 'Because I've got to spend some time this week shadowing Caroline, so I obviously can't do my own workload at the same time.'

'Obviously.'

'And David hasn't had time to recruit someone to step into my shoes yet, so I was thinking, since you're obviously at a loose end, you can do it. I've printed off a to-do list. I know you like your lists.'

Leona held out two sheets of A4.

Jo took them, glancing down the bullet-pointed list.

'All this?' she said. 'Seriously?'

'Is it too much for you?'

Jo looked up from the list.

That smirk again.

There was something about the way that Leona smirked that had always riled Jo.

'Of course not,' she said in the brightest tone she could muster. 'Piece of cake. I'll have it done in no time.'

Despite the additional workload, Jo was the first to leave the office that evening, on the dot of six, her head held high, consoling herself that she might treat herself to a ready meal from Sainsbury's finest range before she rang Gemma. She would text Razz back too, as soon as she got on the train. Ask him if he was free for a drink sometime on the pretext of handing over her letter. It had been a bad day, but it was going to be a better evening. She felt sure of it.

Sure of it, until the moment she stepped out onto the street and heard a familiar voice.

'Hi, Jo. I've been waiting for you.'

She noticed his shoes first. Loakes. Polished nubuck leather with a leather sole.

Several pairs of those expensive shoes had sat alongside her more ordinary footwear on the rack a few years ago.

Looking up, she found herself staring into the face of her ex-husband, Si.

34

'What d'you want, Si?'

'I thought we might go for a drink.'

A drink? After all this time? He'd never contacted her once since their divorce. Not so much as a Christmas card.

She wanted to say no, but then she never had been able to say no to Si. Instead, she said, 'I don't think so.'

She stepped past him, intent on walking on towards the station, but he caught hold of her arm and pulled her back. 'One drink, Jo. What harm could it do?'

She looked at his face. His deep-brown eyes, chiselled jaw, impossibly long lashes. There was still something boyish about him and he was undeniably attractive. And his clothes – she'd forgotten how stylish he was. But he was, she thought now, a little too perfect. A little too groomed. As if he was an actor playing the role of 'handsome man about town'.

'Well…?' he said impatiently.

He hadn't changed then.

'I have to get home.'

'Come on. For old times' sake.'

'No, Si,' she said. She pulled her arm out of his grasp and

fought the urge to punch the air with it. *No, Si.* She had actually said no to him.

Something in the air shifted between them. Si said, 'Aren't you a little bit curious to talk to me again after all these years?' and his tone had softened. It was less demanding now – more cajoling.

And she had to admit that she *was* curious. Why had he sought her out now after all this time? What did he want? Because he had to want something. He wouldn't randomly tip up in her life, not after so long.

'No, Si,' she said again, relishing how good it felt to say no to him. 'I told you, I have to get home. I have to ring Gemma.'

'Gemma!' He sneered. 'Okay, fine. Although it seems a shame when I've come here to see you. And you do look like you could use a drink. Bad day in the office?'

He always had been able to read her moods, she thought. It was one reason why he'd been able to manipulate her so easily in the past. And he was right; she could use a drink. If she just went home now, she'd spend the entire evening either brooding on what had happened at work or wondering what Si had wanted.

'One drink,' she heard herself saying. 'And I mean it, Si. One drink.'

'Fine by me. I know a little place...'

'No, Si. I'll choose where we go.'

She was surprised by how assertive she sounded. Si looked surprised too, but he acquiesced and said, 'Sure, Jo. Whatever you like.'

She led him to Wetherspoons on Deansgate. Partly because it was on her way to the station, but mainly because she knew he'd hate it; he was a snob, was Si. The kind of man who prided himself on *never* setting foot in a 'Spoons. Probably too worried about the leather soles of his precious Loakes getting tarnished on the sticky carpet.

'Mind that patch,' she said as they walked towards the bar. 'I think someone's spilled their beer.'

They hadn't, but she enjoyed the frown on Si's face, the way he steered clear of the spot she'd indicated. What had got into her? She wasn't normally like this.

'So why now, Si?' she said, when he'd bought their drinks and they'd settled themselves in a quiet corner. 'After all this time.'

He looked like a fish out of water. For the first time in all the years she'd known him, she sensed that she was more comfortable than he was. It was a delicious feeling, one to be savoured. All those times he'd taken her to places that were a bit too posh, a bit too upmarket, and she'd sat there, conscious that her clothes weren't quite right and she didn't know what to say.

'There was an article,' he said, 'in the *Yorkshire Post*. You ran a little event. I read it and thought it would be lovely to catch up.'

'It wasn't a little event,' she said. 'It was a festival. A Scrabble festival.'

He frowned again. He'd never liked that game. Not since their fourth date anyway, when she'd asked him to play and he'd discovered he couldn't beat her at it. Si was a man who liked to win.

'Yes, my *little event* turned out to be quite big in the end,' said Jo. She was surprised at the sound of her own voice.

She never used to contradict him. And she sounded – well – confident.

'That's great, Jo.'

He spoke in a way you'd speak to a child who'd brought home a terrible painting from nursery but you wanted to encourage their efforts. Jo felt her confidence beginning to melt away again. How did he manage to do that to her? Every single time.

She took a deep breath. She wasn't going to let him.

'Anyway, how've you been?' he said. 'Met anyone new?'

'No,' said Jo, wishing she could say she was loved up with someone but she wasn't going to lie about it.

'I bet I'm a tough act to follow, aren't I?'

She took a deep breath. 'I wouldn't quite say that. Let's say I'm looking for a different kind of guy these days.'

She wanted to add, *And I'd never even go on a date with you; your name only scores 2 points in Scrabble.* But he'd only scoff.

'Yeah, sure.' He clearly didn't believe her.

'Have you?' she said. 'I mean, are you with anyone? Did you remarry?'

Damn. She shouldn't have said that. Shouldn't have given him any indication that she had even the tiniest interest in him or his life. She didn't want him having that satisfaction. Didn't want him thinking that she ever thought about him.

Si smirked. 'Yeah, yeah, I did remarry.'

'What's she like?' Jo couldn't help herself.

'She's lovely. Blonde – I always did like blondes.'

'Yeah, you used to nag me to dye my hair.'

'Not nag, Jo. Come on. I used to encourage you. I wanted

you to make the best of yourself. And I see you *have* dyed it now – though I'm not sure I'd have gone for red. It washes you out somewhat.'

'I like red,' said Jo. 'It goes with my green eyes.'

He looked sceptical but said nothing.

'What do you want, Si? You must want something if you've sought me out like this, but I haven't a clue what it is.'

'I wanted to see you. To remember the good times.'

'There were good times?' she said. She sounded bitter. She hadn't meant to sound bitter. That wasn't good; he'd think she still cared about him, that she was still upset that things didn't work out.

'Come on. There *were* good times. Do you remember when we first met? I was bowled over by you. Desperate for you to go out with me. And you loved the attention, didn't you? Lapped it all up.'

That was true. She had loved it. She couldn't believe it, not at first, that a man like Si would want to go on a date with her. Jo had spent her entire life wanting people to like her and now someone like Si said he did. After only one date. And then there'd been another date and another one after that. She'd felt validated. And he didn't just want to date her; he wanted a relationship. In fact, he had seemed smitten with her.

She remembered the day when an expensive bouquet of roses arrived in the solicitors' office where she worked; her colleagues had been amazed and delighted for her.

Then there'd been the dress: a Diane von Furstenberg wrap dress that didn't suit her as it clung in the wrong places, but Si seemed to like it.

'Much more elegant than what you usually wear,' he'd said.

Jo had thought the gift was romantic. Gemma had been sceptical. 'He's trying to improve you,' she'd said. 'That's not a good sign. He should accept you as you are.'

Jo had dismissed all of her friend's warnings. Si was being kind. She'd never had a man pay her this much attention. Couldn't Gemma let her enjoy it? She was probably jealous; her long-term boyfriend Jack was doing his PhD and didn't have the money to shower Gemma with gifts.

Then there'd been a voucher for an expensive hair salon. He'd insisted on coming with her to make sure that the stylist did a good job.

'Someone's got to look out for you,' he'd said.

She'd thought it was sweet at the time – caring – although looking back, the stylist hadn't appreciated having Si watching every snip of the scissors. And she'd ended up with a hairstyle far shorter than she wanted.

'It's more feminine,' he'd said. 'Shows off your beautiful, long neck.'

No-one had ever told her she had a beautiful neck before.

'And he's controlling,' Gemma had said. 'It's so sad – all your long hair gone.'

She looked at him now; Gemma had been right. He *had* been controlling. And the signs had been there from the early days, hadn't they? If only she'd seen them. If only she'd listened to her friend.

'And remember that holiday in Italy? When we went to Pompeii?' Si was saying.

Jo nodded. 'With your friends. I never did like that boss of yours. What was he called?'

'George,' said Si. 'Fabulous guy. Went to Eton. And our honeymoon. Remember that, Jo? Australia. Once-in-a-lifetime experience. Wasn't it fantastic?'

Not really, thought Jo. With her arachnophobia, Australia had been the last place she'd wanted to go, but he'd insisted.

'The barrier reef – wasn't that amazing?'

Well, yes. She had to admit that. The one and only time she'd gone scuba diving. And it had been an incredible sight.

'And the rainforest? The incredible birdsong. You don't hear birdsong like that here. And those little wallabies in that park that you could feed from your hand. With the babies poking their heads out of the pouches. Remember them, Jo? We had a fantastic time, didn't we?'

Those wallabies... well, they *had* been cute.

'And Sydney. You loved Sydney, didn't you? That trip to the opera – what an experience. We were good together, weren't we, Jo?'

Seeing *The Marriage of Figaro* at the Sydney Opera House – yes, that had been a once-in-a-lifetime experience. And to be fair, they hadn't seen that many spiders on their trip.

'I suppose so,' she said. 'We did have a good honeymoon. But you chose it, Si. I didn't get any say. And I didn't get any say in what furniture we bought for the house. What curtains. What colours we painted each room. You didn't even let me choose the toaster.'

'I bought you a Dualit,' he said. 'Wanted you to have the best.'

Jo had wanted a red one from Argos. She'd thought that red accessories would look good in their kitchen with its black, faux-granite worktops and glossy, white units. But

Dualit toasters – well, they were a design classic. It had been kind of him, she supposed, to buy her something so extravagant.

Perhaps he hadn't been all bad.

'Remember Venice?' he said.

Jo blushed, remembering that long weekend that they'd mostly spent in bed. She'd barely noticed the Grand Canal.

'And Nice?' she said.

'Nice was fabulous. We did have some good times, didn't we, Jo?'

And she found herself nodding. Because they had, hadn't they? She looked at him again – the eyes, the jaw, the lashes – and she could see why she fell for him.

He looked at his watch suddenly.

'Sorry, Jo, but I need to be going,' he said. 'This has been lovely. It was good to catch up. To reminisce about the good old days.'

He stood up. Jo felt wrong-footed somehow. There'd been a shift in the energy between them, and she couldn't quite see how it had happened. She should never have agreed to the drink. Should have gone straight home.

They walked back over the carpet, Si still avoiding the patch that Jo had said was sticky. He reached the door first and held it open for her. Si always had liked to *appear* to be the perfect gentleman, she thought. In public at least.

'Which way are you heading?' he said as they stepped onto the pavement.

Jo indicated towards Victoria Station.

'I'm going the opposite way,' he said, 'but I'd be happy to walk you to the station.'

'Thanks, but no need.'

He kissed her on both cheeks. Not the swift, perfunctory air kisses of two acquaintances, but with tenderness, his soft, warm lips resting for a moment against her skin.

For a second, Jo felt a longing for him, but pushed it away. Things were over with Si – with good reason too – and they had been for years. And he was with someone new.

'Goodbye, Si,' she said and walked away.

When she reached the Station, her train was about to leave. Jo ran towards the ticket barrier, pushing her ticket into the machine to open the gates, then ran towards the platform. But she was moments too late.

She slumped onto a cold, metal bench, watching the train disappear, and realised that she hadn't found out why Si had sought her out after all this time.

'This is Si we're talking about,' she said to herself. 'He must have wanted something.'

Looking back at the evening, she couldn't figure what it was. He'd spent nearly an hour in Wetherspoons, reminiscing about their relationship and trying to make her see things the way he wanted her to see them, not how they actually were. He'd been trying to reframe things.

He'd been trying to make her believe they'd had a good relationship but why?

Because they hadn't. He had spent every day of their marriage trying to mould her into someone she wasn't. He'd controlled every aspect of her life.

Her ex-husband was a bully. He had bullied her throughout their marriage, like Leona bullied her in the office. Like those children at school had bullied her.

She had been bullied by other people her whole bloody life. And it had to stop, Jo decided. It had to.

35

Jo had finished all her work, but it wasn't quite six o'clock and she didn't like to slope off early. So she sat in the office, watching Leona, wondering for the umpteenth time why the two of them had never got on, why Leona picked on her.

Leona clearly hadn't finished all of *her* work. In fact, she looked frantic. Hassled. Her usually perfect hair looked ruffled and unkempt – her regular grooming sessions in the ladies' loos were a thing of the past now she was being promoted – and her mascara had run too. Jo wondered if she'd been crying.

Jo felt a wave of sympathy towards her colleague. She wasn't coping, that was apparent, although David didn't seem to have noticed. Everyone else had, though. Three of the cameramen had phoned up, complaining that their invoices hadn't been paid. Leona was snappy with everyone, not just Jo, and her usually perfect complexion looked pale and blotchy. Jo had even spotted her biting her once perfectly manicured nails.

Jo wondered, as she had several times in the last few days, if she shouldn't offer to help. If anyone else had been struggling, she'd have gone straight over and asked what she could do. But she remembered all the nasty comments directed at her in the past, how she was never invited out for after-work drinks, and, worst of all, how Leona had stolen her programme idea, so she left her to it and went to the ladies'.

She frowned at her face in the mirror.

Why did people like Leona pick on her? What was it about her face, her personality, her *being* that made them do that?

She never stood up for herself, never had the courage.

When Leona had pitched *Love Letters* right in front of her in that meeting, she hadn't said a word. And Leona would have known that Jo would stay silent.

Or on that terrible date with Neil in ¡Tapas! ¡Tapas! He'd made her feel obliged to pay half of that ridiculously expensive bill. She could have said, *Now, hang on, wait a minute, you ordered all that food.*

How had he known that she would say nothing? That she'd do as he wanted and tap her card on the machine?

Did she look like a pushover? Or, worse still, a victim?

People looked down on her. Why was that?

She stared at her reflection.

Was it because she was slightly overweight? Was she seen as inferior just because of a few extra pounds? Were people really that judgemental?

She recalled the words from that article that Gemma had sent: *remember it's about them, not you.*

'It's them, not you,' she repeated to herself.

Yes, it was about them. Those children in the playground years ago with their meanness and their cruelty were unhappy kids who resorted to bullying others to make themselves feel better.

And Si? He was one of those men who liked controlling women. You read about them everywhere these days: in newspaper articles, in magazines, online. He had done it to her. He was probably doing it to his new wife.

Her only 'fault', Jo realised now, was that she hadn't seen it coming, despite Gemma's best efforts to warn her. But even that wasn't *her* fault.

Should she have known? Should she have seen it? How could you tell if the charming man who took you out for dinner and held car doors open for you and bought you gifts was, underneath the façade, controlling, bullying and manipulating?

Because men like Si were clever. They hooked you, reeled you in, literally charmed the pants off you until you were won over, and only later revealed their true colours.

She had thought she was ready for a new relationship, but was she? Seeing Si again had brought it all back: the years of feeling trapped, unable to make her own choices.

Perhaps it was a good thing that she hadn't got together with Razz. She didn't *think* Razz would ever be like Si, but could she ever be sure? She hadn't thought that Si would be how he turned out to be. What if Razz had been duping her too? Playing Mr Nice Guy with his quiet, gentle manners and his Scrabble club. Even his fear of heights – well, that could have been an act. It had been odd, arranging that trip to Gaping Gill, ensuring that she went down first then not making the descent himself.

She didn't know anymore. It was so confusing.

Si had got inside her head again. Made her doubt everything and everyone. Made her doubt her own mind.

What she wanted, Jo realised now with sudden clarity, was for this to *stop* happening to her. She wanted to become someone like… like Gemma. Or Kate. Someone who felt sure of herself. Someone who had confidence in their own judgement. Someone the bullies ignored. She didn't want to be the centre of attention – although that had been fun at the festival. She wanted to get on with her day-to-day activities, quietly, without anyone interfering or commenting or criticising or judging. She wanted them to leave her alone. But they had always sought her out, those bullies, and would do in future. She knew that. And she couldn't change them, so she had to change herself.

'What is it about me?' she asked her reflection. 'And how can I change it?'

She took out her phone, and scrolled through her messages until she found the link to the bullying article that Gemma had sent her all those weeks ago:

How to Handle Adult Bullying

She scanned down the list of suggestions.

Avoid places and situations where the bullying might happen.

Impossible when it happened in your workplace.

Remember it's about them, not about you. Bullying is a reflection of their insecurities, not your shortcomings.

Leona? Insecure? Hardly. She'd acted like she owned that office from the moment she'd walked in.

Surround yourself with cheerleaders.

Cheerleaders?

Jo harrumphed. Cheerleaders! Honestly. Who came up with this stuff?

Acknowledge that it's okay to feel bad.

No. No, it wasn't okay. She had felt bad for far too long, Jo thought.

'How can I change it?' she said again.

Kate. She wanted to be a life coach, didn't she? Perhaps she'd have some advice. It would be embarrassing, shameful even, to admit all this stuff to someone she'd only know for a short time, but if there was a chance Kate could help... well, it would be worth it.

Jo hastily rearranged the cushions, placing one over the stain on the sofa. She'd never been to Kate's place but assumed it would be smarter than this.

But Kate, when she arrived, didn't seem at all fazed by the scruffy little underdwelling.

'This is lovely, Jo,' she said, staring out of the window. 'What a view.'

The view was admittedly beautiful. Jo had stopped noticing it now, but when she'd first moved here, she'd often gazed out of the window at the town below and the higgledy-piggledy streets criss-crossing the opposite hillside.

'Tea? Coffee?' said Jo. 'Or wine. I think I've a bottle of red lurking at the back of the cupboard.'

'Lurking red,' said Kate. 'My favourite vintage.'

Jo went into the tiny kitchen, poured the wine, took a large glug of her own for Dutch courage, before topping her glass up and going back into the lounge where Kate was now reclining on the stained sofa.

'Cheers,' she said, handing Kate the glass and sitting down beside her.

Kate took a sip then placed her glass down on the floor. 'Better not have too much of that. I need to keep a clear head. In your text, you said you needed my advice.'

'Yes, I do,' said Jo. She took another large glug of wine and placed her own glass down. 'Oh, Kate, I don't know where to start.'

She poured it all out. How she'd been teased – no, bullied – at school. Relentless name-calling. People hiding her stuff.

'It probably sounds trivial,' said Jo, 'but it didn't *feel* trivial.'

'It doesn't sound trivial,' said Kate. 'Children have taken their own lives because of school bullying. And these days – with social media – it's worse than ever.'

'It stopped when I met Gemma. Well, it got better. But it still happens to me now. And I'm an adult. You know my Scrabble TV programme idea? I left it on the printer and Leona must have found it. She pitched it at our team meeting as if it was her idea. David didn't believe me when I told him. He says I've got a downer on her. But it's the other way round – since she joined the team, I don't get invited out for lunch or drinks after work. She's dumped her workload on me. She gossips about me behind my back. Laughs at me.'

'She's a bully, Jo.'

'I know. But why is it always me who gets bullied? What is it about me? And then my marriage, Kate. He stopped me seeing Gemma and my other friends – I actually had a few by then. I had to dress the way he liked, wear my hair how he liked it.'

'He sounds dreadful,' said Kate. 'Controlling.'

'He watched everything I ate. Said I only had to look at a chocolate éclair or a fish 'n' chip shop to put on six pounds. I know you like salad, but I hate it, yet he made me eat mountains of the stuff.'

Kate leaned over and took Jo's hand. 'It sounds like coercive control. You could report him for that.'

'Report him?'

'To the police.'

'I don't think so. It would be my word against his. And they wouldn't believe me, that's for sure. Like David – he didn't believe me about the Scrabble programme being my idea. Gemma sent me this article about overcoming adult bullying, but it's useless. It says it's about them, not me.'

Kate nodded. 'I'd agree with that...'

'But how can it be, Kate? Because I'm the common denominator here. I'm the one that people pick on. It must be something that I do, something about me, that makes them all do that. Like the weak animal in the pack that all the others turn on. The hen that all the other hens peck.'

'Show me Gemma's article.'

Jo wiped a tear from her cheek and pulled out her phone. She held it out to Kate and waited as Kate read, biting her lip and worrying at a hangnail on her thumb. 'What do you think?'

'Hang on,' said Kate. 'I haven't read it all yet.'

A couple of minutes later, Kate put the phone down. 'It's a good article. I think we need to put some of those things into practice. "Avoid situations where the bullying happens".'

'My workplace? I can't avoid that.'

'Perhaps not, but you could avoid being alone with Leona. And maybe even look for another job.'

'I'm not going to let her drive me away.'

Kate leaned over and took Jo's hand. 'Fighting spirit. I like that. Keep a record of the stuff Leona says and does. A written record, with dates and times.'

''Spose. I could have a special section in my Filofax.'

Kate looked back at the article. '"Kill the bully with kindness". Hmmm. Not sure about that one. Could you bring yourself to be kind to Leona?'

'She'd throw it back in my face.'

'How about this one? "Practise self-love". That sounds like a good idea, Jo.'

'It sounds a bit new age.'

'It isn't new age. I'm no expert but perhaps you have low self-esteem. You don't think enough of yourself and they pick up on that somehow. You said it yourself; in a pack of animals, there'll be one that the other animals see as weak and that animal gets set upon. But that can change. We need to work on how you see yourself. Follow the suggestions in the magazine.' She paused and glanced down again at the article. 'Spend more time in nature. Regular exercise. Hot, soothing baths. Eat nutritious food. I could give you some info on ayurveda.'

'Er, not sure about that one. And I'm not sure how having a hot bath will stop Leona pinching my ideas or laughing about me behind my back.'

'On its own, it won't, Jo. But like that ad says, you have

to start believing that "you're worth it". Do nice things for you. Take good care of yourself. Buy yourself a gift every now and again. They needn't be big things. Some handwash that smells amazing. A bunch of lilies from the supermarket. Warm gloves – you'll be glad of those. It gets cold here in the winter. Don't eat ready meals because you don't think it's worth cooking a meal for one. Cook yourself something delicious.'

It was true, Jo thought. She did eat a lot of ready meals; how had Kate guessed that? And that evening when she'd cooked a meal after her first exchange of messages with Razz, she had enjoyed it. The cooking as well as the eating. Although, she had admittedly cheated a bit and used a cook-in sauce.

'And you honestly think that could change things?'

'I think it's worth a try. And I'm going to help you, Jo. You're not in this alone. We'll go shopping together for lovely things. We'll go for walks in the countryside – it says to take regular exercise and enjoy nature so that'd be killing two birds with one stone. What do you reckon?'

Kate's face was full of enthusiasm, Jo noticed. 'Are you trying to practise your life-coaching skills on me? Testing out your potential new career?'

'Yes and yes. But I also want to help you because I like you. So, are you up for it? Ready to give it your best shot?'

'Yes and yes,' said Jo. 'I've never been more ready.'

36

Of all the things that Kate had her doing, Jo enjoyed the hot baths most. It was rather lovely, she thought, luxuriating in soapy bubbles – she'd bought herself a lavender-scented bubble bath – with Radio 2 in the background or sometimes an audio book.

She wasn't faring too well with the nutritious food. Kate had insisted on working out what Jo's type was and had given her an ayurvedic eating plan but Jo loved cakes far too much to stick to it. She had ditched the ready meals though, and was cooking herself hearty dishes of stew and dumplings and chilli con carne. It was the sort of food you'd normally crave in winter, not early summer, but it was comfort food and Jo loved it.

She had to admit she felt better, and although there was no noticeable difference in the way anyone was treating her at work, Jo did think people were kinder to her in the outside world. One day, a man offered her his seat on the crowded 8.37 to Manchester; for one horrific moment, Jo wondered if her belly was so bloated from all the kidney beans in the chilli that she looked pregnant, but looking at herself in the ladies' loos later that morning, she decided that she didn't; he was simply being nice. And when she reached the check-out in Sainsbury's Local at the exact same moment as a young woman with dreadlocks and a nose-ring, Jo was surprised when the other customer insisted that she went first.

'You look more confident,' Kate proclaimed as they set off on one of their walks. They were going three times a week now; either through the woods and up onto the moors or along the canal to Essendale.

Jo stepped around some particularly aggressive-looking Canada geese. The bullies of the avian world, she thought. They were always stealing the bread off the mallards.

'We could go and have a cuppa in the (Not So) Little Board Game Café?' she said. 'See your best friend, Emily.'

'My *other* best friend,' said Kate and squeezed Jo's hand.

Jo felt her eyes welling up. She knew Kate and Emily had known each other since their schooldays, like her and Gemma. That would always be a special bond. So it was a big deal that Kate was now putting her on a par with her old friend. A really big deal.

Jo could hear Leona sighing all morning. She shuffled papers about on her desk. She frowned at her computer screen. She summoned Hannah over and the two of them frowned at the screen some more.

Jo heard Hannah say, 'Sorry, Leona. I haven't a clue. You could ask…'

Hannah glanced over to her and Jo pretended she wasn't listening in.

Jo wasn't surprised she was struggling. Leona had only been at Pop! Productions for a few months before she'd been promoted and then she'd had to take over suddenly too; Caroline's morning sickness was apparently so bad that she'd left much earlier than expected and had decided not to return until after her baby was born, so there'd been no proper handover period. And Caroline did have her own unique way of filing things and keeping budgets. It had taken Jo a while to get used to them.

Kill the bully with kindness, Gemma's article had said.

Jo sidled over to Leona's desk, not quite believing that she was doing this. Assisting the woman who'd made her life miserable? And nicked her big idea? She must be mad.

'Can I help?' she said.

Leona looked baffled. She looked behind Jo, as if suspecting that she was up to something perhaps. Or making sure that David wasn't around.

'I'm not saying you're not capable or anything,' Jo added. 'Caroline sometimes files things in an unusual way and it can be pretty tricky to locate stuff.'

'I'd have been fine,' she said, 'if she hadn't gone so suddenly. If I'd had the proper handover like David promised.'

'Of course you would. Now what are you trying to do?'

'The most urgent thing is this programme budget,' she said. 'I've found the file – I can't make head nor tail of it.'

Jo leaned over, one hand on the desk, the other pointing at the screen as she talked her colleague through all the figures, helped her fill in the missing bits and ensured that everything added up.

'Make sure you save that spreadsheet, Leona,' Jo said. 'I didn't save my work once and it got me into a whole load of bother with David.'

Leona kept her eyes fixed on her screen but Jo could tell

from her expression that she'd been right in her suspicions: Leona *had* deleted that spreadsheet.

Then they heard voices; David and one of the producers were coming back down the corridor. Leona shot Jo a horrified look.

'Thanks for sorting that out for me, Leona,' Jo said, straightening up. 'It makes sense now.'

'No problem,' said Leona.

Jo went back to her desk.

Was this the right tactic? Not only had she helped Leona, but to conceal the fact from David, she'd made out that Leona had helped her. And the woman hadn't even said thank you.

Nevertheless, Jo kept it up all week. Every time she heard even the slightest sigh from Leona's corner of the office or saw her eyebrows furrowed, she'd scurry over to her side and say loudly, 'Leona, could I run something by you?' To everyone else, it must have looked as if Leona was helping Jo out rather a lot, when in fact the opposite was true.

'Clever,' said Kate when Jo told her as they walked through the park one evening. 'Letting her save face. I bet she's squirming. She must feel awkward. She gets promoted above you, then she can't do the job so you're constantly having to help her out.'

'Yeah, but how long should I keep it up for?' said Jo. 'I haven't had so much as a thank you yet. Although she has stopped gossiping about me. Or at least, I haven't *caught* her gossiping recently.'

'And she hasn't nicked any more of your ideas?'

'There haven't been any to nick.'

On Friday morning, Leona emerged from David's office looking very relieved. As she passed Jo's desk, she said, 'Don't suppose you could make me a coffee, could you? That budget meeting was hell.'

A coffee? Who did she think she was?

'Please?' she said imploringly.

'Just this once,' Jo said and headed for the kitchen.

So much for learning to stand up for herself.

She was spooning some instant into two mugs when Leona appeared by her side.

'I'll do that,' she said taking the spoon. 'This was an excuse. I wanted to speak to you without everyone watching. To say thank you. You saved my bacon this morning. You should have got Caroline's job, not me.'

'Well, it would have been nice,' Jo said, 'but you've got it now and that's that.'

'I won't keep it for long. I managed that meeting but it's only a matter of time before David realises he chose the wrong person. I'm struggling, Jo. Even with your help, I'm really struggling.'

Jo paused for a second. She could offer to stay late and talk Leona through everything – it would be far easier in an evening when everyone had gone home – but she'd intended to go along to Scrabble club this evening; she missed them all. And she couldn't avoid Razz forever. So what if he was dating someone else? She had to move on.

On the other hand, it would be hard to walk in again after her absence; practically as bad as walking in for the first time. Everyone would be sure to ask her where she'd been and what would she say?

Perhaps she'd go *next* week.

Kill the bully with kindness.

'Are you and Hannah going out tonight?' she asked.

Leona hesitated.

Perhaps, Jo thought, she's afraid I'm going to invite myself along.

'Not tonight, no,' said Leona. 'Hannah has a date.'

'Stay on after the others have gone. We can run through it all properly, sort out everything you need to know. We could even reorganise Caroline's files so they're easier to find. I've been itching to do that for ages.'

'Why? Why would you do that?'

'Because I'm a kind person.'

The words hung in the air between them. Along with the unspoken words that Jo had wanted to add but hadn't. *And you're not.*

For once, everyone left on time and, when only the two of them remained, Jo pulled her chair across the office to Leona's desk and they went through it all: the budgets, the invoices, the schedules, the forward-planning documents.

Mona stared down at them, a disapproving look on her face. Jo knew what she was thinking as she was thinking it herself. *Why are you helping her, Jo? She got the promotion that should have been yours.*

I'm killing the bully with kindness, Jo told Mona silently, though she was still trying to convince herself. Was this bonkers? Helping someone who'd been so mean to her?

Although maybe it wasn't. Something had shifted. It was subtle, hard to put her finger on, but she realised that she no longer felt afraid of Leona. Giving up an hour or two of her evening was well worth it just for that.

'Thanks,' said Leona when they'd finally gone through everything. 'Did you er... want to go for a drink? I mean, I owe you. Big time.'

'Another time,' Jo said and tried not to notice that Leona looked relieved.

It was nearly half past eight when Jo left the office. There was a train in fourteen minutes; she might make it. She had a spring in her step as she strolled along the edge of Deansgate. She knew that job should have been hers and that Leona still didn't like her much, but despite that, Jo had helped her colleague and she felt rather good about herself.

She dodged grumpy commuters, an elderly woman wheeling a small suitcase along, a group of young men on a night out. She passed the Wetherspoons where she'd had a drink with Si and ¡Tapas! ¡Tapas! where she and Neil had gone for their first – and only – date. She glanced inside.

She'd gone past before she realised what she'd seen. She took a step or two backwards, like a film rewinding, and looked again. Zoey. Leaning across a table, caressing the face of the man sitting opposite her.

And that man wasn't Razz.

It was Neil.

If she hadn't stayed late to help Leona, she'd never have known.

What were the chances?

Well, they were all fishing in the same pond, weren't they,

on those dating apps. All around the same age, looking in a similar geographical area.

But what about Razz? Had he and Zoey split up? Or had they never been together? After all, Jo had just assumed but she'd never known for sure.

And then the thought occurred to her: what if Zoey was cheating on him?

Ought she to warn him?

There'd been no messages from him for weeks now. Jo had stopped going to Scrabble club, initially because she was worried that Zoey might be there, then later because once you stopped doing something for a week or two, it was difficult to walk back in. She and Razz hadn't had any contact since... Jo wasn't quite sure when. He had stopped texting her. She'd assumed he'd been busy with Zoey and she'd been preoccupied with all the stuff going on at work and her self-esteem project.

She scrolled through her phone, looking back through her messages. The last message they'd exchanged had been from him: *No idea*, he had written. She hadn't replied. He *hadn't* stopped messaging her, she realised. She had stopped messaging him.

Leona had interrupted her, she remembered. Had dumped a load of work on her when she'd been about to text Razz back. And then Si had tipped up that same evening, and that had totally derailed her.

Poor Razz. He must think she'd ghosted him.

She would get back in touch. Offer an apology. Hold out an olive branch. Explain what had been going on with her and see if their friendship couldn't be rekindled.

But before she talked to Razz, she decided, she would

talk to Kate. Find out what was actually happening between him and Zoey. If they were together, she would warn him that Zoey was cheating on him.

And if they weren't?

Well, she'd cross that bridge when she came to it.

Jo rattled off a quick text to Kate suggesting they meet for a drink, but hesitated before sending it. It was Friday evening, prime dating night. There was no way her friend would be free.

But on the other hand, there was no harm in asking. She clicked 'send'.

The reply came back surprisingly quickly.

Yes, I'm free this evening. Matthew's visiting his mum for the weekend.

Great. Can you meet me in the pub at half nine?

Sure. See you then.

Kate was late.

Jo bought herself a Pinot Grigio, found a table, took out her phone and clicked on WordPals. She hadn't played much on the app recently; it wasn't the same somehow. She didn't feel the same excitement that she felt when playing Scrabble against living, breathing opponents.

Well, okay. So her opponents were living and breathing. They just weren't living and breathing in the same room as she was.

She'd nearly finished the game – she was losing horribly

as she couldn't focus – when Kate arrived. She typed her final word as Kate bought herself a drink.

'So, what's so urgent?'

'I saw your friend Zoey with a man.'

'And?'

'What about Razz?'

'Razz? Your Razz? What about him?'

'He isn't my Razz, Kate. He's with Zoey. I mean, I saw them flirting at the Scrabble speed-dating. And then she ticked his box and he ticked hers, so they obviously liked each other. And then, well, he's been quiet recently so I assumed they were dating.'

'Zoey? Date Razz? You've got to be kidding.'

'Why not? He's lovely. I saw them together. She was flirting. And she did tick his box, Kate. I went through all the forms.'

'Okay, here's how it was. Neither of us fancied playing Scrabble all evening but I wanted to come along to support you. We thought it would be more fun if we had a drink or two beforehand. Actually it was more like three... or four. By the time we turned up, Zoey had her beer goggles on. And she has a thing about doctors. She flirted with him a bit. She wasn't expecting that they'd be a match.'

'So she turned him down? Poor Razz.'

Much as Jo didn't want him dating Zoey, she didn't want him feeling rejected either.

'Why are you so bothered anyway?' said Kate.

'He's a good friend. I saw her with someone else and well... I didn't want him getting hurt.'

'Hmm. And the rest.' She raised an eyebrow. 'Anyway, you needn't worry about Razz. Zoey didn't turn him down. She didn't have to. He never got in touch.'

37

She'd been avoiding him for absolutely no reason, Jo thought next morning, as she drew up a schedule for the following week's shoot: a documentary following some actor from *EastEnders* as he went on a mission to rescue an endangered species of bird.

Why had she just assumed that they were together?

It had been her own insecurity talking, convincing herself that she had lost him.

And why on earth hadn't she asked Kate for clarification in the first place?

She'd been too afraid of the answer – that was why. She didn't want to ask for fear of hearing how loved up the two of them were.

Ludicrous. It seemed totally ludicrous now.

She decided to text Razz.

Fancy meeting up tonight? Drink? Or dinner even? My treat.

And then she waited.

His reply took a whole three hours and seven minutes to arrive. Jo had almost given up hope.

Sure. New pizza place in Hebbleswick. Fancy it?
8 o'clock?

Perfect.

'I wasn't sure if you'd say yes,' Jo said to Razz.

They were sitting opposite each other in Emily's latest venture, Garlic 'n' Games. Her (Not So) Little Board Game Café had been such a big success in Essendale that she'd decided to expand her little empire.

'I nearly didn't,' he said. 'We were so close, Jo, and then you...'

There was a cough. Jo looked up to see the waitress standing by their table.

'Do you need a few more minutes?' she said.

'No, thanks,' said Razz. 'I'll have a margherita, please.'

'Aren't we having starters?' said Jo.

'No starter for me. The margherita and a sparkling water.'

The waitress looked at her.

'Pepperoni please, and a glass of Pinot Grigio.' Jo glanced down at the menu again. 'And I fancy some dough balls.'

'As a starter or with the mains?' the waitress asked.

'With the mains, please.'

When the waitress had gone, Razz looked round at the huge board games pictures on the walls.

Jo followed his gaze over to the shelves, stacked high with games. 'No Scrabble,' she said. 'I checked whilst I was waiting for you. A board game café – well, pizzeria – with no Scrabble.'

'I can't imagine why anyone would play a board game that *isn't* Scrabble.' There was a pause, then he said, 'What happened, Jo? We became friends. We organised this massive event together and it was an enormous success and then wham! You disappear.'

Jo was about to say that *he'd* been the one who'd disappeared but the waitress was back again, setting the drinks down in front of them.

Razz murmured, 'Thank you,' then took a sip of his water. 'That first Scrabble club after the festival... well, it was such a shame you didn't turn up. I'd asked Annie to bake a special cake for you as a kind of thank you. For all your hard work. And to celebrate how well the festival had gone.'

'A cake?'

'Yeah, it was fantastic. Like a showstopper from *The Great British Bake Off*. With a little figurine of you on top.'

It sounded amazing, thought Jo. When was the last time anyone had baked a cake, especially for her? Not since the last time she'd spent a birthday with her parents, so long ago now that Jo couldn't even remember when it was.

'I'm gutted I missed that,' she said. 'What happened to the cake?'

'Well, obviously we ate it. It was delicious.'

'And the little figure of me?'

'Cosmic wanted to eat that too but we saved it for you.' He reached into his pocket and pulled out a little parcel, wrapped in tissue paper. 'It might be a bit squashed. With hindsight, my trouser pocket probably wasn't the best place to put it. Hope it hasn't melted.'

Jo unwrapped the tissue, revealing a little model of herself, made entirely out of sugar paste icing, complete with red hair, a T-shirt and a pair of jeans and carrying a Scrabble box.

'That's so lovely,' she said. 'Thank you.'

'Well, it was my idea but Annie did the hard work, so you should probably thank her. Oh yeah, and there's this.' He handed over an envelope. It was white, with poppies in one corner, and someone had written *Joanne Knox* on it. Si was the only person who'd call her Joanne and not Jo, but she didn't recognise the handwriting.

She was curious, desperately curious, but decided it could wait. Getting her friendship with Razz back on course was the most important thing this evening. She slipped the letter into her Filofax, and the figurine into her bag.

'So, what happened, Jo? You disappeared after the festival without saying goodbye and...'

'I disappeared? You disappeared. I had to help Mr Morgan with something and when I came out of his office, you'd gone.'

'You were in his office?'

'Yeah.'

'Oh.' Razz bit his lip. 'The one place I *didn't* look.'

'And then you didn't get in touch,' said Jo.

'I was mad busy. Catching up on all the paperwork I'd fallen behind with because of the festival. And...' He hesitated for a moment. 'But then you didn't get in touch either.'

'I thought *you'd* left without saying goodbye.' Jo paused too, wondering whether to be completely truthful with him. A month ago, she wouldn't have had the courage. But now – well, she definitely felt more able to speak her mind these days. 'To be honest, I thought you'd rushed off to be with Zoey.'

He spluttered, choking on his water and showering the table with little drops. 'Zoey?'

'Kate's friend. The gorgeous one. She came to Scrabble

speed-dating. Come on, Razz. You know Zoey. I saw you flirting with her at the speed-dating…'

'I wasn't flirting. I was being friendly.'

'And then you ticked her box. And she was the only one you ticked. You didn't tick me.'

'Ah,' he said. 'I forgot you'd see the forms.'

He took another sip of his water.

'Look, Jo. She was sweet. I enjoyed talking to her. And you're Kate's friend and she's Kate's friend. I wasn't going to tick her, but when she stood up, she looked down at my sheet and it was blank and I felt obliged to. I was being nice. I don't like disappointing people. I didn't expect her to tick me too, for us to be a match.'

'But you didn't tick me?'

'I thought the whole point of speed-dating was to get contact details for people you wanted to see again. I already have your phone number, remember?'

'Did you ever hear from Zoey?'

'No, I didn't contact her. She didn't contact me. But even if I *had* been dating her, what difference would that make to you and me? We're supposed to be friends.'

Friends.

He was clearly putting her in the friend zone.

'I felt like you were ignoring me. Blanking me. It hurt, Jo.'

'I wasn't ignoring you. Things were… well, I went through a difficult patch. In any case, you blanked me once. After our first date. I thought it had gone well, but then nothing. Nada. Zilch.'

Zilch, she thought. Good word: 19 points.

A cough again. Jo moved her hands from the table and the waitress placed their pizzas down.

'Any black pepper?' she said.

They both shook their heads.

As soon as she left, Razz said, 'I didn't think you'd *want* to hear from me again.'

'Why ever not? I had a great time. I loved going down Gaping Gill. It was so thoughtful of you to arrange that.'

'Yeah, when I wimped out... At one point, I thought I was going to vomit in front of you. Just at the *thought* of going down there.'

'You were a little pale.'

'And with you loving adventurous activities – you must have thought I was a right wuss.'

'I *said* I loved adventurous activities but... well, I don't. It was Kate's idea. She said my profile sounded boring and I needed to pep it up a bit.'

'So basically, you lied?'

Jo nodded. 'Lied is a bit strong. I tried to keep it vague. Adventurous activities could mean anything. And art – well, who doesn't like looking at waterlilies and sunflowers?'

'You're not into art either?'

'Er... no. Not really. My only hobbies are playing Scrabble and watching *ER*. Sad, I know.'

'*ER?*'

'Yeah, it's a medical drama.'

'I know what it is, Jo.'

He took another sip of his water.

'So I took you to Gaping Gill, and you pretended that you loved it...'

Jo opened her mouth to say that she hadn't been pretending, she *had* loved it, but he was speaking so quickly that she couldn't get a word in.

'…and the whole time, I felt like an idiot because I was too scared to do it. I planned that afternoon especially for you because I liked your profile.'

'I liked yours too,' she said.

'What did you like about it?'

Damn. It was ages ago, and she hadn't paid that much attention to his profile. Only his name, and the number of points that it scored. She might as well come clean.

'Well, here's the thing, Razz,' she said. 'You'll love this, being a Scrabble fanatic. I kept choosing the wrong men, so I invented this little rule: I'd only date men whose names would score highly in Scrabble. It was a way of leaving it up to fate to decide, I suppose. But I kept getting guys called Neil and Dan. And then you came along.'

'You only agreed to a date because my name was Razz?'

'Actually, you said your name was…'

'So if I'd been called… Ron or… Del, you wouldn't have dated me.'

'Well, no but…'

She'd been about to say that she wouldn't date someone called Ron because could you imagine screaming Ron in a moment of passion? And Del sounded like something from an '80s sitcom. '90s medical dramas were one thing, but '80s sitcoms? In her head, this all sounded funny, but judging by Razz's face, this wasn't the moment to be cracking jokes.

'Razz, I…'

'You went out with me because of my name. I went out with you because I liked you, and when I met you, I liked you even more. I wanted to make a good impression and I was gutted, absolutely gutted, when I couldn't manage to go down that hole. And then afterwards, I was convinced

I'd blown it with you. I was so embarrassed, Jo. No, more than that. I was ashamed. And that whole time, you were pretending. Putting on an act. Saying you liked adventurous activities when you didn't. Deciding whether you liked me not because of my personality but by whether my name scored highly on a Scrabble board. Is dating some silly game to you, Jo? Because it isn't for me. I was hoping to find someone I could share my life with.'

She'd never heard Razz make such a long speech, let alone such a passionate one. So much to take in. He'd liked her. Had wanted to make a good impression. Thought he'd blown it. She didn't know quite where to begin. 'But you said your name was...'

Her voice trailed off as Razz stood up and put two twenty-pound notes on the table.

Oh. He was leaving. About to make a dramatic exit unless she said something to stop him.

Only words failed her. Ironic for someone who loved words so much that when she needed them most, they didn't come.

So Razz made his dramatic exit. Although it wasn't actually that dramatic. He didn't shout and throw his napkin on the table with an angry flourish, before strutting out, slamming the door behind him.

Not Razz. He'd practically tiptoed out: he pushed his chair neatly under the table, walked quietly towards the door, and held it open for an elderly couple who were coming in, before going out himself.

Gone. She thought. She had lost him. Again.

38

Jo sat by herself in the pizzeria for what was probably a couple of minutes, but it seemed like an age. She felt as if every pair of eyes were on her but when she glanced round, the other diners were all eating, chatting or playing board games and no-one appeared in the least bit bothered by Razz's departure. She half-heartedly munched on a dough ball, but, even though nobody was paying her even the slightest bit of attention, she felt self-conscious sitting there on her own.

'Is your friend coming back?' said the waitress.

'Er, no. I don't think so. 'Fraid I've blown it with him. Can I have the bill please?'

'Sure, I'll fetch it.'

She stood up and put on her coat. She barely glanced at the bill when it arrived; the money Razz had left more than covered it, so she handed over the notes and mumbled, 'Keep the change.'

She was halfway to the door when she thought about the pizzas. Heart-broken or not, she'd need to eat. It was a shame to leave two perfectly good pizzas to be thrown into the bin, along with eleven dough balls. Especially when her fridge was full of lentil bolognaise and overnight oats thanks to a recent attempt at following Kate's nutritional advice. And let's face it, when you needed comfort food, flax seeds and beluga beans didn't cut it, whereas pizza...

She walked back to the waitress who was beginning to clear their table.

'On second thoughts, could you box those please?' Jo said. 'Seems a pity to waste them.'

'Sure.'

The waitress returned with three boxes, two square flat ones containing the pizzas, and a smaller one with the dough balls.

By the time Jo reached Hazel Lane, she'd lost her appetite. The house seemed even emptier than usual. She turned on the TV and flicked through the channels, settling on a film that had only just started. A rom-com. But she found her mind drifting off, replaying the evening's events. Wondering if she couldn't have handled things better, phrased things differently. Might there have been another outcome? Or were she and Razz destined not to be together? Was she doomed to stay single?

She turned off the TV. That left only two activities to help pass her Saturday evening. Eating. And WordPals.

She went to the fridge. She wasn't particularly hungry – not pizza hungry – but decided to make a stab at the cold dough balls. Returning to the sofa with the box – no point creating washing up when you were eating alone – she picked up her phone and opened WordPals.

She was about to start a solo game against the app itself, when she realised she had a game request from Dazzle, a player she hadn't seen before. She clicked accept.

Five minutes and three dough balls later, he made his

first move. It was an ordinary game. She had a reasonable selection of vowels and consonants, the Q but sadly no U. The scores were pretty even and it was hard to tell who would win. Or it was until Dazzle played ZAX.

She'd only ever seen one person play that word, and that person was Razz. Of course, it could have been a coincidence. The word mightn't be in everyday parlance – unless you were a roofer – but keen Scrabble enthusiasts might know it, since it appeared on several websites listing high-scoring words.

But even so… this was *too much* of a coincidence. Razz. Razzle dazzle. Could Dazzle be Razz?

He had said he was on the app, although he only used it occasionally. Might he be on it now, barely two hours since she'd since him disappearing through the doors of Garlic 'n' Games and thought he was out of her life forever? He would know it was her – she'd put her actual photo on the app – but she still wasn't sure if it was him as he'd used an avatar.

If it *was* him, then perhaps he didn't want to sever *all* contact. That was a good sign, wasn't it?

The game ended. He won by over twenty points. Jo sent him a message via the app –

Thanks for the game

– but a minute later, the green dot disappeared from under his avatar. Dazzle was offline.

Jo hardly slept that night.

How could she get him to talk to her again, if he wouldn't even reply through WordPals?

Assuming Dazzle really was Razz.

She tossed and turned, wondering what her best course of action should be. Another apology? Turn up at the Scrabble club and hope for the best? Send flowers to the surgery? Not that last one. He'd be mortified.

Next morning, she got up, went into the kitchen and put the kettle on. She made herself a mug of instant coffee, opened the fridge door to get the milk and saw the pizza boxes sitting there. And that was when it struck her.

In one of those first messages that they'd exchanged on Buzzz, those messages which had cheered her up so much after that terrible week at work, he had said that his favourite breakfast was cold, leftover pizza.

She messaged Dazzle through the WordPals app:

Have you had breakfast yet? Because there's a cold margherita here with your name on it.

Ten minutes later, when he still hadn't replied, she tried again.

I know it's your favourite!

Still no reply. She poured the milk in her coffee and waited, praying she hadn't sent a weird message about cold pizza to a random stranger.

But two minutes later, the doorbell rang. Jo sprung up from the sofa, where she'd been idly flicking through pictures on her phone. Her heart began to pound. It had to be Razz, didn't it? She took a deep breath, wished she had a mirror in the lounge so she could check her appearance, but it was too late; he was here now.

She had thought their first date was awkward – the beginning of it, at least – but opening the door to Razz that day was awkwardness on a whole other scale.

'Hi,' she said. Her mouth had gone dry.

'Hi.'

Silence. Awkward, obviously.

'Do you want to come in?' she said, at the very same moment as he said, 'I'm here for the pizza.'

She stepped aside as he came into the hall, pushing a brown paper bag into her hands. She gave a slight shudder although she wasn't cold.

He followed her into the lounge. She was conscious of the scruffy furniture and how bare it all looked.

They stood facing each other. Jo clasped the paper bag in one hand but wasn't sure what to do with the other. Suddenly her limbs felt like they didn't belong to her. She shifted her weight uneasily from one foot to the other. 'Tea or coffee?'

'Coffee, please.'

'Have a seat.' She gestured at the stained sofa; she still hadn't got round to buying that throw. 'Would you like your pizza heated up?'

'Now look,' he said sternly, 'I was offered cold pizza. My favourite breakfast.'

She scrutinised his face, trying to work out if his stern tone was in earnest or if he was winding her up, but she couldn't tell.

'And since I'm getting my favourite breakfast,' he

continued, 'I thought I'd better bring you yours. Look in the bag.'

She'd forgotten she was still holding the brown paper bag. It felt warm in her hands. She peeped inside. Croissants and pain au chocolat. He must have called in at the bakery on his way here. Fancy him remembering; those first messages they'd exchanged – well, they'd been ages ago. The cold pizza had stuck in her mind, she supposed, so the croissants must have stuck in his.

He'd brought her croissants.

No, she told herself. *Don't read too much into that. Friends often bring gifts when they visit each other. That's all it is. Don't get your hopes up.*

'How did you guess I was Dazzle?' he said.

'When you played zax.'

'So, I gave my secret away for a measly 19 points?'

'And the game.' She smiled. Her heart rate was finally beginning to return to normal. 'It won you the game.'

'Not much of a Cyrano de Bergerac, am I?'

'Nope. Although you do have…'

'Yeah, I know. A big conk.'

'I like your nose. It's rather Roman. Distinguished.'

Razz digested this for a moment before he said, 'Look, I'm sorry I walked out. I was annoyed about the adventurous activities thing, but I know how persuasive Kate can be. She made me delete Scrabble from *my* Buzzz profile.'

'Kate did?'

'Yeah. Emily – you know, my colleague Ludek's other half – suggested that Kate took a look at it for me. Reckoned she was some kind of dating guru.'

'She is.'

He harrumphed. 'Maybe.'

So Razz had originally written Scrabble on his dating profile? Imagine if Kate had never made him remove it, Jo thought. Imagine if Kate had never interfered with *her* profile. Things might have worked out so differently. They might have played Scrabble on their first date and lived happily ever after.

'But then also,' he said, 'I was in a bad mood anyway that evening. I'm sorry – I shouldn't have taken it out on you. But I'd had some terrible news.'

'Did someone die?'

'I'm a doctor. I'm used to people dying. It's worse than that.'

'Worse? What's worse than death?'

'Well, not really, but we're losing the church hall,' he said. 'This Friday's Scrabble club will be our final session. And I don't know how I'm going to tell everyone.'

'Let's eat,' she said, 'then we'll think of a solution. Another venue. Pepperoni or margherita? Plate or box?'

'Margherita, please. In the box.'

Later, when he'd finished over half of the pizza and Jo had eaten a croissant and one and a half pains au chocolat – or should that be pain au chocolats? She would never win at French Scrabble – she said, 'So why are we losing the hall?'

'The vicar has decided to rip all the pews out of the church and convert it into a multi-purpose space. He's selling off the hall for development. You know, I wouldn't mind quite so much if it was for affordable housing. I saw three patients yesterday – three in one day – who were in temporary accommodation. But it isn't. They're applying for planning permission to build two executive homes.'

'That's terrible,' she said, looking around her lounge. Okay, so this house was an underdwelling – and, like all underdwellings seemed to be, it was a bit damp – and the sofa was stained, but the view was amazing and she knew she was lucky to have it. 'How about we move into the new space in the church itself?'

'He's putting the rent up too. To cover the cost of the work.'

'Seems a bit mean. He'll be rolling in it once they've sold the hall off. Why does he need to put the rent up?'

'The church needs a new roof. That's why he decided to sell the hall in the first place. If we hold the Scrabble club in the new multi-purpose space in the church, we'd have to start charging for entry. I can't keep funding it – not at those prices. But I don't want to charge. I don't want money ever to be an obstacle to people attending.'

'We'll find a new venue,' Jo said.

'Like where? Where could we accommodate thirty people...'

'Thirty?'

'Your festival worked. We're getting more and more people each week. Where in Hebbleswick could we find a room that will fit thirty people, maybe more, with tables big enough for Scrabble boards at a reasonable cost?' he said. 'Or even better, free.'

'How about we go to a pub? Loads of them have free function rooms.'

'None of them will want us on a Friday evening. And

I don't want people feeling obliged to buy drinks. Not everyone can afford it.'

'If I find you a venue, will you forgive me for the whole dating app debacle?'

'I suppose I might,' he said and Jo could tell from the warmth in his voice that he'd forgive her anyway, probably already had. 'You'll need to find one quickly. If we have to cancel, even for a week or two, I fear the group will lose its momentum. People won't come back.'

'Is the hall already sold?'

'I don't think so.'

'I'll persuade the vicar to give us a couple more weeks in the hall, at least until it's sold, and that'll buy me time to find us somewhere else to go.'

'There *is* nowhere else.'

'What about the school? It's central. Might even be free. Mr Morgan liked the festival in the end.'

'I thought of that already,' said Razz. 'He said no. He liked the idea but said a member of school staff would have to hang around then lock up afterwards. He doesn't want to – especially not on a Friday – and says the teachers won't either.'

'How about Mr Timms?'

'The caretaker? He does salsa dancing on a Friday evening.'

'We should introduce him to Linda. How about we run the club on another evening?'

'He does salsa dancing every evening.'

'Salsa? Every evening? Are we talking about the same guy?'

Jo couldn't imagine Mr Timms doing his finest *Strictly* impression.

'There'll be a solution, Razz,' she said. 'There always is. And when I find it, you'll forgive me and we can put that dating profile stuff behind us and go back to being friends.'

He paused. 'Sure. We can be friends.'

She was relieved but also perplexed. Because she couldn't fathom the look that he gave her when he said that they could be friends.

39

'You idiot,' said Gemma when Jo phoned her next day. 'I can't believe you told him you wanted to be friends.'

'I didn't say *just* friends.'

'No, but that's what he'll assume. Just friends. And nothing more. You should have told him how you felt.'

'But Kate says…'

'Kate. Kate. Kate. I am sick of hearing about what Kate says.'

'Hang on,' Jo said, putting her hand over the phone for a minute. She could hear footsteps outside. And David's voice getting closer. And then getting further away again. 'It's okay,' she said. 'My boss was going past but he's gone now.'

'Are you in the stationery cupboard again?'

'I might be. The thing is, Gemma, Kate knows a lot about dating.'

'You should take my advice for a change. I've known you longer.'

'But you've never even been on a date.'

'I did once. Dan took me to Burger King.'

'Doesn't count,' Jo said. 'You were only fifteen.'

'Anyway, what's the point of dating?'

'Hang on...'

She could hear Leona walking past now, talking to someone.

'Okay, go on,' she said as the voice receded into the distance.

'What do you mean, what's the point?'

'I mean, what's the point? Why do you go on dates?'

'Because I want to meet the right person and get into a relationship.'

'What you need,' said Gemma, 'is someone who's done that successfully themselves. If you knew someone like that, someone who was married to the love of her life, wouldn't that be the kind of person whose advice you should seek?'

'I guess so.'

'I am that person, Jo. I'm the person who is happily married. In other words, I'm the one who understands relationships, not Kate. Isn't time you listened to me?'

'I suppose.'

'Lesson number one. Men are human beings. They feel lonely sometimes. They get scared. If you read those books of Kate's, you'd think they were a different species...'

'...or even from another planet.'

'Exactly. And they're not, Jo. I mean some of them – the Tarquins of this world – might behave in a way that you or I would never dream of behaving. But you don't want a guy like that. You want a Razz. Ask him for a drink after the next Scrabble club and tell him how you feel.'

'I'll think about it,' Jo said, 'but right now, I've got to go. There's only so much time I can conceivably pretend to be looking for Post-it notes.'

When she got back to her desk, David was standing in

the open-plan office talking loudly on his mobile. 'Caroline, there's no need to worry. Everything's absolutely fine here…'

He paused as Caroline spoke. Jo couldn't hear what she was saying.

'She's taken to it like a duck to water,' he said. 'Haven't you, Leona?'

He looked over at Leona, who gave him a thumbs up.

'Caroline, at this rate, we won't be wanting you back at all!' said David. He laughed, but it seemed like an afterthought. An attempt to reassure her that she *would* be welcome back and he wasn't one of those bosses who discriminated against new mothers.

Jo glanced over at Leona, who smiled. She actually smiled.

David returned to his office, closing the door behind him, and Jo turned her attention to her computer; it was high time she got on with some actual work. It was then that she noticed it: the shiny, gold wrapper of something poking out from under one of her notebooks. She lifted the notebook to reveal a family-sized bar of Galaxy. There was a Post-it note stuck on it that simply read, *Thank you.* She looked back over at Leona but her colleague now had her gaze firmly fixed on her screen.

On Friday evening, Jo decided she would go the Scrabble club. After all, it might be the last one ever if she couldn't find an alternative place for them all to meet or persuade the vicar to let them stay on in the church hall until it was sold; she had an appointment to see him the following day. She made an effort with her appearance: her best jeans, her clingiest top, a hint of mascara and she even tried to blow-dry her hair so that it was straight.

When she walked into the church hall, she couldn't believe her eyes. The place was full. Full!

'It's been really busy recently,' said Razz. He didn't seem to have noticed the change in her appearance. Perhaps it was too subtle.

'Such a shame about...'

'Don't breathe a word,' he said. 'I haven't told them yet.'

'But tonight's the last night, isn't it? Unless I can persuade the vicar tomorrow. And that's a big if. You'll have to warn them at least.'

'Yes, so I don't want to spoil it. I'm not going to tell them till the end.'

It was only half past six. Apparently, Scrabble club started at half past five these days. Until seven o'clock was 'family time'. Everyone was welcome, but the Junior Scrabble boards were out along with the adult boards.

Jo recognised several familiar faces from the school. Alfie was there, of course, along with his pushy mother. He was playing with three other children, all younger than him, and appeared to be helping them rather than trying to win the game himself.

Mr Morgan, the head teacher, was there too. He came over as soon as he saw her.

'Great, isn't it?' he said.

'Yes, it's wonderful.'

'It's had quite an impact at school too. The children are mad for Scrabble. We have two lunchtime clubs and an after-school group. And I shouldn't tell you this...' he lowered his voice '…but Mrs Hamilton-Jones has been a much less frequent visitor to my office lately.'

'And yet you can't accommodate the club on a Friday?'

'Jo, I told you…' began Razz.

'As I explained to Razz,' said Mr Morgan, 'a member of staff would need to stay. Partly to lock up afterwards and partly for insurance reasons. And no-one wants to give up their Friday evening.'

'Did someone mention insurance?' said Malcolm from across the hall. He began to head towards Mr Morgan, almost tripping over a small, blonde-haired girl who jumped up suddenly from the table where she'd been playing with Alfie and ran towards Mr Morgan, shouting, 'Daddy! Daddy! I won!' She flung her arms round his legs. Jo had never realised he had children of his own.

'Best get this one home,' he said, ruffling his daughter's hair. 'Come on, sugarplum.'

As the parents and children left, and the Junior Scrabble games were packed away into their boxes, more people began to arrive. The usual crowd – Cosmic, Sylvia and Florence were the first – plus some new faces Jo didn't recognise.

'It's great that it's so popular,' Jo said to Razz. 'It's exactly what you wanted. People from all walks of the community, all different ages, gathering together, playing a few games and getting to know each other. Becoming… what was that phrase you used?'

'Socially embedded,' he said.

'Exactly. Becoming socially embedded. Personally, I feel very socially embedded right now.'

She tried to say that in a flirty way, a tiny hint of emphasis on the 'bed' of 'embedded.' Hoped it made him think that he might want to be embedded with her, but he seemed oblivious. He glanced round the room, his shoulders hunched slightly, an air of defeat about him.

'Pointless though, isn't it?' he said. 'If we can't find somewhere new, it will all have been for nothing.'

Later, when most of the games were drawing to a close, Razz stood up and tapped his coffee mug with his teaspoon.

He cleared his throat.

'If I could er… have everyone's attention please,' he said. 'I have an announcement to make.'

Everyone put down their letter tiles and swivelled round in their chairs to face him.

Then Mr B stood up.

'Yeah, me too,' he said. 'But after you, Doc.'

'No, I insist,' said Razz. 'You first, Stan.'

He must be dreading telling them, Jo thought. He was putting it off for as long as he could.

'As you all know,' said Mr B, sweeping his eyes across everyone in the room like a practised orator, 'by some miraculous fluke and several exceedingly fortuitous selections of letters, I managed to find myself the winner of the inaugural Hebbleswick Scrabble Festival tournament…'

Inaugural? thought Jo. Why did people keep assuming there was going to be another one?

'…and the lucky recipient of a spa weekend at a rather swish establishment in North Yorkshire. A spa weekend for two.'

A collective 'ooh' ran round the room and Cosmic Ray shouted, 'Can I come?'

Stan smiled at him. 'Much as I would love to avail myself of your offer, Ray, I have my sights – or rather my heart – set upon a different companion for the weekend.'

Jo looked around the room. Linda was running her fingers through her hair, sitting up straight and sticking her chest out even more than usual.

'Florence,' Mr B said. 'Florence, I relish arguing with you over made-up words, proper nouns and whether aperitif is an admissible word in an English game of Scrabble. Florence, you have that certain *je ne sais quoi* that I adore...' he said adore with a French accent '...and I'd be delighted if you would accompany me to North Yorkshire for a weekend of sparring and spa-ing. I'll bring the Scrabble.'

Jo half expected him to go down on one knee at Florence's feet. The room fell silent now, awaiting her answer. Jo wasn't sure about everyone else, but she for one was holding her breath.

'As long as it's separate rooms,' said Florence.

'I can arrange that,' said Mr B.

'In that case, yes, I'd love to come. Thank you, Stanisław.'

Mr B clearly besotted with Florence – how had she not realised this before? – and far too old for Jo, but she still couldn't help herself from doing a quick calculation and working out that Stanisław was 12 points. At least it was if you counted the Polish ł as one point like the English letter l.

As Mr B finished his little speech, saying how delighted he was that Florence had accepted, a cheer went round the room. Cosmic Ray, Jo noticed, didn't join in. It seemed his heart really had been set on that spa weekend in North Yorkshire.

'Stan, you might want to get insurance for your trip,' said Malcolm when the room was quiet again.

'Thanks, Malcolm. I'll bear that in mind,' said Mr B.

'Can't believe she's asked for separate rooms,' whispered Razz to Jo. 'She's fancied him for ages.'

'Playing hard to get,' Jo said. 'Kate says it's the way to a man's heart.'

'What utter bollocks! Hope you don't buy into all that nonsense.'

'Course not. But Kate does. She's even got books about it.'

He harrumphed. 'No wonder dating is so hard, if there's women out there who actually believe all that stuff.'

Jo wondered if he wanted to add, *And women who lie on their profiles.*

But the room had fallen silent again and everyone was looking expectantly at Razz.

'Your announcement,' Jo said.

He grimaced at her.

'Sorry, everyone,' he said. 'Must be a sign of old age, but I've completely forgotten what I was about to say.'

When everyone else had left and Razz and Jo were doing a last check of the room, making sure there were no escapee letter tiles lurking under radiators, Jo said, 'Why didn't you tell them?'

'I didn't want to spoil the mood,' he said. 'I reckon everyone – except perhaps Linda and Cosmic Ray – was delighted by Stan and Florence going away together. It would have been a shame to ruin the moment.'

'But they might turn up next week to find the hall locked.'

'I'm counting on you, Jo. To persuade the vicar to let us stay until the hall is actually sold and to line up a new venue ready for when it does.'

40

'Couldn't we stay,' Jo said to Reverend Stone, 'until it's demolished? Or at least until it's sold?'

He shook his head. 'The estate agent says it would be better if all the groups who use the hall relocate as soon as possible. He thinks if it's still being used, it might put potential buyers off.'

'I don't see why,' Jo said. 'What would we do? Hold a Scrabble sit-in and refuse to let the bulldozers in?'

'No, no, no,' he said. 'Of course not.' He smiled but it was a fake smile. The kind of smile Jo could imagine him fixing to his face when a child screamed its head off during his sermon, when he was marrying a bride with a visible bump or when a family chose a particularly loud rock track to play at a funeral, claiming it was the deceased's favourite.

'Why? What harm could it do?'

'I don't know,' he said. 'I'm no expert in these matters. Something to do with vacant possession or the like.'

There was a tap at the door and a woman in an apron poked her head round.

'More tea, Vicar?' she said.

Jo couldn't believe someone had actually said that phrase in real life but she was too wound up to enjoy the moment.

'No, thank you, Mrs Green,' he said. 'Joanne was just leaving.'

She had no intention of leaving. Not yet, anyway. She sat back in the chair and crossed her legs. She was staying put.

'Actually, I'd love another cup,' she said defiantly. 'And it's Jo.'

Mrs Green looked nervously from Jo to the vicar. He rolled his eyes and nodded. She disappeared.

'Isn't vacant possession more a residential property issue?' Jo said hopefully; she hadn't a clue what she was talking about. 'No-one is going to be *living* in the church hall. We'd play our games and then disappear like we always do.'

'You're going to have to find somewhere else anyway,' he said. 'This week. In two weeks. In six weeks. What does it matter?'

'The longer we have, the more chance we have of finding somewhere suitable. If you kick us out and we haven't found anywhere, we'd have to cancel our meetings for a few weeks.'

'I see,' he said, but she knew that he didn't.

'Our club is about community. I'd go as far as to say it's a lifeline for some of our members. People who are lonely. Isolated. Struggling with mental health or money problems. Some of them go home on a Friday evening after Scrabble and they don't talk to another soul until Monday morning. Can you imagine how hard that is? What that's like?'

'They could come to church,' he said.

'That's true, they could. But not everyone believes in God, do they? Church isn't for everyone.'

'We welcome everyone,' he said, but looking at his tight-lipped face, Jo found that difficult to believe.

'Please, give us a few weeks,' she said. 'I promise we'll leave the place tidy. As we always do. You'd never even know we'd been in there. And we won't make any fuss when they want to start demolishing. I can sign something if you like? A legal agreement? It'd mean the world to us. Please. Let us stay.'

He looked dubious. He put his hands together as if he were going to pray and for a second, she thought he might ask her to get down on her knees. But he didn't. He strummed his fingers against each other and looked pointedly at the door.

That second cup of tea had never materialised, Jo realised.

'Well,' he said, folding his arms. 'I suppose I could talk to Tarquin. See what he thinks.'

'Tarquin?' she said.

'The estate agent.'

Tarquin. There couldn't be two, could there? Not with an unusual – and, let's not forget, high-scoring – name like that. He'd said he worked in property. She'd assumed a developer or something, but could he be an estate agent?

And then she remembered what he'd said on their first date: when she'd mentioned that there was a shortage of housing in Hebbleswick, he'd said something about checking it out, seeing if there were any opportunities. Was that what he'd done? Had a scout round the little town, come across the church hall and persuaded the vicar to sell? In other words, was it her fault? She felt sure that it was and even more determined that she would be the one to fix things.

★

It didn't take her long to track him down. A quick search on Rightmove and she found the sales details of the hall and discovered where he worked: one of the larger estate agents in Huddersfield, which dealt with commercial as well as residential property.

Jo stood outside the window, peering at him through the glass between the sales blurb of a three-bedroomed terrace with a view over Greenhead Park and a high-tech apartment near the Royal Infirmary.

The sight of him made her shudder. Her hands were shaking and her legs felt weak underneath her. This was the man who'd tried to force himself on her. Was she mad to be confronting him for the sake of a few more weeks in the church hall?

But it was about more than that. She'd been strangely pleased when she'd discovered the estate agent was the same man she'd dated a few months ago; this was a good excuse to seek him out and to face up to him. This wasn't only about having a venue for the Scrabble club; it was about putting the past behind her. About drawing a line under things and acknowledging that never again would she allow a man like him to come anywhere near her. Sure, he wasn't a Si – well, he might be, but she couldn't know that as she'd only met him three times – but he was definitely a player. And he hadn't shown any respect for her or her feelings.

Later, she wasn't sure what made her record the conversation. It was a spur-of-the-moment decision. She didn't trust him, not one little bit. He might well say yes to her face, then renege on it afterwards. She pulled her phone out of her pocket, clicked on the voice recorder app and pressed the red button, before secreting it into her open handbag, balanced on top of her beloved Filofax.

He didn't look up as she opened the door. His eyes were fixed on his screen, some frantic mouse action going on as he scrolled.

'Hello, how can I help you?' said the woman at the desk next to his. She wore a neat navy shift dress and far too much make-up.

Jo's mouth felt dry. 'I've come to see Tarquin.'

At the sound of her voice, he glanced up and mumbled something to his colleague. It sounded very much like, 'Here we go.'

'Darling,' he said, getting up and air-kissing her on both cheeks. 'Take a seat. However did you track me down?'

'Er, your name's Tarquin,' Jo said. 'It's not exactly common.'

'Yes, it means…'

'Ruler. I know.'

She sat down opposite him, putting her bag on his desk, and looked him squarely in the eyes. She'd thought his brown eyes were beautiful once, but now she preferred blue eyes. You'd think that blue eyes would be cold and brown eyes warm, but somehow Razz's eyes managed to be warm and Tarquin's appeared cold. Maybe it was less to do with the eyes themselves, and more with the face surrounding them. The way a genuine smile caused wrinkles to form at their corners. The way they looked directly at you, hiding nothing, rather than shifting about.

He was wearing the same suit he'd worn on their first date. How easily impressed she'd been. His appearance was immaculate. Tanned skin. Fake tan, presumably. Every hair gelled into its perfect position. Not a hair out of place. It struck her suddenly that he was, like Si, a little bit *too* perfect. How had she not spotted that similarity from the start?

'Tarquin,' she said, wondering how she had ever fancied him.

He paused.

'It's Jo,' she said, forcing herself to smile.

'Jo, we don't do rentals, I'm afraid. Only sales.'

'When you said you worked in property, I didn't realise you were an estate agent.'

'Yes, I'm the manager here.'

'*Acting* manager,' Jo heard his colleague mumble under her breath.

'How can I help you?' said Tarquin. 'I'm afraid we've not got much at the lower end of the market. There's a little studio flat near the centre of town, but it's leasehold with less than fifty years to go.'

'I'm not looking to buy anywhere.'

He nodded. 'I thought as much. Jo, we had fun. I can understand you wanting to rekindle things, but I've moved on now. It isn't appropriate to come to my place of work and...'

'Sorry, can I stop you there? I'm not here to rekindle things.'

Jo glanced over at the woman in the navy dress. Funny how you could tell when someone is listening to a conversation even when they were pretending not to.

Tarquin's eyes followed her gaze.

'Ginny, could you have a look through the files in the back office, please?' he said. 'Dig out the details of that farm near Golcar?'

'Sure,' she said.

When she'd gone, he said, 'Shit, Jo. It isn't mine.'

'What isn't?'

'The er... I mean, we took precautions. Didn't we?'

Jo was baffled for a few seconds. Then she realised.

'I'm not pregnant. We didn't actually...'

'We didn't?'

'No.'

'Oh, shame.'

It wasn't, Jo thought. But never mind.

'Tarquin, I wanted to talk to you about that church hall you've got on the market. The one in Hebbleswick. With planning permission for two executive homes.'

'Moving into property development now, are you?'

'No, of course not. That church hall is where we hold our Scrabble club.'

He snorted. 'Scrabble club?' He laughed, then called through to his colleague in the back room, 'Ginny, cancel the marketing on that church hall that's up for development. Jo holds a Scrabble club there.'

He laughed again.

'It's not funny,' Jo said. 'Loads of people come to those evenings. Families. Older people. People who are lonely.'

'Hmm. Wouldn't be my scene.'

'A few more weeks. That's all I'm asking. I know we can't stay forever. I know it's going to be demolished. But if we had a bit longer, we'd have more chance of finding a suitable alternative without having to cancel any of our meetups. Please, Tarquin.'

He looked thoughtful for a moment, then Ginny appeared and put a file down in front of him.

He didn't thank her, Jo noticed. Typical.

'I'm popping out for a few minutes,' she said.

He nodded and watched her go, then his eyes turned back to Jo.

'What's it worth to you?' he said. 'I mean, would you sleep with me if I agreed?'

'I thought you'd moved on,' she said.

'I have. I'm seeing a couple of women. But I could always use a – what's the phrase? A friend with benefits? A fu—'

'Let me get this straight. If I agree to no-strings, casual sex with you, you'll arrange for the Scrabble club to continue in the church hall on Friday evenings?'

'Yes, and I'll sort that with the vicar,' he said, 'but only until I find a buyer. Do we have an agreement?'

41

Razz's head was throbbing. He rubbed at his temples. He wasn't usually prone to headaches but this one was a belter.

It had been a tough day. A stomach bug was doing the rounds in Hebbleswick and Ludek – the other GP – had called in sick so Razz had had to see quite a few extra patients. In theory, he could fit everyone in *and* finish on time, if he allocated four minutes to each patient, but Razz liked to give people a little bit longer than that. The trouble was that some people came in to the surgery and said that one thing was wrong with them, but often it was something else entirely that they were worried about. If you gave them a little bit longer, they'd get to it eventually, only like every GP surgery these days, Hebbleswick and Essendale Group Practice was stretched to the hilt and Razz never felt there were enough hours in the day to give each person the time he felt they deserved.

And then there were other patients who didn't have anything physical wrong with them at all, but who were just lonely and wanted someone to listen to them. They didn't really need his medical skills, but the thought of sending someone away without giving them a few minutes of his time broke his heart, so he'd sat and listened whilst Mrs McCardle told him that she often felt tired. He'd suggested a blood test just to be on the safe side, then asked her how she was managing since her husband had passed, patted her hand as her eyes welled up and then nudged the box of tissues across his desk towards her.

'The trouble is,' she'd said, 'I'm lonely. I don't really see anyone these days.'

And Razz had wondered about suggesting she might come along to the Scrabble club. He had no idea, of course, if she liked word games, but he could imagine Mrs McCardle fitting right in with Florence and Sylvia and the others. But really what was the point? They hadn't got anywhere to play Scrabble anymore. Their Friday evenings were about to come to an abrupt end. Jo had said she'd find another venue, but if there wasn't another venue to be found... well, even Jo and her amazing organisational ability couldn't rustle something up that wasn't there to begin with.

There were very few places in Hebbleswick that were large enough to accommodate them. He'd wondered about the upstairs function room at the George, but the landlord wouldn't commit to a regular event on a Friday evening – even for the doctor who'd cured his mysterious rash – and, in any case, as he'd told Jo, Razz didn't want the Scrabble club attendees to feel obliged to buy a drink. Some of them, he knew, were strapped for cash. And in any case, Scrabble club was more cake and tea than G and T, and Razz wanted it to stay that way. If Mr Morgan had agreed to let them use the school hall, well, that would have been ideal, but he'd been adamant that it just wasn't possible.

It was such a shame that they couldn't stay in the church

hall until it was sold. That would have bought them a little more time at least to think of an alternative solution.

Not that there was an alternative. But still...

Razz looked at Mrs McCardle's sad, grief-stricken face and longed to have something to offer her, a nugget of hope.

'Are there any social clubs you could join?' he said.

'Not round here. Not for folks my age. If we lived in a bigger town...'

'The Not So Little Board Game Café in Essendale have board game evenings.'

'That would be lovely, Doctor, but I'm not confident getting the bus on my own at night. I did wonder about coming along to your Scrabble club but I heard that's finishing soon. Now the church hall is being demolished.'

Gossip, Razz thought, spread through Hebbleswick even more quickly than a vomiting bug.

To his embarrassment, Razz's own eyes welled up at this point and Mrs McCardle stretched over and patted his hand, then nudged the box of tissues back towards him.

'Yes, I would have suggested that,' he said, dabbing his eyes, 'but you're right. I'm not sure we can continue for much longer.'

'Such a shame,' she said. 'I missed your festival as I was visiting my grandchildren that weekend, but I heard it was a great success.'

At least she had grandchildren to visit, Razz thought. That was some consolation. But still he felt bad that he hadn't been able to come up with anything for her.

The Scrabble club had always been about more than just the game. He'd started the group because he was new to the area and wanted to find people to play his favourite game against, but he also saw it as his way of giving something to the community. Isolation had such a detrimental effect on physical as well as mental health, and Scrabble was a great way to meet other people, especially for introverts like himself. Ludek said much the same about his partner Emily's board game café. There was something about a board game, Scrabble or Monopoly or even those fancy ones in the board game café. There was less need to make small talk if you had a game board in front of you, which was great for anyone suffering from social anxiety or who was just a little shy.

'Yes, it's such a shame about the church hall,' he'd said to Mrs McCardle.

The headache had come on soon after she'd left his consulting room.

He was writing up his notes, reading letters from hospital consultants and signing off on a pile of repeat prescriptions when his phone rang.

'Reverend Stone's here to see you,' said the practice manager.

'But surgery's over,' said Razz.

'He's not after a medical consultation. He said it was personal. That he had some good news for you.'

Good news? Could this be about the church hall? Might they have got a reprieve?

As Razz put the phone down, he didn't dare allow himself to hope.

He stood up when he heard the knock at the door and went over to open it. The elderly vicar shook his hand warmly. 'Doctor Rasmusson.'

'Vicar.' Razz nodded. 'Do sit down. How can I help you?'

'Actually, I think it's more a case of how *I* can help *you*. I've come to tell you that there's been a...' he cleared his throat '...let's just say, there's been a change of plan, and you and your Scrabble group would be more than welcome to continue to use the hall until the building has actually been sold. Of course, I have no idea how long that might be. It could be weeks. Or months.'

Razz wanted to jump out of his seat and hug the man, but thought that might be inappropriate so said simply, 'That's wonderful news. Wonderful. Thank you so much, Vicar.'

There was a silence. Razz wasn't sure what to say next. Had he been grateful enough? Did he need to gush a bit more? Invite the clergyman to join them one Friday evening?

'Doctor, I was wondering...' began Rev Stone. 'I know this probably isn't the time, but I have this strange rash...'

A few minutes later, the vicar left, clutching a prescription for Canesten. Razz sat back in his chair. The Scrabble club could continue, for a few weeks at least. And with a bit of luck, either he or Jo would come up with a more permanent solution during that time. He wanted to phone her, to tell her that they could stay in the hall for the time being, but then maybe he should tell her in person, over a drink perhaps. He texted to ask if she was free, then dialled Mrs McCardle's number. He told her the good news and asked if she might like to come along to the Scrabble club the following Friday.

'I've been talking to the vicar,' said Razz, 'and I have good news.'

He'd asked Jo to meet him in the pub for a celebratory

drink, so here they were now with a small Sauvignon Blanc and half a shandy. He'd even pushed the boat out and bought a packet of Walkers cheese and onion, which sat open on the table between them.

'Don't tell me you've found Jesus?' Jo reached into the bag and pulled out a crisp.

He laughed. 'Not that kind of good news. We can stay in the hall until it's sold. Better still, he's agreed to waive the rent.'

'That's great, Razz.'

He was disappointed by her response; he thought she'd be happier about it. Then it dawned on him that this wasn't news to her at all. She had already known.

He looked at her face as she crunched on another crisp. She looked rather pleased with herself. She'd had a hand in this; he felt sure of it. How on earth had she managed to persuade Reverend Stone?

'I can't help wondering if this is your doing?' he said.

'Maybe,' she said cryptically.

He studied her face. She wasn't usually this mysterious. Well, however this had come about, he felt very grateful to her. Perhaps he should have splashed out on two bags of Walkers. Did one look a bit stingy?

Jo delved into the bag for another crisp. 'We can't rest on our laurels, Razz. We still need to find somewhere else to go once the hall is sold. The future of the Scrabble club still isn't safe.'

42

'You didn't sleep with him?' said Kate the following evening as they walked along the canal. 'I mean, I know you want Razz to forgive you and I know the Scrabble club means a lot to you, but sleeping with an estate agent... well, that'd be taking things too far.'

'Of course not,' said Jo. 'The vicar was most interested in the recording of my conversation with Tarquin. I had to explain what 'friends with benefits' meant. Bless him, he'd never heard of it before. You should have seen his face! He was horrified when he realised that his estate agent was trying to bribe me into having sex.'

'Thank you for bringing this to my attention,' he had said to her. 'If you'd like to leave your phone number with Mrs Green, I'll be in touch. See if we can't arrange something regarding the hall. Now, would you like another cup of tea? And a biscuit, perhaps?'

He had promised to change estate agents, to find one who'd be amenable to all of the community groups staying on in the hall until it was sold.

'It's a great result,' said Kate. 'I bet Tarquin was hopping mad. Losing a client and a potentially lucrative deal. Bet you wish you could have seen his face.'

'Yeah, definitely.'

You couldn't beat a bit of schadenfreude (23 points, although it was German so probably not allowed). Admittedly, it wasn't one of her better traits, but after the way he had treated her...

'But you've still got to find somewhere,' said Kate. 'For when the hall is sold? It probably won't take long. There's such a shortage of housing round here. A developer is sure to snap it up.'

'I know. Trouble is, there *isn't* anywhere else. Not that we can afford, anyway. And I've got to think of something, Kate, because the future of the Scrabble club depends on it. And Razz said he'd forgive me for the fibs I told on my internet dating profile if I do.'

'Ah yes, those fibs,' she said. 'They were my fault. And I've a confession...'

'Go on.'

'Razz had written that he was a big Scrabble fan on his Buzzz profile, and I told him to remove it, but it was ages before I met you, Jo, I promise. He was having lunch in the (Not So) Little Board Game Café with Ludek one day and I went in to see Emily. And you never actually told me that you liked Scrabble or I'd have set you up on a date. I'm so sorry, Jo.'

'It's fine. He already told me. Although I can't help wondering how different things might have been.'

Alongside her day job and Project Self-Esteem – walks with Kate, hot baths, healthy eating and chanting, 'It's not you, it's them' twenty times a day in front of the mirror – Jo now embarked on Project Find-a-New-Venue. She made lists. She started a spreadsheet, with columns for the venue name, address, contact phone number, name of person she'd spoken to, availability and price per hour.

The availability column mostly consisted of one word: NONE.

When there was availability, the figure in the price per hour column was way out of their budget.

She drew a complete blank.

No-one wanted them. There was nowhere they could go.

One possibility was the Quaker meeting house, but the only evening they could offer was a Tuesday.

'That won't work,' said Razz when Jo told him. 'We have so many kids and parents now for the session at half five. They mightn't come on a school night.'

It was back to the drawing board.

Jo was scouring the internet one lunchtime – as she often did – for a new venue in Hebbleswick. There was no point in looking too far afield; many of the Scrabble group members didn't have their own transport. There were buses, of course, but Jo couldn't envisage the older ones wanting to take the bus at night.

'What are you doing?'

She turned round to see Leona standing behind her.

'It's my lunch hour,' Jo said defensively.

'I wasn't accusing you. Just curious.'

'The hall where our Scrabble club meets is being demolished. I'm looking for a new venue. But it's hopeless. Truly hopeless. Anyway, how can I help?'

Leona glanced round the office, empty now as the rest of the team had gone out for lunch. 'Would you mind checking over a spreadsheet for me? I've a meeting with David this afternoon.'

'Okay.' Jo nodded. 'Email it to me. I'll look at it later. When my lunch hour's finished.'

'Oh, of course. Thanks.' Leona turned to go.

Jo took a deep breath. 'Will you tell me something, Leona?'

'Yes, sure.'

'Why *were* you so unkind to me? You disliked me from the word go.'

'I'm ambitious.'

'So?'

'And when I first got the job, David and Caroline both went on and on about how perfect you were. The best production co-ordinator ever. They both said it. So good at organising. They said I'd do well to emulate you, to learn from you.'

'I don't get why that made you so mean.'

'It was irritating. I'd wanted to work in telly for so long so discovering that someone else was not only doing the exact same job as me, but she was very experienced and never made a single mistake. I thought you'd be bound to show me up.'

The article had been right, Jo thought. It *was* about Leona, not about her.

'So you bitched about me,' she said. 'Spread gossip. Laughed at me behind my back. Turned my colleagues against me. Were you trying to make me leave?'

'I dunno. Maybe. I didn't think it through. It wasn't a conscious thing.'

'And deleting my spreadsheet from the hard drive? Was *that* a conscious thing?'

'I wanted you to appear a bit less perfect.'

'Well, you succeeded there. And then you stole my programme idea.'

Leona looked down at the floor, then said, 'I didn't know it was yours.'

Jo harrumphed. 'Oh, come on. Who else round here plays Scrabble? And even if you *didn't* know it was mine, you knew it was someone else's. You could see how much thought and work had gone into that idea, and yet you just took it. Whoever it belonged to, that was a really low thing to do.'

Leona looked up. She was quite pale, Jo noticed. In fact, her whole demeanour had changed.

'I... I just wanted to make a good impression on David,' she said.

'Yeah, me too.'

'But he already thinks the sun shines out of your backside. He always has.'

'Has he?' Jo had never felt that her boss thought she was anything special. She'd just got on with her job, that was all, and never thought anything of it.

'Yes, he has. And my whole life, I've always been the also-ran. Whatever I've tried to do, someone has always outshone me. At school, I came second at everything. Second in spelling tests. Second on sports day. Second in the art competition. I was good at gymnastics but my sister won the county championships.' Leona wiped her cheeks on her sleeve. 'And then I land my dream job, working in telly, and I turn up on my first day, determined to shine, and there you were, Little Miss Perfect, already shining. Doing the job so well, I could never live up to you, let alone do it better.'

'Shining?'

Really? *Shining?* Jo had never shone in her life, not to her knowledge, anyway.

Tears were rolling down Leona's cheeks now. Jo reached into her handbag and pulled out a pocket-sized packet of Kleenex. Leona tried to pull one out. 'Take the whole packet,' Jo said.

'Thanks.' Leona sniffed and blew her nose.

It dawned on Jo for the first time that she was not the only insecure person in the Pop! Productions office. Leona had always seemed so confident, so outgoing, but under the surface, that clearly wasn't the case.

'It was never a competition,' said Jo softly. 'We could have been friends. Worked together. I wasn't trying to outshine anyone. I was just doing my job.'

'I felt…' Leona sniffed again. 'I felt inferior.'

'Inferior? To me?'

Odd. Jo had always thought that Leona looked down on her.

'Yes, to you. I don't think you know how good you are. And you're right. I knew *Love Letters* was your idea. It had to be. I also knew you wouldn't dare stand up for yourself in front of everyone and say so.'

Jo shook her head, at a loss for what to say. She *should* have stood up for herself in that meeting. Why did she always hold back?

344

'Look, I'm sorry,' said Leona. 'I'm genuinely sorry. I felt terrible about it as soon as I'd done it.'

'Apology accepted,' said Jo, and then she decided to be generous. 'To be fair, you pitched it far better than I could have done. Speaking in meetings makes me nervous.'

'No, you're just being nice, and that makes me feel even worse about it. I feel terrible about Caroline's job too. It should have been yours. I think we both know that.'

'It doesn't matter. I want to move on in any case. Make a fresh start somewhere else.'

Jo was surprised at her own words. She hadn't known that was what she wanted but as soon as she said it, she realised it was true. It was time to move on from Pop! Productions, to remove herself from what had become a toxic environment, and find herself a job where she'd feel appreciated. Because she *was* good at her job. She was good at organising, and, she'd realised recently, she was creative too. And someone somewhere would value those skills.

43

After work, Jo decided to try the pubs in the hope of finding a new venue for the Scrabble club. It was pointless, really; there was no way that they'd want to commit one of their function rooms every Friday night for a few families, a group of teetotal pensioners and a man who only drank halves of shandy. But she donned a pair of trainers, planned the most expedient route and set off for her own little pub crawl.

The Fox and Hounds said no immediately. A flat no. Didn't even give a reason. The landlord of the George apologised, but said he had to keep his function room free for more lucrative events.

She almost didn't go to the Packhorse Inn. She knew it would be futile. And it was.

'Sorry,' said the landlady. 'I'd love to be able to accommodate you. My grandson went along to your event at the school. He had a wonderful time. We bought him his own Scrabble set for his birthday and he's always pestering us to play. But Friday's one of our busiest nights. If you could switch it to a Monday…'

Jo thought for a minute. Monday wouldn't be a disaster, would it? It was better than nothing. But Razz had been adamant that he wanted the group to continue on a Friday.

She shook her head.

'Have a drink whilst you're here,' the landlady said. 'On the house.'

Jo hesitated. Drinking alone in a pub didn't appeal, but her feet were aching and her heart was heavy with disappointment. A glass of wine might perk her up.

'Go on, then,' she said. 'A small Pinot Grigio, please.'

'Coming right up.'

She poured Jo's wine then turned to serve another customer. Jo perched on a bar stool, feeling a bit out of place. She'd drink this then head home. See if Razz was online and fancied playing on WordPals.

'Jo?'

She looked across the bar and saw Mr Morgan.

'Hi,' she said.

'Are you by yourself?' he said. 'Or waiting for someone?'

'By myself.'

'In that case, would you join me? I wouldn't normally come for a drink after school but I've... oh, I might as well be honest. I've had a terrible day. Can I get you another?'

A drink with Mr Morgan wasn't exactly her idea of a fun evening but since he had let them use the school for the festival, she felt she couldn't say no. She would have one more glass of wine and listen to his problems, should he care to share them.

They took their drinks to the quietest corner of the bar, Mr Morgan looking round anxiously to make sure there were no parents around.

'So, why's your day been bad?' Jo asked.

'The school manager – she's been off sick for a while – but now she's decided she isn't coming back. She's taking early retirement.'

'Good for her. I mean, if she doesn't feel up to it...'

'Yes, I can see it's the right thing for her, but it's not so good for the school. I don't know how we'll manage – how I'll manage – without her. I interviewed six people today and none of them were suitable. The governors are putting pressure on me to appoint, but I want to re-advertise. See if there's anyone else out there.'

'I'm sure you'll find someone.'

He picked up his glass, swirling the honey-coloured liquid around, then putting it back down on the table without taking a sip. 'I'm not the most organised person. I want to focus on the children's well-being and their education so I need a manager who'll get on with the rest of it, without running to me every five minutes for a decision on the service contract for the photocopier or how many teabags to order for the staffroom. Someone who'll sort out all the admin and the paperwork. Keep on top of everything.'

'And none of the applicants fitted the bill?'

'One of them maybe. But she was a bit too... austere. It'd be good to have someone I can get on with at the end of the day. Someone with ideas too. A bit of creativity.'

He was staring at her now. Looking into her eyes. Oh, God. He didn't fancy her, did he? Was this why he'd asked her for a drink? But he was married, wasn't he? She'd seen his little daughter.

'Jo, I don't suppose...'

'No,' she said. 'Definitely not.'

'You haven't heard what I was going to say.'

'I don't have affairs with married men. Call me old-fashioned, but that's how I am. And besides, I'm in love with someone else.'

'I'm not asking you to have an affair,' he said. 'I'm offering you a job.'

Jo nearly fell off the bar stool. Her face grew hot and she rooted in her bag, pretending to look for a tissue in an attempt to conceal her embarrassment.

'I'm so sorry,' she mumbled, still looking in her bag. 'I just assumed… but it doesn't matter. You said a job?'

'The role of school manager. I'd still have to advertise, of course. And you'd have to apply.'

A new job? Landing in her lap like that when it was only a few hours since she'd realised that she wanted to move on from Pop! Productions?

Coincidences like that didn't really happen, did they?

Jo thought back to the Your Best Life talk where she'd first met Kate; perhaps the woman with the Marge Simpson hair had been right after all. Perhaps the Universe *was* listening.

But work in a school? A few months ago, that would have been unthinkable. She had promised herself that she'd never set foot in a school again after all the teasing – bullying – she'd endured, let alone work in one – schools brought back too many bad memories – but Hebbleswick Scrabble Festival had changed all that.

'I've no experience of working in a school,' she said.

'That wouldn't matter. I've seen how organised you are.'

He took a sip of his drink. Whisky, she thought, 19 points. Though it could have been brandy.

'Ignore me, I'm being silly,' he said. 'It's the drink talking. You wouldn't want to give up your fancy job in Manchester for a little primary school in Hebbleswick. You work in TV, don't you? Must be glamorous.'

'It isn't glamorous at all. I sit in an office. And as it

happens, I am looking to move on to pastures new. But there'd be a condition.'

'Go on.'

'Could we use the hall for our Scrabble club on Friday evenings? I mean, if I was an employee and I guaranteed that I'd stay till the end every single week, that'd cover things with the insurance, wouldn't it?'

'I think we could arrange that. Why don't you come and spend a morning with us? Find out a bit more about what the job entails.'

'Sure, I've still got some leave to take.'

Jo reached into her handbag and pulled out her Filofax.

'How about... next Monday?' she said. 'I'll have to square it with my boss but it should be okay.'

And would get her out of attending the team meeting, she thought.

'Sounds perfect.'

As Jo scribbled a note to remind her to ask David about taking the time off, something fell out of the back of her Filofax. Mr Morgan jumped off his bar stool and retrieved it from the floor, handing it to her.

It was the white envelope with the poppies in the corner.

The letter that the mystery woman had given to Razz, asking him to pass it on. She must have been carrying it round since their visit to Garlic 'n' Games but had forgotten all about it after Razz had 'stormed' out.

She waited till she was back in her own little home before opening the letter.

Dear Joanne,

I hope it's okay to contact you. You don't know me but we have something – or rather someone – in common. Si.

He swept me off my feet and we married about a year after you and he divorced. It was wonderful at first but then… well, I'm sure you can imagine what it's been like. I suspect you will have had the same terrible experiences as me. He tries to control every aspect of my life.

I finally plucked up the courage to leave him a few weeks ago. I also reported him to the police for coercive control. They said it can be difficult to prove a case, that it basically boils down to my word against his unless there is anyone who can corroborate my story.

I didn't know how to find you, but then I saw an article in the Yorkshire Post *about your Scrabble festival – that sounded wonderful, by the way. I recognised you from the pictures; Si still has an album with photos of you in. (Hope that doesn't creep you out too much.)*

I know that it's a big ask. If you go to the police and they do decide to press charges, it could mean going to court and telling a judge and jury about the whole thing. I'm under no illusion – that would be difficult. But if I get the chance, I want to do it, if only to prevent his next wife from going through the same thing that I have. That we have. So I'm hoping you'll consider it too.

I'll write my number at the bottom of this letter in case you'd like to talk it through.

Kind regards,
Sarah

44

It was all too much to take in. Mr Morgan had as good as offered her a position at the school, subject to the necessary formalities, of course. And then, within an hour of that happening, she'd discovered that she wasn't the only woman whom Si had bullied. After years of her life staying the same – single, often lonely, stuck in a job where she didn't fit in or feel particularly appreciated – things suddenly seemed to be changing at a rate of knots. It was exciting – but also frightening.

Jo had no doubts about accepting the job. She liked Mr Morgan. And from what she'd seen of the staff, parents and children at Hebbleswick Primary, she liked the school too.

But going to the police about her ex-husband? That was something she'd have to think carefully about. Did she seriously want to explain what had happened to her to a total stranger? To make her personal life the subject of scrutiny?

Jo read the letter again. And again.

Someone else – this Sarah – had been through the same ordeal as her. Si was the common denominator, the one with the problem. In other words, it had *never* been about her. Gemma's article about overcoming bullying had said that, of course, but it was one thing to read it, another thing to believe it.

This, she realised, was why he'd sought her out. Why he'd waited for her outside Pop! Productions. Insisted they went for a drink. He must have known that Sarah had found her and had guessed his second wife might try to rope his first into testifying against him. He'd been trying to find out if there'd been any contact between the two women. And when it was clear that there hadn't been, that was when he'd suddenly lost interest and left.

She wanted to reach out to Sarah, to talk to that one person who, more than anyone else, would understand what she'd been through, yet at the same time, she wanted to rip the letter up and forget about it. Because the thought of sitting across a courtroom from Si and saying what he'd done to her in front of a judge and jury terrified her.

She needed to talk this through with someone.

'So, what did you want to talk about?' Razz said.

They were sitting in their usual pub, a half pint of shandy and a glass of Pinot Grigio on the table in front of them.

Jo took a sip of her wine for Dutch courage, but it didn't work quite as quickly as she'd hoped. It had seemed a good idea earlier, when she'd asked him to meet her. With his job, she figured, he'd have heard this kind of thing before. Abusive relationships were sadly all too common; you could barely turn on the radio these days without hearing about gaslighting and love-bombing. There'd even been a storyline in *The Archers* about coercive control.

'We're celebrating,' she said, putting off the moment

when she explained the real reason she'd wanted to meet and trying to inject some brightness into her tone. 'The Scrabble club has a new venue. From September, we'll be able to use the school hall.'

'On a Friday?' Razz sounded as if he didn't quite believe this.

'On a Friday.'

'I don't know how you do it. First the vicar agrees to let us stay a few more weeks and then Mr Morgan said we can use the school on Friday evenings. They both said no to me.'

He paused, waiting for Jo to explain, but she said nothing. She was lost in thought, twiddling the stem of her wine glass, watching the pale liquid moving around the glass.

'Are you okay, Jo? You seem a bit distracted this evening,' Razz said.

She looked up. 'Yeah, I'm fine, thanks.'

'I thought we were celebrating. We have a venue, thanks to you, but you don't seem that happy about it.'

'I'm tired, that's all. And I have stuff on my mind.'

He was right, though; she should have been ecstatic; in a few weeks, she'd be leaving Pop! Productions behind and making a fresh start, and the Scrabble club had a new venue. But all she could think about was that letter.

'Is there anything I can help with?' said Razz. 'I'm a good listener, Jo.'

She hesitated. She wanted to tell him about the letter and she wanted to ask him what Sarah was like. Razz had actually met Si's current wife, when she'd come to the Scrabble club looking for Jo, but would he remember her? And was it such a good idea to share her own troubled relationship history with the man she wanted to be in a relationship with? Suddenly, she wasn't so sure.

'I'm fine, Razz. Honestly.'

Judging by his concerned face, she knew he didn't believe her.

He took a sip of his shandy. 'You know, if you ever need someone to talk to, about anything, ever, well, you can count on me. You know that.' He paused for a moment, then clearly recognising that she might want to change the subject, said, 'So are you going to tell me how you pulled it off? Mr Morgan was adamant that we *couldn't* use the school hall on a Friday evening.'

'The school's getting a new manager,' Jo said, 'and she loves Scrabble so is happy to stay on Friday evenings. Which sorts out the problem with the insurance.'

'God, that's a coincidence,' said Razz.

She looked at him blankly; she couldn't believe he hadn't guessed. 'Razz, I *am* the new manager.'

He laughed. 'I know. I was just kidding you.'

She slapped his arm. 'I can't believe you kept a straight face! You should play Poker instead of Scrabble. Anyway, I made it a condition that the Scrabble club could play there when I accepted the job.'

'You're not leaving your job in TV to work in a school because of the Scrabble club?'

Jo shook her head. 'Much as I love Scrabble, Razz, I'm not that daft. I'm not happy at Pop! Productions. I don't feel valued. I got passed over for a promotion recently. And I like the school. I like the atmosphere. I think I'll be appreciated there.'

She took a sip of her wine.

'Well, congratulations on your new job.' Razz picked up his shandy and clinked glasses with her. 'And the vicar? How did you persuade him?'

'I dunno.'

'Come on, what did you say? I know it had something to do with you. Did you agree to go to church every week for a year?'

'Nope.'

'You shagged him?'

Jo shook her head. 'He's a vicar.'

'He's still a man. I know, you promised your first-born daughter will become a nun.'

'Don't be silly. The estate agent happened to be someone I'd dated. And he said that if I had sex with him, he'd sort it for us to stay on in the hall until it was sold.'

'Shit, Jo.' Razz shook his head. 'I never meant for you... I mean, taking the job at the school was one thing. But...'

'Hang on, I didn't do it. I recorded the conversation on my phone and played it to the vicar.'

Razz sighed and downed the remains of his shandy. 'I think I might need something stronger. I thought for a moment you'd...'

'Razz, I'm not that sort of person. Casual sex... well, it's not what I'm into. And definitely not with Tarquin.'

'Tarquin? Don't tell me, you dated him because his name scored 16 points?'

''Fraid so. He wasn't nice to me either. I seem to have a habit of picking men who aren't nice to me.'

'I was nice to you. And I always will be.'

His words hung in the air between them. Jo wondered how to respond. How come she could think of the right words when it came to laying them on a board, maximising her points, working out how to use a tricksy letter like a Q or an X or a Z? But when it came to saying the right thing to the man she loved, once again, words quite literally failed her.

'Let's not talk about Tarquin,' she said. 'Let's talk about happy things. My new job. The Scrabble club's new venue.'

'Yes, we should. Look, why don't we do celebrate properly? Saturday night. Dinner somewhere posh. What do you reckon?'

'I'm not sure it's even a date,' Jo said to Kate.

She still wanted to talk to someone about Sarah's letter. She hadn't managed to tell Razz the previous evening so had invited Kate over for a chat and a cup of tea. They were sitting on the sofa, now covered by a luxurious, red, velvet throw that Jo had decided to treat herself to. It had been expensive, more than she'd normally spend, but it brightened her little lounge up no end. But instead of asking Kate's advice about the letter, Jo had found herself telling her about Razz.

'Of course it's a date. Posh restaurant. He's picking you up.'

'No, it's a celebration. I found us a new venue for the Scrabble club.'

'Just words, Jo. Semantics. Date. Celebration. The important thing is, the man you like...'

'Love.'

'Love already?'

'Well, I think I'm falling.'

'Okay, the man you lurve,' Kate rolled her eyes but she was smiling, 'is picking you up and taking you to a posh restaurant. You make yourself look good. You sparkle and twinkle at him all evening. You pick the right moment and you tell him how you feel. It can't fail.'

'I don't feel that sparkly at the moment.'

'We can sort your clothes. Go shopping. Find you a new outfit.'

'No, I don't mean that. I mean, inside I don't feel sparkly. I've had this letter... Hang on.'

She stood up, went into her bedroom and rummaged in the drawer of her bedside table. She had hidden the white envelope at the bottom, hoping that by putting it out of sight, she'd be able to put it out of mind. But it hadn't worked. She hadn't been able to think of anything else.

She went back into the lounge and handed it to Kate. 'Open it.'

'You sure?'

'Yes, please. Read it.'

She watched her friend's face as she scanned down the page.

Kate sighed. 'You've really been through it, haven't you, Jo? I cringe looking back, thinking how I gave you all that silly dating advice.'

'It's fine. I *wanted* the dating advice. I wanted to meet someone.'

'So what are you going to do about this? Are you going to agree to testify?'

'I don't know. I'm torn. I'm not sure I can face him across a courtroom. It would be my word against his. And he's good at twisting the truth, at making people believe his version of events. He's had a lot of practice.'

'Is there anyone who'd corroborate *your* version of events? Anyone who witnessed what you were going through?'

'Gemma did. I mean, he stopped me seeing her after she sent me an article about coercive control, not long after we got married. But she kept sending the articles. She *still* sends me articles – she likes articles as much as you like self-help books. I printed some of them off.'

Jo stood up and went to the bookshelves, pulled off a dusty pink cardboard folder and handed it to Kate.

Kate shifted from sitting on the sofa to kneeling on the floor, spreading the printed pages around her and surveying them, like a detective studying an evidence wall.

'Wow,' she said. 'Here's someone who has properly looked out for you.'

Jo knelt down beside Kate. 'Yeah, she has, hasn't she?'

As they sifted through the articles, Jo saw that over the years of her marriage, Gemma had been giving her the tools she needed.

How to Leave an Abusive Relationship

Should I Leave Him? How to Decide if Your Marriage is Over

Do I Want a Divorce?

10 Signs That Your Relationship is Abusive

'We need a conference,' said Kate. 'Can we ring Gemma? Or better still, let's do a Zoom.'

A few minutes later, Gemma's face appeared on the screen of Jo's laptop.

Jo felt more than a little anxious, wondering if her two friends would get on. Gemma had always been a bit dismissive of Kate's dating advice, after all. But she needn't have worried.

Gemma's voice was full of her usual warmth. 'Kate, it's lovely to meet you. I've heard loads about you.'

'Likewise,' said Kate.

'So, Jo, tell me about this letter,' said Gemma.

Jo read it out loud, then said, 'I want to help her. I can't bear the thought of him doing it to someone else. But I'm not sure I can face him in court. He'll have some fancy barrister who'll interrogate me and twist my words.'

'What do you think, Kate?' asked Gemma.

'I think it would good if we could both support Jo so that she *can* do it. Not only in the hope of stopping Si from hurting anyone else like this, but I think it might be good for Jo. It might give her some closure.'

'Agreed,' said Gemma. 'Of course, I'll support you, Jo. I always have. If you did decide to testify, I'd be there in court, with you. I'd testify too if they ask me to. And if you don't want to do it, that's fine too. No-one's forcing you. It would be absolutely fine to say no. Wouldn't it, Kate? Jo has to do what's right for her.'

'Absolutely,' said Kate. She turned to Jo and took her hand. 'But you haven't said no. And the fact that you've kept the letter makes me think that at least a part of you wants to do this.'

'Exactly,' said Gemma, 'but how do we help you make that decision? What do you need from us, Jo?'

Jo shrugged. 'I don't know.'

Kate looked thoughtful. 'What's the obstacle, Jo? What's stopping you from doing this? Is it the thought of seeing Si again? Because I'm sure they can arrange for these things to be done over video link, can't they? It'd be like talking to Gemma now, over a screen.'

Jo thought. What was it exactly?

'It isn't the thought of facing Si,' she said slowly. 'It's all those other people who'd be watching. Knowing him, there'd be some fancy, hotshot lawyer, who'd twist my words even more than Si himself used to twist them. Who'd confuse me with question after question and make me sound stupid. They'll say I don't remember things clearly. And they'll try to deny what I suffered, to negate it. It took me so long to acknowledge and accept what I went through. You tried to tell me, Gemma, but for the whole of our marriage, Si duped me into believing his version of events over my own reality. And him and his lawyers – they'll try and get a jury to believe his version and some of them will. They'll sit there, making judgements about me. So that's the obstacle. If it was me and Si and no-one else… well, I think I could do that. I think I'd *like* to do that. I'd like to go… face to face, head to head with him. To tell him how he made me suffer. To tell him that I no longer believe his lies and that I will never be controlled by him – or any other man – again. I've wanted to do that for so long, but I've never had the courage before. But in recent months… well, I've been down a bloody great hole in the ground, I've done a live interview on the radio, faced all those awful childhood memories and gone into a school – accepted a job in one, in fact...'

'A job in a school?' said Gemma.

'Yeah, I forgot to tell you that. I'm leaving Pop! Productions. You're looking at the new manager of Hebbleswick Primary School. And I've stood on a stage in front of over a hundred people, organised a festival, faced that slimeball Tarquin and stood up to the office bully. So I'm ready to face Si. But I want it to be just him and me. I want to tell him what he did and what a terrible impact it had on me. To say how small he made me feel, how useless, how stupid, how ugly, how vulnerable... If I can manage that, I'll go to the police. And then maybe I'll find the courage to testify in court. Assuming they bring the case.'

'Are you sure, Jo?' said Kate. 'You're happy to face him on your own?'

Jo paused for a moment. 'Yes, I'm sure.'

45

Either Si had changed his number or he was ignoring her. She had texted him six times. No reply.

It was worse than waiting for messages on Buzzz, she thought ruefully. Far, far worse.

She looked up at Mona, still staring down at her from the wall.

'Bloody men,' she said.

She could have sworn that the Mona Lisa's enigmatic smile got the tiniest bit broader.

Jo couldn't settle to anything. At lunchtime, she'd gone for a walk round the shops, hoping that some fresh air would help her restless legs. She'd idly browsed through racks of clothes in TK Maxx in the hope of finding something a little bit special for her date with Razz at the weekend. If it was a date. She still wasn't sure. And, in a way, she hoped it *wasn't* a date. Much as she wanted to be with Razz, she wanted to get this business with Si over with first. To close that particular book before starting a new one. Anyway, she still didn't know if the feelings with Razz were mutual, though she suspected that they were.

The fresh air hadn't helped. She sat at her desk now, trying to plough through as much as she could. Despite how Leona had treated her, she was determined that when she left, she wouldn't be leaving a huge mound of work for Leona to deal with.

'Jo,' David called, sticking his head out of his office. 'Have you time for a chat?'

His tone was mellow. Friendly, even.

Not a missing spreadsheet then, she thought.

'Yeah, sure,' she said. 'I'll be there in a minute.'

A few weeks ago, she'd have jumped up immediately if he'd called her. But now, she was going to finish typing her sentence before making sure to save her document.

'How can I help?' she said.

'I owe you an apology. I went into your computer at lunchtime, whilst you were out, looking for a document…'

Oh. So there *was* another missing spreadsheet? Was she in trouble again?

Jo was surprised to realise that she didn't feel nervous.

In fact, *he* was the one who seemed nervous.

'And did you find it?' she asked. 'The missing document? I'm sorry if I filed something on my own drive that should have been on the shared drive.'

'No, it's not that. Leona told me about *Love Letters*. She confessed that it was your idea, not hers. And I found the original document on your drive, which proves it. I owe you a huge apology, Jo. I should have believed you. After all the years you've loyally served this company, you deserve better, and I'm sorry.'

Jo was surprised; that was the last thing she'd expected. It must have taken a lot for Leona to admit her mistake. Hats off to her. She stood up to leave. 'Thanks, David. Apology accepted.'

'Sit down, Jo,' said David, then added, 'Please. Leona also said that stepping into Caroline's shoes was proving too much for her.'

Jo decided she would be magnanimous. 16 points. 'She'll pick it up. She's more than capable.'

'Actually, she's agreed to step down,' he said. 'So I'd like to offer you the job.'

She should have told him there and then, she thought, that she wasn't going to take it. That she was, in fact, leaving Pop! Productions altogether and had already drafted her resignation letter. But she hadn't; instead, she'd asked if she could slip off early, have a bit of time to think about it and he'd readily agreed.

She'd switched off her computer, picked up her bag and headed out of the office. It was fantastic timing, she thought, managing to wangle an hour or two off right when she needed it. And it wasn't as if she wouldn't make up the time. Anyway, she'd done more than enough hours of unpaid overtime for Pop! Productions over the years. Leaving the office at five past four was hardly a biggy, was it?

She walked through Manchester, past the statues of the giant Vimto bottle and Archimedes springing out of his bath, seconds after his eureka moment, and reached Piccadilly Station out of breath. Because of her fast pace, perhaps? Or at the thought of what she was about to do?

The next train to Liverpool Lime Street wasn't for fifteen minutes. Jo bought a ticket, then waited on the platform, hopping from foot to foot. She glanced at her watch: still another few minutes. Would she be on time, she wondered?

The train to Liverpool took a little under an hour, which meant she'd arrive at about half past five. And then, when she got there, she'd have to walk through the city and down to the smart office block near the Albert Docks. What was that? A ten-minute walk? Fifteen, perhaps? She'd be cutting it fine.

It was five forty-three when she reached Gillespie Accountants Limited.

She stood beside the revolving glass door and waited. Unless he'd changed – doubtful, as he was a creature of habit – he'd be out any minute.

Was she really going to do this? she wondered. Doorstep Si like this?

But what other way was there, if he wouldn't reply to her texts?

And after all, he had ambushed her, hadn't he, when she was leaving the office? So it seemed only fair that she played him at his own game.

The doors began to turn. With her back to the wall, she peered down at the ground, at the feet stepping outside. Loake shoes. Black ones this time. But unmistakably Si's.

'Hi, Si,' she said as he emerged into the late evening sunshine. 'Have you changed your mobile number? Only you haven't been responding to my texts.'

He was reluctant, of course. Said he had somewhere else to be. That he had a mountain of paperwork to plough through that evening. That his wife would be worried.

'Will she?' said Jo. 'Only I heard she'd left you?'

Si scowled. 'What do you want, Jo?'

'I want to talk. One drink. After all, when you tipped up in Manchester, I went for a drink with you. Play fair. You owe me that much.'

The trendy bar beside the river Mersey wasn't quite the place she'd have chosen for a showdown with Si, but it was the closest place.

Choose your battles, she thought, remembering one of Gemma's articles. It wasn't worth arguing about *where* she did this. The important thing was that she did it.

She opted for a sparkling mineral water. A Pinot Grigio would have been nice, to take the edge of her nerves, but Gemma and Kate had both counselled her to keep a clear head.

'You'll need to have your wits about you,' Gemma had said. 'You know what he's like.'

'What do you want, Jo?' said Si again.

She took a deep breath, had a sip of the water and paused. She could do this.

How had they agreed she would start?

'I want to talk about our marriage,' she said. She was surprised at how confident she sounded. Strong, even. 'And how it was for me. How you treated me.'

Si rolled his eyes. 'I suppose you've been talking to Sarah?'

'I had a letter from Sarah, yes.' Jo focused on keeping her tone calm, but firm. She was determined not to shout. Not to bully. Not to stoop to his level, in other words. Just to be clear and state her truth. 'But I haven't spoken to her. I wanted to speak to you first.'

He stood up. 'I suppose you're going to side with her. Trot off to the police. Your mind is already made up, isn't it, so there's not much point in us having this conversation.'

'Sit down, Si,' she said, surprising both him and herself at how forcefully her words came out. 'I said, sit down. I spent years obeying *your* orders. For once, you can do something I ask.'

He didn't sit down. 'Obeying my orders? Don't be ridiculous, Jo. I never gave you orders.'

She could feel the indignation bubbling up inside her, but took a deep breath and said calmly, 'You told me what to wear. What to eat. Told the hairdresser what hairstyle to give me.'

'That was for you, Jo. All for you. Didn't you want to look your best?' He sounded cold, but then his tone changed, his face softened. 'You look lovely this evening, by the way.'

Jo couldn't help but glance down at her outfit. Her usual jeans and shirt. The kind of stuff she wore to the office every day of the week.

No, it was a line, she thought. He was trying to manipulate her. Again. But she'd wised up to his antics now. 'None of that was for me, Si. You wanted to change me. To dominate every little aspect of my life. You controlled what I spent. How I looked. Told me what to do. Stopped me seeing my friends.'

He sat down again and leaned across the table towards her, derision written all over his face. 'Friends? You mean, your old colleagues? Were they real friends, Jo? I mean, how many of them have you heard from since?'

Not one, she thought. She'd lost touch with all of them. This felt like a tennis match and Si had just served an ace.

'You stopped me seeing Gemma,' she said.

'Pah, Gemma! You say that *I* wanted to change you, but

Gemma was the one sending you all those self-help articles about how to improve yourself.'

'She wanted to help me.'

'Yes, and so did I. What's the difference? Your friend saying you should learn to love yourself or take control of your destiny, and your husband encouraging you to get a new haircut and make the most of yourself?'

'She had my best interests at heart,' said Jo.

Si harrumphed. 'Debatable. I was the one with your best interests at heart, Jo. You'd never have amounted to anything without me. Who was it encouraged you to get a job in television in the first place? And you've loved it, haven't you? Working in a prestigious industry? Most young women would kill for a job in the media.'

Jo thought back. Admittedly, it had been exciting when she'd landed that first job in TV, but she'd been happy before that, working in the solicitor's office.

'You wanted me to work in TV,' she said coldly, 'so you could show off to your colleagues. I never wanted to leave the solicitor's. I fitted in there.'

'But you've got a proper career, now, Joanne. That's all down to me. You'd never have amounted to anything without me.'

The tiniest doubt crept into Jo's mind – perhaps he was right, perhaps she wouldn't have got anywhere in life without him – but she pushed it away. Of course he wasn't right. She had organised a successful festival, hadn't she? How many people could say that?

'Pop! Productions,' he was saying now and he looked proud.

She couldn't believe it. He actually had the audacity to look proud.

'I often see their programmes on the telly,' he continued, 'and I think, that's my Joanne doing that. Making those shows.'

'I'm not "your Joanne".' She practically spat the words out at him. 'And I'm leaving the TV industry anyway. It was never really me.'

His expression changed, flicking from pride back to derision in an instant, as quickly as changing TV channels. 'Fine, do what you want. You're nothing to me now.'

Jo took a deep breath. She wouldn't rise to the bait, wouldn't let her anger show. 'You love-bombed me, and I was so keen to meet someone and have my happy ever after that I let you. That was my mistake. And then as soon as I had that engagement ring on my finger, you changed and you tried to change me.'

He opened his mouth to speak but she held up her hand to stop him. 'You told me left was right, and right was left – literally. Remember that day we argued over the way to Formby beach? And I said to turn left, but you turned right. And when we ended up lost, you blamed me. Said that *I* had said to turn right. But I hadn't. You could have told me black was white and I would have believed you. You isolated me from the people I loved spending time with. We never socialised with Gemma and Jack, only with your friends. You told me I was fat and that it would be best for me if I went on a diet. You told me my clothes were frumpy and bought me new ones that I wasn't comfortable wearing. You tried to mould me into the woman that you wanted me to be. If you didn't want me the way I was, Si, you should never have dated me. Should never have married me. Because I know now that I am worthy of being loved for who I am, Si. I always was.'

The words were tumbling out now. She took a deep breath, expecting him to try to interrupt again, but he didn't. 'They call behaviour like yours gaslighting these days. Gaslighting. Coercive control. But as far as I'm concerned, the word for it is bullying. You're a bully, Simon. Perhaps the truth is that you're insecure, you don't feel good enough yourself, so you make yourself feel better by making other people feel small.'

'Have you quite finished?' he said coldly. 'It sounds like Gemma's been filling your head with all of this crap. Given you another one of her articles, has she?'

Of course, she'd known he would try and twist things, try to tell her that things weren't how she saw them.

Suddenly, she realised that he believed his own lies and that whatever she said, he wasn't going to accept it. She could never convince him that their marriage had been a sham, that he was a bully, that he tried to control people and that that kind of behaviour wasn't love at all.

There was a kind of freedom in this realisation. She had told him her truth, but he'd never believe her. But maybe other people would. Jo knew at that moment that she would go to the police. Would testify in a court of law if things got that far. But she also knew that even if he was convicted, Si would never believe her version of events. He'd think there'd been some huge miscarriage of justice and that he was the victim in all of this.

'Right, is that it?' He glanced at his watch. 'I'm a busy man. I don't have time for female histrionics.'

He stood up again.

Jo felt... what was it she felt? It wasn't anger. It was a feeling she hadn't anticipated, hadn't expected.

Pity.

She felt sorry for him.

Two failed marriages, neither one of them based on real love, and he hadn't even turned forty.

'I feel sorry for you, Si. I didn't expect to – but I do.'

'Sorry for me? Pah.'

'Although not sorry enough to stop me reporting you.'

'I knew that's what this was about. Bloody Sarah.'

He was speaking more loudly now; not shouting exactly but Jo saw several people glancing round.

He clenched his right fist and thumped the palm of his left hand several times. Jo wondered if he was imagining thumping her.

'And that damn Scrabble festival,' he growled 'That's how she tracked you down. That bloody game. I never have understood why you're so obsessed with it.'

'You've never understood me at all, Si. I'm grateful to Sarah. I'm glad she got in touch. I'll be making a statement to the police. It's something I should have done a long time ago.'

With that, she stood up and left. Without a backwards glance.

46

'And he let you have your say?' said Kate.

'Eventually. After a few minutes of trying to convince me that it had all been for my own good.'

It was Saturday morning. They were walking through some woodland on the slopes of a steep-sided valley a couple of miles from Hebbleswick. Jo's initial scepticism had faded now; she had to admit that the combination of exercise and getting outside in the fresh air definitely made her feel better.

In fact, she was feeling fantastic. She had done something she'd fantasised about doing for ages and confronted Si. She'd reported him to the police, who'd been far more sympathetic than she'd expected. There was a chance – although no guarantee – that they might press charges against him. Having statements from two women who'd been married to him – rather than one – might make all the difference, they'd said.

She felt like everything was finally coming together. David had been suitably remorseful when she told him she was leaving Pop! Productions and said he didn't know how they would manage without her. And best of all, Razz was taking her to a fancy restaurant in Leeds that evening – not too fancy, Jo hoped – to celebrate her new job and the new Scrabble club venue. Jo couldn't remember when she last felt this good about life. About herself.

'I wish I could have seen you in action,' said Kate. 'And seen evil Si getting his comeuppance.'

'He hasn't got his comeuppance yet. In fact, the CPS haven't decided yet if they're going to pursue the case. And even if they do, a jury would have to find him guilty. He might still get away with it.'

They reached a stile and Kate went ahead, climbing over first. 'Yeah, but I bet this has scared him a bit. He'll think twice before bullying someone again.'

'Maybe.' Jo wasn't too sure. In any case, Si needed therapy rather than a criminal conviction if he was to have any chance of changing his ways. But that was something he needed to realise for himself. And perhaps he never would.

This really was the perfect morning. The leaves were such vibrant shades of green. The river was babbling away below them and a chiffchaff was singing its characteristic song somewhere nearby. The sun was shining and the air was warm; warm enough, in fact, that Jo thought she might soon take the plunge and remove her cardigan.

'It's far too nice a day to be talking about my ex,' she said as they strode along. Rays of sunlight streamed down through the trees, dappling the path ahead of them. Crepuscular, Jo thought, 17 points. Not that you could ever make an eleven-letter word in Scrabble, but if you could, it was a good one.

'How are things with Matthew from Scrabble speed-dating?' she said. 'Are you still seeing him?'

'A bit,' said Kate. 'And he's lovely but he's a bit geeky.'

Jo punched her friend gently on the arm. 'Oi, I'm a bit geeky. And isn't your friend Emily a bit geeky too? She runs two board game cafés so she's bound to be. Anyway, there's nothing wrong with geeky.'

'No, but I'm not geeky. And I'd rather not date a geeky man. He bangs on and on about computers. He's even building one. He spends hours on it. I mean, why would you build one yourself when you can pop into Currys and buy one?'

'Perhaps he enjoys the challenge. So you're not that keen on him then?'

Kate sighed. 'That's the problem. I am. Super keen. I wish he paid me as much attention as he pays his hard drive. I've had blokes in the past who were devoted to their mothers, but this one is devoted to his motherboard.'

Jo laughed. 'Talk to him about it, Kate. Tell him how you feel.'

Listen to yourself, Jo thought, full of relationship advice when you aren't even in one yourself.

Yet.

But fingers crossed, tonight would go according to plan.

'And Razz?' said Kate, as if she could read Jo's mind.

'I'm hoping that tonight's the night.'

'It's bound to be. There's nothing stopping you from getting together, is there?'

'I still don't know if he likes me. Not in that way. I think he does, but then I keep coming back to the fact that he didn't ask me for a second date when we first met. Although he did say that he assumed I wouldn't *want* to see him again. But I dunno... I wonder if he just likes me as a friend. And that's good too. Because a few weeks ago, I didn't feel that I had any friends. Not local ones, anyway. And now I have you and Razz and all the people at the Scrabble group. Wow, look at the view.'

They stopped and stared for a moment. They'd wound their way high above the river. The path was narrow now – too narrow for them to walk side by side – and the edge fell away sharply, down to the river below, and the ruins of an old mill, complete with a water wheel.

'We should get a selfie of the two of us together,' said Jo suddenly, keen to preserve this perfect moment for ever. This moment of friendship and new beginnings and the unaccustomed feeling that she was right where she belonged.

'It's called an "usie",' said Kate.

'An usie?'

'If it's two or more people together.'

An usie. Jo liked the sound of that. She wanted to be part of an usie.

They turned, their backs to the river and Kate slung her arm around Jo. Jo lifted her phone high above them, trying to position it in the perfect place to capture both their faces and the water below. It was a good shot, but not quite the right angle. Kate looked smaller than her – well, Kate *was* smaller than her, but not that much smaller – and the old mill wasn't in the frame.

'Careful,' said Kate. 'We're quite near the edge.'

Jo moved the phone slightly. She could see the river on the screen now, but not all of her face. She moved a little, edged nearer to Kate, then leaned back slightly trying to squeeze herself into the shot. And then she took a step backwards.

It was the tiniest of steps, only an inch or two, but her heel didn't meet earth. It met air.

She felt Kate's arm grip her shoulders but it wasn't enough to stop her falling.

The river was a long way below, but Jo didn't tumble straight to the bottom. Luckily, the rocky slope broke her fall, and she part tumbled, part rolled down, banging her head on a tree stump as she reached the edge of the river. And then she passed out.

47

Jo could feel the cold, wet ground beneath her. She opened her eyes and moved her hand in front of her face. It was covered in mud. Her head ached, but other than that, she couldn't feel any pain anywhere. No, wait; her ankle was beginning to throb now too. Jo tried to wriggle her toes and they all seemed to work perfectly well. That was a good sign, wasn't it? She wasn't seriously injured. Just stuck. Getting back up to the path was going to be a bit of a challenge.

She could hear the sound of the river, babbling happily away to itself as it rolled down the valley. And from above, she could hear a familiar voice. Kate. She seemed to be on the phone, but Jo could only make out snatches of the conversation.

'...an accident... rung for an ambulance... mountain rescue... on another call... she's come round now... yes, she was unconscious but only for a minute or so. Could Ludek...?'

Jo tried to sit up but her head was spinning.

'Hang on, I think she's trying to get up,' she heard Kate say. 'I'd better go.'

She lifted her arm and waved.

'Jo?' Kate called. Can you hear me?'

She tried to speak, but her mouth was dry. 'Kate,' she croaked.

'Jo? Can you hear me?'

'I'm down here.' She managed to speak a little louder this time.

'Yes, I know. I watched you fall. I can see you, but I don't think I can reach you. Are you hurt? Yeah, well, obviously you are. But are you in pain?'

'A bit. Head hurts.'

'You hit a tree stump – it broke your fall. Do you think you've broken anything?'

'I don't think so. Ankle's sore. I'm not sure if I can stand.'

'Don't try yet. Just hang on down there, Jo. Mountain rescue are coming, but they're on another call so there'll be a slight delay. I rang Em but Ludek's visiting family in Poland for the weekend.'

Jo closed her eyes. She felt woozy and wanted to go to sleep but knew she probably shouldn't. She remembered vaguely that you weren't supposed to sleep if you had concussion.

Concussion – 14 points.

She needed to stay...

...awake – 12 points.

Damn it. Tonight was her date with Razz. She wouldn't make that if they took her to hospital. And she'd been so looking forward to it.

Razz – 22 points.

The man for her. She was certain of it. Well, as certain as she could be when she wasn't sure if he liked her too.

'Oh God, Jo,' she heard him say.

No, how could she hear him? He wasn't here. Was she unconscious again? Asleep? Dreaming?

'Jo, are you hurt?' he said.

The voice seemed to come from above her. She opened her eyes again and saw Razz standing beside Kate up on the path, peering down at her.

Was this her imagination? Or a hallucination? Perhaps she'd hit her head harder than she thought. Or was he actually there?

'Mountain rescue are on their way,' he called. And then to Kate, 'How long did they say?'

She couldn't hear Kate's response, but heard Razz say, 'Oh shit. That long?'

'Jo,' he called again. 'Where does it hurt?'

'My ankle.'

'Anywhere else?'

'And my head,' she called. 'And I'm cold.'

'Stay there. I'm coming down.'

His words didn't register at first. She looked up and saw him arguing with Kate. Then he headed a couple of metres back down the path, to a place where the slope to the river wasn't quite as steep, before beginning to scramble down the rocks, slipping and sliding towards the bottom.

'With you in a second, Jo,' he called.

This was Razz, she thought. Razz who was frightened of heights. Razz who'd been too scared to sit on a chair wearing a hard hat and be winched perfectly safely down Gaping Gill. And now here he was, negotiating his way down a steep, rocky slope with a river below, and no helmet or rope, in order to reach her.

'Ow, bugger,' he shouted suddenly, and she watched

in horror as he lost his footing and tumbled the last few metres down to the river, a short way downstream from her.

Her heart pounded. Watching him fall was every bit as frightening as falling herself. What if he was injured? It'd be her fault, all because of that stupid usie. What had she been thinking?

'Razz?' she called. She managed to sit up so she could see him. 'Are you hurt?'

He was getting to his feet now, she saw with relief, but he was wincing, clearly in pain, his left hand on his right shoulder. He stumbled along the side of the river until he reached her, then knelt down beside her. He struggled out of his coat and, using only his left hand, slipped it around Jo's shoulders. 'Are you okay, Jo?'

She pulled it around her; it was still warm from his body. 'Thank you. I think so. I was a bit dizzy, but I'm okay now. Apart from the ankle. I'm not sure if I can stand on it. Are *you* okay?'

'Don't worry about me…'

'But I feel terrible. You've injured yourself because of me.'

'Cuts and bruises. That's all.'

'Are you sure?'

'Well, okay. I admit I might have broken my collarbone.'

Jo gasped. 'Your collarbone? Oh, God, Razz. I'm so sorry. This is my fault.'

'I only said I *might* have broken it. And if I have, a broken collarbone isn't usually serious. A few weeks in a sling and it'll be fine. And look on the bright side. You've managed what several weeks of expensive therapy didn't manage – I've conquered my fear of heights.'

★

The Mountain Rescue team arrived twenty minutes later and were somewhat bemused to find that they had two patients to rescue, and that one of them was the local GP.

'Next time, wait for the professionals,' they told Razz.

'I know, I know, but I couldn't leave her down there on her own,' he said. 'She was getting cold.'

They were whisked off to hospital. Aside from a few scratches and a hole in the leg of her jeans, Jo just had a mild concussion and a sprained ankle. Razz, as he'd predicted, had broken his collarbone. When they'd both been checked out and X-rayed, Kate picked them up and drove them home, Jo insisting on sitting in the back so Razz could take the front seat, because it would be quite tricky to climb out of the back of a small three-doored car with only one functional arm. It was hard enough with a sprained ankle.

'Would you mind if we postponed our date this evening?' Razz said to Jo. 'I'm happy to meet up, but I don't want to go to a fancy restaurant when I can't cut up my own food.'

'Sure,' she said. 'Why don't we get a takeaway instead? To be honest, I'm more of a fish 'n' chips out of the paper than a fancy restaurant kind of a person anyway.'

'Sounds good to me.'

Jo caught Kate's eye in the rear-view mirror and gave her a wink. Then she leaned forwards, stretching the seatbelt as far as it would go, and whispered into his ear, 'We could play Scrabble. If you're up to that with only one arm.'

48

Kate dropped first Razz and then Jo off at their respective homes, declining the offer of a coffee at Jo's, insisting that her friend should get some rest.

Jo unlocked her front door and it swung open easily. She thought of how Razz had fixed it, how kind he'd been, but that was nothing compared with scaling down a steep slope to rescue her. Or at least, he'd *tried* to rescue her. Despite his fear of heights.

She went to look at herself in the bathroom mirror. A purple bruise had formed above her right eye and her cheek was scratched, but aside from that, she didn't look much worse after her fall. A little make-up would hide the bruise this evening.

One thing she hadn't asked him, she realised, was where they were meeting. At his place? Or at hers?

She recalled the image she'd sent to Tarquin of the letters spelling out YOUR PLACE OR MINE on the Scrabble board and the upside-down C with a dot turning it into a question mark. She could recreate that, she decided, for Razz.

She dug out her Scrabble board and set the letters up again, but then, on the spur of the moment, she limped back upstairs and rummaged in her underwear drawer until she found a solitary black, lacy stocking. She never wore stockings these days; why would she when tights were so much more comfortable?

She draped the stocking across the board, took out her phone and took a snap. This was perfect; nothing said 'Let's get out of the friend zone' more than a silky stocking draped across a Scrabble board. Well, to a Scrabble fan at least.

She giggled to herself, imagining Razz's face when he saw it, but then she hesitated. He might realise what she was trying to tell him, or he might see the funny side, which would be good, too. Or he could equally be terrified. She knew him well enough now to realise that Razz was no more confident around women than she was around men. He might find the picture a bit too full on, intimidating even, and that wasn't what she wanted at all. She decided to play it safe, and sent him an ordinary text saying,

Want to play at mine or yours this evening?

I don't mind. But might it be easier if I come to yours since you have a sprained ankle?

After fish 'n' chips, which they both ate with their fingers – Razz because it was easier with his right arm in a sling and Jo to keep him company – Jo set up the Scrabble board on the table in the window of her little house on Hazel Lane. The town of Hebbleswick lay beneath them, golden in the evening sunshine. A busker stood, strumming his guitar in the square – which was more of a triangle than a square to be honest, but everyone called it the square – and passing pub-goers tossed the occasional coin into his cup.

The game got off to a slow start. Razz drew an A from the bag so was starting player. His first word – WILL – scored 14 points as it was on the double word star in the centre of the board.

Jo took an early lead making WHY for 16 points using his W. He then played YOU scoring a measly 6 points.

'You must have bad letters,' she said.

'I have.'

Jo made HOPEFUL going down the board, using the last L of WILL. It summed up how she felt about the evening – about her life in general, right now in fact – and scored her 31 points as both her H and F were on triple letter scores.

'There's only going to be one winner here,' Razz said, placing a G in front of the O of hopeful to make GO. The G was on a double letter but it still only scored 5 points.

'That can't be the best you can do.'

'I told you – bad letters.'

On his next turn, Razz fidgeted as he thought about which word to make, rooting around in his pocket, pulling out a tissue and dabbing his nose.

'Hay fever,' he said. He used the U of HOPEFUL to make OUT.

'Why not make POT with the P? It scores more. Can't believe you didn't spot that. Allow me.' She leaned over and rearranged his tiles. 'Must be tricky without your right hand.'

Jo scored 33 points – with bonuses – on her next move, placing SWEATER on the board. Razz's score for the entire game so far was only 31 points. She was going to walk this one.

He was rooting around in his pocket again so Jo passed him a tissue from her handbag. He wiped his nose and put down an O and a U making OUT using the T of SWEATER.

'You've a limited vocabulary this evening,' she said.

'It's the hay fever. I can't concentrate. And I've got bad letters.'

'Can't you prescribe yourself something?'

'There's no cure for bad letters.'

'For the hay fever.'

'Yeah, I'll sort myself out on Monday at the surgery.'

It was boring when a game was this easy, Jo thought as she laid her next word, but things were going to get trickier now as she picked up the Q from the box. There were only two tiles with a letter U and both were already on the board, in places where she wouldn't be able to use them. She racked her brains for words that contained a Q but no U.

Razz, she noticed as she weighed up the possibilities, was fiddling with his sling.

'Is your shoulder okay?' she said.

'Yes, a little uncomfortable. Bit itchy.'

'I thought people got itchy under a plaster cast, not a sling.'

'I'm a bit hot, that's all.'

He was twitchy, Jo thought. She turned her attention back to her letter rack, rearranging the tiles, considering the options. Razz made WITH for 10 points.

'Is there nothing better?'

He shook his head. 'Can't see anything.'

'You really are struggling this evening,' she said. 'Have you lost your touch? It's me who's got concussion, not you.'

She placed WIDGET for 22 points on a double word score. Then she chose her new tiles and was surprised to see a U amongst them.

'That's odd. I've just picked up a U. But there are already two on the board and there are only two in a set.'

'Weird,' said Razz. 'Perhaps some extra letters got mixed up and found their way into your box at Scrabble club last week.'

'Yeah, they must have,' Jo said, but she couldn't really see how that could have happened; they were always careful not to muddle sets up when they packed away after Scrabble club. She frowned at the board. 'There are definitely tiles in here from another box. There's three Ws as well. We'll have to check every set. We don't want Florence and Mr B getting extra letters. All hell will break loose and she'll accuse him of cheating.'

'Yeah, imagine,' he said, placing an M in front of the E of WIDGET to make ME. He looked at the board, then looked at Jo expectantly. 'Come on, Jo. Have you ever known me play so badly?'

Suddenly she clocked the words he'd been making. 'WILL – YOU – GO – POT – OUT – WITH – ME,' she read out loud.

Will you go out with me?

'You rather ruined it putting POT when I wanted to put OUT,' he said.

Her heart was pounding. She gaped at the board. 'Did you plan this?'

He smiled. 'I might have done.'

He was asking her out.

Actually asking her out.

As in, on a proper date and not just going out with friends.

And he hadn't asked her in a boring old text message like anyone else would do.

'How did you know you'd pick the right letters?' she said.

'I had spares in my pocket and my sling. Getting them out without you spotting me was the tricky bit.'

She couldn't quite believe this. He'd gone to so much effort. For her.

'You don't really have hay fever?'

'No, no hay fever. And no itch. I was trying to find the W in the sling. I wanted to ask you out and this seemed like a good way.'

Jo remembered the photo she'd taken earlier. 'Great minds think alike. I nearly sent you this. Not exactly asking you out, but a strong hint.'

She pulled out her phone, found the stockings-and-Scrabble image and clicked send. Razz's phone beeped and he opened the message, his face creasing with laughter.

'Brilliant,' he said. 'You're so creative, Jo. I wish you'd sent it. It would have saved me a lot of effort. And the humiliation of losing so badly. I've been wanting to ask you out again for so long. But I wasn't sure how you felt about me.'

'And I wasn't sure how *you* felt about me.' Her voice came out in a kind of squeak. 'So why didn't you?'

'Because I didn't think there was a cat in hell's chance you'd say yes. Like I told you before, I was convinced I'd blown it when you sailed down Gaping Gill like it was nothing, and came back up with a beaming smile on your face, whilst I sat at the top like a quivering wreck. And even when you admitted you'd told a bit of a fib...'

'That's being generous. It was an out-and-out lie.'

'...a bit of a fib, well, I still felt like I'd been a complete wuss that day. I thought I'd conquered my phobia of heights, but I clearly hadn't.'

'But when the shit hit the fan today and I fell in that ravine and hurt myself, you put your fear aside to help me.'

She thought back to earlier that day. To the shock of tumbling down. Her throbbing ankle and aching head. Looking up at Kate and wondering how on earth she was going to get out of there. And the relief when he was beside her: strong, reassuring, comforting. And also wincing at his own pain, but still, he had been there for her. The next moment, her eyes were welling up and the tears began to roll. They were tears of joy, relief, delayed shock – she wasn't sure what.

Razz walked round the table and knelt beside her. With his good arm, he pulled her in, holding her against his sweater. Cashmere – 15 points. If you were going to weep against knitwear, cashmere was best as it was softer against sore eyes. He took his arm away, pulled a tissue from his pocket, and offered it to her, scattering two letter tiles onto the carpet.

She reached out to pick them up: P and A.

'Was there another word?' she blubbed.

'PLEASE. I wanted to spell out, "Will you go out with me please". Shame there's no question mark. I wasn't clever enough to think of a back-to-front C with an added dot.'

Jo buried her face in his sweater again. He planted small kisses on the bruise above her eyebrow. Much as she wanted him to kiss her lips, rather than her forehead, she had little desire to move from her comfortable position resting against his chest. It was the calmest place she had ever been in her whole life. He was shorter than she was, his hair was scruffy and his dress sense was even worse than hers – although this jumper was rather nice – but none of those things mattered. Jo wanted this man to stay by her side like this. Forever, probably. But she wasn't going to rush into things. She knew she had to take it slowly this time and planned to savour every moment. She breathed in his scent: eau de fabric conditioner and shower gel with a definite hint of manliness.

She tilted her face up to look at him. Razz gently stroked her scratched cheek with his fingers. Her eyes met his. Their big romantic moment. There was hesitation, a delicious hesitation, as his face drew nearer to hers.

He's about to kiss me, thought Jo, and he's drawing out, making the moment last like they do in films.

He went to brush a stray hair from her face, and Jo closed her eyes, longing to feel his lips on hers. Only he didn't brush the hair, he pulled it.

'Ouch.'

'Sorry, I didn't realise it was still attached. Thought it was a loose one.'

Okay, so it wasn't quite as romantic as in the films, but was it ever?

'Kiss me, Razz.' As she said his name, she couldn't help herself from thinking, 22 points.

Although… well, even if he'd spelled it Ras, she'd still have wanted him.

His soft lips touched hers, gently at first, then slightly more insistently.

'Does this mean you'll go out with me?' he said, pulling away slightly.

There was only one way to answer that question.

'I've a slight problem,' she said.

'Oh.' His face fell. 'I've left it too late, haven't I? You've met someone else.'

'No, it's not that. I haven't got a Y.'

He looked puzzled for a minute before breaking into a smile. She loved that smile; he was one of those people who seemed to smile with his entire face, every muscle joining in. He rummaged in his sling, pulling out a letter tile.

'Here you go,' he said, offering it out to her. 'I hid this in there, in case I needed it.'

Her fingers brushed his as she took the tile off him. Soft skin, she noticed. Skin she'd like to explore more. But that would have to wait. There was a game to finish. She looked at the tile he'd given her; it was a blank, a tile that could be used in place of any other letter but wouldn't score anything.

'Perfect,' she said. 'Thanks, Razz.'

She could answer him now, and there could only be one answer. He was a kind, compassionate man, she fancied him like crazy and she loved spending time with him. Especially time playing Scrabble.

She spelled out BLANK – E – S on the board.

'I think you'll find that's 2 points,' she said.

'Only 2 points?' he said.

'Yep. Best 2 points I have ever scored.'

Epilogue

It was September and the end of her first week in her new job and Jo was exhausted. It wasn't that the work itself was demanding; it was the sheer number of new people she'd met. A stream of mothers who'd popped their heads round her door. 'Just saying hello,' they'd all said.

There'd been hordes of children too. Jo had a whole collection of hand-made *welcome to your new job* cards, lining the walls around her desk.

She'd felt at home in the staffroom straight away. In fact, she'd been the centre of attention, the teachers and teaching assistants all keen to know if it was true that she used to work in telly and why had she left a glamorous job like that to work in Hebbleswick Primary of all places? And had she met many celebrities?

The change of scene had done wonders for Jo's confidence. It was ironic, she thought, that now she finally felt able to assert herself, she was in a job where she didn't need to.

And ironic that now she was happy to stand up for herself, she had a kind-hearted man who believed in conversations and compromise. She had confided in Razz about her past, and he had listened quietly, holding her hand, then said, 'If I ever do something that you don't like, you have to tell me. Promise me, Jo. Because I never want to upset you.'

And then he had held her. And kissed the top of her head then her eyelids and her cheeks and every inch of her face as if he were trying to kiss away all the hurt from her past. And then one thing had led to another, and he had made love to her, touching her more tenderly than anyone had ever touched her in her life and Jo had thought she might explode with happiness.

She opened the wardrobe doors now, wondering what to wear this evening. It was a Friday evening, which could only mean one thing: Scrabble club. But tonight was no ordinary Scrabble club.

If only she'd thought sooner, she could have popped into the hospice shop one lunchtime to see if they had anything suitable. It would have been nice to wear something special that evening.

Too late now though, she glanced at her watch. They'd already be closed.

Although... well, there was the Scrabble dress. She'd bought it because she liked it, never imagining she'd have the occasion to wear it, but there would never be an evening more appropriate for the quirky pinafore than this one.

She slipped off her work clothes, put on a plain T-shirt and pulled the Scrabble dress over it. It was a perfect fit; it showed off her curves, curves she was proud of. She took out the new lipstick she'd treated herself to the previous week and put a little on, smiling at herself in the mirror.

'Because I'm worth it,' she said to herself with a smile.

And she believed it. Well, sort of. She was halfway there. It wasn't the new lipstick that made her feel that way. It wasn't Razz either. Yes, he made her feel loved but she knew now that self-worth was called *self*-worth for a reason; it was something you had to find within yourself. She was getting there; a lifetime of believing herself inferior wasn't going to change overnight.

If you'd told her a few months ago that she'd walk into a party – because tonight was a sort of party, wasn't it? – wearing such an eye-catching and unusual dress... well, she'd never have believed it. She'd always sought to blend into the background, to go unnoticed, but walking into the school hall in this outfit would be sure to attract attention.

And it did. Every head turned as Jo walked in. She hadn't realised there'd be *quite* that many heads either.

The original members of the Scrabble club were all there, along with lovely Mrs McCardle and several other new members. Mr Morgan and most of the other teachers were in attendance. And the Pop! Productions crowd and Caroline, with her rather large bump. Jo had never imagined she'd see people from her old workplace here in her new one. Annie was handing round trays of her letter-tile biscuits. There were a few people whom Jo recognised as parents of children at the school, and Linda had already managed to find one of the single fathers and was flirting desperately with him in one corner. And everyone – well, except for Linda – seemed to stop talking as she walked in.

She felt self-conscious. On second thoughts, the dress had definitely been a mistake.

But then Leona suddenly appeared at her side and said, 'Jo, I *love* that dress. You look fantastic.'

Within seconds, a small crowd gathered round her; Mrs

McCardle oohed and ahhed over the fabric, and Razz said, 'I've never seen you in a dress before. Wow. Just wow.'

'It's a lovely dress,' said Cosmic and immediately blushed, the colour of his cheeks clashing dreadfully with the orange of his hair. Perhaps he'd never paid a compliment to a woman before.

'Thanks, Cosmic,' said Jo, 'and Malcolm, before you ask, I think it's covered on my contents insurance.'

Malcolm laughed. He looked a little less geeky when he laughed.

Jo spotted Kate in a corner, chatting with Emily, Matthew and a tall, athletic man whom Jo presumed must be Ludek. She excused herself and went over to them.

Kate looked at Jo in astonishment, and then at Emily.

'You're wearing my dress,' said Emily.

'*Your* dress?' Jo didn't put two and two together.

'I donated it to the hospice shop.'

'And I bought it.'

'What a weird coincidence,' said Emily. 'Have you worn it much?'

'This is the first time. I nearly wore it to the festival but I hadn't quite got the bottle.'

'Wow,' said Kate. 'I'd never clocked before that you two are such a similar size. It looks like it was made for you, Jo, when in fact, it was made for Emily.'

'It was this dress that made me move to Hebbleswick,' said Jo. 'I know this sounds ridiculous, but when I saw it in the shop window, I thought it was a sign from the Universe that this was the place where I should be.'

'You sound like the Bouffant,' said Kate. 'But maybe it *was* a sign. Look how it's worked out for you here. You found Razz. You've organised a festival and landed yourself a new job.'

Jo laughed. She wasn't sure she believed in signs anymore. Or rather, it wasn't so much she didn't believe in them; she didn't find she needed them. For the first time in her life, she trusted her own judgement when it came to making decisions.

'And all thanks to a dress,' Kate said triumphantly. 'Which means, all thanks to me.'

'You? You mean, all thanks to Emily. If she hadn't donated it...'

'All thanks to me. Because *I* had that dress made for her.'

Kate had had the dress made? When? And why? And why had Emily given it away? She was about to ask when there was a tap on the mic and the screech of feedback as Mr B began to speak.

'Hope you don't mind,' he said. 'David – who for those of you who don't know is the executive producer of Pop! Productions and our host today – has kindly allowed me to hijack the microphone for a few minutes to make an announcement. This evening is a double celebration, because last weekend, I asked the lovely Florence to marry me and she said yes.'

The whole hall erupted into applause, with Matthew whooping, even though he barely knew Mr B, and Kate yelling, 'Way to go, Stan!' and everyone hugging Florence.

'Thank you, everyone,' said Mr B. He was blushing; his face was now the same colour as his crimson bow tie. 'And now I'll hand over to David.'

David walked up onto the stage and took the mic.

'Congratulations, Stan and Florence,' he said. 'And

thank you, everyone, for coming. You're all in for a treat this evening as Pop! Productions is delighted to share with you the pilot episode of *Love Letters*, a game show based on the popular word game Scrabble. Before we start, I'd like to express my thanks to the members of Hebbleswick Scrabble club who were kind enough to be the guinea pigs – or rather, contestants – for this special episode, and to Mr Morgan for allowing us use the school hall this evening for our screening. But most of all, I'd like to thank the wonderful Jo Knox, because she came up with the original idea for this game show and she devised the format and we're enormously grateful to her.'

He was about to continue when Razz suddenly piped up, 'Actually, David, could I say something too?'

David smiled and Razz scurried up onto the stage, tapped the mic nervously, then began to speak. 'I wanted to add my thanks to Jo. She worked tirelessly last July to make Hebbleswick Scrabble Festival an enormous success,and then she found us this wonderful venue when we lost the church hall. Without her, there would be no Scrabble club. Oh, yeah, and she happens to be my girlfriend.'

He looked down from the stage at where Jo was standing and mouthed, 'I love you' to her.

For a few seconds, they were lost in their own little bubble, as if no-one else was present at all. The short, scruffy-haired and rather shy doctor with his Roman nose and warm eyes, and the smiley, red-haired, curvaceous woman in the quirky pinafore dress gazed at each other. Then she mouthed back, 'I love you too.'

David looked at Razz; he wasn't quite sure if the doctor had finished his impromptu speech – there wasn't going to be another proposal was there? – but the man seemed to have ground to a halt, so he eased the mic out of his hand and said to the watching audience, 'I think what Razz and I would *both* like to say is, could everyone please give it up for Jo?'

The applause, the whoops, were even louder than they had been for Stan and Florence's engagement. Someone shouted, 'Three cheers for Jo.'

As the first 'hip hip hooray' echoed round the hall, Jo gave Kate a quick hug, then she too climbed the steps onto the stage, her cheeks reddening.

She walked straight into Razz's open arms. Over his shoulder, she could see David, holding the mic out to her now. Oh God, she wasn't expected to make a speech, was she?

The crowd shouted the third and final, 'Hip hip hooray.'

And that was when it dawned on her. She had not only found her tribe and her man; she had found her cheerleaders.

Acknowledgements

This book is the story of Jo finding not only love, but her tribe too.

And in recent months, since my first novel, *The Little Board Game Café*, was published, I realise that I have finally found mine. Although I've always loved reading, it's only through becoming an author that I've discovered a wonderful community of readers, reviewers and other writers; it's been incredible, and I owe a big thank you to each and every one of you. There are so many great books in the world by well-known writers, so I was amazed and grateful that so many people were willing to take a chance and read a debut novel by an unknown author like me.

Thank you to all the wonderful readers' groups who've supported me on Facebook. There's too many to name them all, but I have to give a special mention to the members of Jenny Colgan and More Great Books, including admins Marian Girling and Sarah Price; and Wendy Clarke and the team at The Fiction Café Book Club. And a massive thank you to Sue Baker who organised a virtual publication party for me with some wonderfully imaginative posts.

I owe so much to all the authors who have offered encouragement and advice, especially Pam Rhodes, Kitty

Wilson, Katherine Mezzacappa, Faith Hogan, Rowan Coleman, Suzanne Snow, Julie Houston, Sophie MacKenzie, Heidi Swain and Jessica Redland. A special thank you goes to Trisha Ashley and the Novelistas for welcoming me into their midst.

This time last year, I didn't know what a blog tour was, but I do now, and I want to say a huge thank you to Rachel Gilbey of Rachel's Random Resources and all the wonderful bloggers who took part on The Little Board Game Café blog tour.

I owe an enormous debt of gratitude to Rachel Faulkner-Willcocks. She very graciously offered a feedback session in a charity auction; I won the auction and sent a very rough draft of Love Letters (as it was then called) to her. One thing led to another, and Aria then offered me a two-book deal. Without Rachel and that auction, I would probably still be tapping away on my keyboard, wondering if I dared submit my novel to a literary agent.

Whilst writing is a very solitary occupation, there is a whole team of wonderful people beavering away behind the scenes. I am very grateful to everyone at Aria: Emily Champion (production), Meg Shepherd (design support), Amy Watson (marketing), Zoe Giles (social media), Jo Liddiard (marketing), Ayo Okojie (publicity), Karen Dobbs (sales), Dan Groenewald (sales), Victoria Eddison (sales), and Nikky Ward (digital sales). A massive thank you to Jessie Price for designing beautiful and eye-catching covers for both this book and The Little Board Game Café. Thank you too to copy editor Helena Newton for your helpful suggestions, and proofreader Emily Reader for all your hard work.

I'm very fortunate to have Bianca Gillam as my editor and am so grateful to her; not only is she a wonderful editor, but she's a very patient person too – I'm sure I ask far too many questions!

Many thanks to my fabulous agents, Rebecca Ritchie and Florence Rees at AM Heath Literary Agency for always being there when I've needed you. Like Bianca, they've had to put up with a lot of questions. As a new author, there was so much I had to learn, and they have gently guided me through all of it.

Thank you to my many friends, who put up with me rambling on about my plot dilemmas for hours on end, especially Robert Smith, Michelle Riley and Janis Knox. Special thanks also go to Rachel Wetz-Gill and her lovely husband Martin; they read a very early draft of this novel (and made the appropriate encouraging noises as friends do, even though it was far from polished) but they were also in part the inspiration behind the story – they both love Scrabble, almost as much as Jo and Razz. Martin also hosts my website for me and is my go-to person when I'm confused about IT stuff – thanks, Martin!

A big thank you to the Craven Pothole Club. I loved my trip down Gaping Gill as research for Jo and Razz's first date and can honestly say that Razz missed out! A special thanks to club member, Glenn Costin, for his help with this chapter. Any errors are entirely my own. If you'd like to see for yourself the spectacular wonder that is Gaping Gill, the club organises a winch meet every August.

My mum very kindly gives everything I write an extra proof-read; she's a retired English teacher and knows her passive from her subjunctive, so that's very much appreciated.

And finally, a huge thank you to Hermi, my lovely husband, who's cheered me on every step of my writing journey. He had faith in my ability to do this when I didn't have any in myself.

About the Author

JENNIFER PAGE wrote her first novel – a book about ponies – when she was eight. These days she prefers to write about romance and her debut, *The Little Board Game Café*, was published in 2022. When she isn't writing, Jennifer can usually be found playing board games. She has worked as a television producer, a music teacher and has even run a children's opera company. She lives near Hebden Bridge in West Yorkshire with her husband and his large collection of games.

If you'd like to find out more about Jennifer, please visit her website at https://jenniferpage.co.uk where you can subscribe to her newsletter and receive a free epilogue of *The Little Board Game Café*.

You can also follow her on social media:
Instagram: @jenniferpagewrites
Facebook: @jenniferpagewrites
Twitter: @jenpagewrites
TikTok: @jenniferpagewrites